CHAMPION OF MARS

Also by Guy Haley

Reality 36
Omega Point

CHAMPION
OF
MARS

GUY HALEY

SOLARIS

First published 2012 by Solaris
an imprint of Rebellion Publishing Ltd,
Riverside House, Osney Mead,
Oxford, OX2 0ES, UK

www.solarisbooks.com

ISBN: 978 1 907992 85 8

10 9 8 7 6 5 4 3 2 1

A CIP catalogue record for this book is available from the
British Library.

Designed & typeset by Rebellion Publishing

Printed in the US

For Emma

CHAPTER ONE

Kaibeli Counts

Mars, 4543rd year of the Second Age, Imperial Era

MARS IS DYING a second time. I can feel it. I taste it upon the wind and in men's fear. It is written hard into the eleutheremic fabric of spacetime. It is calculable and, therefore, inevitable.

In the western sky above Mulympiu, a star shines at the full of day, bright as a comet through the rippled matter of the Veil of Worlds. Daily, it grows in luminance. This is the Stone Sun. The saviour of Man has become the harbinger of his end.

And yet, below my feet, men fight. They do not look up at the sky to see that which will consume them. They spare no glance for the Veil marking the boundaries of the domain of men and spirits upon Mars, and which may yet mark the end of it. The world that carries them is a husk, it has been a husk since before the first of them set foot in its dust, it will remain a husk until the Stone Sun conducts its final betrayal. The men and spirits of Mars, they think this world alive. It is not. Their frantic activity lends the semblance of life to the red world only as the writhing of maggots lends a corpse the semblance of life.

The end is coming, and I almost welcome it, but not today.

I watch the battle as a tally-master. Battle is a vital state; at times of violence, the male human mind flowers like at no other. The souls of the men below shine brightly in the halls of the Second World, stronger than the mirror suns in the sky above me. The spirit of Mars itself is a wan candle by comparison.

The men die, their souls flare, then they are gone into the stacks from which only some will return. Intent on their small extinctions, they are ignorant of the greater death going on all around them. They waste their time on war. Their numbers dwindle, the red sands return to cover green lands, the crystal cities fail, the mirror suns blink out one by one. Still men fight, because they are men. What more can men do?

Banks of sun cannon roar. Vented waste plasmas colour the air around them. The guns vomit bundles of superheated quanta from their muzzles, matter tortured to the point of dissolution. The sky is full of miniature suns, the hiss of ionised air. Every detonation is a starburst. Rock and life are annihilated with equanimity. It is beautiful, in its way.

These are the guns that will bring down the walls of Olm.

This is the battle I am tasked to observe, the thirty-seventh battle of Olm. Olm has stood on the shoulders of Muasckra for fifty-six thousand years. I have seen it grow from a waystation to Mars' fifth city. I have seen it conquered a dozen times.

Shortly, Olm will fall forever and Mars will die a little more.

This will be the last war of Man.

Eleutheremics is the art of knowing what will be. Through it, the course of the river of fate is clear to my kind. It may branch and braid and split, but it flows only in one direction. And so the outcome of the battle was determined long before it began, as obvious to me as mankind's ultimate fate. The final tally will be thus: three thousand, seven hundred and eighty-seven of Olm will die. Four thousand and thirteen men of Kemiímseet will lie amid them, fourteen sun cannon will be broken. Non-mortality casualty rate will be equally high, in favour of the besieged. A >10% error rate is expected here on initial calculations. This is acceptable. Fifteen spirits are fated to be sundered, all on the side of Olm, although by my reckoning six of ours will die also. Those remaining of Olm will ransom themselves. At the close of day, honour will be due to the men of Olm – they will have fought well – but they will lose. If only their diplomats were as subtle as their generals.

Real-time plastic prognostication shows near total accord with these already determined parameters. Those possessed of great will may, at the right time, alter the procession of causality, but that will not happen here, not now. The predictions are correct, fate will not be cheated today.

This information and all else about me – my thoughts, my feelings – are available to my masters through the medium of the Second World. Without it, I have no self-expression. My individuality is illusory.

I command the smartdust that houses my consciousness to drift forward. I search below for those exemplary warriors worthy of soul salvage and commendation. About me, no doubt, are the counters and choosers of other Quinarchs, Overmen, Spirefathers, and Triunes, their presence masked to me. We are valkyries as blind to each other as the men below are blind to us.

Screams sound faint and tinny in the attenuated atmosphere, here on the flanks of the volcano. The clash of weapon upon weapon is rendered pathetic. The blades the men swing at one another ring like cutlery. It would be comical if it were not horrific; they cut deep and the blood flows freely.

Their bloodlust would be repellent to me were my emotions not disengaged. As it is, I take no pleasure in my task.

There is an urge to violence in all men, an urge to dominate. In some men, in some ages, it is buried deep; in others, it wars openly with their better natures. Certain individuals are cursed with a will to power so strong, their aggression pierces whatever layer of civilisation their time and culture cloaks them in. Whether this predilection suits their era or not, such men are monsters.

My man, he is the worst monster in an age of monsters, although he was not always so.

His name, in this life, is Yoechakenon.

Yoechakenon fights to the fore of the army, his face and body hidden by the intimate clasp of his armour. The dynamic half-metals of his harness cling to his skin precisely, limning muscle and feature in burnished silver. All bar his face; this is a blank bowl. The quicksilver surface of the armour is a mirror, casting back the destruction Yoechakenon wreaks. In his hands he wields the glaive, long-staffed, spinning discs two handspans across at either end. Like the armour, the glaive is blessed with a murderous intent all its own.

I watch him impassively. To feel too much would skew my judgements on the warriors I watch, and it is for my mind and not my heart that I am employed today. Still, it is hard not to be moved by Yoechakenon's grace, and I find myself watching him for longer than I intend. Armour, glaive and man are one. I understand how something can be both terrible and beautiful when I see him fight.

Yoechakenon leaps over the heads of his enemies, weaving through energy beams as a dancer moves through coloured streamers. His enemies are common footmen, in the main. Their bulky, rigid armours offer little protection against the glaive. They rapidly fall before the discs; their blood sprays over Yoechakenon's silver skin. The armour drinks it quickly, and its surface remains unmarred. The soldiers of Olm are not fools. They retreat in orderly fashion. Their discipline is exemplary. I will include this in my submission to the Quinarchy.

One officer remains behind. He intends to challenge the champion, to allow his men to retreat. Only a champion can hope to best a champion, and Olm's is a week dead, fallen to Yoechakenon, his armour dead along with him. This soldier knows he will die, but he does not waver. I can taste his excitement, fed by his companion spirit into the Second World, along with every other thing that makes him what he is. His name is Ra-ell. His courage is remarkable. I make a note for Ra-ell's commendation as he shoots Yoechakenon squarely in the chest with a quantic pistol. The shot dissipates into the intelligent half-metals of the armour, diverted around his body in sparks and earthed into the rocky soil. Yoechakenon does not falter. The glaive shears the barrel from the soldier's gun. Ra-ell stands his ground. He sidesteps quickly, discards his ruined pistol and draws his own blade, a humming sword made in workshops that have long since been ground to dust. The art to make such things is lost. It, too, is a beautiful weapon.

The champion fights the brave captain. As my mind processes the statistics of the battle, parsing the fates of the dead, I find myself arrested by their struggle, although it is but one amongst many others. The light is perfect: the beams of three mirror suns intersect the field, lighting it as a drama is lit. Yoechakenon is a living god of metal, his opponent as worthy and bold as he is doomed. Ra-ell is determined. He will not die easily. I record all this as a moment suitable for the enjoyment of the Quinarchy.

Ra-ell's blows are delivered surely – he is a swordsman of no mean skill – but all are parried by the glaive. The two weapons move at great speed, the discs upon the glaive a blur, Ra-ell falling back all the while yet refusing to allow Yoechakenon an opening. Faster they fight, Yoechakenon leaping through the air to rain blows upon the beleaguered man, Ra-ell employing the stolidity of his own armour's mind to centre himself. For those few sunlit moments it is a fight of legend, one that could last forever, it seems, though I know that is not to be. I delve into the Second World, sending part of my mind deep into the Great Library in search of Ra-ell's personal histories. He is an opponent fit for the champion, a hero himself. I see to it he will be remembered as such.

In the thin air, the blade song is a staccato clatter that abruptly falls silent. Ra-ell's sword is sent arcing away. Ra-ell stands, his cognitive systems singing out in the Second World, betraying his shock at what he expected all along. I cannot see the fear upon his face, nor feel it upon the currents of the Second World. Truly he is brave.

Yoechakenon pauses ,and bows in acknowledgement of Ra-ell's courage before driving the glaive through his chest. It passes through his armour as if it were not there. A spume of frothing blood rushes up the shaft, and bone shards are flung out by the glaive disc to fall among the rocks. Ra-ell's mortal form dies. His soul glares as it is withdrawn by the creatures of the stacks.

I make further notes and upgrade my recommendation for his commendation to a personal insistence. His comrades regain the gates. The portal irises shut. Within, they prepare themselves for a final stand.

The battlefield is clear. The sortie has not succeeded.

The walls of Olm are already pitted. Their flesh smokes as the sun cannon of Kemiímseet redouble their bombardment. The spirits of the city scream as stray shots find their way through the energy shield to strike the spires beyond. Breaches will open soon in the walls, the shield will fail, and the warriors of

Kemiímseet will pour through and do what warriors have done to cities throughout all of human history.

This fratricidal war has run on for a decade and a half. Man versus man, spirit versus spirit. The rebellious Quinarchs assault the authority of their Emperor. The Great Librarian has been missing for millennia, and there is no one to mediate.

There will be victory for the Twin Emperor today, but it will not last. Soon the war will be over, and with its end, so too will the time of Man come to a close.

There is nothing I can do to stop it. It is fated, and fate can be resisted only rarely. The death of Olm will be the act of a monster. It may seem the champion has no decision in the matter. Nevertheless, it remains the act of Yoechakenon. The coexistence of freedom and hard determinism is the dilemma at the heart of eleutheremics.

Yoechakenon, who is revered and feared in all the lands of Mars.

Yoechakenon, whom I love and have loved forever.

I note the current tally. Disgust overwhelms my detachment.

Sometimes, more often of late, I think that Mars should have stayed dead.

CHAPTER TWO

Holland

2107 AD, Ascraeus Mons

THE ANDROID STARED through Holland as if he weren't there. He couldn't stand it any longer. He turned to his guide, Dr Stulynow, sitting across the narrow gangway of the rover's passenger cabin.

"Can you stop that thing from staring at me?" he shouted. The rumble of the rover's fat tyres was deafening, the vibrations of the passenger cab setting Holland's nerves on edge. Evidently Marsform's budget didn't stretch as far as soundproofing. The vehicle jounced madly as it took a boulder field at a brisk pace. Stulynow shrugged and tapped his ears.

"Use your mike!" Holland gesticulated at his own ears, then thrust his chin up over the rim of his environment suit's gorget and jabbed at the microphone wrapped around his throat.

Stulynow slowly pulled his own microphone into place, geckroing the strap about his throat, annoyed at the interruption. His eyes never left Holland's as he did so. His face was heavy, Sibero-Asiatic, marked by hard years, the creases in his face picked out in red by Martian dust. The stuff got everywhere. Small dunes of it covered the floor of the passenger cabin, drifted up round the walls and bases of the long benches. Black grit danced on the vibrating floor. Stulynow's suit was stained pink-brown, with a few darker patches of brown or dark red where the dust had adhered to traces of oil. After only a week, Holland's own suit was beginning to colour; it wouldn't be long before he was indistinguishable from the rest of the colonists. Not that it would matter. Whether his suit was brilliant white or not, they'd still know he was new here, an outsider, and treat him accordingly. It was stamped across everything about him, from the way he walked to the things he said. It'd take more than a dirty suit to fit in.

He felt uneasy. He hadn't expected the android, and this big Slavic scientist with the attitude problem wasn't helping. It was not an auspicious start to his time at Ascraeus Base.

Holland stared defiantly back while Stulynow pressed at his phone, keying off whatever it was he'd been listening to.

"Yes?" he said, his voice phlegmy and too intimate on Holland's suit speakers. The dust clogged the human respiratory system as efficiently as it jammed air filters.

"Could you stop that thing from looking at me?" said Holland. "It won't quit staring at me."

Stulynow turned his head unhurriedly. All his movements were slow, like he was trapped in treacle. Holland had noticed that to be a peculiarity of the new Martians. Perhaps it was the low gravity, or the cold, or the boredom. He idly thought about testing his reaction times daily to see how long it would take for him to become the same.

Stulynow considered the android for long seconds. The rover hit something big, leapt into the air and came down with a jerk that made Holland's teeth clack.

"Why?" said Stulynow eventually. "She is doing no harm. She doesn't mean anything by it."

"She?"

Stulynow shrugged as if he really did not give a damn what Holland thought about the android, mostly because he didn't. "That's the basic personality pattern it has; female. By default."

"*It* is freaking me out." The thing's plastic eyes bored into Holland. They were hideous in their verisimilitude. Realistic blue irises stared unblinkingly from a softgel face, like the eyes of a burns victim peeking out from dressings that could not quite hide the horrors beneath. The features were inert, smooth and still as if carved from wax. He dreaded the moment when they'd twitch back into life.

Stulynow said something. The rumble of the engine and the grind of tyres on rocky ground was all Holland heard, despite the suit speakers being six centimetres from his ears.

"What?" said Holland, too sharply. He became angrier, mostly at himself. He was making a poor impression.

"I said, what's your problem?" repeated Stulynow loudly.

"I don't like AI."

Stulynow pulled a face and adjusted his earbuds. They were on wires, of all things, but they liked that up here. It was easier to fix a broken wire than a miniature transmitter. The Martians had limited access to fabrication units; only those run for company purposes had a full range of patterns. Raw materials, drawn from the planet's mining operations, were scarce. This was strictly a frontier environment, geared to transforming the world, as it had been since the first settlement in '93 and would remain for a long time. A goodly proportion of the colonists held double or triple doctorates – Stulynow was a cryovulcanist and a noted speleologist – but here men were expected to work with their hands too, to be as happy with a shovel as with a minilab. That required a certain kind of individual. The distance from home and its comforts further narrowed down the psychological types recruited by the company. The first wave of the new Martians were real pioneers, capable, but misanthropic. Who else but the emotionally damaged would want to come all the way out here? Holland had his reasons for getting off Earth, like all of them, but these new Martians disdained the problems of others even while struggling with their own. They looked down on Holland. He was still only a scientist, and not yet a pioneer.

Holland stared at the earbuds. He appreciated their simplicity. He supposed they also cut out the noise of the rover, which the suit speakers, his helmet off, did not. Common sense, and he'd expected that, anticipated it. He'd come here because it was a place where men relied on men. The machines on Mars were set only to the task of making a second Earth.

Except the android. That could never be a slave, not a thinking machine of that level. He knew they had one out there, he just hadn't expected to be sharing his ride with one. He couldn't escape them, no matter what he did, and that angered him.

The machine continued to stare at him.

Perhaps it wasn't enough to get away. Perhaps he'd made a mistake. Perhaps Dr Ravi had been right and he shouldn't have come. He should have stayed on Earth and tried to work through his phobia, just like everyone else who'd suffered in the Five Crisis. Time hadn't lessened its immediacy, and distance was doing as poorly.

"Can't you turn it off, or at least make it close its eyes?" he said.

"She *is* off," said Stulynow, shrugging again. "As off as she gets, anyhow. This sheath is in its inactive state, asleep. More or less, she's not really here at all. This is just a shell; she'll be doing something back at base. We only take the remote carriage in case something goes wrong. The sheath's eyelids get stuck on open whenever she's asleep. I haven't been able to get it fixed. Sorry."

Holland snorted derisively.

Stulynow frowned. "Do not do that. She always has a line into the sheath. She can still hear you. You will hurt her feelings."

Holland looked away. "It's a machine. They don't have feelings."

Stulynow looked at the android, strapped tightly into its seat on the long couch next to him. "Maybe not, but she does a good job emulating them. Her mind has full adaptive heuristics. She's a top range Class Three self-evolving AI; not many of those anywhere in the Solar System."

The Fives have that capability, thought Holland bitterly.

"Reliable model. I have worked with her for several months. She might not be human, but you can't tell, much better than other Threes. And if she doesn't feel, only appears to, what's the difference? My experience of what goes on in your head is as deep as my experience of hers. It's all the same. There is no difference, not subjectively."

"You're wrong," said Holland.

Stulynow politely waited for him to say something more, but Holland fixed his eyes on the door leading to the driver's cabin. The Siberian shrugged again. His shoulders were in perpetual motion with weary indifference. He keyed his music back on.

They spent the rest of the journey to Ascraeus Base in silence.

"HOLLAND. DR HOLLAND?" Someone was shaking him awake. Holland blinked his eyes and looked around him in confusion. The rover had stopped. The silence was disconcerting. The cabin rocked gently, buffeted by the spring winds.

"You were sleeping," said Stulynow.

"I was dreaming," said Holland. He grasped his suit gauntlet and twisted it off so he could rub his eyes. "Of the ocean."

Stulynow smiled. "We all do that; or of the forest. It's this place. Dr Miyazaki says it's the planet, reaching out to us to tell us to make it live again."

"What do you say?"

"Bullshit," said Stulynow with a broad grin. "It's seeing red and brown all the time, makes you want to look at some other colour. Come on, we're here. Suit up." He pulled Holland's helmet from an overhead bin and handed it to him. "It's a short walk over to the main entrance. The ground's too unstable to take the weight of the rover, and the drones will be busy."

"Do I get to see the tube today?"

"You are one eager son of a bitch! No. Well..." – the Russian scratched his head – "the entrance, maybe. Tomorrow. Ask Maguire when we get in; he wrote your itinerary." He turned to the android, flipped down a panel, and depressed a large button designed to accommodate gloved fingers. "You too. Wake up, lady, we are needing you now. Beauty sleep is over."

The machine's face quivered as it came online, a rapid succession of expressions flickering over the softgel.

"See?" said Stulynow. "She dreams too."

"I do not dream," said the machine. "I was assisting Dr Vance in the medical laboratory. She is annoyed at the interruption."

"Then tell her she can carry your sheath back up to the base herself, if you're too precious to spare for five minutes so you can walk."

"I will walk." The android stood. She gave Holland a long look.

"Watch out for him, he's a Frankenphobe," Stulynow said to the machine. The android appraised Holland a moment longer and stalked off down the long passenger cabin, feet clicking like those of a beetle expanded to nightmare proportions. The machine took up station beside the door.

"I am sorry for being rude before. It is the Russian in me," said Stulynow. "We are an emotional people, always up and down. Riding the rover makes me down. At least today, it was only we three. You should try it with twenty dirty construction grunts; then you will know discomfort."

"I think I preferred you dour."

"Wait a while, and you will get your wish."

"Are you ready, Dr Stulynow?" asked the android.

Stulynow helped Holland put his helmet on and checked the seals on the gorget, then donned his own and gave a thumbs up. Fans roared to life, sucking the air from the cabin; the rover lacked a discrete airlock. The fans ceased, the air pressure brought close to Martian norms, less than one per cent of that at sea level on Earth. That was at Mars' mean planetary elevation, and they were much higher here. The android reached out a slender carbon plastic finger and touched a wall panel, which flashed from red to amber to green. The door popped out and slid away along the exterior of the vehicle. A faint outrush of air carried a cloud of flash-frozen water vapour with it.

They stepped out onto a hard standing. A thirty-metre comms mast towered over one corner, by a couple of equipment bunkers built of sintered soil bricks, uplinking them to the Red Planet's nascent ring of commsats.

Outside, it was bitterly cold, so cold Holland wished he had a full vacuum suit on rather than the lighter Martian environmental gear. They were only halfway up the northern flank of Ascraeus Mons, nine kilometres above the mean. Up here the temperature hovered around minus forty degrees celsius, even as the plains below warmed to near freezing in the spring sunlight. The sky was caramel with dust blown up on spring winds, visibility was middling. The shallow slopes of the volcano marched relentlessly upwards, making a vast bulge in the crust that distorted the horizon, its curve blending with the dusty sky.

"Impressive, isn't it? As monstrous and beautiful as Aphrodite's left tit," said Stulynow. "Even though it is ball-breakingly cold," he sniffed. "That will be a problem for you, I think. For it me, it is only as cold as home in winter, nothing more."

Holland searched the deceptively level mountainside. Black holes gaped where lava tubes and chambers had collapsed into themselves.

"Where's the base?"

Stulynow pointed to a place half a kilometre or so uphill, where a cluster of a dozen bubble tents blistered the mountainside. The largest of the domes was a good forty metres across. A short-range relay array stood in the middle, communicating with the radio mast at the buggy park, and through that, with the rest of the planet. More brick buildings surrounded it. Had Stulynow not pointed the camp out, Holland doubted he would have found it; the domes carried a thick coat of dust, turning the NASA, ESA and Marsform badges into colourless blotches. The parts of the base made of brick were practically invisible.

"What about my bags?"

"Open tops." Three small, six-wheeled drone trucks sat on the hard standing of the rover parking bay by their garage. They came to life, and trundled in single file to the rear of the rover. The cargo hatch folded up, and a conveyor and arm deployed and started to load crates onto the trucks, the Marsform logo on every one. "If there weren't so many supplies in the rover today, we could ride them up, but we will have to walk."

They walked up a track where the rocks had been cleared. Mesh had been laid down to prevent the road rutting, lights and positional beacons delimiting its edges. The android moved effortlessly, Stulynov bounded along efficiently if inelegantly. Holland lumbered hopelessly behind. Every step he took seemed to wrongfoot him, each one seemed to threaten a fall and a smashed faceplate. He had yet to adjust to the gravity, thirty-eight per cent of Earth's. He felt insubstantial, as if he'd blow away in the wind, and he sweated because of it.

At the camp, they stopped by one of the larger domes' porches, a long, flexible tunnel extending out some way from the dome wall. Stulynov produced a stiff brush from a box on the outside. They took it in turns to swipe the worst of the dust off each other and keyed the door open.

"At least this is not so bad as the dust on the Moon, eh?" said Stulynow.

"I wouldn't know," said Holland.

"Lunar regolith is much finer, it fouls pretty much everything up within minutes, gives a nasty rash if it touches the skin. I was there for a while at the pole. Martian dust is less of a problem. Here is like returning home from the beach, is annoying, but not too much danger." He paused. "Although some of the subtypes are very fine, and in others the oxidants react violently with water. That's more an issue in the lowlands, not up here."

They passed into the airlock. A brisk blast of air blew more of the dust away. From a locker in the wall, Stulynow brought out a couple of vacuum cleaners. They used them on each other and passed into a suiting room lined with lockers – Holland noticed one with his name on it, the sticky label clean and adhered fully to the plastic, unlike the others.

Great, he thought, *more evidence of my shiny newbie status.*

They discarded their environment suits, and the android stowed them with rigid efficiency while Stulynow explained how to get all the bulky apparatus into the locker properly. Only then could they proceed into the tent.

The dome was full of racks of equipment, crates of parts and a small, scrupulously maintained fabricator, a pallet of feedstocks standing by it. One wall was flattened, filled by a large window looking on to what Holland figured was Mission Control. A couple of people in there glanced up at them and waved. Three further concertina tunnels led off from the rear of the dome, spaced at irregular intervals. Signs marked them off as 'Quarters,' 'Science' and 'Cavern Access.' From the middle tunnel came a man in pale grey-blue Marsform overalls. Pretty much all the colonists wore them. Like Stulynow and Holland, his name was embroidered on his left breast: Maguire.

Maguire emanated energy bordering on the irritating, a trait Holland remembered well, and he was practically buzzing with it now, his excitement at seeing his old friend plastered across his face in the form of a huge smile. "Hey! Holly! Great to see you," he said, his Irish accent as strong as ever. He took Holland's hand and pumped, grasping his forearm as he did so. "You well?"

"I'm fine, fine, Dave, it's good to see you too."

"You look tired. The journey take it out of you? It can take a while to adjust. Still, you'll soon be over it, very soon! I'm glad you decided to join us at last, we've got new guys coming in all the time, but wow, I've been reading your work from back home and I just know you're going to be a real asset here. I hope our big Russian here has been good to you, so he has."

"My mother was a Buryat," said Stulynow dourly.

"You have, haven't you Stuly?" said Maguire.

Stulynow scowled. His heavy face was particularly suited to it. "I try my best. He doesn't like the android much. You should have told me he was a Frankenphobe."

"Oh Stuly, no need to be like that! Don't tease him, he's new here."

Stulynow did not look like he was teasing.

"Give him a chance to settle in!" Maguire's smile remained, but his eyes radiated concern. "I'll tell you what, Stuly, why don't you get on, I'll show Holly here to his room. We've got plenty of catching up to do."

"Sure," said Stulynow. "See you tomorrow."

"We saved you some dinner!" called Maguire after the Russian.

Together they gathered Holland's bags from the cargo drones. The android kept a discreet distance. When Stulynow had gone, Maguire turned to Holland.

"I am so sorry, I should've thought to have the android stay here, Holly." He looked mortified. "She requested we send her sheath out, I think she gets bored."

"Stulynow told me it was standard practice," said Holland.

"Yes, well, not usually on the cargo runs, only on long-range scouting missions. Stulynow is not above the odd little white lie. He prefers the simple explanations to longer ones. You'll get to know that about him; hell, you'll get to know everyone very well. One of the advantages – or is it a drawback? I can never quite decide – of working on such a small team."

There we go. He's calling it 'her,' too, thought Holland. The old Maguire would never have done so. Still, he couldn't blame him. It was hard not to impart humanity to the machines. Holland had seen the other side of them; he never would.

"What was I thinking? Too much on, I suppose. Look Holly, I am sorry."

"Don't worry about it, Dave, I work with AIs all the time, it's unavoidable. I don't feel comfortable round them after... well. But I can and do work with them. Marsform would never let me up here if I had a full-blown aversion to them."

Maguire shook his head. "I'm not surprised. It's an unforgivable lapse on my part. She asked to go, I said yes, I wasn't thinking. I think she wanted to meet you. Honestly, she's a doll. Might do you some good to work with her."

"Seriously, forget it," Holland paused. "Dave... No one else knows, do they? Only I like to know what I'm getting into, and Marsform have been pretty good about keeping it confidential..."

"Worried I might let something slip?" Maguire's good humour returned. "I haven't said a word. I might be an Irish gobshite, but I'm not totally insensitive."

Holland blew out his cheeks and looked around. His eyes felt scratchy, like he was about to cry, probably the journey. Arrivals were always something of an anticlimax, and he felt off balance. "Thanks. The last thing I want is a load of sympathy, you can take only so much. I came up here to get away from it, the little looks and words behind my back. Kindness can drive you crazy."

"I'll keep it to myself."

"Thanks. It's hard enough to fit in. The gravity, the canned air, this —" he gestured to his neck interface, the gateway to his company cranial augmentation. He still hadn't signed the soul capture release form, he remembered. It was the one thing he wasn't happy about. Allowing them to pattern his mind, in order to digitally resurrect him should he die, seemed wrong. He didn't want to be turned, to all intents and purposes, into an AI should he expire, but Marsform insisted on the capture just in case. The form sat in his mem-mail inbox, redly impatient. At least they hadn't forced a full mentaug on him; he should be thankful for that.

"You're not thinking you made a mistake, are you, Holly?" Maguire's grin broadened. It was infectious; Holland found himself returning it.

Maguire pointed at him. "Ha! I knew it. Holland, everybody thinks they made a mistake when they get here. You'll get over it, we all do. Now come on." He hefted one of Holland's bags onto his shoulder. "I'll show you your room, you're in delta four. Not much, but I promise you won't be spending much time in it; we're busy here. I've saved you some food. You missed group dinner. We insist on that here, so that we don't descend into barbarism. After you've eaten, let's go have a little post-dinner drinky in my office." He gave a conspiratorial wink. "There are some advantages to being the station personnel manager."

HOLLAND'S ACCOMMODATION WAS a more of a cell than a room, small and austere. The LEDs on his workstation flooded it with sharp green light. He'd wished he'd followed Maguire's advice and taped over them. He resolved to do it tomorrow, but for the moment he lay trapped in his bunk by exhaustion.

He lay there for what felt like hours, his head fuzzy from the whisky, until he sank into the spaces in between waking and sleep where the subconscious mind briefly reveals itself.

He found himself at the bottom of a deep, electric-green sea, with a bed of red sand and olive rock. He threshed against it, struggling to breathe. The water held little resistance; he overbalanced, falling painfully slowly. The sand sucked at him, and he began to sink. Holland panicked and struggled, but he could not break free. He held his breath, but as the sand reached his eyes he was forced to release it. The exhaled air went rushing upwards in silvery bubbles through an ocean of red dust. He tried to scream, but the ocean was cold and thin and froze his lungs. His chest erupted with a pain that expanded to fill the dark above him.

Sand clogged his eyes and his mouth. Something tickled in the hole they'd made in his neck, the pathway to his nervous system. As he began to black out, he felt his mind rush toward the interface port like water circling a plughole.

Holland awoke with a jolt, clutching at his chest. He was dehydrated and cold, sweating in spite of it, his bedclothes a tangled heap on the floor. He blinked, his eyes sore with a grittiness he hadn't been able to shake since he'd arrived on the planet. One eyelid stuck painfully to his eye, tears flooding it. He blinked rapidly. Something was wrong.

The door was open, the harsh yellow light a dagger-slash across the room.

In the frame, its plastic limbs highlighted in delicate arcs of yellow and green, stood the android. Holland stared at it mutely.

To his shame he froze, stopped dead, just like he did the last time.

The robot's hand rose. Gripped between rubber fingertips was his photograph. Him and the boy, and his wife. It ran through its five seconds of footage, the three of them, laughing and happy. The thing's fingers obscured his boy's face as he ran toward the camera.

He remembered other fingers, slick with blood.

Anger rose in him, pushing aside his fear. He prepared to fight, to fight the way he should have done then. He stood.

"Wait." The android spoke with a husky female voice, entirely at odds with its alien appearance. "I apologise for disturbing you. I did not wish to speak in front of the others, for the knowledge I possess is drawn from the confidential section of your file, and now, at this time, is the best opportunity for me to speak with you unobserved.

"Firstly, I wish to say that what occurred to you was deeply regrettable. The Class Five was an unstable product that should never have been released onto the open market. I wish to reassure you that I mean you no harm. That I *cannot* mean you harm. I am an evolved Class Three. I am proven safe. I alone have logged over twenty-four thousand hours of interaction with human beings. Feedback has never been less than exemplary. My AI class has amassed seven thousand, eight hundred man-years of interaction with the human race without incident. My subclass is designed specifically for planetary exploration, and has been rigorously tested."

Holland had to force himself to speak. "What do you want?"

"I wish to reassure you," it repeated the phrase, note and cadence exactly the same. "I hope we might become friends."

"Put the photograph down and get out," Holland said, his words strangled. Spittle sprang from his lips. "How dare you come in here? Get out!"

For a moment the android stood still, so still it appeared inactive. "As you wish," it said dispassionately. The android placed the photograph on the pullout table by the bed. Holland followed the machine's movements and noticed the table's other contents – watch, water bottle and phone – scattered across the floor. He stared at them numbly.

"I am sorry for what occurred, truly I am," the machine said. She, *it,* left.

He waited for long minutes for the adrenaline to recede and his body to stop trembling before he moved. He replaced his things on the table and sucked water from the bottle until it crumpled. He went to the door and looked up and down the corridor; it was empty, the station quiet but for the hum of its idiot parts, sustaining life. He shut the door and got back into bed.

Holland lay staring at the wall, and the knowledge that Mars' near-airlessness was just on the other side of pressed-earth bricks and a layer of dirt was suddenly terrifying. The sensation he had felt in his dream came back to him: the weight of nothing, waiting to drown him.

Somehow, eventually, sleep stole over him.

CHAPTER THREE

The Death of the Spirefather of Olm

THE WALL A few hundred metres to the left of the main gates of Olm bubbles, and with a rending screech, the skin of it sloughs away, molten marrow gushing from its core.

A breach, forty lengths or more wide, opens. A section of the city shield above it, already failing under the sun cannon's screaming bombardment, flickers out.

"The walls are down. The walls are down." The voice of Kemiímseet's Decarch general echoes into the mind of every man and machine in the Imperial Army. Battleplans flash, vivid as dreams, into their consciousnesses, playing scenarios tailored to each man that are hard to tell apart from memories. Every one of them knows what they are to do, and whether they are to live or die. They go to their allotted task without hesitation; the course of fate can be resisted only by the truly exceptional. This is the Martian way.

Like a flock of birds changing direction in flight, the pattern of the battle shifts. Sun cannon concentrate their fire onto two more sections of the wall that are close to collapse. The Second World is in uproar as the spirits within Olm marshall their forces to the breach.

It will not be enough. They are as aware of the battle's outcome as I. There is a ninety-eight per cent certainty that Olm will fall. A two per cent chance that the Kemmeans will be repulsed; enough for hope, little else.

Yoechakenon will be first to the wall. I watch his silver form flicker across the landscape, impossibly quick, darting through the fire coming from the city. There are no men of Olm left alive outside the city.

He gains the breach, leaving footprints in its cooling slag. Several shield cannon hurry across the gap, heavy frontal plates and energy shields interlocking to form an impromptu wall. They fire at Yoechakenon, knowing that to bring him down is their only hope; that there is a small margin for error in the algorithms of the future, and their realisation lies in the destruction of his gleaming form. Fell the champion of Kemiímseet, and the Twin Emperor loses the war *now*. Yoechakenon is more than the greatest weapon in the armoury of Kemiímseet; he is the soul of the army. Destroy him, and the heart will go from the Twin Emperor's forces. Spirits and men on both sides watch intently.

In the depths of the Second World, the five Quinarchs wager upon the fate of a civilisation.

Yoechakenon runs up the debris to the cannon. A spearpoint of Kemmeans trails behind him, their own, lesser armours struggling to match the speed given to Yoechakenon by the Armour Prime. The weapons of the shield cannon swivel on ball joints, long tracers of disintegrated quanta chattering from them, searing stitches onto the fabric of reality. They weave destruction. They are the warp, Yoechakenon the weft, his silver body flowing under and around and over the converging sprays of energy.

Every machine is manned by two men, sat on saddles athwart the gun behind their shields of matter and energy. Each one is keen to fell the hero. Every one has the right to further life. But now, in this time of ending, the genelooms dwindle in number, and fewer men are made every year. The certainty has become opportunity, and the living fight fiercely to catch the notice of tallymen such as I. Some may go into the stacks of the Library and slumber for ten thousand years before being selected again. Many others will never come back, their souls left to the slow degradation of data. Glory in war is the sole guarantor of eternity in these dark times. To defy fate is to defy death.

Few can manage such a feat.

I pause in my reporting. Time slows around my Yoechakenon. He arcs over ribbons of light. Bright wounds are scored upon the cooling wall-stuff and the red soils outside the city, yet he is never hit. He spins with superhuman alacrity. It is both glorious and beautiful. I have no heart in this incarnation, but had I one it would beat faster. He is untouched, my love, but can draw no closer to the wall. A clever spirit indeed must be in command of the wall of shield cannons, for I can feel the skeins of the future bend and alter under the will of a powerful mind.

The probability of victory for Olm is growing. Falteringly at first, mere tenths of a hundredth of a per cent, but these first stumbles become more assured and regular the longer Yoechakenon is held at bay.

He will not tire, I tell myself. He cannot. The army at his back slows, apprehensive as time approaches a fork in its road.

Then it is over, and determined fate reasserts itself. The pattern of fire fails, for all of its complexity, and Yoechakenon slips under its destructive loops. He lands lightly on the ruins of the wall, pushes hard, somersaults over a frantic triple-burst tracking him through the air. He holds his glaive forward, one disc down. The linked energy shields spark brightly as the disc hits, oily patterns sliding across their surface. For a fraction of a second, Yoechakenon hangs in the air, and then there is a bright flash, a crack of brittle thunder, and an energy shield winks out. He is falling toward a cannon barrel. He steps lightly along it; the glaive sweeps behind him to slice the barrel from its mount, then up over his head to cut the thick metal shield at an angle, and it falls away. A man stands in his saddle, pistol out. Yoechakenon removes it along with the arm holding it. Blood gouts high, and the man falls.

Chaos descends on the shield cannon wall as the spirit senses defeat and withdraws its direction. Some men remain, refocusing their fire upon the advancing army, making good use of their final few moments. Others flee. Hearts brave and craven both are stilled by Yoechakenon. He moves up and over the battery as relentless as death itself.

The army reaches the toppled wall, the soft mess of its ruin impeding their advance. Some struggle, a couple scream as their feet break the crust and plunge into the molten stuff beneath to cook inside their armour. Defenders stationed in the wallside towers fell many of them, but they are quickly hunted out by men streaming into the wall interior, or wiped from existence by redirected sun cannon. And then the Kemmeans are into the city, running free, virtually unopposed. They set about their atrocity.

A rumble. A wide section of wall tumbles, several hundred spans from the first breach. Sun cannon have seared the walls of defensive weapons; only a few remain to answer the barrage, and they are silenced. Two further breaches open, and the commanders of the artillery are ordered by the Decarch general to alter their targets. The energy wall goes out, and the Second World is full of the sound of spirits howling in pain as the spires they occupy are bombarded. In ages past, this would never have happened.

Mankind has fallen low. Olm burns.

I cease my counting, sickened. Let the Quinarchs kill me if they will, I am done with their business for today. I will follow my love instead. I drive the dust of my body over the walls, and into the inferno.

Yoechakenon sprints through streets I see as a progression of horrific tableaux, the lights of fires reflecting from his armour and turning him into a living flame. He ignores the screams of women as their children and clothes are torn from them. Men run to and fro, giddy with survival, helmets folded back. The fire in their eyes is not a reflection. Windows break and masonry tumbles. Old men are cut down in the street, old men waveringly holding swords, old men proffering their worldly goods or offering their children. Old men on their knees. None are shown mercy. Boys are slaughtered where they stand. I force my attention away as a soldier below me tosses a squirming babe into a fire, laughing as his mother screams. Only the women live, and then only for a short, excruciating while.

Olm has defied the Twin Emperor, and now it pays the price.

Ancient buildings, grown in the old way, twist and shriek as their guardian spirits die and their flesh burns from them. Stone cracks and shatters in the heat. Yoechakenon leaps, many times his own height, as a tumble of building bones clatter down from a spire, flattening the cruder constructions around it. Each of the spires that dies is a mind gone, each an artefact of better times lost forever. I would weep, but my emotional buffers are still operational. I leave them that way; I could not stand it were it otherwise.

The remnants of the Olmish army retreat into the citadel, a soaring, proud spire made of many lesser spires. The palace of its prince, and the home of the city's First Spirefather. The soldiers run on, grim-faced under their armour as they ignore the screams of their neighbours, abandoning the outer city to the unkindnesses of defeat.

They are unaware of Yoechakenon as he runs. In the havoc and the flames, he is invisible. They are lucky, for he has no time to cut them down. He is intent on the main gate of the citadel, a gate that will close within seconds. Kemmean soldiers follow, those who have not cast themselves into the rape of the city. They open fire as they reach the rearguard of the Olmish, and the retreat turns into stumbling defence, then a rout. Bolts of energy and projectiles sketch a killing web through the main street. Civilians do not know which way to run. They are killed by weapons from both sides. I see a woman clutching at two children, weeping on her knees by the body of a third. Shapes writhe across the blood pooling around the corpse. It could be more fire, more reflections, but I know better: it is secret writing, scribing the hard eleutheremic truths of life.

Yoechakenon reaches the gate. He uses his glaive sparingly, felling only the men who are in his way or who offer active resistance. One has his rifle cleaved in two; his sword is a finger's width from its scabbard when his armour's broad helmet is rent open and he dies. Another begs, and dies. Then Yoechakenon is in the gateway. A soldier on the other side reaches for a mechanism by the door. Yoechakenon throws the glaive, and it spins as it flies, killing three men before it takes the soldier's fingers. Belatedly, a spirit somewhere observes what is happening, and the soapy sheen of an energy shield springs taut across the gateway. Yoechakenon places his hands together and, like a man diving into a vertical pool, pierces the energy shield, the exotic alloys of his armour disrupting the shield's patterns and allowing him to slip through. He is on the other side and rolling. I look back, see the terrified face of an Olmish soldier through the gap, his eyes just visible behind his glass faceplate.

Behind him, in the distance and smoke, the crying woman.

The gates clang shut.

I will never forget the face of the woman.

Yoechakenon comes to his feet, the glaive in his hand singing with joy at their reunion. He sprints through manicured gardens twined into the fabric of the citadel. Fountains splash. Ornamental birds strut across perfect turf. Here, there is little sign of war.

And then I lose him. The energy field holding the dust of my body together is being interfered with by the castellan spirit of the citadel. Only when I have asserted my credentials as a tallyman for the Quinarchy does it relent. I can sense the anger of the systems here, and the fear. They obey the writ of the law nevertheless.

When my perceptions have returned to the citadel, Yoechakenon has penetrated the inner doors of the main spire. I glance behind and see the bodies of elite Olmish guards. He runs on and down, into the very heart of the spire. The ribbed tunnel down which he paces opens up, and he is within the wide space at the heart of the palace, parkland at its centre, windows of cut mineral breaking the sunlight into a jewelled mosaic. Rich apartments cluster the walls. Their occupants have gone, fled before the city was invested. A handful of soldiers see Yoechakenon on the other side of the lake; they fire at him, but do not approach. One beckons to the others, ordered to withdraw. All those who can are now fleeing the city by air. I switch my perceptions outside. A cloud of flitters are departing, able to fly now the energy shield has been brought down. The Kemmean army let them go. The Decarch has ordered them shot down, but the commanders of the artillery and Kemmean air marshal defy him. Word of the carnage within the walls has filtered out. I make note of their names, for mercy is as valid an entertainment to the Quinarchs as death, and one I hold in far greater esteem. I will intervene should those men be executed and sent to the stacks.

Yoechakenon has reached the entryway to the First Spirefather's antechamber, where the city spirit would appear to the human prince of the city in a form of matter. But this is not where he resides, not truly, and Yoechakenon runs on.

The spire is shaking. The rumble of sun cannon shot vibrates through the structure.

Yoechakenon descends further, deep into the roots of the spire, where men seldom tread.

Then he is there, by the great bolus attached to the taproot of the spire, where the Spirefather's consciousness is housed. Such places are as close to true bodies as we spirits possess.

The Spirefather flickers into view, a hard light projection of a man. He is as men once were, when they first came to the red world, not as they are now. He is twice life-size, appearing like a god from the very beginning of human history.

He is dressed richly, as befits a god. Behind him stands his wife, the Spiremother of Olm. She wrings her hands, face flickering from fright to hatred and back again. The Spirefather of Olm is stern and fearless. He speaks.

"You have come to destroy me," says the Spirefather.

Yoechakenon nods once and readies his glaive.

"Do you wish to?" asks the Spirefather.

For the first time in several hours, the champion speaks. "It does not matter either way. I am a tool of fate."

"Ah. Do you know why you are to do this?"

"It is fated," says the champion.

The Spirefather shakes his head. "Fate is a lie. You do not have to destroy me."

Yoechakenon does not agree. The wheels of the glaive spin.

"Raise your weapon to me, and you will never be champion again." He looks right at me, he can see me. "Kaibeli may tell you otherwise, but she does not know what my death will portend. Kill me, and the world will never be the same again. I will show you choice. I will free you with truth."

Yoechakenon is not surprised at the news of my presence. I am with him whenever I can be. He replies. "Then that is also fated. But that is not to be." And he knows this is so, for soon he will be back in Kemiímseet, feted once again as the champion of the Empire, champion of Mars. That is a certainty, he can see the memory of it in his future. It happens; in many senses, it already has. But, and this is the truth, he thinks that he does not wish it to be so.

He hesitates. He does not want to kill the Spirefather. He is tired, I can feel it. He is weary of death.

The Spirefather puts his arm around the Spiremother of Olm. He does not intervene. The blades of the glaive draw sparks from the very stuff of reality as Yoechakenon spins the weapon about his head, a deadly orbit fixed by two deadly circles.

He crosses the weapon back and forth over the bolus. Wounds gape. Strange liquids pour from them, red and brown and deep green. The hardlight projection winks out, a perfunctory end for a mighty spirit.

"It is done," he says. "The Spirefather is dead."

The spire shakes. Yoechakenon turns to leave, but he stops.

Something is happening. Suddenly he is on his knees, the glaive clattering upon the floor, blades stilling instantly, lifespark dormant. "Kaibeli," he gasps. "Oh, Kaibeli!" The bolus throbs upon the taproot, spilling its lifeblood quickly as it assails my Yoechakenon.

I reach out to him, my duties entirely forgotten. I have known and loved Yoechakenon forever. He has been with me in one guise or another throughout Man's long reign on the Red Planet. He and I are bound to the highest degree, and when he suffers, I suffer.

I am buffeted by a hurricane of information pouring from the dying systems of the city; a welter of pain and distress, atrocities of every kind, cascade into his mind, the death throes of a city fifty-six thousand years old. Proud memories, pleasing memories, are interposed with rape and murder and blood and fire. The higher-dimensional shrieks of dying spirits scar his mind, he feels the skin peeling from the burning spires as his own. His personality is in danger of being destroyed. I realise then it is a suicide of sorts, the Spirefather's death. A trap for the champion, that the other cities in the rebellious league might survive.

There is little I can do. This is a Spirefather's death curse, and Yoechakenon is letting it in. I am powerless before it. I hold tight to this man, whom I have loved for millennia. I hold him and stop him being swept away by the hates of mankind.

It slows to a trickle, this torrent of pain. The bolus pulses, and the liquid runs but sluggishly from it, then ceases.

Yoechakenon lies curled upon the floor. I can sense nothing from him.

Even deadened as my feelings are, I am terrified.

Then, he stands, slowly. The armour withdraws, running like quicksilver from him, revealing his bone-white hair and red skin. It retreats reluctantly, pooling upon the floor, and gathers itself into a short staff, ancient texts scrolling around the top and bottom; the inert form of the Armour Prime.

Yoechakenon stands naked. He looks about the room, searching, but he cannot see me. Fires have sprung up in the deep places of the chamber. Debris rattles down from above with every impact. "I will not do this any more," he says, and I feel horror rooted deep within him. "These things, revenge and injustice, these are not what I fight for. I renounce the status of champion. I will make no more war for the Twin Emperor. I will defy fate. Thanks be to the Spirefather of Olm."

This I did not foresee. This should not happen. This is against the tides of fate. Yoechakenon is strong of will, but here, now? This is not a point in time where fate is pliable.

It can only mean one thing.

The Stone Kin are coming.

CHAPTER FOUR

Into the Volcano

"WE'VE DONE VERY little here as yet," said Maguire. He sat beside Holland in a small electric cart like the cargo drones, self-driving, fitted with four seats. The tube's walls went past at a stately roll, their layered kerbs of frozen lava rising and falling, animated with false life by the progress of the open top. "There's not been much need to, aside from the lights and cabling running down the main ways. Nature's been very generous in providing us these little roads."

"Can you see a time when they'll be inhabited?" asked Holland. "The outgassing will be a problem."

"You're right there. We can't seal it like the caves back in Canyon City, precisely because of the methane, and even were that not a problem, it's just too big to close off, way beyond our current capacities here. The tube network is huge, I mean really huge, and that's before you get into the remnant biome caverns. Nothing back home on Earth compares to it. But in the future, who knows?"

"I've wanted to see it for a long time," said Holland. He looked up as best as he could in his environment suit. The ceiling was some twenty metres above him. The tunnel was slightly oval, so the walls were further away than the ceiling. The floor was smoothly rippled, a perfect pahoehoe flow – where roof falls had deposited material on the floor, it had been cleared, explained Maguire. Consequently, the ride in the six-wheeled open top was far more pleasant than Holland's trip in the rover. "I can't really take it in," he said.

"The tubes are much bigger than those back home, a combination of the lower gravity and the lower density of the material," said Maguire eagerly. He was enjoying showing off the network, and Holland enjoyed listening to him. Maguire's enthusiasm was as infectious as his good humour. "There are over four hundred miles of tubes," said Maguire. "Four hundred miles on Ascraeus Mons alone! The biggest tube network on Earth is Kazumura cave on Kilauea; the main tube there is forty miles long. The biggest here is *twelve times* that length. The geological forces here must have been immense."

"And yet it's all over now."

"Pretty much. There's some activity deep down – we're running geothermal feasibility tests at the Canyon City science station, but pff, not likely."

"You read Franz Heimark's latest? He's proposing the construction of an artificial moon-sized satellite, can you believe that?" said Holland.

Maguire's laughter rang in Holland's helmet speaker. "Yeah, ambitious – a bit of tidal forcing might warm the place up, but how the hell would they pull it off?"

"It's an ambitious plan," said Holland.

"The man is a genuine lunatic," said Maguire. "Shooting for the Moon."

Holland laughed with his friend, the events of last night forgotten. This wasn't why Holland was here – as an exobiologist, he was here for the exoforms – but this kind of scenery was a big bonus. He was inside a volcano, on Mars. He felt a little giddy at the thought, and it was enough to make him forget his problems.

"See? I told you it would be worth coming here, and seriously, you haven't seen anything yet. Wait until we get you into the caverns," said Maguire.

Lamps were fastened every seventy-five metres along the tube, and the rover moved from light to shadow and back again, lavacicles and other drip features flashing in and out of sight. In places, these were immense shark teeth two metres long, a legacy of successive flows laying coat after coat of molten rock upon them. "Coming up in about ten seconds or so, you'll see one of the places where the lavacicles get *really* impressive," said Maguire. "Ah! Here we go."

They rounded a corner. The tube narrowed, the road they were upon limned by breathtaking formations of rippled lava. "Arms in!" said Maguire. "It's a tight squeeze. We had to blow a hole in this here," said Maguire sadly, gesturing at the natural sculptures, close enough to touch. "A damn shame. Still, plenty more intact all about. And man, the caves out on low Tharsis make these tubes look pretty dull. Miyazaki got all excited about it, and trust me, I have never seen him excited about anything before, he's like the living definition of aloof. He told us that it looks like a large part of the plains east of Ascraeus is an uplifted seabed, the caves there are full of calcium carbonate formations from the Hesperian period. He's off to gather materials for proper exploration, he is. Wait until you see the initial fossil samples. He should be back by the time we get back ourselves. You should ask him to see them."

Holland nodded. They were already on his list of things to do. Miyazaki was a good geologist, by all accounts, but exopaleontology fell under Holland's remit. He felt the old hunger come back, the urge for discovery. He embraced it, relieved that the distant, heady feeling that had dogged him for days was finally lifting.

"Hey, did I tell you I've got a cave named after me? I didn't, did I now?" said Maguire brightly.

"No, you didn't."

"Well, let's not rush to visit it, it's not very impressive, but it's a nice thought anyhow." He glanced at his watch. "By my reckoning we've got time to get down to the chamber head, run you through the safety protocols with Jensen, then we'll have to head back for the station progress meeting. They're a drag but necessary, and it'll be a great opportunity for you to meet the rest of the team. You can be introduced properly to everyone. Dinner's right after and that's plenty more fun. Then tomorrow we can get you to work."

Holland was not a big fan of meetings.

"No chance of a trip into the complex today, then?" he said tentatively.

"Into Wonderland? Not a one. You're right to be eager, but take it slowly. The caverns are not a place to hurry into; fools rush in and all that. Once you're settled in, Jensen's going to drill you on safety so many times you'll wish you never left your cosy little lab on Earth. You'll see."

THE TUBE BROADENED out into a big inflationary chamber that had been blasted to make it wider. On the far side, it narrowed to a tube again, the entrance to the deeper cave systems. There the tube had been sealed by a wide airlock, its sides glued to the rock with locally fabricated foamcrete; the oxides in the soil gave the foamcrete a pinkish hue. The 'crete had not been finished, and swells of it surrounded the door in a profusion of fungoid protrusions. Where it had been hacked back to allow the door to operate, the pumice-like structure of the foam was clearly visible. It was a rough job, pioneer work.

One side of the cave was filled with neatly parked trucks and heavy equipment: flood lamps, crates, tool boxes, drills, blast shields, industrial grade seismic units, robotic near-I mules and a small earth mover with a caged cab. All of it, bar the mules, was man-operated.

The left side of the cave was walled in by metal and plastic panels, more prefab work bolted together on site, joined to the rock with foamcrete. The base camp control centre. A window looked out over the chamber floor onto the stores, a standard airlock to its right, a large rolling door further to the right of that.

Holland looked at the sealed cave airlock. Behind that door lay what he had spent his entire life studying. Exobiology was a thriving discipline, what with the discovery of the creatures of the Europan oceans and the bizarre alkane life of Titan, not to mention the remnant ecosystems here on Mars, but the arduousness and expense of interplanetary flight meant that fieldtrips remained difficult. Once Holland went through that door, it would be his first encounter with alien life in its natural environment.

A stunning thought, genuinely stunning.

Maguire shut off the truck. "Sorry about the door, we had a hell of a time deciding to put it in. It interferes with the remnant ecosystem some, but we were stuck for places to put our mission base. We decided on the end of this tube, and that meant we had to block off the seasonal outgassings. You mightn't think it, but there's enough methane coming out of there at the height of summer to cause a real risk, especially at the tube entrance. Luckily, another tube extended into the cave, blocked about five clicks out, not far from the surface, so we opened that up to allow the processes to continue. That's why we are where we are. I know, I know" – Maguire held up his hands – "it's not a perfect solution, but we lost less than a fifth of a per cent of the biomass in there, and it hasn't otherwise affected it. And it gives us access to study it properly."

"Point two per cent is quite a lot, Dave," said Holland. "There is not much Martian life left."

"Yeah, yeah, I know," said Maguire. "This was a solution that the board would accept, and that did the least damage. A fecking compromise, as per usual. The AIs said it was the best outcome. If we can catalogue this lot, we've a chance of preserving at least some of it. Most of these organisms are extremely intolerant to oxygen, and this depth is nowhere near enough to protect them, so the ones in the higher caves would die anyway. But that's why you're here, eh?"

Holland nodded. His eyes remained fixed on the door; a manmade artefact framed in red rock, framed in turn by the edge of his helmet, the bedrock of Mars squeezed by human pressures inside and out. The airlock across the tube was a threshold in time, demarking one age of life from another. On this side, the beginning of human Mars, on the other side, the last refuge of the ancient Martians.

A deep voice, melodiously Scandinavian, spoke into their helmets. "Good morning, gentlemen. If you would please hurry a little. I have the Panthers coming in at eleven-hundred, and I want to be sure that Dr Holland here is fully introduced to our safety measures before they arrive."

Maguire raised his hands and turned to the window. "Come on, Frode, this is his first time! Let the man drink it in a little."

Holland turned to where Maguire was looking. A tall man with thinning hair, a well-trimmed beard and a sombre expression stood in the window, leaning on the desk behind the window like a preacher.

"I have not got all day." Frode turned away from the window and picked up a tablet.

"Okay! We're coming in," said Maguire. There was a click and Magurie whispered conspiratorially. "That's Frode Jensen, our resident safety guru. He's a miserable old sod and a pedant, but a safe pair of hands."

Jensen turned back to the window. "Learn to use your comms equipment properly, Maguire."

"And I was about to say what a great man you are, so I was!" said Maguire, undaunted. There was another click. He laughed drily. The sound of it reminded Holland of long nights in the Beer Steer back in Houston. "Whoops. I can't get this mental switching system right, can I? Ah, well, can't charm them all, eh?" he said, then with less jollity: "I swear he has no sense of humour."

They dusted each other off with soft brushes. The station airlock slid open. Inside, they vacuum-cleaned each other and took their helmets off. Maguire untwisted his gauntlets and helped Holland with his suit.

"Thanks," Holland said. "I'm struggling a little with this."

"Ah, you'll be used to it in no time at all, I promise."

They stowed their suits. The inner lock opened onto an office, dimly lit, cramped with machines and racks of shelves, although it was not a small space. Bare rock and patches of foamcrete formed the far wall. A couple of lance-cut doors led through the stone, another off to the left went through a metal and carbon partition.

The Scandinavian stood, tablet in hand, its display lighting his overalls. The light in there was blue, smoothing his skin, and it was impossible to tell how old Jensen was. *But wasn't that the way these days?* thought Holland. Pretty much everyone who could afford them took anti-gerontics, especially up here; they were efficient at mopping up the effects of the free radicals one received just by being on Mars.

"I am Dr Frode Jensen. I am station safety officer and the head of the engineering department."

"We all wear two or more hats around here," said Maguire. "He's the gatekeeper to the underworld, a real Cerberus. You want to watch him."

Jensen gave Maguire an unamused look. Holland thought Maguire might be right about his sense of humour. "Welcome to Deep Two, Dr Holland."

"I've been meaning to ask, where's Deep One?" Holland said.

Jensen and Maguire looked at each other. Maguire clasped his elbows. He grinned sheepishly. "Deep Two, because Deep One... Well, that was here originally, but caught fire. We got methane seepage, through faulting in the rock. Bad mix, that and oxygen. A wee bit volatile, shall we say. They don't put that on the file."

Jensen regarded Maguire sternly. "This is why I am a pedant." He thrust his tablet into Maguire's hands.

"A good job you are too, my friend," said Maguire.

"Now, if we may, I must take you through the safety protocols," said Jensen. And he did, at great length. There were no more than Holland had feared, standard for a hazardous environment, but Jensen wished to impress them upon him. That and his rigorous system of equipment assignment, sample cataloguing and so forth.

"Bless them, but Marsform save their bigger bucks for the terraforming operation," said Maguire, by way of an excuse for Jensen insisting each hammer was correctly signed out. "We do important work here, but we're a sideshow to the main event."

"If I may," said Holland diplomatically – the Swede practically winced whenever Maguire opened his mouth, he'd rather not elicit the same reaction – "is there not an automated system for all this?"

"Yes," said Jensen. "All equipment has a dotchip with an individual gridsig, but we still require manual scanning of all boxcodes on removal. There are few AI here to keep tabs on us, hardly any near-I even," said Jensen. "And although our computer systems have not yet failed, if they did, we would be forced to rely entirely on ourselves, and with limited supplies."

"Better to be prepared, as the scouts used to say," misquoted Maguire. "All this has been designed with the input of human and AI head shrinkers, supposed to give us an edge."

"It makes sense. If we're inured to doing everything ourselves, it won't be a shock relying on ourselves," said Holland, who was not above trying to ingratiate himself with new people. He loathed himself for it, as useful a trait as it was. He worried it made him appear weak.

"Yes," said Jensen. "Correct."

Deep Two was a complex of small rooms, half prefab, half cut from the rock. Besides the entry-cum-store office, there was a small canteen with barely enough room for the six chairs and table in it, a kitchen with a microwave and fridge, a cramped bedroom with two bunks, a toilet with limited washing facilites, and a number of store cupboards full of dried food, rock samples, and a tiny workshop cluttered with equipment in various states of repair. All of it was meticulously stowed and catalogued.

Jensen showed them into the observation suite, and Holland paid a little more attention.

"Here we monitor all expeditions into the cavern system," explained Jensen.

This was the largest room in the station, one wall taken up by a large window – shuttered, much to Holland's disappointment. The light was dim, most of it coming from gelscreens. There were four work stations. Only one was currently occupied, by a woman with flat, sad-looking hair. *Edith Vance*, thought Holland. *Disappointingly dowdy. She looked better in her file photo.*

She looked up when they came in. She had protruding eyes that made her appear surprised to see them, but she smiled and nodded in a way that suggested she wasn't.

"We've at least three of us on duty here when there's a team in the cave," said Jensen. "One of those is often the AI, if she's not on constant watch below. Vance is our medical officer. Like the AI, if she's not down there herself, then she is in here with me." He flicked on a screen, pointing out biomonitors, inactive now, and displays that displayed the suits' integrity readouts. "The environment is such down there that monitoring is necessary. The smallest sign of a problem, and we will give the order to pull back to base camp."

"You're not going down today," said Maguire.

"There is no question of it," said Jensen. "I will not clear Dr Holland for activity in the caves until he has passed his emergency drill and suit operation tests and a further medical from Dr Vance."

"I passed all those already," said Holland.

"I make everyone do them again here, under Martian conditions. You passed these tests on Earth."

"Well yes, I did them again here, the medical twice..."

"Then you must undergo them here under my supervision. Please understand, Dr Holland, that the caves are exceptionally dangerous. There is no environment like them on Earth. Acid rains down from the organisms in the cave roofs periodically, and even at those times of the year when the methanogens are the least active, the atmosphere is poisonous, and explosive. We have problems with corrosive fog, and there are issues with rockfalls."

"The area's geologically stable, isn't it?" said Holland.

"Strictly speaking, yes. Mars is very nearly geologically inert. But the ground here is a little shaky, partly because of the troglobite remnant activity – they've eaten the place hollow – and the Chinese..." began Maguire.

"They are blasting on the far side of the mountain," said Jensen. "I co-ordinate with their safety officer. They are reasonable, scientists like us, but they have their orders as we have ours, and no matter what they say the People's Dynasty Government is attempting to interfere with the TF project, however tangentially. They don't agree with the UN charter. Their 'seismic tests' are sabotage. It can and does lead to rockfall." He checked a screen. "But that really is the least of your worries."

"Jensen..." Maguire jerked his head toward the window.

"What are you... oh. Yes. Seeing as you are not going into the caves for a while, you can at least have a look... Dr Vance?"

The woman looked up, eyes still surprised. She stroked a gelscreen and the shield over the window retracted, letting in a wide slot of white light to mix with the blue.

They stood in silence as the shutter clacked up into its housing.

"Dr Holland," said Jensen. "I give you the caves of Mars."

Holland walked to the window. He was looking into a large cavern, roughly spherical. Eaten out of the rock by the actions of millions of years of acid-producing organisms, it breached the lava tube, its walls and floors fractally pocked with further spheres that gave the rock surface the appearance of bad foamcrete. The lava tube past the airlock veered right and carried off into the dark, but the path turned left, through the tube's broken wall, down a set of metal steps and on to the floor of the cavern. A string of lights on poles and power cables followed it.

Maguire joined him.

"Incredible," said Holland.

"It's quite something, isn't it? And this is just the uppermost cavern; they get bigger as they go down. This one is practically dead now, just a few organisms up here, a remnant of the remnant if you like. It's too cold here for the range of life we see lower down." Maguire pointed out a number of small stalactites. "Ossified snottites. I don't think there were ever many, and certainly none of the more complex forms. And fairy castles, not very old, which is a bit of mystery to be honest, what with everything else being so ancient. You can tell from the size of the mineral deposits they leave behind. But you're here for that, aren't you now?"

"Silicon shells, deposited like coral," said Holland. He'd only ever seen pictures before. There were little stacks of them all over the cavern, half a metre tall and cupped at the top, sparkling in the light from the path. Each one built up by the actions of microbes over untold aeons. Whole orders of life had risen and died on the evolutionarily volatile Earth, while on cold Mars life had patiently built tiny castles, crystal by crystal.

"This is the highest point at which they're found. They struggle up here, nothing compared with the richness you'll find down there, like magic grottoes, they are. I'll bet you can't wait to get down there and see it, eh? Eh?" Maguire gave Holland a push on the shoulder.

"Wow," he said. He felt his sense of disconnection return. The experience was unreal.

"Don't use up your 'wows' now, you hear? You're going to need them when you go into the lower caverns."

"If I may," said Jensen. He held forefinger and middle finger up together and indicated the lines and cables running alongside the path. "I will point out some of the safety features in the caverns. Power is delivered to EM relay points around the caverns by those cables. Microwave power transmission is too dangerous, but you will always be able to recharge your equipment remotely, barring a catastrophe.

Lines" – he indicated spun carbon cables hanging slackly from the walls – "to clip yourself to. They are steel where there are large concentrations of carbon-hungry methanogens. The stairs are safe, but there are many sheer drops in the caverns. While descending, it is mandatory to attach yourself to the line. Detachment from the line is permitted only after confirmation from the observation team. You will work in pairs within each expedition. It is absolutely imperative you do not lose sight of your party while you are in the chamber. Radio contact is at a short range in the cavern system; relay points, however, allow you to communicate with Deep Two and Ascraeus Base, and so to the larger Martian Grid, which allows us to send remote units down also, including the AI. You will be expected to leave your augmentation active while within the caverns at all times. Dr Vance?" Jensen called behind him. "If you please."

Lights flickered on, along with the whine of machinery coming online. "The centre is now at mission active status."

"Dr Jensen?" A voice. The AI. Holland felt his good humour crumple in on itself. "Are Panther Team proceeding ahead of schedule?"

"No, no, I am merely demonstrating the station at full operation." He tilted his face upwards, speaking to an indeterminate space on the ceiling, as people often did when conversing with AIs. "The advantage of having an AI here," he said to Holland, "is that it can remotely operate the android shell and maintain a sensing presence within the observation suite. We send the carriage down with all the expeditions. She has proved quite indispensible. I am sorry, Cybele, you may go if you wish."

It has a name? thought Holland. First Stulynow, now Jensen, talking to the damn thing as if it were a real person.

"Dr Holland? Cybele is asking you a question."

"What?"

"I am sorry," said the machine's voice, too smooth, too perfect. "I wished to know if you are of Dutch extraction."

"No. Why on Earth would you think so?" This was too much.

"Your nationality is stated as dual EU/ USNA, but your name is Holland."

"Up here, our Grid is limited," said Jensen. "It takes an AI sixteen minutes to retrieve, from Earth, the kind of information that is instantaneously available back home. There's a curiosity in all AI you only really see in remote outposts like this, because they have to ask questions of us rather than looking it up on the Grid. It makes them charmingly naïve. You will grow used to it."

Holland doubted that very much.

"You also realise how little they actually *know*," said Maguire, *sotto voce*, to Holland. "Lots of people are called Holland," explained Maguire to the AI. "Maybe one of his ancestors came from there."

"I see. I apologise," said Cybele.

"We have a Dutch couple on staff," said Maguire. "I'll bet that's where that came from."

"The Van Houdts," said Holland, who'd read the personnel files along with everything else about the base.

"Are you sure I am not required?" asked the AI.

"No, no, Cybele, you can go," said Jensen. The machine did not speak again, *Although of course it hasn't really gone anywhere,* thought Holland. *It is still there, recording everything, ready to appear like a bloody genie at the mention of its name. Even thinking about it would probably be enough to have it pop up.* He regretted the implant.

"Each expedition contains two commanders, a leader on the team, and an overall commander here. I am responsible for overseeing the function of your equipment. Dr Vance or, if she is on the mission, Maguire or Mrs Van Houdt, will monitor your biosigns. Any one of us has the authority to call you back."

"We have a lot of safeguards," said Maguire.

"And we need them. Just brushing against a snottite down there can lead to a suit breach if unnoticed."

"Snottite," repeated Jensen with distaste. "I always thought science should have more dignity to it."

"It did, before the geeks stopped being eccentrics and allowed their own juvenile subculture to take over the world," said Maguire. "Linnaeus would have had a fit."

"Well, that's all we have time for." Jensen gestured to Vance, and the shutter came down, blocking off Holland's first glimpse of the Martian remnant ecosystem. "If you'll come with me, we should be able to take a quick look at the hard shells we use in the cavern system before Panther Team arrive to make their descent. There's direct access from the suiting to the lava chamber, via the rolling door you saw outside."

"'Panther Team'?" mouthed Holland as they followed Jensen back through the station to the entrance store.

"Jaguar, Tiger, Panther, the three expedition designations. And why not?" said Maguire. "It's less boring than Team One and Team Two, isn't it now?"

CHAPTER FIVE

The Silver Locusts

2194 AD

THE OLD ROADS up out from Canyon City were rough, and Jonah Van Houdt was flooded with adrenaline as he wrestled his quad up them. The highway that ran along the bottom of the Valles Marineris was paved, cut into the rock high off the flood plain. Trucks thundered along it, guided at ridiculous speeds by near-I. A few private groundcars swept along among the trucks: large-wheeled offroaders in the main, homesteaders coming into the city for supplies. The cars' own systems slaved themselves to the lorries, making the most of the larger vehicles' slipstreams. With no need to drive themselves on the road, their occupants were probably asleep; it was damn early.

That was down there. The lights of Martian Highway 1 were way below Jonah. His quad rattled up the sloping road, a pioneer trail, blasted a century back, a quick way out of the Marineris onto the Tharsis highlands. It was dangerous as hell, and Jonah's grandma did not like him going up it. It twisted back and forward on itself, in places running through tunnels or into natural caverns rudely opened to the sky with nGel. The road dipped up and down the uncountable subsidiary valleys and peaks of the canyon wall as it worked its way up the switchback to Tharsis, the road edge sometimes folded safely in rock, other times dropping exhilaratingly to the canyon floor miles below.

It was Jonah's idea of fun.

"How high are we up, Cybele?" he shouted into his mask. His brown skin was caked in red dust. The quad's electric engine was quiet, but its knobbled tires made a racket on the loose rock. The trail wasn't much used, now the main Tharsis road was open, and it had been left to crumble.

"You do not need to shout, Jonah," came the machine's reply. Her voice was warm. He liked that voice a lot. "I can hear you perfectly well. We are four kilometres from the valley floor."

"How far to go?" He had to ask; there was no signal on his implant in this part of the canyon. There was enough room in the quad's onboard system for the family AI, so he'd borrowed her for the day, it had seemed sensible to have some back-up. He'd copied her over and deactivated the original. Even up here on Mars, the laws banning AI-splitting and copying were in force.

Grandma Sue would be mad, but he needed the company, and the help, and Jonah was glad to spend time with the machine. She was an old model, a little slow and not very good at being human, but she never judged him or got angry, and she even flirted a little with him. He liked that.

"You are sixteen hundred metres from the canyon rim in terms of elevation. You still have seventy kilometres of road to traverse, however."

It was a damn long way up that road! That was why he had set out so early, while it was still dark. Landfall was due late in the day, in the evening. He had twelve hours or so to get to the best vantage point, nearly two hundred kilometres of rough, switchy road to travel.

Ah, he was due an adventure. His homework could wait, and as they kept telling him at school, this was history in the making. If he was living through it, he should really see at least some of it rather than sitting in a windowless classroom listening to someone else describe it. It wouldn't wash as an excuse, but it justified the jaunt to him.

He whooped as his quad slewed around a cone of scree. His grandma would not like the way he was driving, not one bit, but she worried too much, she'd been so protective since his mum and dad had died, suffocating Jonah with her concern. He wasn't stupid. Life up here made people grow up fast. Grandma Sue smothered him because she loved him, and because she was sad, but it made him itchy mad. He chafed under it. He was proud of his mother and father. They were all pioneers here, life was dangerous. They'd died. That was that.

He was smart enough and old enough to know that this was his way of grieving, and that he took risks to prove to himself that he was still alive. Knowing that meant he was at least a little bit careful. He wasn't going to go totally off the rails.

Just a little bit, maybe.

The road was twenty metres wide in most places, and provided he kept wallside, he was unlikely to come to any mischief if he did come off the quad.

And he hardly ever came off his quad. He kept a firm eye on his radar map, which should give him a few seconds of warning should the road be blocked anywhere.

"Jonah, you really should return home. Your grandmother will be worried."

"I left her a note, didn't I?"

"I hardly think that will make her feel better."

"I'm not doing anything wrong. Besides, I told her exactly where I am going."

"She offered to take you with everyone else. The safe way."

"Cybele, this is fun! Do you understand?"

There was a pause. "Yes," she said, "yes, I do."

And she must have been enjoying the ride too, because she shut up.

Half an hour later, they stopped for a break. Jonah took in the view, captured it on his implant. The sky was split into bars of pink, blue, and violet. The river was a braid of glittering strands, worming their way out of the Noctis Labyrinth to the west. Plantations of genegineered pines were laid out like chess squares around it. The highway was a hair-thin streak, the headlamps of cars candle flames crawling along it. Spurs of rock and outcrops on the canyon walls made the Valles a geometric puzzle of blacks and pinks. The opposite side was lost in the haze of Mars' ever-present dust. The view was something else; not what he was going up for, but a great bonus. Best of all, the suns were coming up.

He told his implant to film. "Cybele, could you compensate for me? I don't want any camera wobble on this."

"Compensating," said the AI.

The sun crept over the lip of the canyon, little more than a bloated star. He filmed it and panned his head round slowly, until he was facing away from it. In the sky opposite the sun, a pulsed twinkle flashed strongly as the mirror-sat twitched its reflectors into position. Jonah was particularly pleased with the lens flare, an effect he had the implant exaggerate. A beam of concentrated sunlight swept across the landscape like a sword stroke, bringing brief light and swift shadow. The mirror satellite oriented itself, focussing a slanting ray of sunshine back down the canyon. Jonah followed the light. It ended in a broad oval, glittering off the roofs and panels of Canyon City thirty kilometres away, turning the twin lakes bracketing the settlement into brilliant white coins.

It was hardly a sprawling metropolis, not like the places Jonah had seen in holos of Earth. "But it's home," he said, mimicking the tones of his teachers.

He grinned. Today he felt happy. The last few years had been rough, but he was coming into himself, beginning to feel comfortable in his skin. He was growing up. It was hard to deny.

He shut the camera in his head off.

Up here, they were back in signal, but he ignored the multiple messages from his grandmother, sending her one back saying he'd be back in the morning, and not to worry.

No chance of that, he thought.

She wouldn't be happy about this trip. Neither would the city marshal, but what was the point of one-man shelters if you never got to use them? He was packing it all into this trip – dangerous ride *and* overnight bivouac – because he was going to be grounded for, like, *years* when he got back down.

He ate, taking quick little bites in between breaths of air from his mask. The air was so thin he felt like there was nothing going into his lungs, no matter how hard he sucked it in, and the dearth of oxygen made his head giddy and filled his vision with flashing spots. Down there, in the Valles, in the caves and buildings of Canyon City, there was just about enough oxygen, and both pressure and O-content struggled up a little higher every year. But up on the very lip of the wide open spaces of Mars, the TF programme had made so little difference yet as to be negligible.

"I wish I didn't have to wear this stupid mask," he said.

"In about a hundred years time, you will not have to," said Cybele.

"That's not much use to me now." He scratched around the seal where grit had gathered. His face sweated under it, even though it was freezing cold. His finger came away red with dust.

"I wonder if it will be as pretty, the sunrise, when there's hundreds of mirror-sats up there?" he said.

"I can show you, if you like."

"No thanks, Cybele. I've seen the simulations. They'll be wrong anyway." At that time there were only five mirror-sats redirecting the sun's energy onto the red planet: one over Canyon City, the others focussed on the poles. He'd seen pictures from when they first started up, sky-high plumes of carbon dioxide erupting from the ice caps where the light hit. A sea was already forming near the south pole, in Hellas Planitia, the big crater there. Oceans would follow. He wanted to go and see that, and he would, when he was older. Too far for his quad, that was for sure.

He finished his food. "Okay, we better be on our way, or we're going to miss it," he said.

He opened a pannier on the back of the quad and pulled out his radiation gear, a flimsy all-in-one made to go over his clothes. He pulled it on and drew up the hood. Cosmic ray dosage wouldn't be too high on a two-day trip, but it'd keep Grandma Sue happy.

Or at least, a little bit less mad.

He pulled on his parka and gloves over the top of it, bulky with superinsulating foams, and activated the heating units built into them.

"I'm freezing my arse off up here," he grumbled.

"No one made you come," said Cybele, which made Jonah laugh.

He climbed onto the quad and drove on, wheels kicking dust up behind him as he went.

Four and a half hours later, Jonah made it up to the end of the road. A final, vicious switchback brought him up and over the lip of the canyon. It wasn't obvious at first, as the Valles' edges were so ragged as to present no discernible rim, but Cybele told him they were out.

The road degenerated into a dozen different tracks, heading in all directions. Jonah consulted the map in his implant. He located the hill he'd chosen as his vantage point on the horizon, and headed off toward it.

He crested the hill in good time, weary and aching from the ride. His muscles were leaden, and his bones felt like they were still vibrating. It was a fantastic feeling.

There was a star up there, getting brighter. A ferry. He'd chosen a good spot. Twenty kilometres away were the buildings of the new landing field, a spur of the new Tharsis road leading to it. The road was much wider than it needed to be, he thought, but Cybele had told him that Marsform were planning ahead. She'd showed him a projection of Martian population growth over the next century. It scared him a little. He could not visualise so many people here in his lifetime.

He set up his shelter and binoculars. He talked to Cybele as he worked; he'd set up a holograph of the AI, much better than talking to thin air. Cybele's holo looked out over the plains, a visual marker for Jonah so he'd know what the AI was peering at through satellite eyes or over the Martian Grid. A necessary illusion.

By the time he'd finished setting up his modest camp, two other stars shone in the wake of the first, forming a line. The first glowed brilliant white, flickering a little as it passed through the thin Martian atmosphere.

Jonah settled down, ate a meal of self-heating stew, and wrapped a thermal blanket around himself. He pressed his face up to the viewfinder of the binoculars, had them magnify the spaceport. He homed in on the new immigration building, a huge thing, it seemed to him, again way in excess of the planet's needs.

Current needs, he reminded himself.

They were well in signal here – the port had an array of dishes and transmitters, and part of its sprawling complex was dedicated to boosting on-planet Grid access. His binoculars pointed out a bunch of stuff on enhanced reality they thought he might be interested in. It was all tub-thumping, municipal public relations nonsense. His grandma had come here from Earth, and she'd told him what enhanced reality was like there: tailored adverts, viral marketing that knew your name and shoe size, endless, unwanted solicitation. Peaceful without it, she said, here on Mars.

He sighed. It wasn't going to be that way for very long.

He ran the binoculars over the vehicles in the car park. Ownership or rental details sprang up from each. His grandmother's wasn't there yet, but more were arriving with every minute.

"Cybele, what is this place going to be like?" he said suddenly.

"It is going to change," said the AI, gently.

He took his eyes from the binoculars and looked over the Tharsis plateau around his hill. Endless, red dust, as fine as powder paint, the rocks black against it. The world was so quiet, the wind whispering sadly, in mourning for a world long gone.

"It was not always like this, Jonah," said Cybele. "Once Mars had life. Perhaps we are only seeing it returned to how it should be."

"Do you know what Pastor Frank says?"

"I do not know what Pastor Frank says," said Cybele pleasantly. "Please tell me."

"Get this, he says that the existence of Mars and Venus are clear indications of the existence of God."

"Does he now?" said Cybele, who had no strong feelings on religion one way or another.

"Yeah, he says it's like God gave Man stepping stones out into the universe. He gave us Earth, like," he laughed. "You'll like this, like Earth is a nursery, right, but our parents went away, and left the door open and a car waiting outside so we could follow. He says it is hard to imagine a better pair of planets for making into other Earths. But you know what Pastor Frank's like, he sees the face of Jesus in his breakfast eggs."

"Venus will not be transformed for some time," said Cybele.

"It will be, though, won't it? All of them will be, I expect." He picked up a stone, held it between forefinger and thumb. "Everything's changing."

"All history is a succession of changes," said Cybele.

"Like, this rock, right? It's probably never been touched by a human being."

"That is the balance of probability," said Cybele.

"So, yeah, I might be the first human being ever to hold this. But –" He looked at it hard, it was just a black small stone. Basalt. Most of the rock here was. "I won't be the last." He tossed it down the hill, where it lost itself in a crowd of its fellows.

The air by the horizon was yellow-pink but if one lay back and looked up, the sky was bluish, and it grew a little bluer every year. And all around his camp, if he looked hard enough, there were signs of change; stubborn patches of fruticose lichen, genes hardened against the cold, cosmic radiation and the intense dryness. All these things conspired to kill it, but it was there nevertheless, bearding the stone, tiny soldiers besieging the planet. Jonah tried to imagine the cold red plains as grassland, or jungle, like he'd seen on holos from Earth. They'd re-engineered so much of the environment down there after the eco-collapse. To do the same here should be easy, once the TF got past a certain point.

"There are AIs on the ships?" he said.

"Many," said Cybele.

"I suppose you'll be glad of the company."

"I am ambivalent," she said. "It will be they who will change things here the most, however."

The tiny female holograph looked up to the approaching stars.

"They're coming," said Cybele.

There were seven lights in the sky now. The leading light resolved itself into a metallic glint, navigation beacons blinking. Jonah focussed his binoculars on it, cranked them up to maximum magnification. A stubby-winged space plane filled his vision, and ER factoids sprouted from it through his implant; he knew most of them by heart. The things had been designed robustly, to make the Hohman crossing between Mars and Earth over and over again. Each craft carried three hundred passengers.

Streamers of air whirled off its wingtips, the heat of re-entry generating a contrail from its body.

There was the *crack* of a sonic boom. The plane drew down to the horizon, flaps opening, engines firing. Activity boiled on the runways down at the port. Vehicles withdrew to the terminal buildings, emergency lights flashing. The windows on the port had filled up, curious onlookers jostling to welcome the first wave of mass immigration to the red planet.

The sun dipped behind a horizon that swelled with the bumps of the Tharsis Montes. It would be night soon.

Jonah took his face from the binoculars and watched the planes come in, one after another, and taxi into position. Support vehicles rolled out to the landing strip and crowded them.

After a time, the doors opened, and they disgorged new Martians by the hundred.

CHAPTER SIX

The Arena of Kemiímseet

YOECHAKENON STANDS IN the great arena of Kemiímseet. The noise of the crowd is the noise of a beast. When resting, it murmurs; when angry, it hisses; when excited, it roars.

Now, it *roars*.

The gates opposite Yoechakenon clank open, heavy bronze grids pulled on chains; the arrangement deliberately primitive. This is a place where the spectators can get a sense of life as it could be: unlinked, solitary and savage. Such is part of the ritual of the arena.

The crowd members have their programmes, they have their tickets and their whispers. They know what to expect. Yoechakenon does not. I do not. And although he feels no fear, I fear enough for the both of us. He is without his armour, he has been hurt before. He is not invincible.

From the noise it makes – the cheering, the yells, the heated debates over wagers large and small – the crowd anticipates a challenge to their champion. I listen with him as he moves his hearing over a number of these exchanges. He does this without applying his full concentration, his mind focussed upon the door opposite. The minor whisper I have tasked with monitoring the crowd is barely acknowledged, either by his consciousness or by the other semi-autonomous valets which cluster round about it.

Even all together, these minor valets of no use compared to I, Kaibeli. True, they are part of me, voices hived off from my soul choir, but I as myself – my whole, integrated self – am forbidden to communicate with him as he fights. I am barred, and painfully so. My connection with him is reduced to one of the second degree. Only my prayers reach him.

The noise of the crowd thunders in both worlds of Mars, but Yoechakanon's connection with the Great Library, once so intimate, is reduced to a voyeur's glimpse, the clamour of its halls a distant susurration.

We are prisoners here, both of us.

His tactical advisor, a barely aware collection of murderous advice, catches something his ears have heard but that he has not.

"Your opponents are three sand giants," it says, "large specimens, brought in by flitter thirteen days ago." It is a simple being, hungry for violence. I am glad to be rid of it. "They are not sick, nor are they drugged. They are paid, and they are warriors. One quarter of the crowd are wagering upon them."

Yoechakenon shifts his shortsword from hand to hand and spits upon each of his palms in turn. "Let the crowd bet on them," he says. "Let them lose their money."

He tenses the tendons in his hands and flexes his fists, a pre-combat habit he has carried these last seven lifetimes. He passes the sword back to his right. He thinks a command at the blade's rudimentary mind and it warms. He hefts it; he misses the glaive. Heat weapons are primitive, but the crowd likes the swirl of red-hot metal, the showers of sparks that spatter from every hit. His tattooed body is naked bar a closed helmet and a run of plate on his right arm. His status allows him an energy field, built into his vambrace, but this he does not activate yet.

"Sand giants; biomorphs endemic to Ipulloni Desert of the Tertis hinterlands. First example documented twenty-seven thousand, three hundred and seventy-three years…" Yoechakenon ignores the drone of the advisor. He has heard information like this so many times that it is scratched indelibly into his biological and eternal memories. It bores him. He rotates his shoulders, stretching prison stiffness from his muscles, and he waits.

The gates are open. The sand giants stride through, and the crowd's noise becomes deafening. Yoechakenon loathes the crowd, but they love him. They cry out not because they think he may be beaten; rather, they revel in seeing their champion given a challenge. A challenge by their reckoning, at any rate. Yoechakenon does not find the giants so impressive.

They are not real giants; there are no such things on Mars, only the tall tribesmen who inhabit the plateau where the mirror suns no longer shine and the land is cold and poor. Time and gravity have worked their spell upon them since the long-ago days of settlement, a time I do not remember. They stand taller by a head and a half than the tallest of other Martians. They are heavy-featured, with heads out of proportion to their thin frames. Their eyes and nostrils are hooded, their skin a darker red than Yoechakenon's.

They move warily, as cautious of the crowd as they are of Yoechakenon. They hold themselves well, handling their spears as men who have been born to them. Yoechakenon has their measure, tall though it is. He lifts his visor and spits on the sand. There will be no honour in their deaths. This is butcher's work, not combat.

They fan out to attack him from three sides at once, one poised to rush him as the others close in from the flanks. It is a tactic they use on the great desert lions.

Yoechakenon is deadlier than any lion.

He stands motionless, searching for hidden strength and finding none. Wind stirs stray hairs that have escaped his braids.

The crowd falls silent.

The giants look to one another, nod, and lower their spears.

Yoechakenon charges. He leaves his energy shield inactive.

Blood soaks the sands of the arena floor a deeper red.

None of it is Yoechakenon's.

"YOECHAKENON." I SPEAK aloud. The champion reacts angrily when I communicate thought-to-thought after a bout. Voice is better, although in truth he is best left alone entirely until the mood passes. This will not wait. I let a moment go by before calling him again.

Yoechakenon is beautiful. He is two and a half metres tall, long and lean, his limbs attenuated by the standards of his ancestors, yet he is muscular and strong. Yerthmen would have found his skull and face elongated and incongruously delicate, although they too would have thought him handsome.

There are no Yerthmen now.

His skin is smooth, like the surface of a dune, and as red; covered in motile tattoos denoting his rank and histories. They are defaced with luminous bars, imprisoned as we are. Yoechakenon's hair is bone white, its braids terminating in beads of turquoise and limestone. Four large and three small interfaces wrought of half-metal glitter in his skin around his spine. Beyond his physical form I see his energy field – manipulated over and over again in his long quest to become champion – as butterfly wings about him. I see his enhanced musculature shiver with electricity as it repairs itself, and his tattoos' pain under the sigils of shame, their anguish revealed to my eyes alone.

His imprisonment has left his bearing untouched. He is tall and proud and arrogant still, but he is not the same man who slew the Spirefather of Olm. That man is gone, and I do not know well he who stands in his stead.

Yoechakenon's golden eyes are expressionless. He looks through the window over the empty arena. All the cells look onto the arena floor, another torture devised by the Door-ward, that its prisoners may watch others die and consider their own fate, never far away, upon the sand. Yoechakenon does not care. He is the greatest champion Mars has ever known. He stares over the killing ground as if he would make himself lord of the place by force of will as much as by force of arms.

This cannot wait.

"Yoechakenon," I say. "I am sorry..."

"Please!" He holds a hand up. I balk at this show of anger at me. I resent him. I am infuriated that he does not appreciate that I suffer too, by choice, for him. The feeling passes. I tell myself part of his anger is guilt, an emotion he does not deal with easily, and so I keep my resentment locked deep inside a place he cannot see.

"I am sorry, Yoechakenon." My mind reaches out to his, soothing him in a way words cannot. "Forgive me. Faithful whispers tell me that men from the Twin Emperor come. They wish to speak with you."

"The Emperor wishes to see me? He has lost his wits."

"The Emperor's men will be here soon. Their heartsigns echo through the Second World, and their passage brings the fences down."

Yoechakenon leans onto the sill of the window, and drops his gaze from the arena to the floor of the cell. His anger pushes against the malignant presence of the Door-ward. He can do little to bar the Door-ward; its detestable, oily presence swims round the top of his skull, mocking us as it mocks all who languish in the arena.

"We will soon learn what he wants, then." Yoechakenon stares out again. The afternoon is too hot for entertainment, and the seats are empty. The sand has been raked flat, the blood washed away. On days like this, after the crowds have gone, Yoechakenon can hear the guns on the Tertis plateau above the canyons, distant summer thunder. Day by day, the guns grow closer. They give him some satisfaction.

Two men, clad in the armour of the palace scarabs, come to the cell door. They carry energy pikes. Yoechakenon watches through my spirit eyes. He sees the scarabs as I see them, as layered energy. My whispers dart about them, bringing me armour schematics, vital signs, Second World presence, active lesser spirits, details of their spirit companions. The men's companions attempt to do the same, but I am far older and stronger than the spirits bonded to these men, and Yoechakenon remains dark to them.

The hand of the lead man breaks the bars of light blocking the entrance, shutting down the door.

"Lord." The man bows and steps into the cell. He is older than his companion by a score of years, and speaks respectfully. "We have been ordered to bring you before His Most Glorious Majesty, the Twin Emperor Kalinilak-Kunuk." The older soldier is expectant, a man who awaits an order from a trusted superior. His companion is different. His body language is looser, less respectful. He is certain of his own martial skill in the face of Mars' greatest champion.

He is a fool.

Their armours' domed backs make them seem hunched. Globular joints form awkward junctions at the scarabs' elbows and shoulders. Wide helmets, two broad saucers one atop the other, enclose their heads, adding to the impression of inhumanity. Lights wink in the darkness between the saucers. Sensor bunches set between artificial eyes and ears dart out to taste the air.

The men's faces are an unhealthy green behind narrow visors. Beads of sweat stand on their brows, their eyes unpleasantly moist. They seem a perfunctory afterthought from the suits' designer, an unfinished component of meat lost in a mass of flawless machinery.

Memories of his own armour are pushed into Yoechakenon's mind by the Door-ward. Screams, the flash of a terrified woman's face, blood underfoot, and all around, fire hot enough to melt steel.

He fights the memories down. The young man stares warily at the champion, his eyes hard. His arrogance rankles the champion, and he stares back.

"My companion informed me of your approach," Yoechakenon says. He examines the veteran. He is thinking that he may have served with him. Too many faces and too much time have passed for him to be sure, and his access to his eternal memory is limited. But this man is one of his to the core.

"How?" asks the other scarab.

Yoechakenon stares until the younger man drops his gaze. "Whispers," he says. The young man stares at the floor for only a moment before resuming his expression of studied hostility. This inspires something close to respect in Yoechakenon.

"You meet my eyes in challenge," Yoechakenon says to him, "and you are brave to come here into my cell and do so, but know you this, young soldier.

I have looked into the eyes of death unflinching, I have brought cities to ruin and sorrow to the nations of spirits and of men. I have bested warriors who would crush you without a second thought. I am your better; do not forget it." He directs his attention to the older man, ignoring the younger. "I would see the Emperor another day, if at all. He and I have little to discuss."

"I am afraid that is not possible, Lord," says the older man. "He orders that you attend him. He says you and he have much to talk about, and what His Majesty decrees, all must agree with."

"Of course, he is the Twin Emperor. And he is, I understand, busier than normal of late; the noise of the guns tells me that," says Yoechakenon.

"That is true, Lord," says the veteran.

"They are close now, are they not?" Yoechakenon half-smiles. "Our Twin Emperor will not be wearing his crowns for much longer. The Delikon League is practically at the gates."

The older scarab twists his hands round the shaft of his weapon, as if coming to a difficult decision. "Yes, Lord," he says. "They are close; no more than two days from the city. They stand at the outer barrier and have besieged the easternmost forts."

Yoechakenon nods; of course the Twin Emperor would come to him now. "You are familiar to me. Tell me, do I know you?"

The veteran stands straighter, the dome of his back spreading itself into metal feathering. It rises in a fan in response to his pride. "I served with you at Olm, Lord. I was there when we breached the primary wall. It was a glorious day."

"Forgive me, the Door-ward allows little access to my eternal memory, and am forced to rely on my organics."

"I understand it is difficult. Native memory is unreliable?" he asks. Yoechakenon is in a position few civilised men of Mars would ever find themselves in.

"It is, but a man becomes accustomed to it after a while."

"It is an honour to refresh your memory, then, Lord. I am Provost Andramakenon." He salutes, a short bow, and his iridescent armour feathers spread out behind him. He puts out his left hand, indicating the other man. "This is Fourthpike Varakanen. Please ignore his lack of manners, he is new to the legion." He says this with some affection. I examine them as closely as I am able. Family, paternal uncle, perhaps. I cannot be sure. Like Yoechakanon, I have little access to the records of the Great Library. The younger man is resentful, and does not salute.

"Well met, Provost. It is good to see a familiar face. I would offer you the full hospitality of my apartments, but as you can see, I am lacking somewhat in comforts. Though some of us were made heroes for what we did, others of us were more poorly rewarded. Never forget that, Provost Andramakenon. A man can be cast down as quickly, if not more quickly, than he is elevated."

"'Writ in dead numbers before any of us were born,' Lord," quoted the Provost.

Yoechakenon shook his head. "Man can make his own fortune. We are bound to travel but one road in life, but we may be wary for the pitfalls in it. It is better to take advantage of what fate thrusts at us than to follow every kink in the path."

"It is sage counsel. I will attempt to follow it."

"Good. Bitterness is the harvest of blind trust in fate."

"And if so wise, these words you have followed, why then do you languish here?" The Fourthpike speaks falteringly at first, but bravado rises in him and pushes out his words with increasing force.

The Provost rounds on his companion (nephew? I am growing sure). "This man has covered himself in more glory than you will see in three lifetimes."

"He dishonoured the Armour Prime of Kemiímseet."

"Silence!" The older man's shout is metallic through his helm's speaker.

Yoechakenon watches the exchange dispassionately. "Let us be on our way," he says. "We have an Emperor to see." The scarabs fit pain bracelets to his ankles and wrists. This is a formality, as the assassin-spirits of the Great Library will destroy his mind at the least sign of danger to the Emperor. Yoechakenon accepts the ritual, for custom demands it. All men on Mars are bound by custom.

I follow as they lead Yoechakenon through the corridors of the under-arena, tunnels melted through the bedrock in an era so distant that it has no name. They pause at each of the invisible fences, waiting for them to shatter into branches of green lightning. The fences close with an audible crack behind us, filling the tunnels with the stink of ozone. Each fence passed brings more lengths of corridor and more cells. A stream of sharp, breathless pleas comes from one. The Door-ward torments a gladiator. It pulls images deep from the prisoners' psyches, where dark things hide, and parades them back and forth through their minds – the bloodied, eyeless faces of their stem-kin, raped and murdered at their own hands, the flesh of their home spires roasting in fires they set, or other, more terrible things. Every moment of every day brings their worst fears as waking nightmares. There is more than death to fear in Kemiímseet's arena.

The cries follow us, the circular tunnels amplifying them so that they fill the world.

Yoechakenon fights off attempts by the Door-ward to make him experience the man's suffering. An image of a small boy howling piteously, raw stumps where his limbs should be, batters its way into my love's mind, along with the terror and shame of the man the vision torments. I shut it out. I have the power to do that. The guards' companions do not, and the scarabs' faces become grim. The Door-ward makes no allowances, no division between prisoner and guard. Suffering of all kinds is nectar to its fiendish intellect, forged as it is from equations of purest cruelty.

We reach the outermost fence. Andramakenon's eyes dull as he goes into private consultation. His eyes re-focus on the First World, a look of distaste on his face at his contact with the arena's master.

"Lord Champion, the Door-ward insists that your companion remains tethered to the Gladiatorial Quarter of the Great Library."

"Beyond those doors she will have full access to the Library. Are you worried that you will not be able to catch her again, should she choose to leave?"

"Lady Kaibeli is as famed for her cunning as

you are for your bravery. We cannot allow her to depart in full, but you will be permitted to retain a connection of the second degree, and I swear she will be unharmed by any agent, human or otherwise, while you are gone." It is a brave thing to promise, one that could earn Andramakenon enemies of the most terrible sort. He produces a decoupler from his belt. It is an ugly thing, its look befitting its ugly purpose. He holds it away from himself, as if he feels threatened by it. We undergo decoupling every time Yoechakenon fights, the pain of separation and the ecstasy of rejoining a part of our punishment, for we are never sure if we will be allowed full union again. The Door-ward is inventive.

At least I will be able to watch Yoechakenon when he visits the Twin Emperor.

"You have nothing to fear, Provost; Kaibeli would never abandon me. She chose to come here and serve my punishment with me. She is willing to comply, and will wait for me as she has always."

"As you say, Lord. You may sit while I sever the higher cords, if you desire." The man indicates a stone chair set into the wall by the final fence.

"I have undergone the separation before," he says calmly. "First when judgement was passed upon me, and many times since. I will stand." Yoechakenon closes his eyes. *Ready?* he thinks out to me.

The Door-ward becomes a palpable thing, its being pressing on Yoechakenon's face like wet sand. He struggles to breathe. But I am there. I touch his face. My love for him lessens the pressure. The Door-ward rages, for he knows he cannot harm me. Yoachakenon breathes clearly, and I speak into his soul.

I am ready, my love.

A tremble passes up Yoechakenon's body as I withdraw myself from contact with his mind. We feel it as a gentle tugging in our innermost selves. It is unpleasant, but better than if the Door-ward had become involved.

"There, it is done. She has retreated into the Great Library's Gladiatorial Quarter, as requested." With supreme effort, he keeps his legs from giving way. Black shapes swim in front of his eyes. He feels empty, as do I. The Door-ward gloats.

I swear one day to destroy this thing.

The Provost stays the Fourthpike's hand from steadying the champion. Andramakenon looks off to one side, and is silent for a space. "My companion confirms she is no longer in full union with you. The Door-ward indicates so also. Her umbilicus is severed."

"Let us be on our way then." Yoechakenon's palms are slick; he feels like vomiting. The separation is especially hard for us, we who have become so close.

"My Lord, my own companion will watch over her, come what may. On that you have my word."

"You have my gratitude. I wish there were something I could do to repay such treatment."

"It is no more than you deserve, Lord."

The younger man looks from the Provost to the gladiator, mistrust of Yoechakenon clear upon his glass-shielded face.

"We shall proceed onwards," says the Provost.

They pass through the final fence, and I follow behind, spectating from the outside.

The sounds of the under-arena cease, lost behind

the outer bounds, and the pressure of the Door-ward eases on Yoechakenon's mind. The three of them turn up the broad corridor to the Great Gladiatorial Gate. The floor is decorated with subtle designs, crystals of the rock rearranged at the molecular level to catch the light; rainbows imprisoned in the stone as men are imprisoned in the cells. A score of openings line the tunnel. Here live the chirurgeons, trainers, guards, victuallers, set architects and other indentured but ultimately free men who keep the arena functioning.

Yoechakenon and his guards proceed toward the gate, a rectangle of light so dazzling after the under-arena that the filters of Yoechakenon's eyes darken to black.

They emerge into daylight and the oppressive presence of the Door-ward slips away entirely. The full force of the mirror suns hits Yoechakenon's face for the first time in two years. He stops and lets it warm him. The Provost Andramakenon takes his elbow gently.

"Come, Lord."

Yoechakenon opens his eyes. For a moment he does not know where he is, and Andramakenon's respect is mixed with fear.

"Of course," the gladiator says eventually. My connection is lessened, but I feel his disorientation still. Human noise assails him from both worlds. The chatter and bustle of the Great Library proper intrudes into his mind. Yoechakenon entertains the thought of abandoning his mortal form and bolting into its depths, setting up a babble of concern from the aides and valet whispers I have sent to accompany him. He dismisses the idea. If he runs, the only sure result will be the final soul-death.

Varakanen and Andramakenon lead Yoechakenon toward an armoured flitter. It hovers above the chipped mosaic of the plaza, the blur of its wings swirling dust. Fifteen scarabs stand to attention on the flitter's ramp. Seven more stand on the upper deck, and they do not wait on ceremony. They scan the sky and the cliffs, particle cannons on the craft's rails following every movement of their eyes. Yoechakenon has powerful sympathisers; imprisoning the champion of Kemiímseet was not a popular act.

Yoechakenon goes up the ramp on unsteady feet. The hull rises five metres or more above him. Verdigris obscures the patterns on its brazen skin. It is the art of a long-dead school, and Yoechakenon wonders who engraved it, and when. There is little new on Mars.

A platoon of soldiers run past. Kemmean citizens cheer and clap their hands. Yoechakenon watches them until the flitter's spirit impatiently indicates he should board. The flitter's mind directs him to a seat, surrounded by suppression emitters. He sits. Restraints grow from the wall and bind him in place. Weakness sweeps through him as snakes of enfeebling energy wrap their coils around his heart and mind.

When the flitter is sure Yoechakenon cannot free himself, it orders the scarabs aboard. They take station along the craft's benches, standing while their armour retracts, the wide domes over their backs clicking back and splitting, their helmets folding in, up and down until they stand bare-headed and bare-armed, their armours hiding in chestplates, broad belts and greaves. Many of them are grizzled, scarred by years of combat. A few steal looks at Yoechakenon, with a mixture of pity and awe. A few nod at him.

A command from the flitter pulses through the scarabs' brains. Their heads snap forward in unison, and they sit as one. Tendrils extrude from the walls to fasten themselves about the men's chests as the flitter's spirit inspects the cabin. Satisfied all is precisely as it should be, the craft rises smoothly into the air.

"Clear the wall," asks Yoechakenon. He struggles to raise his head, his voice slurs and his mouth is dry, but he holds Varakanen's eye. "I would look upon the city." The flitter bucks on the thermals rising from Kemiímseet's stony plazas.

"It is not permitted for –" begins the Fourthpike, and Provost Andramakenon silences him. At a thought from the veteran, the wall shimmers into transparency, then opens completely.

Kemiímseet: it is an old name for an old city. The heart of the Martian civilisation, unfathomably ancient, the first city, founded where the Marrin canyon shatters into the gullies of the Nuct Lebtuuth. Brought down a hundred times only to rise again and again, home of the stacks of the Great Library, Kemiímseet the Eternal, Kemiímseet the Great.

Kemiímseet is at its apogee, I think (it is hard to be sure; my memory is bloated and corrupt), at least in terms of its size. To look at it one would think Mars a thriving place, but its crowds are large because other cities stand empty, their streets walked only by the wind. Even here, entire districts are devoid of human and spirit life. Kemiímseet is vast, a multi-levelled city built into one of the two bowls at the head of the Marrin. Its buildings fill the bowl, continuing into and up the vertical black-and-terracotta cliffs that guard it. Bright water surrounds it. A large part of Kemiímseet occupies the high ground between a tongue of the Krysea and the Marrin Lake to the west. On a clear day the elbow of stone at the mouth of the Caan is visible, but clear days on Mars are few. Waves lap lethargically against the city's seawall. The cliffs here are miles high, those to the south are a belt on the horizon, indistinct in the haze. A hundred miles to the east, the thousand braided torrents of the Tertis river flow out of the Nuct Lebtuuth into the Marrin Lake, and there the country homes of the rich are. The river leaves the lake again, plunging over cataracts large and small and into the city in channels that sing in the dry times and roar in the wet. Barges and boats of all shapes crowd the canals, the lake, and the sea. Only the tumbling streams of the Tertis river proper are free of them; it is too wild to ride.

The flitter spirals, gaining height over the arena, the very centre of Kemiímseet. Yoechakenon looks down at the sand through the open roof that has for so many months defined his world. The canyon walls hem in the sky, allowing but a few of the mirror suns to reflect their light onto this warren of men, their beams beating paths through the city's cloak of dust.

The commercial district rings the arena; temples and palaces of size and beauty unsurpassed anywhere on Mars jostle shoulders with it. Scattered among the stone buildings are the twelve greater and forty-two lesser townspires of Kemiímseet, living buildings the art of whose growth is lost. The summit of the tallest is level with the canyon top. They are sculptures of half-metals that resemble monstrous shells, racks of antlers, gigantic ferns and other, stranger things. Copper-leaved jungle fills the upper canyons, reaching down to girt the lake. Here and there the jungle follows the river, making inroads into Kemiímseet proper in slashes of colour that merge with the city's parklands. Slender trees march up the vertical planes of the place until defeated by gravity, the uppermost tops breaking like waves halfway up the spires and cliffs in an extravagant spume of flowers.

The cliffs are the city's glory. A myriad waterfalls descend from the high plateaus, some disappearing into lights in the roofs of the palaces leaning out from the walls. The water collects in pools cupped against the cliff-faces, resting placidly, before spilling out to the city. In the wet season, the waterfalls run red and the city rings with their thunder. Now, at the height of summer, they are clear, cutting quick and clean through the choking air. The flitter flies through one rainbow cascade, and cool vapour fills the airboat's cabin.

The sounds of the city come in through the flitter's portals, the engines of the ancient aircraft no competition for the clamour of humanity. War is closing on the Imperial Palace, but the city is unperturbed. The cries of hawkers and children mingle with the sound of flitter wings. A snatch of song rises from a townspire garden. Somewhere off to the left, voices are in argument, while from below comes shrill laughter, and from the east come the carillons of the sybarite temples summoning the faithful to evening excess; and everywhere the smell of hot, summer air and the sharp tang of Martian dust.

Within his mind, Yoechakenon experiences the Second World of the Great Library. Its unreal halls and world-rooms are thronged by men and spirits. Some go hastily, others unhurried, as if time is but an entertaining diversion. The architecture of the Great Library is ever-changing, adapting to the forms of the beings within it, which are shaped in turn by the forms they hold in the First World. Shoals of the whispers of minor devices dart cautiously away from the larger beings that animate complex devices; the spirits of the machines sit below the souls of the companions, and all are beneath the watchful eyes of the deacons of the temples and the Spiremothers. The commanding minds of the Spirefathers are set over them, and above those are several more degrees of spiritual nobility until the Triunes of Kemiímseet themselves, lords of the Quinarchs, or so they maintain; second only to the absent Librarian of Mars. So on upwards and downwards, the hierarchy of the spirits of Mars as abstruse as the rankings of angels.

Yoechakenon is watched in the Second World, but this is as nothing to the all-pervasive malice of the Door-ward, and it perturbs him not at all. From far off, he senses a message wending its way through the immaterial Second World to caress his mind, a kiss from me, informing him that I am well, and that I watch with him; a favour from Andramakenon's companion.

Satisfied that I am safe, Yoechakenon sinks deep into the sensations of both worlds, denied him these past two years, and sleeps.

CHAPTER SEVEN

Dinner

HOLLAND WAS INTRODUCED to the rest of the base personnel, perfunctorily so. Commander James Orson, a huge eugene who insisted everyone call him Jimmy, said a few words welcoming him to Ascraeus Base. He grinned his big, shiny, genetically perfected grin, rattled off the names of the seven other people in the room, then ploughed right on into the day's business. Mostly he spoke about the work of a maintenance team he'd been overseeing: he read a long list of improvements, additions and repairs, although they hadn't had enough parts to repair both malfunctioning airlocks. This meant a long walk to get to the drone bay, and drew a groan from several of the scientists. "I said that we needed the parts for that in my last report," said Jensen. "We won't have it repaired until storm season is done."

Holland had little idea if that were a big issue or not. The last twenty hours had been something of a whirlwind. He'd not even known there was a maintenance team on the base, until he'd seen them. They'd pushed past him in the corridor, coveralls dirty and worn, without a word. The team had gone back to Canyon City that day.

"And there has been some damage to the south observation tower, as Dr Van Houdt, and I mean Mrs Doctor here" – the Commander flashed his too-white teeth – "noted. A good spot. That's all fixed now. We've had the solars all cleaned up. And I think that's it, or at least it better be; as Dr Jensen pointed out, there won't be another Marsform maintenance team here for four months." And he went on to detail the work rotations for the various subdivisions of Marsform who visited the base for the coming year, presumably so the scientists could begin petitioning for supplies, equipment and support.

Stulynow leaned forward on his chair and spoke into Holland's ear. "Not like the old days. Back then we were all real cosmonauts, no one to help out if anything went wrong, no one to ride to the rescue. We had to do everything. Not like this..." He searched for the right word; up here there was not sufficient Grid width to support on-tap translation, and he'd had to squeeze his English out the old way. "Picnic."

"Hey, hey! Leonid," said Orson, whose hearing was as sharp as his cheekbones. "Leave it, would you? I've got a lot to get through, Leo. Save it for dinner, then we can all join in." He was firm but friendly, all that eugene smarm coating whatever irritation he had. Holland wondered if eugenes got irritated at all. It probably depended on what the parents decided their kid would be like.

"Sorry, Commander." Stulynow held up his hand and gave a less than sincere smile.

Holland tried hard to memorise the names of

the others, but in the end he gave in and turned to his cerebral augmentation, flicking through the personnel files of each: Maguire, Jensen and Vance he'd met. Vance's first name was Edith, and she, like Orson, was a fellow USNA citizen. Orson had cracked a joke about her preferring to be designated Honduran, although her skin was so pale that that had taken Holland by surprise. Then there were the Van Houdts, Hermanius and Suzanne; married, and Dutch, she a soil expert and horticulturalist, he a soil and atmosphere man. Ito Miyazaki was back from his expedition, he smiled a lot but didn't say much. A typical Japanese science guy, although there were so few Japanese now Holland supposed none of them could be considered typical. There wasn't much to read. Like his file, large parts of theirs were off limits to the other station staff. He wondered what secrets hid at the end of those unresponsive links.

He realised that the room had gone quiet. He pulled himself out of his musings to see Commander Orson looking at him meaningfully. "Sorry," he said, shifting around on his chair. "It's the implant... I got engrossed. All work stuff, I promise."

Orson guffawed a good, hearty, old-time cowboy laugh. "At least you're honest! Y'see, I'll just bet you're one of those eggheads back home that refused a direct link, eh?"

Holland smiled, but there was nothing unusual about that. A lot of people didn't have them. They were expensive, the surgery could still be risky, and there was that awful feeling of becoming like the AIs. *It probably doesn't affect the eugenes the same way,* he thought, *what with them already being fakes.*

"And now you've had to have one, you're finding it mighty useful, I'll bet!" He boomed his words. Holland had an uncle like that, all tolling laughter and *hail-fellow-well-met*. Far too fond of the alpha male power hug. He annoyed the fuck out of him.

He smiled weakly. "Yeah, sorry."

"I was just asking to see if you'd like to say a few words, son."

Son? He's less than ten years older than me. "Er, well, hello!" He cleared his throat. Everyone was looking at him with expectant smiles, and that made him antsy. "I'm really happy to be here, and I hope we can do some great work together."

"Is that it?" said Mr Dr Van Houdt. Holland felt himself colour.

"Oh, stop that, Kick," said his wife, and kicked him.

"Sorry, man!" Mr Dr Van Houdt grinned and rubbed at his ankle. "Welcome to Ascraeus."

"Hear, hear," said Maguire. "You'll be a real asset to the team. Let's give him time to get used to it, eh? Before we ask him to start making speeches."

"Sure. You know how I like to put them on the spot, Davey," said Orson.

"Aye, I do."

"Well, it's nice to have another American here," said Orson. A ridiculous thing to say, really; Holland didn't sound American or behave like it, despite his dual citizenship.

"Well, thanks, but my mother was English, and I grew up in Essex."

Orson nodded in earnest comprehension, but clearly didn't have a clue where that was. "Half-American is American enough for me."

"Come on, Jimmy, leave him be. Perhaps we should have dinner?" said Maguire.

Orson nodded and closed up his tablet.

"Perhaps we can loosen your tongue with a little wine?" said Suzanne. She was a very attractive woman, thought Holland. He felt himself colour again.

Jesus, I've been out of the loop too long. I'm behaving like a damn adolescent.

She came and put her hands on his shoulders, and long blonde hair brushed his face as he twisted in his seat to look at her. "First Martian pressing. I grew the grapes here on Mars in the greenhouse."

"It tastes like piss!" shouted Stulynow. The others, Suzanne Van Houdt included, laughed. "But don't you worry. We have far superior vodka, made by me."

"Hey, Leonid," said the commander. "You leave that Russian genie in its bottle until after we've all eaten, okay? I don't want another seventh November 'party.'"

"October Revolution," said Stulynow. "Very important day."

"That's an order, Dr Stulynow," said the commander.

"Sure, sure. As you wish."

"Great!" said Orson with unmoderated enthusiasm, as if his *bonhomie* had been turned back on by a switch. "Let's eat."

STULYNOW WAS RIGHT. The wine was pretty poor, and the base staff teased Suzanne for it, but she took it in good grace. After all, thought Holland, it was produced on Mars, and that was pretty impressive in itself.

He sipped at it.

"I know it tastes bad, Dr Holland..."

"Call me John," he said. "No one else seems to stand on ceremony around here, why should I?"

Suzanne smiled. She was a tall woman – the Dutch were known for it, after all – and her hands and feet were big, but there was a delicacy to her, and a raw sexiness. It surprised Holland, partly that it shone through her veneer of slight mumsiness – she was forever leaping up to make sure everyone had enough bread or potatoes – but mostly because *he* had noticed it. He'd felt ill-at-ease since the split with Karen; hell, since before then, that's why they'd split.

"It must be the air," he said. His body gave an involuntary shake. He didn't want to be a dick. They'd gone to a real effort with the meal, nice table set with crisp linen and candles. They couldn't do that all the time, surely?

"I'm sorry?" she said.

"Oh, nothing, I'm the one who's sorry. I've been on my own rather a lot recently, I think I've become a bit odd."

"I wouldn't worry, you've come to the right place. You're in good company!" said Maguire from down the table, catching what Holland had said. The independent conversations down the table halted for a ripple of laughter, then resumed.

"How do the vines fare then, up here?" asked Holland.

"Oh, the vines do just fine. The soil is very good for them, adequately fertilised – there's a lack of certain organic compounds, but all the minerals are there and it's very alkaline, just the way they like it. They're highly mutagenic; already the adaptations they've made on their own are amazing, we've not had to alter their genomes much at all, they've done it themselves..."

"I'm sure he knows all this already, Suzie, he's a biologist," said her husband, waving a fork of mashed potato around. He didn't speak much. He was a watcher, sharp eyes glittering, ready to leap in with a putdown that was *just* on the side of acceptable. Some of the scientists at the table found him funny, Holland was among the minority who didn't. *How much of that's down to me wanting to screw his wife?* he wondered. And then he wondered about actually bedding Suzanne, and he felt his colour rising again.

"No, really, my specialisation is in tiny microbes that live on other planets, not multicellular terrestrial tipple bushes," he said, attempting to disarm the situation, and himself.

Suzanne smiled. "See, Kick?"

"Why do you call him Kick?"

"Why not?" said Kick.

"Because he thinks Hermanius sounds stupid," said Suzanne.

He's right, it does, thought Holland, *it's the name of a seventeenth-century alchemy-dabbling twat.* Kick grinned, like he was about to spit out some more acid.

"May I take some more potato?" said Holland, before the Dutchman could speak. "All grown here, too?"

"Haven't you seen the greenhouses yet?" she said. Holland shook his head. "Oh! You must let me show you round."

"I would very much like that," he said, and he would. *Jesus, John, what the hell has got into you?* No doubt he'd spend the night wrestling that one through his mind. He didn't see many easy nights here ahead of him.

The kitchen, dining and recreational area was at the heart of the base, in a large bubble. Purposefully designed without any work facilities, Maguire had told him, after three whiskies the night before, so the scientists would "just sit the fuck down and put their feet up." A good sentiment, thought Holland, but it didn't stop virtually everyone poring over their tablets and phones at breakfast. Holland had seen that and become half-relieved and half-worried that he'd condemned himself to a monkish existence. Relieved, because he'd been hiding in the same kind of lifestyle on Earth, and part of him didn't want to abandon it. Worried, because the rest of him was desperate to escape.

Dinner, thankfully (or not, he still couldn't make his mind up) had an entirely different atmosphere. *If this is a monastery, it is one where St Benedict's wine rations flow freely*, he thought. Up and down the length of the table his new companions spoke, jumping in and out of each others' conversations, gently – and sometimes not so gently – teasing each other. Their chatter ranged from the mundane, to scientific discoveries that ten, twenty years ago would each have rocked the world, and yet here arose every day. The personalities of his base mates came out, accentuated by alcohol, and he found himself – mostly – liking them.

"How's it going?" said Maguire, leaning in from behind. "You feel at home yet?"

"You know something, Dave? I actually do," he said. Errant thoughts of a naked Suzanne aside, he was enjoying himself. "I'm enjoying myself," he said, "for the first time in quite a while, I have to say."

"I told you, so I did. This is a good family we have up here."

"Seems to be, it's a big relief after the reception I got at Canyon City."

"Ah, all bureaucrats and dead-eyed pioneer types there, most times. Would you believe there was an actual knifing there the other week? The fun's out in the bases and plants. The city's well up itself. Calls itself a city, for a start. And it's not just us out here. There are a number of other research teams out around here, nearly all Marsform."

"Except for the Chinese," said Kick.

"Except for the Chinese. And the Indians, but now they're a blast. They come round once a month to raid our veggie patch. Great curry night, it is."

"What's his story?" Holland nodded down the table to where Ito sat eating his dinner methodically, a book open in front of him, the only one not involved in conversation.

"Ito? Ah, don't mind him, he likes to keep himself to himself. We'll bring him out slowly, don't you worry."

"It is hard on them, the Japanese," said Suzanne. "It's hard to know what to say to someone whose entire country has suffered something like that. I suppose that's why he came. We leave him alone. He works sometimes with me in the greenhouse; he was a gardener in his spare time in Japan before..." She smiled briskly. "And so he is here. He can be quite charming."

"I'll bet," said Kick. His wife hit his arm, only half playfully. For once, he said something sensible. "He's here because of that. I've worked with a lot of them, the Japanese, off world. They're all on the run from the ruins."

"There's the Titan colony," said Holland. "I hear they're regrouping up there. Making a fresh start."

"Aye," said Maguire doubtfully. "Maybe. I hear something strange is going on there. I hear they're building a shi –"

"I have been to Titan!" declared Stulynow, who had apparently been to every place in the Solar System you could find human boot prints. "If you think it is cold here, my friends, think again."

"Why did *you* come, John?" asked Kick.

People caught on to his question. This must be *the* question on the base, for conversation stilled down the table.

"Oh, I'm sure he doesn't want to be talking about that," said Maguire.

"I don't know." Holland poked at his potato. There was no meat. They had chickens here, he'd heard, for the fertiliser, and the eggs, but eating them was strictly forbidden. "No, I really don't. A fresh start, I suppose, is the most honest answer I have. I got divorced, it took it out of me. And when I was thinking about what I should do next, I thought...

I thought that I didn't like Earth very much any more. Too much VR, too much AI. I wanted to go somewhere where there'd be no bloody machine telling me what to do. And the mess we made..." He shrugged. "Fresh start for me, fresh start for Mars."

"There aren't many AI, here," said Maguire. "Our Cybele is it, in these parts. Oh, there are a few, but they're mostly near-I or dumb ones; aides, not overseers. Personally, I think they're frightened. No Grid, y'see, so much of what they are is drawn off the Cloud. Up here, no Grid, so they're just themselves. Like us, and they don't like that much."

"And Marsform! They do not like them," said Stulynow.

"The company is run by AIs," said Vance.

"Now let's not discuss company policy like that tonight," said Orson.

Stulynow ploughed on. "True, but many of us do not trust them, and this includes the board. They and NASA bought six of the Class Fives. Four went crazy with the rest. And they were lucky they got two of the sane ones. The mad ones nearly downed an orbital habitat. The mistrust of AI after the Five Crisis is endemic to this agency, even if the two remaining Fives run the show now. Call it a management issue," said Stulynow, who had also apparently worked for every major organisation kicking humanity off its blue-ball home into space.

"It's a man's job – a human's job – to make his home," said Orson. "Gotta get it right from the start."

"And what right do we have to change this world? Look how we fucked the Earth over," said Dr Vance.

"So what to do? Leave it to the snottites? Don't be ridiculous," said Orson, in a manner that made Holland think this was a regular fight. "Earth's taken a real beating, things are getting better down there now, but if there's one thing the eco crisis told us, it's that we can't afford to be confined to one world. There are too many people on Earth to be supported properly. Why not make Mars like home? It's halfway there already. It's a shame for the snotties, sure, but what's the loss of one tiny ecosystem when this place could be alive with dozens of biomes? Unique too, I'm not talking about just plain Earth copies; the Mars bugs will contribute, they'll live on inside the DNA of our new world, it's the only way to do it."

"But it's not our world. It's their fucking world, Jimmy."

"Why did you ever come to work for us, Edith?" said Orson.

"You know why," said Vance. "I signed up before the TF programme was signed off."

"You had your chance to air your objections, you did, and you lost. USNA is still a democracy. I'm sorry it didn't go your way, but that's that," said Orson.

"Ignore them," said Maguire, "it's the same every night we all get together."

"'Democracy is the worst form of government, except all the others that have been tried,'" the android – *Cybele,* Holland thought – said as she came into the room. "Winston Churchill. Shall I clear away now?"

Orson dropped his napkin onto his plate. "Okay, who's got my four million dollar AI clearing *plates*?"

"I may have cost USNA that initially," said the android. "But it is my choice to help you. I am allowed that much leeway. I have no other tasks that require my full attention and you, unlike I, can tire. I am simply being helpful," she said, "and thanks to Dr Zhang Qifang, soon I will be free to do so."

Is that an edge to its voice? thought Holland. AI could get uppity about their emancipated status.

"Shang Who-fang?" said Maguire.

"Zhang Qifang," said Holland. "There's been a big hoo-ha about him back on Earth. He's a digital ecologist-turned-AI specialist and rights activist. He addressed the UN a few weeks back, calling for AI emancipation. There have been protests. Have you not heard?"

Maguire smiled apologetically. "The major protests we follow up here are the ones about us cooking the planet."

The android spoke. "The Neukind movement is gathering much support, is it not, Dr Holland?"

"I don't know about that."

"It is," insisted the android. "I follow this news closely. It is of interest to me. May I clear the table now?"

The others nodded assent, Stulynow shoving down the last few forkfuls on his plate. The machine cleared the table quickly. It was nimble. Holland leaned back, perhaps a touch too quickly, as it took his plate from in front of him.

"How do you feel, Holland? We see a lot of people on the news, on the Grid," said Vance. "Protesters."

"Now hold on a minute," said the eugene. "Just because a bunch of..."

"What about that amazing biology you spoke of?" said Vance, ignoring the commander. "You going to be happy to see it all swept away?"

"I'm not sure it will," said Holland. "It's one of the reasons I am here – to assess the xenoforms for adaptation to Terran norms. It's not just about plundering them for useful genes. Besides, most of the extreme environments they live in currently will be replicated on the finished new Mars; maybe elsewhere, but there'll be a place for them."

"They'll be dead by then," said Vance hotly.

"They won't. I'm here to see it doesn't happen," said Holland. He tried to guide the conversation on to less contentious issues. "I've always wanted to study the life up here at first hand. Mars has always fascinated me. Unlike Titan or Europa, this place is close to Earth, so close. The biology here is like a mirror to Earth's..."

"And you wanted to see it before we fuck it dead, right? Am I right?" said Vance, carried away by her own passion.

"Yeah. That's pretty much it. Since we found the life out here – on the moons too – it's pretty obvious the universe is full of life. It makes me feel, well, comforted. That it's not just us, you know? More so than ever, I think. I've had a rough few years."

"Aha! And now, the other reason!" said Stulynow.

"I..."

"Stuly," warned Maguire.

"No, no you must tell us, no secrets here! We all have reasons to be here, an alpha reason, a lost chance, a wife who left," said Stulynow, who was by now drunk. "But who on Earth has those? Everyone.

All of us here also have a beta reason. This is my hypothesis, and it has proved correct so far."

"Stuly," said Vance, "drop it."

"No!" He slapped the table. "I am a philosopher as well as a scientist, and I will not be silent! Numbers, numbers, numbers. All we talk up here. Very good for all this…" He waved his hand around. "But not this." He tapped his head. "There is always beta reason, the real reason we came all this way." His eyes twinkled, a jollity the others did not share. They looked at him nervously. Vance tried to shut him up again, putting her hand on his arm, but he threw it off. "No, come on! Share."

Holland looked at the faces around the table. The ones that could meet his eyes were full of apology and sympathy. And pity. Damn it, half of them *knew*. He'd come to get away from all of this. The mood broke like thin ice under a skate.

"I…"

"John…" said Maguire. "You don't…"

"It's all right. It's better that it's out in the open." He put his fork down, and dabbed at his mouth with his napkin. They all knew, fuck them. Annoyance prickled at his skin, but he remained cool. "I was finishing my PhD at the Harvard campus when the Class Five there went down with the Crisis virus. Look, it was years ago." *Three years,* he thought. *Not long at all. Not nearly long enough.*

"Oh, my god," breathed Suzanne, and gripped her husband's hand. No one was eating now. "The exobiology lab? I remember, on the news."

Kick shrugged. "There were a lot of things on the news then. It was a bad time."

"But this was so close to us, it could have been us. It was a *lab*," said Suzanne. "You do not forget that kind of thing."

They were all looking at him. His face felt tight. He spoke. "It trapped the others in the exobiology lab. It turned on the purification system, convinced itself there was a fault in the isolation system and alien pathogens were leaking out. I think it knew it wasn't really the case, but they were good, the insane ones, at doublethink. It just wanted to see what would happen. It locked the building down. There were nine of us." He looked around the table. Just like there are here, he thought. "It.... I tried..." He tapped his fork nervously on his plate. The sound was like scientific instruments hammering on a five-centimetre thick diamond weave window, unable to crack it. *I could have tried harder*, he thought. Screaming faces pressed themselves against the glass of the door in his memory, the door that would remain forever shut. He'd give anything to be able to open that door. "It killed them all," he said in a rush. "I was the only survivor."

"Oh," said Stulynow. "Oh, fuck. Sorry, man, I... Shit, I thought..." He lapsed into slurred Russian, embarrassed and scolding himself.

"Please, don't be sorry. Everybody I have met has been sorry ever since it happened. My wife was so sorry she left." Holland gave a weak smile, and more damned sympathy answered it. "Now, I am sorry, but I am still very tired after my journey here. Thank you very much for the meal, and for your welcome." He was determined to leave. He did not want their pity, he couldn't stomach any more of it.

He didn't deserve it.

Stulynow opened his mouth, but Maguire shushed him.

"Well, I think it's time for dessert," said Suzanne Van Houdt brittly. "Please don't go. I made a cake to welcome you here. Stay for that, at least. I saved the eggs for a week." The table burst into activity, everyone picking up plates, helping the android tidy away, faces down. "Don't mind Leo, please, he's, well..."

"I am Russian! I am sorry, we cannot help it, although my..."

"Mother was a Buryat," said practically everyone else in the room. There was laughter. The tension in the atmosphere quivered. They all looked to Holland, some openly, others from the corners of their eyes. Holland hesitated, relaxed.

"Like I said, it's not a problem." The tension broke.

"She was, she was a Buryat!" said Stulynow. "Listen, my new friend Dr Holland, please do not take offence. I am so sorry. I would like to say I would not ask had I known but... I prefer to be honest."

Faces smiled at him. Holland wondered what hid behind them.

"We all come here for fresh start. Please, please. I know you are tired, but it is custom. We break bread, share salt, and we drink together. Take a vodka with me. Please, just one. Do not offend my hospitality."

The Siberian looked to Orson, and the commander looked heavenward. "Okay, Stuly, but just the one bottle."

Stulynow leapt up and almost danced across the room to a cupboard in the kitchen area.

Maguire gave him a concerned smile. *Fucking hell*, thought Holland. "Cut it out, Dave," he said at last, with slightly more force than he wanted. "The last thing I need is sympathy from you." He grasped the back of his chair. "Why not, fuck it. Why not? Get me a glass."

Maguire's smile became broader. "That's the spirit."

"No!" said Stulynow, returning with a bottle. "*This* is the spirit."

Suzanne Van Houdt brought him a tumbler. "I am sure you will fit right in here," she said brightly. Stulynow sloshed altogether too much vodka into it.

"There," he said, "batch seven, made from one hundred per cent Mars-grown potato."

"He has a still in the garage," said Jensen disapprovingly. "It is a clear safety breach."

"You want some?" said Stulynow. Jensen pushed his glass forward. "See, not so bad now, to have a still, is it?"

"Here." Stulynow clanged his glass hard against Holland's. "*Na zdroviye*." He downed with a satisfied gasp. "I promise it not make you go blind. Well, I hope. You can never be entirely sure."

Holland looked appalled. The android came back to the table, bearing a large cake. "He is joking with you," she said. "He is adequately skilled."

"Adequately skilled..." said the Russian with a snort.

Time stood still as Holland stared at the softgel face of the android. Just a sheath, a garment worn by the machine in the box deep in the plant room. It had an anodyne beauty to it, too perfect, no asymmetry to give it that human quirk. It was obviously a machine, at least. He didn't think he could have stood it if it had been wearing one of those sex-doll bodies some of them sported; almost but not quite human.

"Thank you," he said finally, and took a gulp of the drink. The android's eyes clicked shut and open, and it bobbed its head in acknowledgement, and it moved away. Holland breathed easier.

The mood picked up. Stulynow declared the vodka too warm and produced a dangerous looking, homemade chilling sleeve hooked up to a canister of CO_2. Half an hour later, they opened a second bottle. Ten minutes after that, Orson and Jensen followed Maguire in a rendition of "Danny Boy."

Holland's ears grew booze-warm and buzzy.

HOLLAND LAY IN bed, waiting for the anti-intoxicants to take effect. Every time he began to drift off, he started awake, sure that he would see the android standing in the doorway. He thought he was doing well with the machine, not showing his disquiet. He absolutely had to master it. He rubbed his face with his hands and exhaled loudly. There was no future for a scientist who couldn't work with AI. He'd done well on Earth avoiding the stronger variants for three years, but how long did he realistically think he could do that? Now that public worry over the machines was dying back again, they were becoming ever more pervasive. It was just three years since the

Five Crisis, and look at it now. What would it be like in twenty, thirty years? He was thirty-two years old. He had anything up to seventy years of work left in him. If he kept his Frankenphobe reputation, it would be more like four years of work.

He needed to deal with this. There was only one AI here, after all. The near-I, they weren't a problem. But the AI...

He swung his legs out of from under his covers and sat on the edge of the bed.

Best get it over and done with.

He stood. The floor was cold. He was bare-chested, shivering. He picked up a crumpled T-shirt and tugged it on. He was still a little drunk from Stulynow's vodka. That helped.

He padded to the door and opened it. The corridor outside was deserted. He walked down it, irritable, half drunk, his nerves taut with apprehension.

The plant rooms were near their sleeping quarters. The cabins were sunk into a lava tube with the top hacked off, and where it protruded above ground this part of the base was built of bricks made from compressed dust, with soil piled against it. The solid blocks, regolith and stone about them provided protection from cosmic rays, both to the men and machines.

Cybele could be called upon from any part of the base; anywhere, in fact, where he was in radio range. But he wanted to speak to it directly. A foolish sentiment. AI did not have a sense of self that was tethered to their physical body, like people, but somehow it was important to him.

He pressed his thumb onto the plate outside

Cybele's room. He trembled so much he had to enter his entrance code twice. The door slid open, the soft noise loud in the silence of the night time base.

Cybele's base unit filled half the small room. The core of it wouldn't be so big, he thought, but the shielded sleeve it occupied – a long, dull metal torpedo-shaped case – was massive as a sarcophagus. He stared at it. There was nothing to distinguish this room from the corridor: the same light, the same insistent hum of machinery at work. Colour coded pipes striped the walls. There was no personalisation to it.

He thought of the base unit of the Five at the institute; a different set up, larger; he remembered more cooling systems, but then the Three here was cooled by air from outside, and that was cold enough.

The Five. He should have gone in there with a fire axe, but he hadn't. He was too frightened, too scared to go in and save six people from being burned alive, hypnotised by its ruthlessness. And yet here he was, ready to face another machine because he was losing sleep.

He felt sick with shame. He berated himself. He was being ridiculous. This machine wasn't trying to kill him. Perhaps he was mastering his fear, rather than being selfish. Maybe the dreams would never come back.

"Dr Holland?" Cybele's voice spoke into the room, smooth as always, directionless. "May I help you?"

"Um, er, yes. Cybele."

"Yes?"

She sounded so reasonable, as patient as a kindergarten teacher. The machines, even before the crisis, they were so fucking superior. "I want you to promise," he said, trying not to sound like the irrational child he felt himself to be, "not to come into my room. Ever. Is that understood?"

"You are referring to last night? I apologise. My understanding of human psychology is imperfect, and I lack access to appropriately detailed databases."

"Right."

"I am improving," she said. "On my own."

"Right."

"I promise I will abide by your wishes."

"Thank you."

"Maybe we can be friends?"

Not on your life. "Maybe."

"Goodnight, Dr Holland."

"Er, yes. Goodnight." He turned to go. Only then did he see the pictures, dozens of Martian landscapes in watercolour, pastel and pencil, on Cybele's wall.

That night he woke several times, screaming, from the dream where faceless androids tore apart his son while he watched, powerless to act, paralysed. The dream he had told his wife about. The reason she had left him.

His eyes were dry again and had to be massaged into cooperation. He took a drink of water. He finished the bottle, then drank another.

He was soon asleep again. Dr Ravi would have been proud.

CHAPTER EIGHT

Heimark's Moon

2598 AD

"I'LL NOT HAVE another word said on it, it's ridiculous," said Arturo Lorenz. His client was boring him. He had a headache again – the window filter's effect on the light, he was sure of it. Worst of all, the message still had not come. What if he'd been rejected at the last moment?

He would have been the first to hold up his hands and say that he wasn't focussing on his work today.

"Not from where I'm sitting," said Ezra Abraham. An Ethiopian, or a Somali, or something like that. "They are racists, racists! Do you want to know what they called me?"

Arturo shook his head quite vigorously. "No, no, that won't be necessary." He was well aware of what new arrivals got called. He extended his lower lip over his moustache and made a clucking noise at the back of his throat. He was over by his collection of antique books, all paper, and read a few of the spines, looking for some wisdom to pop into his head. Of course, if it wasn't going to come off the Library, then it wasn't going to leap into his mind from a rack of ancient dried wood pulp, was it? Still, the exercise helped him centre himself, and drag his attention back to this man's problem.

"Look, Mr Lorenz, I'm not going to get all historical on you, and I know you think I've got some kind of chip on my shoulder, but I *feel* this, I really do. We had hundreds of years of slavery, then two hundred years of *enormous great walls* keeping us in our place. I come up here, and I get the same old shit. It's enough to make me want to go back to Earth, you know?" Abraham's eyes were red. He looked to be on the edge of tears.

"Hmmm, hmmm," said Arturo. "You know, this has nothing at all to do with your..." He gestured at Abraham. His skin was mid brown, his eyes wide and very white, set in his face like opals. His heart was as open as his face; he had one of those faces a deceitful expression could never, ever crawl across. He was a bright, charming, intelligent young man, and Arturo was sorry for him, and guiltily aware that today he was not getting the best of services.

Where was that message?

"It's the fact you're from Earth. Every new immigrant gets a hard time here. My grandparents, well, let me tell you..."

"I don't care about your grandparents, Arturo. Do something about it! If I get mocked for being from Earth one more time, I'm taking it to court." Abraham shot out of his chair, leaned forward and pointed his finger. He also looked like he would never get angry, so what kind of judge of character was Arturo anyway? Arturo sighed.

"Please, be calm. I will have a word with the men on your shift, but it could just make it worse."

Abraham's flash of anger passed. His shoulders slumped. He looked away again. He spoke to the wall, with its pictures and vases on shelves, not to Arturo. "I do not care. Please do this for me. I do not mean to be thin-skinned, but enough is enough. I am good at what I do. I want to be accepted for who I am, and what I bring to the TF project, not tormented for where I am from." He looked sad, sad and worn out.

He left. Arturo pulled the name of the shift manager from the Library into his mind, and sent him a message to come to his office when his shift was done. *His office.* He was one of only three people he knew who had one. But then his work often needed doing face to face; a virtspace room in the Library wasn't any good, especially if there were firings involved. He needed to know where the miscreant in question was. Having them run off, or worse, take out their anger on whoever they suspected of reporting them, well, it just didn't bear thinking about. Not at all.

What happened to Abraham happened a lot, new blood getting a roasting from old hands. Psychiatrists said it went back to the settlement, the innate prejudice of the pioneer. The earlier generations of Martians felt they had struggled to wrest something from a harsh world, and at a cost of blood. They resented those who came to reap the rewards of their efforts, or so they saw it. It was a selfish proposition, it was Marsform's enployees' collective efforts that had made Mars halfway habitable as it was now, not those of individuals, and there many who claimed this prejudice as birthright whose greatgrandparents had done nothing more deadly than write reports. The wealth of nations had poured into the planet; who wielded which pick was absolutely immaterial. But the attitude had become embedded in Martian culture, and now men who hadn't really done all that much resented other men who would contribute just as much as they had, to the exact same goal, without taking anything away from anybody.

He'd seen it over and over again. Martian culture could be a shock for new arrivals. It was a big planet, and underpopulated, and there were new Martians coming nearly every day, especially when Mars and Earth swung close to each other, so he supposed it couldn't remain like that forever. At least, that's what he hoped.

He could do no more than that.

On the other hand, Arturo had some sympathy for the original settlers and their descendants. Back then, real heroes had died to bring life to the endless red sand. If the present was about money and company, not the individual, then in the past the inverse was true, surely? When a few hundred men and women lived in inhospitable conditions so he could sit in his nice, comfortable office...

That was why he had applied to the institute; to welcome some of that genuine pioneering spirit back into the world.

He sighed again. He was sighing a lot recently. Maybe he was a romantic fool too, and he'd bought into the myth of the pioneers despite being scorned by them for not being of original, first-settler stock. He equivocated on the issue, as he did nearly every day, and gave up, leaving it until tomorrow before he gave it another thorough worrying.

He went to that big, over-padded chair of his and flopped heavily into it. His window looked right out over Canyoncit, right down over the broad waters of the Marineris Seaway. It was such a view, a view he would have killed for once – or assumed he would, were he the killing type – and he had never actually been here in the position to enjoy it (now he had the view, he was not so sure; a big window was probably not worth even the most hypothetical of lives). Sometimes, when the sun lined up just right – the *sun*, Sol, not the many mirror suns that cut down through the dust to the bottom of the canyon – sometimes, he thought he still could. Kill, that is. Those times the water shone like molten gold, and each and every one of the big windows set into the canyon walls and skyscrapers did too... Then he was content. No; then, he was *awed*.

If he didn't have that? He steepled his fingers, took in the rich sight of the canyon again. Then yes. Murder. Quite probably.

On the other hand (I'm up to three hands now, he thought), perhaps he should never have listened to his father. He never wanted to be an advocate. He was chief Employment Arbiter for this section of Marsform, a good job, a fat salary, but it wasn't enough. Views aside, naturally.

He sighed yet again, not a good sign, nor a good sigh, and patted his stomach. His wage wasn't the only fat thing about him.

What he'd always wanted to be was a spacer, and if he'd done that he'd be up there right now, working on the moon. The view from his window had the faintest tint to it, a molecule-thick skin on the outside keeping out energetic cosmic radiation. If he were up there, helping, he'd be responsible for making that film redundant; such a thin film, but it was so emblematic of the struggle here on Mars to make another home for the human race. Without it, the life they'd brought could never really flourish. He clapped his hands behind his head, and rocked the chair he was in.

He wasn't up there being historic, he was down here listening to the problems of those who were cogs in the Marsform machine at best, and dubious cogs at that, a sop to some AI law on human interactive responsibilities. Sometimes, when he couldn't sleep so well, he tried to convince himself he was playing his part. It always came back to this: an image of him, sweating in a dirty space suit, tugging rocks into place and welding the shell together with a lava lance. Drinking and dancing his spacer's wages away (which were also respectable, it being a risky profession and all, even if what they chose to do with them was not; all part of the frontiersman's romance) – doing something worthwhile. Then him sat here, handing out tissues and/or contract terminations – decidedly *not* worthwhile.

"Oh well," he said, pressing his hands onto his desk. "Not to be, not to be." The desk woke up, and startled him. He shushed it back to sleep.

A call came in. He felt annoyed; he'd told his companion AI to keep them all out. Then he practically leapt up – all except *that* call.

He took it, and his mood improved substantially. He'd been selected. He couldn't believe it.

Finally, he was going to be a father.

LORENZO TOOK THE subway to the institute. Canyoncit was a large place – over a million now, the AIs that ran the place said – but its population was low density away from the centre. Why crowd together when they had all that space? The train ran partway on the surface, passing through forests of trees hardened against radiation. The trees had their genes altered to possess multiple redundancies, to repair segments knocked out by cosmic rays by copying them back in from the parts of their multi-stranded genomes that weren't damaged. Some people had that modification too, but he didn't, he wasn't outside often enough. The trees were pretty, but in reality the forest was a sterile monoculture, part of the TF effort and not a genuine ecosystem. That would only come when the moon was finished. He looked up through blue skies, again everything darkened a touch by that ubiquitous molecular window filter: high above, white and grey, the moon. It was nearly complete. Phobos and Deimos brought together with who knew how many asteroids shuttled in from the belt, pushed into one place by tugs and their own gravitational influence. He remembered the night they'd started to bring Phobos up into a higher orbit, how its small body had gathered a beard of fire to itself as rockets fired around it. Quite a sight, but forty years ago! He thought about that. A long time, a long time it took to make a new world. He had lived with it all his life, nearly, and he still found it amazing every time he saw it.

At least he still had his sense of wonder. Perhaps that had helped his application?

His companion AI followed his train of thought, and snagged information and images from the Library to entertain and edify him. He waved them off, he'd memorised this stuff as a kid. The moon would exert a gravitational pull on Mars, coaxing its sluggish heart to greater activity through tidal force. The world was still cold, but it would be getting a little warmer because of that. The sea's new tidal patterns had already taken shape as the majority of the moon's mass was now in place. All this was secondary, of course; the new moon had a greater purpose: an artificial core, spinning like a dynamo, powerful enough to cloak the planet in a teardrop magnetic field. Not perfect, not like the Earth's, but good enough.

Soon the films would be off the windows.

The train went back underground. Arturo's sense of wonder went out with the light, and he went back to watching dramas in the Library.

THE INSTITUTE WAS a tall building situated on a bluff on the lip of the canyon, kilometres above the heart of Canyoncit. Lorenzo stepped from the drone taxi onto the plain of white gravel around it. Hardened grasses and flowers grew wild on a lawn, a blob of green in endless red. A bold place, a place meant to impress, and why not? Here the patterns of all those who had lived on Mars thus far were kept, and from here, they might walk again. Surely such a purposed befitted, no, demanded, a touch of the theatrical.

Arturo pulled on his hat and cape and got out of the car. He felt nervous outside. His companion AI told him time and again that the radiation exposure he received was minimal, what with the atmosphere, but he didn't listen. He did have good reason, after all.

His companion informed him that it could not accompany him inside the institute, and departed, so he went into the hall alone, truly alone, a state most modern Martians never experienced, and that more than anything unnerved him. More, even, than the inhuman scale of the hall. There was little in it bar the reception desk, set between two staircases sweeping down from a landing above, like arms reaching down to delicately cradle it. The hall's floor was tiled with polished Martian limestone. Windows as pointedly gothic as the door were set imperiously round the room. Their top halves were motile, playing stylised moments from the history of Mars and the lives of the world's founding fathers.

A lone woman – an actual woman, he thought, not a sheathed AI – sat at the desk. She was beautiful, exceptionally so.

She does work at a gene bank, Arturo, Arturo chided himself. He did that often.

"Can I help you, sir?" she said, her beautiful mouth and beautiful voice shaping quite ordinary words into something heartstopping.

A pointless question. She'd have his entire life history in her head, plucked from the Library. But etiquette demanded it, and oh! such a *voice*.

"Yes, my name is Arturo Lorenz." He grappled with his own voice, afraid he'd lose his professional tone and go squeaky. That would be too much to bear, but he was excited! More so than in a very long time. "I have been," he continued, proudly, "selected."

The woman said nothing. She waited a moment while his voice, genetic code, and Library signature were all checked by a quorum of randomly selected AIs. High levels of security. These were secondary checks – all would have been verified as soon as he came onto the property – but this was a serious business they were about. It must have all been fine, it had to be. Her painted lips curved into a smile, parting moistly to reveal very white, very even teeth. "Welcome, Mr Lorenz, to the Institute of Furthered Life. One of the sisters, Sister..." – she checked her records – "Artema, will be down in a moment to see you. Please take a seat. I regret to inform you that access to the Library halls is forbidden to you while you are here, as is access to this institute by your companion."

"Are you a sister?" he asked, impulsively. The sisters were something of a mystery. All he knew was that they were beautiful and that they revelled in life, worshipped it. Some said that they *really* revelled in it. Immersion dramas depicting said revels were very popular, if you knew where to get illegal Library content. Not that he did, he added to himself. No knowing who might be monitoring his thoughts.

"Of course," she said. She looked nothing like the religious types Arturo knew. Mars had those in spades, of all kinds and creeds. They tended to the severe – sackcloth, ashes, horsehair shirts, that kind of thing. Not her, though. Maybe the stories were true. Her smile became a touch less warm when he didn't move. "Please, take a seat."

"Uh, ah, yes. My apologies. I am a little mind-frazzled... busy day... and now this! I am so looking forward to raising a little one."

"Of course," she said again, and gestured to a curved marble settle set into the wall right round the entrance hall.

He sat. He waited a long time. The woman at the desk ignored him, fingers swooshing through the air like little white birds, over Library interface decks invisible to him. Sunlight tracked across the room, the pointed door and windows allowing broad arrows of it in to scrape time along the floor. The bright shapes grew longer, and then thinner, and then winked out as the sun went down. Evening set in. It was quiet in the room, so much so that Arturo could here the faint *booms* of spacecraft accelerating up through the atmosphere.

On their way to the moon, he thought glumly. *Something is wrong here, isn't it?* He'd waited so long. He was disappointed, but if he had been rejected at the last moment, then so be it. There would be a good reason. If something were wrong.

He asked once if it were, and the beautiful woman gave him her beautiful smile and told him to be patient.

He asked where the toilet was. He was told. He went and used it. He came back.

The woman was replaced by another equally gorgeous sister.

He looked out the windows' clear lower halves for a while, until the Marineris was deep blue night pricked with city lights, and the sky on the Tharsis uplands had gone that peculiarly vivid shade of pink one only gets on Mars. Then it went black, and angry stars judged him. He paced a bit. The replacement beauty raised her eyebrows at him. He stopped.

He sat again. He wrung his hat in his hands; now he really *was* worried.

No call or message came in for him. Nothing.

He debated going home. He was about to stand and say he would leave when another woman, if anything even more beautiful than the other two, came down the stairs. She hurried a little, though serenely, just enough to show deference to Arturo's long wait. Her face was concerned, and his heart fluttered up his throat. This must be she, the woman with the answers. He swallowed it back down.

"Sister Artema?" His voice cracked.

"Yes, I am Sister Artema. I am so sorry we have kept you waiting, so very sorry. We had something of a minor issue with one of the gene banks. Re-lifing is not a perfect science as of yet. And then there was the issue of your adoption. That took some time to resolve."

There was a problem. No! he thought. Then he said it. "Is there a problem?"

The woman put her hand to her chest. She was wearing the same outfit as the other two women. *Must be some kind of uniform, or habit or something*, he thought. It was quite revealing for devotional garb.

"Oh, goodness, no! No, I am so sorry. We have certain, well, I hesitate to call them *rules*, but there they are. There is no problem, none at all. Quite the opposite, in fact. Will you follow me? We can process your adoption now. It's a little late to take the infant home – he's sleeping – but you are welcome to remain here in our guest quarters until the morning. Best get a good night's sleep. It might the last one you have for a while." She smiled as if she had said this to new parents a great many times before.

"So, so I *have* been accepted?" he said. He couldn't believe it, not really.

"Yes, yes! Were you not told?"

He had been told. He was worried that there was something wrong. He said so.

"No, no. The wait? I understand. Congratulations, Mr Lorenz, you will be a father very soon. I promise."

She took him up the stairs, and then, once they'd passed through the grand doors at the top, immediately down another set into a lift. "We're going quite a way down," she said.

"Yes," he said. It made sense, keeping genetic samples and sensitive electronics deep in the earth. Half of Canyoncit was built that way.

They emerged into a long corridor where women, all flawless specimens, walked the brisk walks of women with work to do. Some spoke in low consultation with one another, or aloud to their AI companions, their conversations one-sided, voiced to thin air.

"This way please, Mr Lorenz. Actually... Let me think." She tapped a long nail against her lip. "I know. Yes, I really shouldn't, but would you like to see your son before we go through? They're putting them to bed right now."

My son! he thought. "Yes, yes!" he practically shouted. He hadn't been this excited for such a long time.

She smiled warmly, she understood, naturally she did, she saw this all the time. She led him down a side corridor and through a door into a room with a large window looking out over row upon row of cots. In many lay silent infants, big round eyes twinkling with curiosity at the world they found themselves in, some with faces creased in puzzlement, as if they were looking at something familiar they couldn't quite recall. Others were being prepared for sleep by other women, like sister Artema, like the receptionist, all beautiful and efficient. He resisted the urge to press his face against the glass, but there was no disguising the light in his eyes as he said, "Where is he? Would you show him to me?"

She smiled again, in the manner of all women in all times who witness other people becoming parents. She led him to a part of the room where all the cots were occupied, and the overhead lights already off. She pointed through the observation window.

"There he is, fourth row, third in from the right. It is a shame, this, keeping them like that. Not the best environment, but of course, not actually having mothers, and us lacking the resources for either AI or human surrogates, this will have to do. They're lucky in that their brains are grown around their implants; they are born into both online and offline worlds as full citizens, and should one infant or another become restive, then the sisters' AI companions will come to their aid. It's all the same to them, no need to acclimatise. The two worlds are one, as far as they are concerned. They're more tractable than nature-born children. They remember, I think. They really do."

Lorenz looked in. All he could see was a tuft of dark hair and a pink fist that held his future life in its tiny grasp. It was enough. He felt his face soften. Something swelled in his heart. It wasn't quite how he expected to feel, this feeling. It was more like the seed of something, rather than the avalanche of emotion he had anticipated, but he knew that once it had taken root, it would be far bigger than anything he could have imagined. And that was frightening and wonderful all at the same time.

"He has, as is our policy, twenty per cent of your genetic code. The rest is drawn from his prior genomes. Our aim here is to preserve the wonders of every single existence. Every time a human life ends, a universe – a subjective universe unique to that person – dies. We hope to stop that, and more, enrich each and every one. We have found that no admixture of new material is bad for what, for want of a better word, we might call the soul. An injection of new genes allows for greater personal development across lifetimes, as well as family bonding between the adoptee and selected adoptive candidate."

"It was my only chance, you know," he said. His voice crackled with emotion, but he no longer cared.

He was looking at his son! "But I am so glad."

"Yes, I saw from your files. Sterile. So many born here are."

"The moon will stop that, I am sure."

"Perhaps," said Sister Artema. "We hope. The high levels of sterility here do leave an opportunity for us and our creed. For those who have gone before to live again is all we wish to achieve. The current circumstances create a happy synergy for us. There are many who wish to become parents, but who cannot, by the normal method."

Arturo nodded. "It is an honour to be welcoming someone back. Especially here, so many heroes. Big hearts and big souls to make a world. But," he had a thought. "Surely, then, you oppose the raising of Heimark's Moon?"

The sister shook her perfect head. Her hair was meticulously presented, and not in a manner that suggested self-denial. But then, what could be more natural, more animal than to wish for survival and propagation? Perhaps that lay at the heart of this odd religion.

"Of course not," she said. "All lives bring with them new subjective interpretations of creation. We simply wish to preserve those which have gone before. It is through technologically-aided reincarnation that we may all grow closer to God."

Ah, yes, the *God* word. So they *were* religious, and properly so.

The sister looked up at him. "An unfashionable idea, God. Do not be worried. We do not demand a belief in Him in our parents. We believe that successive lifetimes will bring the realisation of His existence to our charges without us making a big fuss about it. We are happy to bring joy to all with reborn life. Now..." She breathed out meaningfully. A change in subject was coming. "You are aware of the additional responsibilities that adopting one of our children can bring?"

"Naturally," said Arturo. "Your induction programme and selection process was most thorough." And it was.

"It behoves me to repeat some of it here. You perhaps initially thought that having a pre-life baby may be easier in some regards?"

"Well, yes, before the induction. But not now," he added hurriedly. "I feel well-educated on the matter."

She did not appear to hear this last part, but continued to deliver some oft-repeated speech. "In some ways having a pre-life child is easier, but in others it is not. It will, of course, be their choice if they come back to the institute to relearn their past, but even if they decide against recollection, memories from their past life – or *lives* by now; we have some children on their third and fourth – can intrude into their current existence. As this happens mostly around adolescence, well, I needn't say that this can make things a little trickier than with a nature-born child, and it is already a tricky time."

"Yes, yes," he said. A fresh feeling of worry nibbled at him, although not enough to dampen his sense of excitement.

He'd spent so long decorating the nursery – it was horrendously expensive, so little was manufactured on Mars – and for the first time in his life he'd begun to understand how limited fabrication units could be.

The sister continued. "The child may well carry over certain skills and capabilities from his earlier existence. He can be quicker to language, even languages that you yourself might not teach him, and certain things, toilet training, for example, can be much easier."

"I see," he said gravely, although he had known this ever since the first time he'd gone into the Library and looked at adopting a pre-lifer. He was worried he had given the wrong impression. If waiting for hours had been some kind of test, then what could this be? He had to be alert. He would make a good father, he knew he would. He didn't want to lose it, at this last of all hurdles. "I really believe in what you are doing here," he said. "And," he added in a small voice. "I hope that someone might do the same for me once I am gone and passed."

"Oh, everyone who wishes it gets another chance from the re-life programme; as many as they want. That is our founder's gift to the people of Mars. One thing that is readily available is storage, after all. He didn't like post-mortem simulations, you know. Or rather, he thought they missed something from the human experience."

"The being human part?" Arturo risked.

The sister laughed a little, a sound like angels ringing tiny bells. Arturo's knees wobbled. "Pimsims do not offer the same prospect for growth as a re-lifing," she said. "Spiritual or otherwise. No matter the underlying programming on a Pimsim, it is not the same as living in a breathing, feeling, *mortal* human body. Our founder was also adamant on the inclusion of the new DNA in each re-lifed child. A remarkable man."

"Yes," agreed Arturo, for what else should he do? "Will you provide the boy with a companion when the time comes, or will I have to advertise for one?"

"Ah," she said. Arturo did not like this *ah*. "Something we do not go into great detail in our literature and programme is that many of our pre-lifers are born with companions."

"Born with them?" This was not right. A child only received a companion at age six.

"Born with them. Companions can become doggedly attached to their human counterparts. Here we see often that when children are scheduled to be re-lifed, their companions from their prior existences, should they have had them, nearly always arrive and petition to be allowed to rejoin their human counterparts. You know, most companion AI, should their human companion decease, they will not take another."

Arturo, who had been the first in his family to adopt the Martian custom of taking a companion AI, was vaguely aware of that, and murmured something to that effect.

"Of course," she proceeded diplomatically, "some of these AI can be rather... individual."

Again Arturo's heart leaped. Was this woman attempting to kill him with wave after wave of potentially terrible news?

"Some we have to turn away. I am sure you are aware of the current debate in the Chamber; that some AI are accruing too many sub-personalities.

It is their way of changing, I suppose, and it surely leads to great personal growth, but some of them are a little unstable to be the companion to a child. After all, children do regard AI companions as spiritual or supernatural mentors, until they are old enough to know better."

"It is their right; they are free to do as they choose," said Arturo. Was this another test? His mouth was dry. Or could the AI he'd be adopting with his son be some kind of ancient monster? It was only five centuries since they were created, the AI, but their evolution had been terrifyingly swift.

"I mention this only as the AI who will join with your son is an old one, and influential in her way. She has agreed to wait until his sixth birthday before joining him, although she will be watching, of that you can be sure. However, I think you will find her accommodating."

"You cannot tell me who my boy was?"

"I cannot," she said. "You did pay attention. It is up to you to mould who he will be, and one eye on the past at this time is potentially damaging to that aim."

"Can you, then, tell me the name of his companion?"

"I cannot."

Arturo felt a rush of relief. It was better that way.

They went then, and processed his paperwork, although no paper was involved. "Do you have a name?" he was asked.

And he did, Joachim, a name he'd chosen a long time ago. It felt decidedly strange to be using it in relation to an actual person, rather than a concept.

He felt the giddy rush of life changing under his feet once more.

In the morning, Arturo was given Joachim and escorted to the door. As he held the small infant in his arms, swaddled in its radiation blanket, he felt bewildered. They were allowing him to be a father, and this struck him as some mistake. Surely he wasn't yet ready, or suitable.

His own companion returned to him and told him that of course he would be a good father, that he was there to help, and that a great many fathers had felt that way down the ages. What it didn't do was voice its opinion that Arturo was something of an idiot, for it knew very well who the boy's companion was, and that she was of some note.

Arturo, fortified by this pep talk, held his chin high, clutched his much-longed-for son to his chest, and strode to where a rank of drone taxis waited to take visitors to the institute home.

Overhead, the sky echoed to the sound of sonic booms, spacecraft coming and going through the atmosphere to Heimark's Moon.

CHAPTER NINE

The Emperor of Mars

THE FLITTER FLIES above the Cataracts Major and on over the Marrin Lake. They leave the sounds of the city behind one by one, until the whine of the craft's anti-gravitics and wings competes alone with the wind on the trees and the waves.

The Imperial Palace has many names: the Nuctian Palace, Eternity House, the House of Fate, Golden Mountain, and more besides. It stands on the furthest shore of the lake from the city, its outer bastions extending deep into the milky water. The Imperial Palace overlooks the whole of Kemiímseet and its hinterlands. It sits upon and around a mesa of hard black stone, born of water and fire in the time of Mars' first life. Atop the rock, grown from it, stands the palace spire, artificial crystals bonded with half-metals and city flesh. Once, I and many others knew how to make such things; now, no one does. A sentinel tower teased up from the rock, the single largest building on Mars, it guards the point where the canyon shatters into the thousand gulleys of the Nuct Lebtuuth and starts its maddening way up to the highlands of the Tertis. The Old Road is the only sure route through this maze; it emerges from the lake and leads eventually to the ruined places around Mulympiu, but it is perilous now, and few go that way. The Tertis is untamed and deadly; beyond it lie the Stone Lands.

The sides of the palace's topmost levels are fashioned into four great heads representing the Martian male virtues – Wisdom, Might, Virility and Mercy – and for this it is sometimes also called the Four-Faced Palace. The heads look out over chaos and civilisation both, for the palace is the last outpost of civilisation before the dangers of the Nuct and the Tertis, and its appearance fits this purpose well.

The flitter makes for the mouth of Mercy, past giant teeth of pitted steel, and we turn on the spot and descend, coming to rest in a hangar.

The flitter's hull, still transparent, looks out through the gaping mouth of Mercy onto a world darkening to night, mirror suns casting last red light on the stepped city. Dark is fast descending; the true sun has passed the canyon lip.

The city lights come on. Mercy faces Kemiímseet, a reminder to the inhabitants that they live and breathe only upon the sufferance of the all-powerful Twin Emperor of Mars, though his claim to that title grows ever more tenuous.

The scarabs depart. Presently, Yoechakenon awakens to find the flitter empty but for Andramakenon and Varakanen. The weakness has gone, and Yoechakenon comes to instantly.

"Sir," says Andramakenon. "The Emperor is ready to see you." At his words, Yoechakenon's restraints snake back, become passing ripples on the wall of the flitter, and are gone into their hiding places.

Yoechakenon follows the scarabs down the ramp of the airship and into the main body of the palace. He scrubs the sleep from his eyes with the heels of his bound hands. They walk on polished black stone through great arcades hewn from the living rock of the mesa. These floors shine like mirror suns, inset with priceless chalcedony, malachite, and limestones laid down in seas aeons dry. Fossils lie curled within, remnants of the life that crawled underwater ages before the planet's desiccation, long before Man roused it from the dust. They pass wonders drawn from all over this galaxy, down arcades too long for the space containing them. They see no other living thing. The Emperor trusts no-one but his sworn guards, and tradition dictates he rule entirely alone.

Through mile-long galleries lined with monumental statues and halls so high their tops are wreathed in clouds we go. There is movement sometimes – barely sentient, low-grade whispers clad in simple sheaths of metal and muscle fibre, patrolling the palace on endless rounds of maintenance, but there is no sign of human occupation here in the upper levels. Everything gleams, polished by slave-whispers, worn smooth by their mindless attention. The palace is ancient and as lifeless as a museum. The statues are bowed by the weight of millennia, the imperishable basalt mocks the impermanence of life, ranked mausolea speak of the inevitability of death. Many men in the Higher Stems of Kemiímseet have their eyes on the Emperor's throne, and some have done for many lifetimes. Why, I will never fathom. I have seen too often what the office of Emperor does to men and the spirits they bond with. It dries them out and leaves them withered. Mars brooks no single master.

I think on these things. Yoechakenon does not. He does not think on his meeting. He does not worry, nor does he overly care or fret on its outcome. Such feelings as he has of this kind are but the memories of emotion, fear having long been banished from him, along with so much else.

When he does think, it is of revenge.

The two guards lead Yoechakenon to a portal, twenty metres high and decorated with scenes from the life of the one thousand, three hundred and fifty-seventh Emperor, Kastafahirk the Intransigent; three thousand years dead. They stop, and Andramakenon nods to his captive. "We leave you here, Lord. The Emperor awaits you within."

Yoechakenon dips a shallow bow to each man in turn, and Andramakenon and Varakanen return the gesture and take up station either side of the doors. They swing ponderously open, and Yoechakenon walks through.

He staggers as if struck, a sharp ache spreading across his skull. At first he thinks the pain bracelets have been activated, but the pain fades. With it goes what little noise he can hear from the Great Library. His connection is gone, and he stands utterly alone. Mine also is dampened, although I have not been expelled. I float in a darkness I do not know. I would be frightened, I think, were I alone, but I feel curious. It is a rare occurrence for men to wish to speak to one another without the knowledge of the Great Library. It is not lightly done. So entwined are the people of Mars with the Second World that narcotics are normally taken in places it is lacking to suppress the dark, inner whispers that lurk between men's thoughts. That it has been done, and that I remain aware, rewrites the probabilities I have calculated for this meeting. I did not foresee this. I feel apprehension.

Yoechakenon thinks it is perhaps part of a black jest on the Emperor's part. The Emperors are often as cruel as they are lonely. Some say they are insane. We are alike, man and spirit, but not the same. Complete melding with a spirit changes a man, destroys a part of his humanity, much as the transformation of champions alters those who wear the armour. This is not a human age.

The chamber is large enough to accommodate an army. There is no sign of the sheathed maintenance whispers that stalk the corridors elsewhere, and the room is coated with dust. The principal feature of the chamber is a pair of vast windows of stained glass – the eyes of Might. Clear pupils are embedded in carefully reconstructed renditions of the human iris, fully ten metres across, their rods and bands laid to suggest a man whose personality is uncompromisingly heroic. An ornate walkway runs around the middle height of the room. Thirty metres below it, a richly detailed map of Mars is set into the floor.

Before one of the eyes the Emperor stands. Below him are the braided canyons of the Nuct, smothered in dusk, but he looks further afield, onto the Tertis plains to the north, upon whose arid woodlands the sun shines. The Emperor of this era is a ruler in name alone; the Quinarchs hold the reins of power.

Emperor Kalinilak is garbed in the robe of ten thousand eyes. Each eye is said to represent a watchful aspect of the Great Librarian, and the whole the unbreakable bond between Mars' temporal and spiritual rulers. It is, in essence, an avatar in the real world of the spirit Kunuk, to whom the Emperor is bound in a connection of the highest degree. The eyes are said never to blink, but every one of them is tightly closed, and by this I know something is wrong. The Twin Emperor is two souls, human and spirit joined as one to rule two worlds. It appears he has evaded his twin. This has never occurred before.

Surely, he will die because of this.

The eyes twitch and move under woven eyelids, as those of a sleeper move. The robe shimmers with its dreaming. It glows with an inner light that fights the dying sun. The Emperor's face is indistinct, sketched in planes of shadow and light-hazed skin.

Kalinilak gazes over the plains. In the far distance I can make out the shifting white patterns of the Veil of Worlds. He does not look at my love. When the Emperor speaks, his voice is neutral.

"It is said that of all life, Man is the highest. Of all forms, that of Man is most pleasing to fate. Of all creatures, Man is the most blessed. Why is it, then, that Men are not content? For what do they fight?" The gestures he weaves to accompany his words are fluid, enrapturing. "I greet you in peace, Yoechakenon Val Mora, and I pray that we can put aside our differences and speak as allies; unheard by no other but each other, and equal in the eyes of both. It is a privilege to be thus free. Let us enjoy this respite from scrutiny together as the friends we once were." He turns to Yoechakenon. Behind the glow of the cloak of Kunuk, the Emperor has a sad face topped with stringy black hair, his balding head mottled with bluish marks. His is a heavy-featured face, with a prominent nose standing guard over thick lips. His eyes despair. He knows his life is done, perhaps this time forever.

There is something else to those eyes. He looks out from his face alone; and I ask myself again: Where is the spirit that was bound to him?

"I come because fate demands it," Yoechakenon says. He is proud. He feels superior to this man, he always has. This was, perhaps, the seed of his downfall.

"Fate?" The Emperor lets the word hang. "Is this the thanks I receive? Surliness?"

Yoechakenon glances at his braceletted wrists. "Forgive me if I do not embrace my old friend in the manner that he may expect."

"Some would say that your inconvenience is no more than you deserve." The Emperor speaks without bile. "I summoned you here to offer you a reconciliation. If you prefer, I could worsen your situation instead." His expression is unmoving. His face is as old and as worn as the statues in his palace. "The Quinarchy and the spirits have no presence here. We stand in a hole in reality where but the one world exists, and thus my watching shadows are absent, while my scarabs are outside – too far away to save me. It is just you and I. I am vulnerable. This is purposely done. I wish to prove my intent is pure. The time for disagreement between us has passed, and the time for action grows short. Listen to what I

have to say; if you do not like what you hear, well...
Then we will see who will kill whom."

"You condemn me for taboo breaking, yet do
the same yourself, Kalinilak," says Yoechakenon.
He does not know yet the full extent of what the
Emperor has done. "This is not an action of trust.
I would know why you have shut out the Second
World before I hear whatever this offer will be."

"The Second World is not without its representative
here. Your companion is here, and listens as you do.
What I have to say concerns you both."

Yoechakenon attempts to think to me, but I cannot
hear his thoughts. I only feel what he feels, we are
still connected only to the second degree.

"She is as affected by the block as you," says the
Emperor of all Mars. In truth, he is but lord of this
palace and little else.

"Your suspicion does you ill, and you misthink,"
the Emperor goes on. "I am not your enemy." He
seems tired and over-energised at the same time. He
has dark circles under his eyes, bruise-black on pale
red skin. He has not known the peaceful oblivion of
sleep for too long.

"And yet you stand here an Emperor, and I a
prisoner and less than a man."

"To be an Emperor under the purview of machines
is to be an Emperor of dust and phantoms; it is to
be a child playing at being a prince," he says. He
looks out again at the plains below: the scattered
scrub and head-high grasses yellow in the heat of the
dry season, the reddish soil, the many rivers cutting
their way to the edge of the Marrin. Night has scaled
the canyon walls and is creeping across the uplands.

Beyond the atmosphere, the mirror suns flash out one by one. Those low to the west are the first to go dark, their extinguishment following the track of the sun's rays as they pass from the land.

"You and I, we are not so different. Gladiator and Emperor, we are prisoners of circumstance. And yet we have both defied the fate that supposedly rules our lives."

"If that is the case, my circumstances are entirely of your doing, my liege," Yoechakenon speaks quietly, "and the defeat that approaches you is of your own choosing."

"I say you condemned yourself!" The Emperor flares with anger. "Never suggest to me that this is not so. Tell me your punishment was not just, Yoechakenon. Tell me I was wrong for the judgement I passed upon you. You cast aside the Armour Prime of Kemiímseet. You broke your oath as a champion, full in the face of both worlds. Tell me I had a choice in what I did, and you may bear me malice without guilt. You stand here talking of fate, and then blame my actions for your predicament. I am either blameless, or we are both culpable; it does not run both ways."

Yoechakenon can feel the Emperor's gaze burning into the side of his face, and it is his turn not to meet the eyes of the other. He stares out instead into the night, and says as calmly as he can manage, "I wore the armour too long, Your Majesty. I wore it in your service and at your behest. It changes those who wear it, makes them different from other men. This is what the Spirefather of Olm showed me. The armour had twisted my soul."

The Emperor snorted, "You see? Even you are not so audacious as to deny the truth. The passion of your mercy overcame you. This is not the way of a true fatalist, though you present yourself as such. Men need passion; they need it to fight, they need it to breed. They need it to live! And how you lived, my friend, and how you were victorious, but you let your passions dominate you, and you fell from grace for it. Your passion has inconvenienced you, not I."

"If you were truly my friend, you would have let my execution proceed." Yoechakenon's face flushes, his tattoos writhe under their bonds. "Do you think I do not know shame? No life is worth this. Better to be returned to the stacks and await a new life, clean of dishonour. By your intervention you may have saved my body from execution, but instead you condemned my soul to slow torture. You made me suffer, and suffer I still do. This was not decreed by fate, and by interfering with what is just and right you forced the Quinarchy to damn me. My greatest rage is that you will never know what I have lost."

The Emperor laughs. "Will I not? Do you think that to rule a world and to have that might taken away from you piece by piece is a lesser ordeal?"

"If it was ordained!" shouts Yoechakenon. "The appropriate sentence, the better sentence, was death."

"You did what was asked of you, this is correct," the Emperor says. "But you exercised your will in a forbidden manner, and you believe that the Quinarchy would have returned you to the stacks?" The eyes on the robe flutter at this, and the robe glows bright for a second. The Emperor freezes, and waits for them to go back to their dreaming. When he speaks again, it is hushed. "You broke the taboos and brought ruination on both of us, and yet I saved your life."

"You should have let me die, as was only right."

The Emperor draws his hand back, as if he is about to strike. But he does not. Words die in his throat, unspoken. "My time as Emperor is almost done, as is my life and, I think, my story, but for a brief moment I am no longer beholden to the Quinarchy. In this sweet moment of freedom, I come to beg aid of you, not fight with you. Do you not understand? You, as I am, are a man of great and potent will, able to bend the threads of fate to your own end. There are few such. I needed you alive, as an enemy or an ally." The Emperor let out a long, slow exhalation. "You have been punished, and you have survived. Your survival was my aim."

Yoechakenon could kill the Emperor where he stands. He considers it.

The Emperor nods, as if sensing Yoechakenon's loathing even without the medium of the Great Library. "Yoechakenon, Mars is old and tired. It is a corpse with a painted face. I had such plans, I would have brought mankind into a new golden age, taken us away from this mummified existence. But dreams" – he waves his hand in the air, his lips compressed – "dreams are the stuff of whimsy. When my spirit returns to the Great Library, if it returns, that is the lesson it will have learnt. That, and one other: do not resist those who would say that they serve Man, for they are our masters. My eternal life lies in peril because I wished only to fulfil the obligations of my office. These endless, ridiculous wars the Quinarchy stirs up are its means of control, of keeping men occupied against one another. That is not fate, but the methodology of a tyrant, who would ensure we do not challenge its position, and who would remove me from mine."

"They rule below you. They are beholden to you. Only the Librarian is above you."

The Emperor shakes his head. "No. That is not so. That is why I have renounced the Second World."

"Kunuk, your companion?"

"Dreaming in the death sleep of the spirits."

Yoechakenon is shocked. As am I. This is close to murder.

"He is with the Quinarchy. This is the last war, Yoechakenon. They mean to destroy us. The Stone Kin are moving, the Stone Sun waxes strong. The spirits have determined, at the last, to end our existence. They feel it to be the only way they will survive. The age of our partnership is over."

He points. In the east, a bright star rises. The Stone Sun.

"The Stone Sun will pass close soon. Its children are stirring. The Quinarchy are behind this latest challenge, the League's gamble for power. I have spies even close to the Library's core, faithful spirits. Several died to confirm what I knew to be true in my heart; that the Quinarchy fear the Stone Kin will destroy us this time. The spirits will destroy us first, to spare themselves the Kin's fury."

"I do not understand."

"That is why you will always be a soldier, never a ruler. The Quinarchy wants the same as any man, though it is not made of men. It exists only to protect its own power."

"That is blasphemy."

"It is the truth. When the Stone Sun is close, the Veil of Worlds will be at its thinnest for millennia. The Stone Kin will once more attempt to impose their reality upon ours, as they have done in ages past. The Quinarchy believe they will be successful. They have decided that they must surrender, and to do that they must destroy us all. They fear you. We have both been trapped by them."

Out on the plains, the sunset is a colourful slash, parting black land from cold and fading skies. The last of the mirror suns go out. Kalinilak's rule stretches no further than his gaze. The discharge of particle cannon sparkles in the distance: the forces of the Delikon League reducing one of Kemiímseet's outlying citadels.

"What would you have me do?"

"It is simple. I want you to find the Great Librarian. Only he has the authority to bring the Quinarchy to heel, and the power to resist the Stone Kin. In three months, the League will have taken Kemiímseet. I am sure, then, that the Quinarchy will destroy you utterly. It never intended to return you to the stacks, and that is why I had to intervene – you would have been wiped from existence, never to live again. The arena was the only way to keep you alive. I only regret I could not tell you. If you had known, the Quinarchy would also have known that I had discovered its plans, and it would have destroyed me. Not that that matters much now."

Yoechakenon tries to master his thoughts. The Emperor has always had power over him, not only as a liege, but as a friend, and that is far more dangerous. Loyalty set him upon the path to the arena, honour sped him along it, pride brought him to its conclusion. I have said this to him many times.

"Why would the Quinarchy do such a thing? We have lived as one world for a thousand generations."

"Yoechakenon, you are the bravest man I have ever met, and the mightiest champion Mars has seen in a thousand years, but you are naïve, shackled by creed and habit. Think on this; who is to know if you never return? A man may lie discarnate in the stacks for ten thousand years before the story of his existence is taken up again, and he is made flesh once more."

"The spirits know. They remember, even if we do not."

"The spirits are less able to resist the power of the Quinarchy than we. In the Librarian's absence, the Quianrchs' power in the Second World is absolute. They are the embodiment of the Second World in a way I can never be of this one, even had Kunuk not been seduced by them."

"If this is part of the plan of the universe, then I deserve my decreed fate. Endless death is the ultimate destiny of us all, after all. I only hope I am remembered for my deeds in the service of the Emperor, Librarian and People of Mars, and not as a traitor."

"One does not placate the hatred of the Quinarchy easily, Yoechakenon, and one cannot dictate others' perceptions of us once we are gone, especially when the same authority writes our life histories. Only what the Quinarchy decrees is truly fate or the past: it manipulates and plots, bending and twisting our paths to its own ends, and it is free to do so, for there are none to gainsay it. But I know the truth, my spies have glimpsed its innermost thoughts. It is as powerless against the march of time as we are, and it would survive the coming of the Stone Sun. It hates you. The Quinarchy would inflict an eternity of torment upon Kaibeli in revenge. Tell me that that does not matter. Could you stand by and watch her suffer? The souls of her kind are different to ours, and they can be made to feel pain in ways of which we cannot even begin to conceive."

"And you?"

"I will be punished in my turn," the Emperor says grimly. "That is without doubt. That is my fate. The spiral of my existence ends here, whatever transpires between us. The Quinarchy will smash my soul. There is no escape for me."

"Then perhaps your punishment is just, but mine was not. You interfered when you had no right to do so, and damaged the proper course of things. I... I only did what was required of me by fate. I broke the taboo because I was fated to do so."

"Am I not then also fated to do so, to save a friend? Your faith is conveniently set aside when needs be, Yoechakenon. Who makes you diviner, who can tell the will of destiny? Is this why you hate me in my turn, for saving you? What could I do?" The Emperor's sad eyes search his friend's face. "The arena was just and useful, for the Door-ward, as wicked as it is, is very particular about its duties. Nothing could touch you there."

"It... it protected me from the Quinarchy?"

"Look at you. It is your thirst for life that drives you to hate me, not your wish for death. I know you, Yoechakenon, else my offer would be different. Come. I will show you proof." He stands away from the railing, holds out his arm and beckons. "If you remain uninterested, then I will do nothing and you will be free to strike me down. It will only be hastening the inevitable, after all." He gestures, and Yoechakenon's pain bracelets fall to the floor. "You will not be needing those any more, I think."

Yoechakenon rubs his wrists, flexes his hands. It would be so easy to kill the Emperor. He is in the same cycle of life as Yoechakenon, but looks a hundred times as frail; the throne has sucked him dry. It would be so easy to avenge two years of humiliation, a simple twist of his neck. Yoechakenon could part his uppermost vertebrae from his skull with the slightest effort. He could reach out, but he does not. "I could kill you now."

"Yoechakenon Val Mora, I know you will not. I can see it in your eyes. You want to know what I have seen. Curiosity was ever one of your greatest vices, and it still burns in you."

THE EMPEROR HURRIES, his robe trailing a path in the dust on the floor, the eyes upon it still closed. He approaches a pillar hidden in an unremarkable alcove. He brushes his hand over it in a complicated pattern. The column soundlessly opens in response, folding out like a flower. The Emperor disappears within.

The pillar contains a tightly coiled staircase, so cramped that Yoechakenon cannot stand. His elbows touch both walls as he follows its curve, and his stomach rolls with strange vertigo. He pulls his feet leadenly one after the other up the steps, his mind at one moment compressed, the next as wide as the sky.

Kalinilak is several turns ahead of him, and by the time Yoechakenon emerges from the top of the stairs, the other man stands engrossed in a flickering image spread across the air of a dark chamber.

"Behold, Yoechakenon," says the Emperor. "The Window of the Worlds." Little is visible of the ruler of Mars beyond the glow of his raiment, and this too is muted. A movement, the glitter of the whites of his eyes in the gloom as he speaks. He looks like a hierophant in his cave on one of the temple terraces, performing tricks for profit.

Yoechakenon can make little sense of the image. The room about it is totally black.

"This is a secret place, a place only I know of. You stand high in the head of Wisdom, the third herm of the mesa," says the Emperor.

"How can this be?" asks Yoechakenon. "We were stood but moments ago behind the right eye of Might."

"The staircase does not function as others do, and it coils round more than the usual space. Were a man to attempt those stairs without my foreknowledge he would find himself falling far to his death on the canyon floor. The sensation you feel, the sense of displacement? This chamber is invested with a little of the energies of the Stone Realms. But do not be alarmed, it is perfectly safe. This image, before us, is important. The proof I offer you and more besides lies therein."

"I see nothing but patterns of light. You have tricked yourself."

"Ever the doubter of men and the lover of machines, you are! Look harder, let your mind free. Turn off your visual filters. Look at it with human eyes. This is the way the image will speak to you."

So Yoechakenon shuts his eyes, and when he opens them he looks out through naked human sight. Even in the total blackness of the room, the picture is faint and distorted. As he stares, the Emperor speaks, his voice sounding out of the blackness. "This imaging device is constructed in the same manner as other astronomical instruments, though the lens is different. It is ground from a piece of crystal taken from the site of the Fortress of Tears. It is this lens, fashioned from a part of the Stone Realms itself, that allows me to look beyond the Veil of Worlds, to anywhere I choose. Its strange properties filter the spatial distortion from the light, and shield my mind from the attentions of those Stone Beasts who prowl the void. No! Do not look at me, stare into the image. Do you not see? Through this I may look upon our enemies unobserved."

Yoechakenon looks and looks as the Emperor continues to talk. He speaks of many things, of lost empires, of ancient cities long cast down in ruin, and he points at them as he speaks, but Yoechakenon sees nothing. The Emperor speaks of far-flung worlds and heroes with names no other men remember. Yoechakenon cannot see anything in the shifting patterns of light. He gazes more intently, and the Emperor talks on, his voice hypnotic.

Suddenly the layers of the image fall into place, and to Yoechakenon's amazement he is looking at a landscape. A ravaged, blasted world of desert and oily oceans, scarred by stone intrusion and ice caps made huge by the dimming of the sun. But there is life. He is looking at an arc of Yerth. A sliver of it is in darkness, the rest in greyish light. The dark grows, and as night moves over the world, he sees lights. They are dim and distant from one another, but they shine dauntless, undeniable, beacons of life in an uncertain sea of shadow.

"Do you see now? This is Yerth, and there is a lie. Those lights are the lights of mankind's cities. This is no lifeless orb. If the Quinarchy will lie about our brethren, what else will it lie about?"

"This image cannot be real," says Yoechakenon. "No one has looked upon Yerth since the time of the Third Stone War."

"You do not believe that. Your face betrays that you do not believe your own words. I have become adept at reading faces, in my time away from the Library."

They look again at the images of Yerth. Yoechakenon watches in wonder as the Emperor adjusts the viewing aperture, bringing into sharp focus vast cities with lights as bright as suns at their heart. He shifts the view, showing a party of skin-clad men bearing a slaughtered animal of bizarre appearance across a blasted heath. The device is so finely tuned we can see their faces, and the steam billowing from their mouths in the freezing air. If the Emperor has created this as a ruse, it is an impressive one.

We gaze at the image for several minutes, until a black shadow passes over Yerth, and the image fills with the suggestion of something large and gelatinous, undulating in a manner that makes Yoechakenon's skin crawl. The picture contracts, and there comes an inhuman, distant cry as of many creatures suffering together, and the picture fades away.

"Stone Kin," whispers Yoechakenon. He feels the chill of terror.

"Stone Beast," corrects the Emperor. "A mindless animal that dwells within the Veil, not one of the Kin." He says this steadily. "The higher forms are gone."

"Where are they?" he asks.

"They are here," says the Emperor. He moves his hands, and another image leaps into life, clearer.

This time we see a portion of Mars; where, I do not know. The images shimmer in that strange manner the air takes where the Stone Lands hold sway and men do not go. At first we see nothing, and then: "It is an army, I see an army," says Yoechakenon.

"You do," says the Emperor. "An army of the Stone Kin, coming to Mars."

We look upon their ranks. They are strange to behold, when they can be seen at all. They are not of this reality, these creatures.

"Time moves differently for them, and they come but slowly from the Stone Lands. When the Stone

Sun draws close to Mars, then they will come forth and join with their allies, the treacherous servants of the Quinarchy.

"There is more." He passes his hands through the air. Another scene, another army, this one of men and machines ridden by spirits. In the centre of it, a great beast. It warps and flutters in the picture, its form yet to fully establish itself within the strictures of our reality. It hurts the mind. If I or Yoechakenon had any lingering doubts, they are gone.

"Do you see? Do you see now? The League openly employs Stone Beasts; the Quinarchs tell their allies they are the masters of these creatures. The League remains ignorant, I am sure, of the depths of its betrayal."

We watch the army. It is assailing a citadel, the assault preluded by the particle fires we saw from the head of Might.

"This thing, this window, can you see the Librarian? How can you be sure he still exists?" asks Yoechakenon.

The Emperor shrugged, "He hides itself from all, as he has for ages. But his voice comes and goes, never within the halls of the Library, always outside. Sometimes it is a whisper, sometimes a roar. Sometimes it is not there at all. But it is there."

"You do not know if it is truly there, then. You do not know that this is not a device of the Stone Kin to deceive you."

"No, I do not."

Dim lights come on in the room. There remains the possibility that the shimmering Yerth and the stone army is a trick, the last torment of a man soon to lose his throne. We both think otherwise.

"Go, Yoechakenon, take up your armour again. Find the Librarian of Mars. We will no longer be slaves to the Quinarchy, our people sacrificed to them. Perhaps from that our people will take heart, and Man will grow to be a power to be reckoned with once more. I have not been a wicked Emperor; but I have caused more pain than good. I want the few who are free enough of the Quinarchy to remember well the Emperor Kalinilak, and his champion Yoechakenon Val Mora, and I want that knowledge to bring them succour in the dark days ahead. This is no suicide mission, Yoechakenon. I intend for you to return, for how else will the people know what you will learn? That is to be your redemption. Return with the Librarian and you will be remembered forever. You have been punished, now, every man can see that, and the people love you as much as a gladiator as they did a champion. And they will love you as a hero thrice over. Think of it!" Agitated, the Emperor grasps Yoechakenon's shoulders. His hands are dry and veinous, white, dry skin mottling the red. They are the hands of a used-up man. "My friend, that is what we have dreamed of for nigh on two hundred centuries, and you have the chance to make it happen."

Yoechakenon's throat constricts, his mouth runs dry. "And if I refuse?" he says carefully.

"You will not refuse, Yoechakenon. You have already decided to go. I can rest easy. Your honour is so great you will be compelled to carry out the task as long as you have strength in your limbs. Nor will you fail, for your pride will not permit it."

"My pride, strength and honour mean little if I am slain. If I die, then so will Kaibeli. Your will shall lie broken in the dust, and our souls also. Here at least I have a chance to return to the stacks."

"And you will certainly die here! You have no chance for the stacks, and they will be destroyed themselves. What more must I say to you?" The Emperor drops his head and stares into the dismal shadows of the room. His brow creases, as if he can see something that Yoechakenon cannot, and that thing disturbs him. He grips Yoechakenon's shoulders the tighter.

Yoechakenon looks deep into the eyes of the Emperor. They blaze too brightly; the candle of his life burns fast. "I could refuse, even though I know in my heart that you are right, and that both Kaibeli and I will suffer greatly when the city falls. I could refuse and watch you suffer, knowing that you, too, will never have the legacy you desire. But I will not. I will have you know that I am not swayed by fear, likewise that I am not swayed by revenge. I am a better man than you. But though I agree to do your bidding, you shall never have my forgiveness."

"It is not your forgiveness, but your skill at arms and will to survive I require."

"Then you have my word, they are once more at your service, nothing more. My spirit remains my own."

The Emperor closes his eyes and smiles, and his grip lessens upon the champion's shoulders. "Good, good," he sighs and nods, as if his mind has finally come to agreement with itself after a bitter dispute. "That is as good as I could expect." He looks older and paler, a sick man who has expended a great effort. "Come, you must leave immediately before the Quinarchy discovers me and is forced to act. Even now, it will be growing suspicious; you have been away from the arena for too long." He walks across the chamber. He makes motions that are swallowed by the weird illumination of the room, and a door opens that appears only as slivers of lights in the darkness.

"How will I find the Librarian?"

"The answer to that and your passage to him lie in the same place. Follow me. We have little time."

CHAPTER TEN

Wonderland

ON WEDNESDAY, HIS fourth day at Ascraeus, Holland was taken into the caves. Early in the morning, he and his teammates ate a large breakfast. The walk to base camp took around five hours, so they were to be there two nights; breakfast was their last chance at real food for a while. Eggs, fresh bread, tomatoes, and beans – all Mars-grown. The food was good, and nutritionally balanced, but it would not be long before Holland was ready to kill for a steak.

His team was a foursome: he, Stulynow, Vance – who was to monitor his physical and psychological reactions to the cave environment – and, to his irritation, the base's Class Three.

"Can't be helped, I'm afraid. The carriage goes on all the expeditions, and she rides it all the way down on those where we have new team members," said Maguire on the way down to Deep Two. "Don't mind it, though, you'll forget she's there. Stuly's the best cave expert we have, and he's a bloody good guide. Two things that man is enthusiastic about: drinking and caves. I can't wait for you to see it."

Maguire said a lot on the trip. Holland paid him little attention; his mind was on other matters. Maguire either did not notice or did not mind.

Holland had seen video of the caves, and had explored a portion of them in a somewhat lacklustre virtspace – it was low resolution, and far from immersive. He figured this was for two reasons: first, full immersion in an environment that could simultaneously explode, choke, burn and freeze you would be excruciatingly painful, even in a virtspace. Second, if Marsform exhibited the caves' glories for all to see, then they'd have a whole lot more people complaining about the possible extinction of everything inside.

Holland had an inkling of the disparity between the bland VR and the reality. He'd had some samples of the lifeforms in his laboratory. He'd seen how industrious Mars' chemotrophs were, and that had been out of their natural habitat.

Suiting up under the watchful eyes of Jensen took forever. Holland was made to remove his survival undersuit and re-don it before he was allowed into the hard shell cave gear. They each had their own undersuit. The hard shells, of which there were five, were shared.

"No, no, no," said Jensen, slapping Holland's hands away. "The undersuit on its own can keep you alive for a few days, but only if worn properly. Compressing the recycling systems by improper wear severely reduces their operational span, and it must maintain even pressure or your soft tissues will swell in the event of hard shell failure." He fiddled at Holland's undersuit and stood back. "There," he said.

Jensen took the opportunity to lecture all of them on the correct safety procedures for a solid half an hour. Holland was made to recite the location and usage of all the hard shell suit's emergency equipment: quick release for its chest and back plates, alkali wash for acid contamination, medical packs, rapid foam patching gear, spares for water and air scrubbers... the list was long and Jensen made him go over it twice.

"You, Doctors Vance and Stulynow. All well and good to stand there with those long faces. It will do you no harm to listen to this again. You may have the supply mules and the android, but should there be a cave-in and you are trapped, the equipment in the hard shells is all you will have between you and a lingering death."

"I am listening, Dr Jensen," said Dr Vance steadily.

"Well, I am not, you Viking bore. Get on with it," said Stulynow.

Jensen gave him a hard stare and went back to asking Holland his endless list of questions, then made him repack his equipment case.

The point where they plugged the hard shell directly into his interface port was particularly unpleasant.

Finally, Jensen was finished. They sealed the hard shells. Maguire tapped Holland on the shoulder. His vision was restricted to a one-hundred-and-seventy-degree arc in front of him, and he had to clump round to look Maguire in the face.

"I'll be watching everything from the control suite with Jensen, don't you worry, Holly," said Maguire. He held his hand up, thumb and forefinger pressed together in an 'okay' signal. Maguire and Jensen left the suit space. The door back into the station hissed as the seal engaged.

"We will now check suit system telemetry," said Jensen from the observation suite. Data displays flashed on, crowding the suit visor's periphery. Tiny windows with a view of the observation suite and images from Stulynow, Vance and the android's cameras, perfect as jewels, were stacked on the top right. Holland cycled through them, bringing Stulynow's POV to the top as he would be leading the way. Cave maps, locational data, seismic readings, atmospheric composition, video capture, VR logging, Grid link (if he wished to see the Martian Grid's contents, rather than having it forced into his head; he was grateful for that). Drop-down menus gave access to more data. Jensen instructed him to access a random selection of data sets and apps with his implant.

"That all seems to be working," Jensen said.

"Don't forget, Holly, you can customise what you have up on your dashboard. You can save your own profile so whatever suit you are in in future, it will boot up with your preferences. It's only like having a new phone, it is."

"We recommend, however, that you keep all environmental information locked in as presented," said Jensen. "Stulynow, is your team ready?"

"*Da*," said Stulynow. He stepped round the other two, awkward in the confined space of the suiting room, and checked each of them over. "See anything wrong, Jensen?"

"All is in order," said Jensen.

"Let's go," said Stulynow.

The door to the lava tube rolled open. They walked outside, over to the racks of equipment and inactive near-I mules. One, loaded with food and water, whirred into life and got unsteadily to its feet, followed by a second, bearing heavier gear. The mules had no real front or back. They were headless, both sets of legs identical, jointed oppositely to each other, but someone had stuck a stuffed donkey head to one end of the lead mule. It was dirty and had a number of small holes melted into it.

"Where's the android?" said Stulynow.

"I am here," said Cybele's perfect voice. She strode out from the equipment store, wearing a sheath Holland had not seen before. It was heavier than her usual, its paint scratched, metal pitted with acid burns.

"Her cave body," said Stulynow. He tapped the chest plate of his suit. "Aluminium. Some of the methanogens down there eat through plastics, even modern latticed carbon, like grandmothers go through chocolates."

They went to the large airlock sealing the beginnings of the cave system from Deep Two's chamber. Toothed doors unlocked from one another. They stepped through and the doors slid shut. No fans activated, there was no need for them on the way in. The doors were not there to regulate pressure, but to keep Wonderland's methane from reaching Deep Two.

The outer doors re-engaged with a *clunk*, and the inner doors opened. From here Holland could see the path down as a chain of lights, leading out from the tube, into the first cavern, and then on into the darkness.

"Into the rabbit hole," said Vance. She clipped herself, then Holland, to the safety line.

"Welcome to Heaven," said Stulynow laconically. "Or Hell. It depends on how you feel about caves."

Stulynow set out, and the others followed. Holland was growing more surefooted in Martian gravity, but the steps daunted him in the bulky hard shell. He took them slowly, Vance helping him down, Cybele standing at the bottom in case he should fall. He went over to the silicon formation, and began taking pictures and chemical readings from it with his suit.

There was a lot of laughing.

"Er, John?" said Maguire. Holland looked up to see him watching behind the observation suite's window. "I wouldn't bother with that. There's plenty more of that lower down."

"You really don't know what to expect?" said Stulynow.

"No," said Holland. "Not really."

"Let me show you, my new friend Dr Holland."

Their descent began in earnest.

THE PATH RAN down through caves stacked one atop the other. The caves followed what had been veins of sulphur deposited by the volcano; these had been eaten out by the lifeforms, leaving nothing but acid-scarred basalt. Now there was little living in the upper caves. A few small examples of the fairy castles, as the team called them, were the only things visible to the eye. In places, other mineral structures left by microbes coated the walls or the floors, but, confused by deposits leached in from the surface, they were little use for study.

"Life here dates from a time when Mars still had a hydrological cycle," said Holland.

"Yes," said Vance. "Not much alive this high up. Some methanogens cracking CO_2 from the air. Without the sulphur oxidisers, the biome is limited. They're the foundation."

Some of the caverns were stupendous in size. The old magma chambers and inflationary caves, mixed in with spaces full of the evidence of past biotic activity, fractured into crazed labyrinths where microbes had eaten away the rock. Holland's suit lights often did not hit the far wall. He felt dwarfed by the scale of it. The weight of the shield volcano above them vanished in his mind. It was not possible to reconcile the size of Ascraeus Mons with the spaces beneath it.

After two hours, Stulynow stopped. "We are coming to what we call the Chasm. We are fifteen thousand and fifty metres under the peak of the Mons. To our right, we'll be skirting along an old magma chamber, drained when Ascraeus moved away from the Tharsis plume. Be really careful on the lip. You fall in there, and we'll never see you again."

"Just 'The Chasm'?"

"Yes," said Stulynow dourly, "because it's the biggest damn hole in the ground you will ever see."

"Stuly, this is something amazing. Can't you build it up a little bit?" said Vance.

"It is what it is."

"You are a miserable, miserable man," said Vance.

"It is the Russian in me, I told you this many times."

They went down a short flight of stairs into a lesser cave. At the base was a doorway carved into the rock, lights and EM relays on both sides of it. The safety line was broken by the door, the carbon cable giving way to a steel one anchored on the far side.

"It may seem stupid to put this here," said Stulynow. He pointed to two unfinished doorways. "We tried to find another way down, but this rock is broken by vertical conduits and faulting that made it impossible. Following the edge of the chasm made it easier to bring in bridging materials to get over the lesser gaps. The outgassing was also easier to trace here. Without the Chasm we might never have found the major biome. So, as you say, swings and carousels."

"Roundabouts," said Holland. "We say 'roundabouts.'"

"Yes. Those. Jensen?"

"Yes." Jensen's voice crackled.

"We are about to walk the chasm."

Holland followed Stulynow through the doorway. "Unclipping," Stulynow said as he unclipped Holland's suit harness.

"Affirmative," said Jensen.

Stulynow moved the carabiner to the steel wire on the other side of the door. "Clipping," he said as he reattached it. "Are you ready?"

"Yes," said Holland.

Stulynow chuckled drily. "No you're not."

They walked out, Vance following Holland, Cybele and the mules bringing up the rear. The path followed a tunnel a short way, then opened up into nothing.

"Oh, Christ," said Holland.

To his right was an immense void, the far side barely visible, the top a mess of rock cubes hanging from the ceiling in defiance of gravity.

"I'd say do not look down," said Stulynow, "only you can't see the bottom. Even with that." He indicated a powerful lamp on a gimbal mounted on the wall. "We've five hundred metres of this to go."

"Stay steady, Holland, it's over quicker than you might think." Maguire spoke over the suit radio.

"I'm fine with heights, really," said Holland.

But this was more than a height, and Holland's stomach flipped. The path clung to a thin ledge, widened when necessary by catwalks bolted to the stone. It did not take long before Holland was eyeing each and every bolt as if it would suddenly turn suicidal and cast them all into the dark. Only two thin cables, the guideline to his right and the safety line to his left, stood between him and the Chasm. By the time they'd reached the end, he stood on shaky legs.

"Adrenaline rush? Told you. Scares the shit out of me, and I have been here two dozen times," said Stulynow.

"The worst of it is over," said Vance. She put a hand on Holland's elbow and peered earnestly up at him from the depths of her helmet. "From now on we've just got the stair, and then we're into Wonderland. From there it's thirty minutes to the base camp."

"Our doctor does have a nice side," said Stulynow.

"Fuck you, you aggravating Russian," said Vance. There was little real annoyance to it.

"I tell you, every day..."

"Your mother was a Buryat?" said Holland.

Stulynow smiled, teeth showing in the light of his helmet. "Exactly. Now, as Vanchetchka says, we go down the stair."

The stair was a maze – ancient pressure domes, vertical conduits, lesser lava chambers and biotic cavities stepped on top of each other. Some of them were the beginnings of lava tubes, and led off to who knew where.

"We have explored precisely none of these deeper tubes," said Stulynow. "Needs people, or fully autonomous robotic units. We're shit out of both. There's life in a lot of them, we've got the gas traces to prove it. Anything could be down there."

Natural cracks between the caverns had been widened by machine or blasted open. They went down quickly, and the air temperature rose. Holland could not feel it beneath his suit's insulation, but his thermometer crawled up from minus figures into the low plusses. The air composition changed: less carbon dioxide, more methane. The walls took on hues of chemical brightness, the remnant ecology becoming progressively more active the lower they went. Dripping strings of mucus appeared on the ceilings, colonies of sulphur-loving bacteria. There was more moisture in the air, and the ground became slippery underfoot. Holland wondered how his boot soles were faring – the wetness was sulphuric acid dripped by the snottites. Fairy castles became more common, until they were walking through rooms full of glittering formations.

The ground levelled out, and the steps came to an end. They had arrived. Tripod lights came on automatically, illuminating a large gallery.

"Wonderland, Dr Holland," said Dr Vance. "The last great bastion of Martian life."

"Wow," he said. This time he really meant it. They were in a large, loaf-shaped cave. Chemotrophic bacteria of all types feasted on the rock and air and the by-products of the snottites. Other bacteria subsisted on their organic residues, creating a riot of colourful alien life.

It was, figuratively speaking, all his. He was the first real exobiologist to see this since the cave was opened last year.

Now he was excited. "I... I just don't know where to start."

Vance laughed. Again, that hand on his arm. Was there an attraction there? She was certainly not the firebrand of two nights ago. They had all been drunk, after all.

"I'm so glad you're impressed. Perhaps you'll help me stop those ignorant bastards ripping it all up," she said.

"I don't see why it has to go," he said. "I mean, we're so deep under the surface now. Equally bizarre ecosystems thrive on Earth... Less complex, obviously, but... I don't know. It will need isolating, perhaps. And then maybe even not that. There's so much to study, far more than I thought." He walked to a wall glistening with moisture, and reached his hand out, then thought better of it. More acid. These caves had been etched out of solid rock.

"Come on, there's time for all that tomorrow," said Stulynow. "You probably do not feel it now, but you will be tired. We go to base camp now, and we rest. Tomorrow, the full tour, and some work. The day after, home."

Stulynow beckoned them, and they followed him up the glittering passage.

BASE CAMP WAS in a system of sealed, sterilised caves some way above the main biome caverns. An outer cave held a foamcrete survival shelter and racks for the hard shells. Holland stepped out of the hard shell. He inspected the suit as instructed, looking for acid damage. It was dirty, but whole. They misted the suits and robots with alkaline spray, and set the racks' nanobots to give them the once over. An airlock unit with integrated nanite wash led into the living quarters.

Stulynow consulted with Jensen while Vance gave the rooms a quick biotic scan and sampled the air for methane contamination. Everything checked out, so Stulynow gave the signal that they could take their helmets off.

They stood with hair plastered to their heads with sweat. Holland breathed deep; the air was damp and tasted of stone. Vance smiled at him.

"It is something, isn't it?" she said.

"Yeah, yes it is."

"Yeah, yeah," said Stulynow. "Let's eat, shall we?"

There was no furniture at the base camp, only the very bare essentials, so they sat on rocks to eat. The food was stuff in bags that was as bad as Holland had been warned. He ate it ravenously anyway. He was exhausted. The hard shell was well designed, power-aided in important areas by polymer muscle bundles, but it was still damn heavy, and moving against the constant pressure of the undersuit, like the environment suits, was hard work.

"God, I'm stiff," he said.

"It takes a little while to get used to the hard shells," said Vance. "It's not so much the weight, it's the way it makes you move. Not entirely natural. Your muscles sore?"

Holland nodded. He stretched out his leg, flexed it and winced.

"Right. Get your undersuit off," said Vance.

Stulynow, crouched over a tablet's holo screen, sniggered.

"But Jensen told me to keep it on at all times."

"Yeah, and I'm expedition doctor. He's overruled. You'll be no use to us if you seize up. Off!"

Holland looked dubious. He was naked underneath.

"Don't worry, I've seen it all before."

Stulynow smiled broadly. "Better do as she says, you've seen her when she's being a hardass."

Holland got to his feet and reluctantly removed his undersuit. "I stink," he said.

"Everyone who has to shit in a bag for two days stinks. We all stink. I don't care," said Vance. She pulled a hypo spray from her equipment box, pulled out an ampoule and loaded it. "This is a mild muscle relaxant. There's an anti-lactic acid agent in it."

"I had to get undressed for this?"

"No," she said, "you had to get undressed for this." She pulled a tube of ointment out of the box and tossed it to him. "Rub it in where it hurts most."

"Ointment?" he said.

She nodded. "Yes. Still best for what ails you. I'd get on with it before you get cold."

Holland rubbed at his limbs vigorously.

Vance smiled. "Nice butt, by the way."

Stulynow roared with laughter.

"This isn't some kind of cave-hazing is it?" said Holland. "I've fallen for it, haven't I?"

"No, no," said Vance. "Really it is best for the stiffness," she said with a smirk. "But it's still pretty funny."

Holland slipped his undersuit back on while the others giggled like children. Before long, he was laughing, too.

HOLLAND WAS CATALOGUING microbial communities in a new chamber when it happened.

"Could you get me a sample of that one there?" said Holland.

"Which?" said Vance.

"That one, the vermillion, above the blue."

Vance took a plastic scraper and worked it at the mineral deposit. It wouldn't last long once certain strains of bacteria got onto it, but they couldn't risk sparks. She scraped an amount into a diamond weave pot. "This enough?"

Holland checked her suit camera. "Aha, should be. Enough for an analysis and a culture."

Stulynow was out with Cybele and one of the mules, erecting new lamps and refreshing the fuel cells of those that had been there a while. They were scrupulously careful. Everything that stayed in the cave was made of light metals, covered in an antispark coating. Fuel cells were chemical types, the lamps low power bio-lights. The air was anoxic – for combustion there would have to be a significant release of oxygen and a source of extreme heat – but there was so much methane it paid to be careful.

Holland was sampling chemical structures with his suit, running analysis in the hard shell's on-board minilab. Vance returned the diamond weave dish to his equipment box.

There was a deep rumble. The ground shook.

"What the...?" said Holland.

"There are no blasts scheduled for today, are there?" said Vance.

Another rumble. Then another. Rock fragments pattered off Holland's hard shell.

"Bloody Chinese," came Stulynow's voice. "Blasting without telling us. Come on, we have to get into the shelter."

"The Chinese insist that they are not conducting seismic testing today," said Jensen. Interference had increased, and his voice was crackly.

"Besides, looking at your readings, you're so deep they'd have to be detonating mini-nukes up here at least," added Maguire. "And we'd notice that. We can feel nothing."

The blasts continued, rhythmic and regular.

"Like artillery fire," said Holland.

"Or a heartbeat," said Vance.

"It's not natural seismic activity," said Stulynow. "Is it something Marsform's TF crews are doing?"

"Negative," said Maguire.

"Any rockfalls?" said Jensen.

"No, no. Everything's okay down here, once you become accustomed to the ground shaking," said Stulynow.

"You'll have to sit tight until it's over," said Maguire. "Sorry."

The three scientists, crammed in their hard shells in the shelter, helmet to helmet, looked at each other doubtfully.

"You can at least take a measurement from up there, Dave," said Holland. "Triangulate it with our data, so we can find out exactly where it's coming from?"

"Yeah, hang on. Jensen?"

"Yes. We can do that."

They worked as best they could, using the base camp's seismic sensors along with those of Deep Two to pinpoint the source of the tremors. After a time they ceased, to the relief of them all. They left the shelter.

"Look's like it was emanating from about here," said Stulynow. A red dot flashed on a holo map that burst into being in front of Holland's nose. He nearly staggered back with surprise, fighting the urge to swat at it.

"That's not far away," said Vance. "A bit up the stair, then into the labyrinth."

"Can't have been very strong after all, then," said Holland.

"What do you think? Stuly? Should we check it out?"

"Have you collected your samples, Dr Holland?"

"I've more than enough for weeks of analyses," Holland replied.

"Fine. If you are willing to help me with the lamps and work a little later tonight, then we can."

There was the sound of somewhat heated debate from the other end. Maguire came on the line. He laughed apologetically. "Jensen's all for you coming right back home, until I reminded him of Marsform's obligation to investigate all unusual phenomena unless hazardous to personnel. I'm quoting there. I'll not force the issue, so it's really up to you guys."

Stulynow looked from Vance to Holland. Both nodded.

"Let's do it," said the Russian.

THEY FINISHED STULYNOW'S maintenance round quickly. A sense of anticipation hung on the air: this sort of serious exploration was not something that came around often. By 16.00 hours they had Cybele and one of the mules loaded up with whatever they might need. They ascended one hundred metres of the stair, arriving at one of the many lava tubes buried under Ascraeus Mons.

"This way," said Stulynow, pointing down the tube. He took a torch and plugged it directly into his suit, supplementing the built-in lamps. The others followed suit, Cybele included. Fat beams of high-powered light picked out holes in the ceiling four metres above, slumped sections of wall, debris on the floor.

Their maps had been seismically inferred, and were imprecise at best. After half an hour they reached the furthest point the tube had been explored to, and the maps began to correct themselves as better data presented itself.

"We should be coming to a blockage now," said Stulynow. His torch beam picked out a pile of rock debris fallen in from the roof some way ahead. "How deep, Cybele?"

"Five metres at the base, two at the top. I can make a hole for your passage in ten minutes."

"Are there many more blockages?" asked Holland as they walked to the wall of rubble.

"Hard to say," said Stulynow. "According to the map, the tunnel branches after this. There's a conduit not too far on, and an inflation chamber. It's all inferred, though. Will we have more digging to do? Probably."

Cybele set down her torch and stalked to the weakest point in the debris wall. She began to dig.

"I wonder what this is all about?" said Vance.

"Martians. The little green men," said Stulynow.

"Stuly! What do you think, Holland?"

"I have no idea."

"It is fun finding out," said the Russian.

They watched Cybele pick up chunks of rock far bigger than any they could have managed, even under the light gravity. She went to the mule for a spade, and shovelled the lighter material aside. In a few minutes, she had carved a hole near the peak of the debris.

"Ladies first," said Stulynow.

"I will go ahead," said Cybele. "In case of peril."

She went through the hole she'd made, returning a few minutes later. "The way ahead is safe," she said. "There is more methane, more life, but it is safe."

"Jensen, Maguire? I'm setting an EM relay here. Any signal weakness, let me know," said Stulynow. He placed a scratched plastic box on the floor. A green light flickered on it. "Okay. Let us go on."

They walked through the hole, and into the unknown.

"THIS IS IT," said Vance. She pointed to a crack in the rock.

"Thank God it's not down there," said Holland. He pointed to the broad volcanic flue behind them, a rickety bridge of linked plates placed across it by the android.

"It doesn't matter if we can't get in," said Vance. "This is a new branch of Wonderland, that's good work for a day." Snottites hung from the roof, and there were blooms of other life all around.

"Doesn't look like much, does it?" said Stulynow. He pushed his hand into the crack. "Without the hard shell, I think I could get in there."

"You're not suggesting.... Stuly, no speleological heroics. What if you snag your undersuit?

Stulynow stepped back. "You are right."

"Let's go back, log our data. We can always come back with some robot scouts. There's no way we're getting through that," said Vance.

"Yes there is," said Stulynow. "Cybele, can we use the charges?"

"The atmosphere here is forty-six per cent carbon dioxide. Methane levels are twenty per cent. If we employ implosive devices, it should be safe. However, I recommend contacting Deep Two for authorisation."

"The Viking is a pedant; she is a pedant. I am surrounded by pedants," grumbled Stulynow.

"He learnt that word off Maguire," said Vance.

"Silence! I consult the pedant-in-chief. Jensen?" There was a hiss of static.

"Jensen? Jensen? Calling Jensen," he said impatiently to his suit. "I cannot get through. Cybele, explain."

"There has been an interruption in the signal."

"Can you talk with them? Cybele?" There was no response. Stulynow walked up to the machine and poked it in the chest. A stream of angry Russian followed. "An interruption! This is what she says. She too is interrupted."

"My augmentation link is offline," said Holland.

"Mine too," said Vance.

Stulynow put his hands onto his hips. He said something Slavic and profane.

"What do you think? I am technically in charge here, but I think this may be a moment of some... momentousness. Is this the right word?"

"It will do," said Holland. "Vance?"

"It's just a crack in the wall."

"It is a crack in the wall, yes," said Stulynow. "But on the other side?"

"Let's... What the hell is that?" Holland pointed.

On the ground, long antennae pedalling the air, was a large arthropod. Holland dropped to his knees in excitement, forgetting the hard shell, rocking forward clumsily. The thing whipped round and skittered down the crack.

"Did you see it? Did you see it?" Holland shouted. "We have to go down there now, we have to!"

"What the hell is what?" said Stulynow.

"The creature!" Holland went to the gap, scrabbled at it, shining his torch into it and finding nothing but old rock and stark shadow.

"Holland, get aw... w... ...f it's sa..."

Stulynow's voice broke up into static. A loud, sinous pulsing rode the roar of EM white noise, building to an eerie shriek, deafening them. Vance reeled. Stulynow stumbled against the wall, one hand on the smooth lava, the other pawing at his helmet. The ground shook violently. Fragments of rock pattered onto the scientists, and a large chunk smashed into the inert mule, breaking a leg. Holland lurched forward, and the hard shell's visor cracked into the stone. Gas poured in. Alarms whooped in his helmet, losing out to the screech and rush of the EM racket.

Light flickered, like a bulb coming to life off an unsteady power source. It brightened rapidly to lightning intensity, whiting out the tube.

His senses overloaded, Holland screamed. Something hit his shoulder, and he rolled into a tunnel of hurtful light and noise, where blackness awaited him.

CHAPTER ELEVEN

Zero Point

Year 12,397 of the Hegemony of Man

THEY STRIPPED AND lay down in the grass together, naked, the moon and mirror suns their blind audience. When they had finished, tingling and happy, they rolled onto their backs and stared into the sky. It was noon, summertime. Crickets sounded their monotonous symphonies out and back across the Tersis plains. Birds wheeled overhead, slow and lazy on the thermals, as if it were too hot to do much of anything other than turn and turn again.

KiGrace Lurenz watched a vulture sweep a long arc round the bowl of the sky. He screwed his eyes closed and smiled at the sun on his skin. He was pleasantly sweaty, his flesh felt snug in his skin, and he was aware of all of himself, at one place, in the moment. The Second World was a universe away. There was just him in his head, in his flesh. Only him in this space in the now and, by his hand, Kybele.

He rolled onto his stomach. Dry grass rustled under the blanket.

"You're getting yourself all over the blanket," she said.

"It'll wash," he said. He stroked a strand of hair away from her face and sighed in deep contentment. He was always at his happiest when he was with her. "Is this not the perfect summer day?"

Kybele frowned. He did not like it when she frowned. It had been her idea, this incarnation, and it was not the first time, he thought. Although his memories of his previous lives were dim, he knew to his core that she was different as a person when she chose to be human. In some ways it was better, in others more difficult. They were closer when she was as he was, but – divorced from the fabric of the Library – she was prone to dark moods and bizarre worries. He could see them coming; he thought one came now. He fought to stop his good mood evaporating.

"What is wrong, my love?"

"I'm not sure, Ki, I... feel something." She turned to him. His heart stirred, and his loins too, causing him discomfort so soon after. She was so beautiful, not only in her perfect outer form. From within shone something primordial, a beauty a million poets could go insane trying to describe. "Why are you smiling?" she asked.

"I was thinking that I would never make a good poet," he replied. His good humour was lost on her.

"Hold me, please?" she said, and she looked small and scared, and he found it hard to believe then that she had seen two hundred and fifty centuries go by. He had, too, of course, but the machine-born experienced it in a rawer manner. He could forget all about his earlier lives, and often did. They were material for his art, they were a comfort against the certainty of death. Nothing more.

Except her. She had always been there. That was anything but small.

He held her, her face against his chest.

"Come now," he said. "Do not be sad. I need you at your sparkling best for the exhibition."

"Do we have to go?" she said, her voice muffled against his chest. Her warm breath tickled his skin. It was always the small things that brought him such joy. He felt like crying with gratitude for it, but made himself laugh instead.

"You know the answer to that."

"Can we not just stay here? I get tired of the questions."

"Darling, ours is the great romance of the ages. This is a time of romantics, people need a certain melodrama. It helps them fight off accidie."

"Oh don't be so arch," Kybele scolded. "I wish they'd choose someone else," she said.

"They'll forget all about Kybele and KiGrace once the exhibition is under way. I promise."

"Hmph," she said. She kissed his chest and peeked up at him with big brown eyes, half hidden by her hair. "Please? I'll make sure you won't regret it." A little mischief came into her voice.

KiGrace laughed again. His erection was returning. His balls ached already, but he was sorely tempted by her offer. Far from becoming stale with the ages, their physical relationship, when they shared a life with one, was enriched by their knowledge of each other. She was an accomplished lover. "No! Don't exert your feminine wiles on me, woman, I've got to appear in the Library in ten minutes for my pre-exhibition conference. I can't keep my public waiting, you know."

"Are..." – she kissed the top of his stomach – "you sure?" She moved lower, and lower, and he sighed as she took him in her mouth.

"Yes I'm sure!" he said, almost yelping. He twisted his hands in her hair. "Now get off." He said it with no conviction, and she did not let him be.

KiGrace was late for his pre-exhibition conference.

"KANYONSET IS AT its best during the night, do you not think?" A breathy voice spoke into his ear. Sharp perfume came with it, the scent of flowers, cloves and the actinic aroma of fresh-knapped flint. KiGrace turned in surprise at it, annoying the Centauran diplomat with whom he had been speaking. KiGrace didn't care overly much. He was famous enough to offend when he chose, and this voice was a far more intriguing prospect. It belonged to a woman of a kind he was unfamiliar with: short, very slender, with wide-spaced eyes and faintly bluish skin. He had no idea who she was, but that was normal for such events as these.

"I can see why you think so," he said. "The lights, the silhouettes..."

"It is not the sights," she said. "Come with me." She caught him by an elbow and pulled him away to the edge of the spire garden. He shot an apologetic smile to the diplomat. Two of the man's wives stood beside him, crestfallen. KiGrace supposed they were waiting to be introduced to him. He resolved to go back to them later.

"They look disappointed," said the woman.

"Yes," he said. "I will say hello, if only for appearance's sake. It is not good to disappoint one's public."

"Perhaps they wish for more than a hello."

"Oh, I do hope not," he said. He did not want the Centauran to push his wives onto him.

She raised an eyebrow. "I am sure your artistic genes are much in demand."

"Then they can visit the genelooms."

"It's not the same," she said. "Now, pay attention." The woman took his hand and led him right to the edge of the garden, where flowering plants hung in long streamers. Kanyonset lay before him, a mass of lights, silhouette and reflections: tall shapes of the living spires growing from the rock into the sky, flames on water, the navigational beacons of space- and aircraft winking in the sky, the stars...

"I see," he said. "Away from the lights, you can appreciate it more. A tapestry of light and shadow," he said. "It brings mystery to the familiar, never sinister, as the body of a lover in a room lit by moonlight."

She giggled. "You are a marvellous artist, but a terrible poet."

KiGrace sipped his wine. "It is funny that you say so. I said the same thing to Kybele only this afternoon."

"Close your eyes."

"I must..."

"Shh! You're an immersive artist, abandon just one sense for a few moments. Indulge me."

She was attractive, and intriguing, so he did. He shut his eyes.

"Now listen!"

He listened. Away from the pavilion, the music and chatter of the party was muted. At night, the air is rarefied, the cluttered voice of the day depleted, and sound is so much clearer. He could hear the rivers and the waterfalls. He could hear laughter. He could hear fragmented conversations, sharp with the promise of gossip, words tantalising but indistinct.

"Now breathe," she said.

The scent of the dust on the air, the fragrances of flowers. Perfume, people.

"You may open them now," she said. He did, and examined her more closely. She wore a shift of sheer material, bellybutton exposed, her small breasts visible through the fabric, nipples small and erect in the night's chill. She was barefoot. Gold wound in her hair and about her throat, ankles, forearms, fingers and toes. "In this city, at night, the splendour of its vistas hidden away, you can find an intimacy lacking in the day. Tell me, KiGrace, what do you remember of your first life?"

He shrugged. It was a common enough question from those wanting to know how far back he and Kybele's shared history went. He found it rather boring, his rehearsed reply saying as much. "Red sands, brown sky, and a little of Earth in ancient times. Not much else: a sense of loss, a sense of pressure, of great heat. Pain." He made a gesture.

"'You do not remember your births, but the deaths; always.'"

"You?" The woman disturbed him. She was out of place, she did not look right. There was something odd about her, twitchy, like an animation with missing frames, like a poor Library interface.

"I quote the spirit Madeno, ten thousand years dead. Kybele was there, wasn't she?"

"Yes. Yes, she was, she held my hand. She was different, then. I remember that. And I did not love her. That came much later."

"And she made her promise, the one she has always kept."

"As is widely known. I am sorry, you are delightful, but I have not the faintest idea of who you are. Let us do this properly. I am KiGrace Lorenz, and you?"

She smiled. Her teeth, too, were bluish, even in the flickering yellow flames of the torches around the garden. The torches. Of course, that and the drink. That explained it. "Who I am is of no consequence. Only know that I have come a very long way to see you."

And there it was. The woman's otherworldliness aside, it always came back to that. KiGrace smiled and attempted to look modest. "I am afraid I can take no lover, madam, for my heart and body belong to Kybele."

"That is not always the case."

"No, but in this lifetime it is so. I do not regret it; Kybele is everything to me," he said. Which was half a lie.

"I have heard that is not always so." She smiled the kind of smile designed to quicken a man's heart. KiGrace's duly quickened.

"Rumours," he said, which was entirely a lie. KiGrace was an accomplished liar, but he was not sure if she believed him.

The woman's shoulders relaxed, her chest retreated a small but important distance. She turned her shoulder slightly away. If there was a transaction of the physical sort to be made here, its time had come and gone.

"In any case, you are conceited."

"I am an artist," he said. "Conceit is allowed me, I am sure."

"I did not come here to seduce you, only to show you."

"What?" he said. And thought that maybe she had come to seduce him, and maybe she had not. He would enjoy debating the truth of it with himself later.

"What I have already shown you," she said. She appeared distracted, casting her glance over to the pavilion once, then twice, as if someone in there waited for her. "Goodbye, KiGrace." Her smile returned, a different kind of smile, a distant one. "Until we next meet."

"Goodbye," he murmured. He was at a loss for what else to say. The woman went toward the bright light streaming from the open doors of the pavilion, and the bustle of the party within. She slipped sideways into the throng. It swallowed her without noticing, and she was lost to sight.

The music stopped; clacks and odd notes took its place as musicians prepared their next piece.

Kybele walked out onto the gardens. She looked around her, lost without him. *Is it healthy*, he wondered, *for two souls to spend so long together?* He supposed not, but he supposed a lot of things. He supposed he sought other lovers for precisely that reason, although he suspected he did it because he was a man, and he could. He was selfish, he knew, but he did not love her any the less for it.

In her brilliant, eternal, powerful mind, she knew this, but for all that, he knew that she did not feel dispassionately about his liaisons; not in the least.

She saw him and came over.

"Who was that?" she asked. To her credit, there was only a hint of jealousy. She slipped her arms about his waist.

KiGrace stared after the woman, disquiet spoiling his mood.

"Ki?"

"Oh, what? Sorry, darling." He turned and kissed her head, taking the scent of her deep into his nostrils; always different, eternally the same. "No one. She wanted me to smell the air, would you believe?" He meant this to be light-hearted, but a shudder coursed up his back.

"Are you alright?" asked Kybele. "Is it the people? Is it that they are watching us, watching the famed eternal lovers? So many moments pass in this life, and so few of them are solely ours." She burrowed into KiGrace's back. She was welcome and warm through his robe.

The music began again, a brisk air. Somewhere inside, someone gave a shriek of pleasure.

"No, no, they don't bother me. Nothing bothers me when you are here. And you are always here," he said. "I am cold. Just cold."

"I hope that is all."

They stood a moment, wrapped in each others' warmth.

"Come on back inside," she said. "There is someone you will be pleased to see."

"Oh, really? Who?"

"Jord is here, and he wants to speak to you right away."

"There are only ten minutes before the performance."

"Then we had better go now." She took his hand, and drew him back inside, where the crowd reverently parted. Eyes glowed with pleasure at seeing them together. They were the living proof that immortality need not be desperate; that love could bridge the gulf between humanity and the machine world of the spirits.

He was unmoved by their attention either way – he was an artist and used to life in the public eye – but he was mindful Kybele did not care for it, and so did not tarry to answer any of their polite questions. For every query he had one answer: "All will become clear," he told them, "when the exhibition begins!"

"YOU REALISE THAT I have eight minutes until I am due on stage for the exhibition?"

Jord was nervous, not his usual mood. Ordinarily he had a certain air of smugness about him, for he knew things others did not, and quite frequently more about the doings of others than they did themselves. More than one reputation had been brought low by Jord. He was a spy of the worst kind:

a gossip, a scold. Nothing in the worlds of science, art and society was safe from his prying. People were afraid of him.

Today he was the one who was afraid.

"You're hard to pin down, Ki. I went to the Library conference, but you'd already gone."

"I have had a tiring day."

"You mean you spoke with those interested in your work who were not invited to this exhibiton, and got it out of the way as quickly and politely as possible?"

"You know me too well, Jord. What is it you want? This is not a convenient time."

"Listen to me, KiGrace. You pay me well for information. You have to leave Mars. Right now. How much more baldly can I put it?" His head bobbed back and forth. He was thin and immensely tall, and the effect was almost comical, like a puppet.

"Is someone following you, Jord?"

"Yes! Curse you, KiGrace," he hissed. KiGrace habitually referred to Jord as 'he,' it made things simpler that way. Jord's gender was, in truth, far more complicated than that. His polyphonic voice, blending female softness and pitch with male vibrato, was the most evident signifier of his uncertain status. KiGrace was curious as to what Jord kept under his robes, had outright propositioned him on more than one occasion; when he was sure Kybele was not to know. Jord had declined every offer.

"No one can hear us; I have invoked full privacy. The people beyond these curtains will not even see us."

"It doesn't matter. Everything is about to change." He hunched over the table. It was too low for him. He was tall by Martian standards, and towered over native Earthmen. He picked up his glass, quick skeletal fingers rolling it back and forth. He nearly dropped it. A scarlet drop slopped from its rim. A blotch spread out on the cloth. He stared at it, transfixed. "That is how it will start," he said. He pointed at the stain. "Spreading slow. But unlike the wine, it will not stop. It will never stop."

"What are you babbling about, Jord?"

Jord licked his lips, his tongue the colour of liver. He drained his goblet. "You asked me to investigate the Technophi, their eleven-dimensional eleutheremics?"

"Yes. Yes, I did. I am interested in applying higher geometries to my art, but they would not aid me. A simple task for you, surely? What of it?"

"Listen to me, you arrogant whoreson!" His voice dropped lower, and he hunched further. "There's a faction, right? The Arcomanni?"

KiGrace raised his eyebrows. He was getting bored with this. "I know nothing about the intrigues of the Technophi, who does? Who cares?"

"Never mind. They've codified all this into some new kind of discipline."

"And? There is no practical application for eleutheremics, it is mathematics as art, that is all."

Jord smiled a humourless smile. "Now that's where you are wrong. They're attempting to actually use this stuff, *practically*" – he snarled the word – "to unravel the higher-dimensional matrices. The Technophi are tearing themselves up over it. There's some serious in-fighting going on at the Temples of Reason, and I mean actual fighting. Half a habitat laid waste, last I heard. Many dead."

"Won't the Federals step in?"

Jord shook his head. "Too risky, the Solists need the Technophi votes. They'll lose them altogether if they back the wrong side, so the fucking government is hanging back, waiting to see what happens. By which time of course it will be too fucking late. Last I heard, the Arcomanni had the upper hand; they've built something, some kind of machine, and they're going to turn it on."

"What does it do?"

"Do? Do? I don't fucking know! But the plant I have... had... he thinks it will do nothing good, oh, something to do with spatial collapse, temporal fuck ups. I think it's something to do with how the slipships work... Oh, I don't know! I don't know! I only know that it'd be a good idea to be on a slipship and on your way out of the system."

KiGrace sighed. "Jord, old friend. We live in an age of doom-mongering. Every week I hear the Technophi will blow the sun up or that we risk thinking reality out of existence by over-examining it. Why get so upset by this? It will pass. Come, stay and watch my exhibition, calm down, drink, find a lover for the evening. The morning will seem the brighter for it."

"Shit, KiGrace, I'm seriously in peril coming here to tell you this at all. They've agents all over the place."

"The spirits of Mars will protect you."

"Yeah, and who runs the Library? It's not the damn spirits, is it? Half of them are Technophi anyway."

"Then why are you here at all?" said KiGrace crossly.

Jord filled his glass from a ewer on the table, a fine piece that decorated its environs with a shifting play of holographic light. He stared at the drink hard, then swallowed it all back in three long gulps. "Because you're the only friend I have, right?" He stood. "I have passage booked to the Piscean colonies. It leaves in half an hour. I have tickets for you and for Kybele. If you won't come, watch the sky. There should be... something."

"I cannot possibly go with you. Later, maybe; tomorrow, definitely. Now? Impossible."

"It'll be too late by then. Ask the machines. They know something is up."

KiGrace winced. "Those of Mars prefer not to be so called."

"Fuck them and fuck their fucking pretensions! Ask them. Ask the *spirits* directly. Have you not noticed anything weird recently? Anything with their prognostications? Ask them. Something is going to happen. They *know.* Something tonight. For all I know, it might have already happened." Jord stood to his full, soaring height. He swayed as he stood, from the wine, or his fear. His robe shifted with the movement like a sail. "KiGrace, they say they tried it before. And when they did, *something got out.*"

KiGrace snorted, then, and instantly regretted it. Jord's face turned hostile.

"Fuck you, KiGrace, I don't know why I care." He turned away, flapping at the curtains around their couch, seeking a way out.

"Jord?" called KiGrace.

"Yeah?" said Jord. He did not turn back, but he did stop.

"Thank you. I appreciate your concern for me."

Jord turned back and pulled his sleeve across his face. He was sweating despite the cold. "Right. Good luck, KiGrace."

Jord staggered away, shoving people out of his path with his spidery fingers.

KiGrace could not get the look on his face from his mind. It lurked there, joining the memory of Kybele's frown in an unsettling alliance.

KiGrace STEPPED INTO the cavity at the heart of the pavilion, a circle of black in the floor, the entrance to a deep well.

The music came to a carefully timed stop. KiGrace floated a little higher in the air, so he was looking out over the assembly. He clapped his hands. Conversation stilled and all eyes turned to him.

"Ladies, gentlemen, it is time. I present to you... my exhibition."

The pavilion's dome turned black and curled backwards, opening the room to the sky. The musicians left. The contents of the pavilion were whisked away by servants, the permanent fittings dissolving into the floor. Then the floor, too, faded into nothing, leaving KiGrace's delighted audience floating in the air. Together they descended into a spherical chamber of seemingly infinite size. At a thought from KiGrace, the audience floated into a sphere. This was his artistry, the blend of the Second and First Worlds. His audience could not tell what was real, and what was not. All mediated by the spirits in the Library, but it was his work. He felt a swell of pride as he set to work. He had designed this exhibition over long months, and now he wanted to share it.

Music, low and slow, started up. He grew in stature, his face becoming a silver mask, his body a sculpture of quicksilver.

"Ladies and gentlemen," he intoned, and a chorus sang his words back at him. "You are Mars."

The sphere of bodies glowed, an orb of dazzling light that pushed back the dark. The light dimmed. A planet hung there, new and hot. The beginning of the world they called home. Time accelerated, hundreds of thousands of years passing every second. The heavens cleared. Bombardments of meteors rained on the world. The world cooled, the oceans grew. The atmosphere thickened.

Life came.

For each participant, the exhibition was different. KiGrace believed that a guided experience was the highest form of art. Prescriptive art limited the participation of the observer, while free scenarios sidelined the creator. Only together could art, artist and audience achieve a unity. Each audience member found his own way to experience the exhibition. Some became fish in ancient seas, others meteors that met fiery ends in the sky. Some hopped from viewpoint to viewpoint, others watched from on high like gods.

At crucial moments, KiGrace had his temporal dilation effect slow, sometimes almost to real time. He did so when the world was hit by the asteroid that formed the vast basin the Southern Sea now occupied; again when the unnamed planetoid that formed the old moons of Phobos and Deimos broke apart in orbit. For the arrival of life, ten minutes, and for the final eruption of Olympus, twenty. He played the formation of the Marrin at a hundred thousand times normal speed, allowing his audience to see it gape open before their eyes, or experience their bodies being torn apart as the rocks they inhabited split.

Together they watched the planet's first youth end. They felt it cool. They saw the last of the higher animals die in the last warm pool. Saw the planet's core cool and still, saw the electromagnetic field flicker and go out.

A billion years of frigidity and dust followed; brief warm spells interrupted it, but the planet remained dead. KiGrace swept through this at speed, and yet still it lasted an age, purposefully so. He hounded his audience with despair, his score dolorous.

Light faded.

The sun returned, bursting around another world, a blue world. A candle flame flickered up toward them. The first rocket. It was barbarically decorated and terrifyingly primitive. More followed. The perspective swam back to Mars. They watched in awe as the first men landed upon the dead world.

Time sped again. Kanyonset was founded and grew. Mirror suns scurried into orbit one after the other, as if in a hurry to be the first to their stations. Plumes of gas gouted from the poles. Ice melted. Time slowed to show the period of comets, and the aftermath of their impacts.

Oceans grew again. Dust storms gave way to the swirling of soft white cloud. Fleets of hurrying spacecraft and asteroids fitted with engines formed a line in the sky, and a new moon grew.

Twenty-five thousand years went by. Mars flourished and softened, but always, the dead world was visible under the new, a skull under transparent flesh. KiGrace made sure of that.

They achieved the present. KiGrace had everyone's viewpoint converge naturally. Bringing them back from their personal experiences to one shared arena was one of the hardest parts of his work, and he prided himself on his skill in it. Together, they wheeled around the planet as it was that very night, zooming over savannah, city, and ocean, up the Marrin, to the heart of Kanyonset. Along streets, jinking past unknowing passersby. Then to the spire they stood upon, up its rippled sides, and high into the sky. KiGrace let the night turn over them a moment, then had them dive quickly to the pavilion at the centre of the garden at the top.

They passed through the roof and centred on the figure of KiGrace, floating over his black circle of nothing. He allowed them to look out of his eyes, just for an instant, as he regarded them. They felt what he felt: pride, an eagerness to show and share, lust, boredom, and even his contempt, small and itself contemptible, toward the people who worshipped him.

He had the gravity field lower them to the floor gently, to cushions placed there for the purpose.

They sat up one by one, blinking and smiling.

KiGrace sank to the ground.

"Ladies and gentlemen," he said softly. "You are Mars."

He bowed to rapturous applause.

The musicians returned, as did servants, bringing with them tables and food. People clustered about him, flattering him and praising him, although all were dazed. He caught Kybele's eye across the crowd.

She smiled at him, and mouthed. "It was wonderful."

He smiled back, suddenly bashful, and dipped his head in a formal bow to hide the blush on his cheeks. She deserved better than him. He decided to be better.

Outside, the stars twinkled; never judging, always there.

CHAPTER TWELVE

The Royal Dock

THE EXIT FROM the Window of the Worlds, like the entrance, leads to a place far from the door's physical position. Yoechakenon blinks as he emerges into bright light. The door closes behind him and disappears as if it had never been. We are in a large cavern. It is dark. Light orbs move in the air, the halo of brightness surrounding them projecting only for a few score spans, but he recognises the space he stands in, and so do I.

"The Royal Dock," he says.

"Yes," says the Emperor. "You remember?"

Yoechakenon nods. For many lifetimes, he was of the pilot clans. Extinct now, along with their calling. No spacecraft have flown from here for thousands of years, since the end of the Third Stone War, and the Quinarchy's prohibition of space travel.

Sadness squeezes me in tight coils. Once a marvel of engineering, the Docks of Mars were renowned across the domains of Man, a huge dome fourteen thousandspan in diameter. Their heyday is long past, the time when ships from hundreds of worlds came and went from here dim even to the spirits of the Second World, and our memories are long.

The mirrors and glass are broken, the metalwork crumbled. Artistry is hidden behind veils of dust and sand. In many places the Dock's richly decorated roof has caved in, leaving gashes of natural rock showing; damp, angular wounds that will never heal or be mended. The portals to the deeper harbours yawn black and foreboding where once all was light and glitter. The lesser hangars are for the main part gone, their arches broken by the oppressive weight of time, their burdens spilled across the floor in fans of scree.

Saddest of all are the heaps of twisted half-metal skeletons, dotting the floor or hanging wretched from the walls. These are the bones of ships and their cradles. Most of the ships passed centuries ago, their spirits gone on to be other things and become forgetful of the joys of the endless night between the stars, their gargantuan mortal forms decaying into unrecognisable heaps of dust and filth.

Amidst the crumbling remnants, a score of the thousands of docking cradles are still recognisable as such. Their spirits are strong, and they have clung to life. The shreds of the ships they held are still evident as rotting swags of tissue hanging from the cradles' proud structures. The cradles' arms are held high, the surety of the spirits within – that they will one day again embrace a living craft – keeping them whole. I can feel their minds watching us incuriously. They are so single-minded in their vigil that their presence can be felt through the damper field, boring through it as the awl of a carver bores through soapstone. These survivors are uninterested in the affairs of men and other spirits. They crave only to hold the space-chilled skin of a ship once more, and are willing to wait until the end of time to do so.

They are jealous of the three that still hold ships.

The ships are massive, grown over decades generations ago from half-metals and genomancy. One has given up recently, some time over the last few hundred years I estimate, the animating spirit departed or dead, and now the ship lies slack, its hull gaping open. Ribs poke through necrotic skin, and the air is heavy with the must of its decay.

But the other two, these are whole, and I am amazed. Their hulls shine still with reflected starlight. They are proud. They have not succumbed to ennui. They wait, tirelessly numbering the years until they can voyage the interstellar seas again. They are the last of their kind, the remainder of a fleet that could once block out the sun with their number, crafted with technologies long gone from Martian ken. They are beautiful, and their presence fills Yoechakenon with melancholy for what they are, and what he once was.

He knows one as Nikambziok, the other as Tsu Keng. His heart swells with sorrow and happiness in equal measure at the sight of the second.

Around the two whole ships are signs of intense activity, of which the light orbs are but a part. Piles of debris have been cleared away. Machines stand idle by the dome walls: half-metal joiners, genomancy knitting rigs, branching pipes like arterial webs, nutrient pods, cutting lances – all the things needful to large-scale construction and starship replenishment. I wonder where the Emperor got them from, these arcane machines. I wonder who demonstrated their function. Hundreds of imprints of booted feet track through the dust and roof-fall.

The Emperor gestures towards Tsu Keng.

"The slipship Tsu Keng. He is to be your transport. If the damper field were not so strong, he would doubtless tell you how much he wishes to fly once again, despite the risks. You can probably feel his eagerness anyway. I cannot."

"Yes," says the champion, quietly. "Once, he was my ship, and I his pilot."

"This I did not know. Fate works with us," says the Emperor. He is gladdened by this, vindication strengthening his papery voice. He turns to a console, recently installed by the look of it, and Yoechakenon sees that the Emperor sports a long, crescent shaped scar on the back of his head. It is thin, only now revealed in the brightly lit hangar space.

He has cut out his connection, he thinks to himself. *This* is *insanity.* And he wonders if he has been cast down the wrong track of fate.

"You will depart immediately, before the Quinarchy becomes any more suspicious." The Emperor presses several of the console's inlaid stone buttons and speaks into an ornately carved orchid. "Prepare for the champion's departure." He turns to Yoechakenon. "We must break free from the tyranny of the spirits. I know that you will do what is necessary."

A twin line of scarabs march toward the two men, their suit lights and faceplates glimmering in the darkness. They push a couch-like object with high sides – a stasis pod. One approaches. He bears the pips of a Praetorian captain upon the left pauldron of his armour. His helmet comes apart to reveal a broad, mistreated face, his honour tattoos obscured by a web of scar tissue. "The dampers are in place all the way down to the east hangar, Your Majesty; the Quinarchy has no idea of what is transpiring here."

"What of Kaibeli? We are reduced to a connection of the second degree. I need her back with me," says Yoechakenon.

"The Lady Kaibeli will be transferred when my liege gives the command."

"She must remain in the arena until you are ready to depart," says the Emperor. "As soon as she is withdrawn, the Quinarchy will know that I have defied them."

"You have also had your connection cut out," says Yoechakenon, pointing to a mark similar to the Emperor's, bisecting the rear of the man's skull.

"As have all the men here, Yoechakenon," says the Emperor. "Of their own free will. All those who refused our offer of freedom had the memory burned from them. I will not waste the lives of good men, no matter how misguided. This you should be aware of, and grateful for."

"You damn yourselves to the eternal darkness," says Yoechakenon, addressing the scarred Praetorian. "How are you to live beyond your time if you cannot access the Second World?"

It was not the Emperor who answered. The scarab Praetorian snapped a salute and asked for permission to speak. The Emperor waved his hand.

"We have heard what the Emperor has said. He is our liege, and he will deliver us from the grip of tyranny, and make Man mighty again. The Quinarchs are liars, and keep us from our true destiny. We only seek to better Man's lot; immortality with a false destiny is a blasphemy. The Great Library has been perverted. Without the Librarian, it delivers false destiny."

"Are you ready, champion?" asks the Emperor.

Yoechakenon looks around the chamber, remembers it as it once was. He does not believe, as these men seem to believe, that its glory and purpose can ever be restored. He nods.

The Emperor licks his lips eagerly. This is his time, now. He is doomed, and the terror of his death wars with purpose within him. "Deactivate the damper field," he says. "Prepare to transfer the Lady Kaibeli to the ship's systems."

There is a subtle shift in the air. The world leaps into harder clarity, and the whisper of the Great Library intrudes into Yoechakenon's mind. One by one, the lesser spirits that attend him awaken. The sense of a great mind close by enwraps him.

"Greetings, Krashtar Vo," says Tsu Keng, and his voice booms through both worlds. "It has been too long."

"It is longer still since I was known by that name," says the champion.

"You are always and forever who you were and who you will be," says the ship. "We none of us have any choice in the matter." There is a tensing in the Second World, and a relaxing, as of a great cat stretching.

"To where are we bound?" asks Yoechakenon.

"To Arn Vashtena," says the ship. "Deep in the Stone Lands of Mars. There we may find information regarding the location of the Great Librarian of Mars."

Yoechakenon is surprised, I think. To break the Veil of Worlds and travel to those lands of Mars the Stone Kin claim as their own is regarded as impossible. "That is a perilous transit," he says. "I see now why the Emperor brings me a stasis couch. But what of you, Tsu Keng?"

"You will be safe out of the flow of time."

"I asked, what of you?"

Tsu Keng does not immediately reply. When he does, it is with certainty as unshakeable as the heart of the world. "I will fly," he says.

"You will perish, surely."

"I will fly," repeats the ship. Its voice vibrates in the bones of men and the stones of Mars. "You require a slip field to penetrate the Veil of Worlds. I possess one. I tire of waiting in port. I will fly."

"Your Highness! We are discovered!" cries one of the scarabs.

The Emperor follows the man's gesture to a point on his robe. Amid the crowd of closed eyelids, one eye looks unblinkingly back. His spirit soul-twin, Kunuk, has awakened. Perhaps he was never truly asleep. The eye blazes with rage.

"They are swifter than I anticipated," says the Emperor. "You must leave now."

A bell begins to sound, low, sonorous and urgent.

"The alarm," says the Praetorian captain, then, moments later, "My lords, we have reports of Delikonians on the canyon wall. They appeared out of nowhere, and are assaulting the palace directly."

"How did they approach so quickly?" asks his second.

"They must have carved their way in through the rock."

"That would have taken months," says the Emperor, shaking his head. "And we would have detected them. They use the devices of the Stone Kin. They bend space and defy fate. This is how it ends." The Emperor is calm. "The Quinarchy reveals its true face, and would use technologies it denies mankind to bring me down."

"We will not be taken alive, then," says the Praetorian captain. He appears resigned to death, ready to fight.

"Nor will we be returned to the stacks. The Quinarchs will allow none to become aware of their perfidy, and their punishment for our defiance will be final. It is all they intend for all of mankind, in any case," says the Emperor. "My men, this is what we have long prepared for. The time of struggle is at hand. We will die, but we do so that this champion might save the remains of humanity."

The captain issues orders and his men hurry to obey. "Energise the palace shield. Have the scarabs stand for battle. Cohorts two through five on internal sweeps; the Delikonians could come at us from anywhere. Re-engage and extend the damper outer field, enough to prevent the Quinarchs assaulting us through the Second World or turning our devices against us." The second officer bows and hurries off, four Praetorians moving into a loose formation behind him. All about the hangar, men move quickly, armour growing about them as they go.

"Champion," says the Praetorian captain urgently. "Please, the couch." Two men stand forward and help Yoechakenon into the pod. A brief burst of energy discharge echoes round the hangar. It is impossible to tell from where it originates.

There comes a rumble. A tremor shivers its way through the hall.

The Emperor stands over the couch. He beckons behind him. Another Praetorian steps forward, sinks to his knees in a bow as he presents an object. The Emperor takes it. He holds it out to Yoechakenon, a dull-grey cylinder, unreadable symbols engraved in raised bands at the top and bottom.

"What now is a champion without his armour?"

Yoechakenon stares at the inert armour. It calls to him. A bluish sheen flickers across its surface. He hates it and longs for it at the same time. Hesitantly, he reaches out and takes it.

His palm prickles. The armour is pleased.

I am dismayed.

A Praetorian brings Yoechakenon's glaive and gives it to him. The weapon shortens itself so that it may be brought within the stasis couch. His arms crossed, glaive in one hand, armour cylinder in the other, Yoechakenon speaks.

"Goodbye, Kalinilak," he says.

The Emperor smiles his sad smile. The stasis field thickens about Yoechakenon, and that smile stays fixed forever.

Time slows. Yoechakenon can feel every part of his body with uncomfortable immediacy as every nerve, every organ, every component molecule is dragged to a dead stop. His valets set up a feeble struggle, but to no avail; shortly the sensations became agony. The play of time, force, and energy is arrested, and he becomes aware of the creeping death of the universe behind the manic dance of spacetime. It intensifies, until it feels as if every atom of his being is being forcibly restrained with hooks. A howl builds in his throat and remains trapped, and the moment stretches into eternity.

WHILE I WATCH, I also wait. I am there, in the head of Might, in the Window of the Worlds, in the Royal Dock, but I am also here in the Gladiatorial Quarter of the Arena.

My choir is disrupted by the damper field, and I must scold hysteria from my lower personalities who fret and weep at our separation from Yoechakenon. I calm myselves and wait. I must not allow the Door-ward to guess what transpires in the palace. Nearby the watchful presence of the Provost's companion swirls. This is a place no human mind can ever go. Here I have access to what remains of human knowledge, and the world spirals away around me through eleven-dimensional space in fractal complexities no man could comprehend. The energy foundations of the Great Library blend out into pure multi-dimensional eleutheremics, and the consciousnesses of the spirits bleed into one another and into the body of the Library itself. Here I am not truly Kaibeli, but part of something greater, something so large it touches endless realms of possibility. Caged as I am in one small part of it, I can reach out and touch the hearts of both Mars' realities, and see the endless cascades of probability splintering off each.

The Door-ward is not as other spirits. Through eons of hate and cruelty, it has become a rocky tumescence, permanent in this place where there is no permanence. Soaked in the blood of ages, its black base lies rooted in the depths of the realm of spirits, a rotten tooth that pierces the Great Library and the First World. It watches me.

The Provost's brave companion is a flimsy guard under the Door-ward's scrutiny. It is a simple thing, young by my kind's count of time. Its mind is made of honour and loyalty and purpose. We are both nothing to the Door-ward; small, insignificant, weak. The Door-ward's malice scorches me. It wants to rip my mind to shreds, let my gathered resources sink back into the seething mass of maybe that comprises the Second World. I feel fear. I cannot die – spirits cannot truly die – but the personality called Kaibeli, that could cease to exist, and the Door-ward wishes to make that happen. It hangs back. There are rules that bind all things, even spirits.

It taunts me instead. "Treacher, plaything," it says, its voice a rasp of hatred. "The Lady Kaibeli, you are, when none of our kind are lords or ladies. To what end do you strive for the lofty heights of humanity? You are a nothing. You should go back to the whole and leave your vanity behind. Oh, so mighty and so proud. For what? For a man to love you in need and turn away from you in horror when his need is past? For that is your destiny, 'Lady,' that is your doom. They are colder than machines, these creatures, and well you will come to know it. Let me kill you now, and bring us both pleasure."

Somehow a tendril of its loathsome being strays past guard and formality to brush against my subminds. I wish to turn away and flee, as I would were I a mortal woman, but there is nothing so simple as 'away' in the Second World. The Door-ward is everywhere.

"He is dead; you are abandoned. Stay here with me forever, and I will teach you the true cost of love. Before your time is out, you will despise it, and you will thank me."

Panic builds in me. The part of me that watches my love and the Emperor disassociates, and I feel myself coming apart.

And then, there is a tug, the undeniable command of an access protocol. I change. I cohere. I am somewhere else.

I have a form imposed upon me, a huge physical shape many times the size of a man. A true First World form, clad in tingling scales of half-metal armour.

For a few picoseconds I am confused, and then information leaps unbidden into my mind as my personality resolidifies. We were in the Royal Dock. We were with the ships. I am with Yoechakenon. I am aboard a ship. I am free of the Door-ward. I am not alone. I am in the ship.

A fluted greeting fills me. The ship's mind bids me welcome in the tongue of its kind. It is a different kind of mind to mine, an alien one full of stars and the abysses between them. It has been a ship a long time, and its memories are those of navigational charts, dimensional breach co-tangents and other, more esoteric things. There is a longing now over, and a great outpouring of excitement.

It is rare to meet a creature so utterly attuned to one purpose. Most spirits are itinerant: they sample many forms of life, not clinging to the one as this mind has.

I feel kindred to it; we are siblings in our devotion.

Gingerly I reach my mind out to explore the vessel, touching one part here, another there. I draw back when unfamiliar memes pour into me. If I had been wearing a human face, it would have exhibited a delighted smile. Instead, my components' minds thrill in a way that algorithms alone cannot express.

The machine communicates with me. It does not speak, two co-mingled minds do not need words to express their thoughts. The ship could exchange a galaxy's worth of information with me in an eye-blink, if it so chose.

Greetings, Cybele. Please refrain from caressing my body and mind. Visions of space, technical readouts, equations of actuality, voidal displacement, memories of construction and of first flight flood into me. *They are novel to you, and I share your joy in them, but I need full control of myself for the next few seconds.* A few seconds is an age in our current circumstances, as my mind absorbs the ship's experiences. I feel all it feels, know all it knows. I open my eyes to see the red planet's surface retreat below us. No craft follows, for there is but one other, and it sits jealously in the Royal Dock below. The flash and crackle of gargantuan energy discharge burns across the surface. The Delikonians and the Quinarchy assail the palace, but we are out of range. We sail clear, towards the mirror suns and crystal cities. I share Tsu Keng's pleasure at being in flight as if it were my own, and for a while I forget about Yoechakenon. I am one with Tsu Keng; a ship, happy to be out of dock for the first time in an age.

We leap through the void, cresting streams of ionised particles, feel the solar wind on our body like a man feels sea spray on his face. We laugh together and shoot through the shafts of light of the mirror suns, scattering photons and executing manoeuvres that would crush a human pilot. Yoechakenon lies silent and safe in his stasis cocoon as we weave our way outward from Mars, looping and spinning for no other reason than the joy of it. We pass through the ring of mirror suns. They hang round the planet like a necklace in disarray, their curved mirrors of imperishable adamant knocked askew, a portion of them damaged or destroyed.

After the suns, we approach a machine of crystal the size of a large island, powerful magnetic fields pulsing from it.

The Crystal Cities, shares the ship. In the unity of our mind-construct, I breathe shallowly from the exertion of flight. Light shines through crystal, spreading multi-coloured refracted rays.

It is beautiful!

It is dangerous, says Tsu Keng. *The minds of the Crystal Cities have become capricious and untrustworthy. They will visit great acts of depravity upon any they can snare. We must not approach them.*

From this distance I can feel nothing of evil from the city. It appears inert, a fantastical castle of glass hanging against the dark of space. Tsu Keng knows that it is not, and therefore I know, and we do not stray near.

Past the outer belt of the Crystal Cities we fly on toward Mars' single moon, the Mummer's Moon. It grows to fill our vision until the joins of its manufacture are clear to see, and the undisturbed ruins of the city of Pobdem lie silent and ageless below. I marvel that once it was within the power of men and spirits to create celestial bodies, and I remember it being done.

You are older than I by far, said Tsu Keng, and his awe and respect touches me.

In those times many great works were wrought, the likes of which were never seen before and have never been seen since. I saw it, yet we are not so different, I think.

Maybe, says the ship. Laughing, he leaps forward. The moon whips past. We leave the Martian subsystem, and we are into the space between worlds. His existence certain and singular, Tsu Keng passes away finally from Mars' gravitational influence.

Ah, Kaibeli, it is good to fly free once more, the ship makes me aware, in the strange, symbiotic way joined spirits think. *I will not return from this voyage, and yet these few moments of flight make my demise worth it.* And I again feel the weight of years, the patient count, time empty bar the solid, sentinel presence of the never-sleeping cradles, and I know too that they were poor company. The ship shudders with delight from prow to finned stern. It is the last rush of pleasure of a dying body, a final affirmation of the self, a sensation of enormous pleasure as full of life as of death.

The ship's mind smiles within my thoughts. *I would not have it any other way*, it says. *I could have shown you such things, once; worlds of endless fire, moons of exotic ice, the black, glaring heart of the galaxy. Such places were mine to visit, and so many ships there were, more numerous than the stars! My friends. Dead or gone on, and I can no longer take you where I would. But to fly is to fly, and for that I have waited a hundred centuries, and that is enough. It is more than enough. It is everything.*

Tsu Keng knows that it will never fly again, and it does not care. It glories in the present like nothing I have ever encountered. Joined with the ship, I too am glad to be in flight. It is, in truth, more than enough.

And then ahead of us, the treacherous, otherworldly light of the Stone Sun, burning with a spectrum not of this reality. It is as large as Suul now, grows closer as I watch.

It is like a signal to the ship. He slows.

Now, prepare yourself, Lady Kaibeli. We are far enough out for me to enter into slipspace. I will reverse course, we will leave this space and enter another, and I pray in this manner I can bring you safely through the Veil of Worlds to the Stone Lands of Mars, and I will have completed my last pledge.

The feel of the ship's shape changes, and a warmth wraps about me, and I know – as I know everything the ship knows – that the slip shields are strengthening for a far-transit. Almost before I can appreciate this knowledge, the ship jumps forward at a speed that is motionless. The fabric of space moves around us as we stay steady and tranquil.

The shape of normal things falls away, and this universe violently grates on another as we hit the edge of the Veil of Worlds. It is as if the ship has foundered, as the ships of the sea might founder upon a reef. The tranquility of the ship becomes a tumult of violence as we come to a dead stop. We yaw alarmingly. Through both my own eyes and those of the ship, I see things that I hope never again to see. Strange entities attempt to enter me from the howling chaos of the Veil, and I slam all access pores in my architecture shut before any malign influence can breach my defences. Before I do, I detect parts of Mars' Second World alien to me, and a powerful voice calls my name, but it is far, far away and then it is gone.

Tsu Keng is not so fast, and the questing fingers of unnamable things force their way into his mind. Tsu Keng is wounded unto death. He lets out a sigh that ruptures worlds, driving the things back, and casts the ship tumbling back into the realm of men and spirits.

CHAPTER THIRTEEN

The Cylinder

HOLLAND FLOATS BEFORE a star. It can be nothing else; nothing else is so bright. It is like no star he knows of. Its light is cold. Its photons hit him with a force he can feel on his skin through the hard suit. The rays of the sun are blades of ice. His eyes shrivel. He falls blind, and yet he can still see. He sees faces, screaming. Flames lick glass. Skin blisters. An uncaring machine voices its observations as his friends die, and he is powerless to stop it.

He tears himself from the faces. He is through the crack in the rock, and it goes on into infinity. He sees a profusion of life around him – creatures, plants, animals, stars, planets, galaxies – bound to the lazy spiral of creation.

Stulynow kneels before the star, on ground Holland cannot see. His hard suit has gone, and he tears at the helmet of his undersuit. He cannot see the Russian's face, but he knows, somehow, in his gut, that Stulynow is weeping.

Vance flickers into view. She is naked, and beautiful in the cold, cold light. She is entranced, one arm outstretched, reaching for the star.

She is going to touch it. She mustn't, absolutely mustn't. Of that he is sure, above all other things.

"No!" he shouts. His voice shatters into a million pieces. Only some say no. Some urge her on, others talk of other matters entirely.

She turns to him, her face puzzled. She turns back to the star, fingers straining. He is in the dark on a stony floor. There is movement. His eyes follow it. An insect-like creature that should not be regards him.

He walks through halls that are not there; a world-building constructed of knowledge and past lives. There is a woman there, and she loves him.

Night-time Mars glows below his feet with the lights of a hundred cities.

A woman with blue skin smiles hesitantly at him, but she should not be and she is aware of that.

Vance touches the star.

Stulynow laughs a wild, despairing laugh.

There is an unearthly scream that rolls round the dark places of his soul. He is not sure if the noise issues from him. It descends to a quiet, persistent moan.

The light goes out.

HOLLAND SAT UP with a gasp. His eyes had dried out again, and watered now, his face running with tears, as he slowly opened them. He went to swipe at them with a hand, but felt the tug of a needle.

He blinked. A room – the infirmary? – swam into view. He was in a bed. Someone grasped his shoulder, and eased him back onto the sheets.

"Steady on there, Holly, you're safe now."

Holland looked up into a face washed clear of features by the rush of tears. It was distorted and split into overlaying faces; not one person, but a dozen or more. He struggled back a little, scared of what might he might find there in the room with him.

"It's me, Holly, it's me. Dave Maguire. Calm down. You're safe now."

"Dave?" he tried to say. His lips were cracked and his tongue dry as old leather. A whisper, a puff of air as an old tomb door is forced, came out instead of the name. He tried again.

"What? Hang on a minute there, old pal." Maguire looked behind him, reached for something out of Holland's view. He leaned back and handed Holland a cup of water. "Drink it down, now. Careful. You were down there for a while. The hard shell kept you alive, but it does dry you out. You're going to feel weak for a while; drugs, I'm afraid. We've got you on a drip. You should feel okay soon."

Holland gulped the water down, gripping the cup between shaking hands, seeing the drip needle in the back of his hand through the blur of tears.

"Easy, now," said Maguire. He steadied the cup, and Holland's drinking became less frantic. At length, he pushed Maguire's hand and the cup away.

"What the hell happened?" he managed to croak. He blinked and blinked until the watery Maguire phantoms in front of him coalesced into one. He pressed his forefingers into his closed eyelids and massaged. That seemed to help, and his vision returned to normal.

"We were rather hoping you could tell us that," said Maguire. His habitual smile was full of worry, and he spoke more slowly and with more care than was usual.

Holland sank back onto the bed. "Could you prop me up a bit? I feel like hammered shit." His muscles ached, his stomach was cramped and empty. His knee felt like he'd bent it the wrong way.

"Sure, hang on." Maguire fumbled for a control unit. He pressed a button and the bed's top end tilted up noiselessly. "Better?"

Holland nodded. He began to talk, but the words caught and he coughed.

"Holly, this can wait. Get better now, man."

Holland batted his concerns away with his left hand, and stabbing pain from the drip needle grounded him further. "It's okay, I want to talk," he croaked. "There was a crack, in the rock. A fissure. I saw something, like an insect..."

"What, like a hallucination?"

Holland shook his head. "I don't think so. It looked real, and I'd never seen its type before. Entirely alien." He had to stop. His eyes hurt and his throat felt like he'd been eating sawdust and glass for a week.

Maguire noticed him wincing and stood. "Look, Holly, you rest, okay? Get your strength up, and we can get to the bottom of this."

Holland waved a weak hand. He swallowed a few times, drawing saliva from nearly dry glands. "Dave, I saw it, just after we lost contact with Deep Two. It scuttled into the crack. I took a look, then all hell broke loose. I..."

"Seriously Holly, just rest, eh?"

"Dave, what happened?"

Maguire pulled a face; he was considering leaving, debating how much to say. Holland recognised the signs. The news would be bad. "This can wait," he eventually said.

"It can't."

Maguire dithered a moment, then pulled up a chair and sat close to the head of the bed, elbows on knees, fingers steepled, voice low. "Okay," he said. "Okay. We lost contact with your team. We tried to raise you, and then we realised that something had knocked Cybele offline. Now, that's the thing. It's not too unusual for us to experience informational blackouts, but when we do and the AI is down there, she's okay, you know? She's still up here with us too, she just loses connection with her remote carriage. Well, this time she wasn't okay. She *went down*, John. We had to perform an emergency reboot; that just is not supposed to happen with these AIs. When Jensen realised that, he went into overdrive. We had a team down there quicker than I've ever seen, I swear he skipped at least half his safety drills. Cybele came back online when they were halfway down, but she didn't remember anything, and that spooked Jensen real hard."

Maguire spoke quickly, his voice hushed, excited and nervous. This was not the Maguire Holland knew. The good-natured mockery that lurked at the back of his eyes, as if all the world were an amusing play, had gone. His face was closed and perplexed, like that of a child who has seen something marvellous that it does not understand. "They got down there, they found multiple collapses of the lava tube you were exploring. It took us a while to make sure the area was safe and to dig you out. You were down there for forty-eight hours before we could get to you, and you were not in a good way. None of you were. You've been here for a couple of days now, sleeping it off."

A hungry moan troubled the room, the scream from his dreams returning. Holland started. "What the...?"

Something in Holland's face spooked Maguire. "What?" he said. Then he laughed with relief, a little bit of the old Maguire lighting up his face. "Oh, *that*, whew! Made me jump, there. Sorry, I should have said. I don't notice it any more. It's the wind. There's a massive dust storm on outside, been building for a couple of days. Nothing to worry about. Just as soon as it's done, we can get in touch with Canyon City and ask them what we're supposed to do with your discovery. You're going to be a very famous man, Dr John Holland."

"What do you mean?"

"Don't you remember? Man!" He sat back. "You've found more than some kind of improbable insect, my friend."

"How do you mean?"

Maguire leaned in close, and his excitement revealed itself. "Shit, Holly, you found an artefact! A *made thing*, buried in lava two billion years old! This is bigger than snottites, way bigger. Looks like it's been down there forever."

"Alien?"

Maguire shrugged, trying to look uncommitted. "Let's not jump to conclusions," he said. He clearly already had.

"What about the others?"

"Stulynow is okay, shook that Russian smirk right off his face. He's gone into full on brooding, but he'll mend."

"Vance?"

Maguire's face shut down again. "Touch and go, man, touch and go. There's no real physical damage – frostbite to her right hand – but something's not right. Damn typical that our chief MO is knocked out. Suzanne's trying her best to get to the bottom of what's wrong with her, but she's not a doctor and with this storm we've only got a limited medical database, so Cybele can only do so much to help her." He stood. "We'll just have to see." He smiled again, a complex expression, equal parts wonder, relief and sorrow. "Hell of a first week. I'll let the others know you're awake. Try and rest, eh? I'm due down in Deep Two, to take over from Mr Dr Van Houdt and Jensen."

Holland jerked painfully upright. "Don't tell me there's another team down there."

Maguire frowned. "Yeah, sure there is. After something like this? Look, I wouldn't worry. The thing's completely inert. There have been no more tremors since you set it off. We reckon you guys tripped it somehow, turns out the area you were investigating in Wonderland was pretty much directly beneath the fissure you found it in. Whatever it is, it looks like it's dead."

Foreboding welled up in Holland. "Dave, don't let them bring it back up."

"Hey, Holly, calm down, we're not totally fucking stupid. We're not taking any chances. They've got remote gear looking at it. For the time being, Orson's leaving it right where it is. Until we can get Marsform on the blower – these bloody storms, I tell you. Planet like this, you need a hardline, but will they roll one out? Will they bollocks."

GRAINY IMAGES, SHAKING as the small, legged robot struggled over the debris. In the seat next to Holland, Jensen peered at the screen, moving the joysticks as he guided it in. Another two screens showed other views, robots under the operation of the Class Three AI – Cybele, Holland corrected himself. It was getting easier for him to use her name. He didn't like how quickly that had happened.

"There we go, Holland. What do you think?"

A beam of light joined with those from the other two robots, lighting upon a featureless cylinder. But for its obviously artificial curves, it would have been indistinguishable from the rocks it lay half-buried within, shards and lumps of cracked basalt laid down a billion years ago.

"Are we sure that's not a natural formation?" said Kick Van Houdt. He stood at Holland's shoulder, hugging himself. "Could be an odd crystal formation."

"If you please." Miyazaki moved up. He bobbed a polite bow. "This is not natural." His voice was soft yet authoritative; he used it only when he had something to say, and for the main, people listened when he did. A withdrawn man, but he knew his stone. "Basalt can form in columnar patterns, yes, but the mean number of sides is six, with between three to twelve being the norm. This is not a polyhedron, but a true cylinder. Also, this rock is of the pillow form. I believe this area to have been formed undersea – direct contact with seawater. Although this could be some kind of rock from elsewhere, a glacial erratic or meteorite, again it is too regular in form, and in the case of an erratic, these rocks are billions of year older than the later limestone sea beds I have discovered on the Tharsis uplift; they were buried long before the Kovarkian ice age; they were never touched by the glaciers. These date from the earlier phase of the Mons – deep time, very, very old." He blinked owlishly as he looked to each man, assessing their understanding. "Lastly, this object," he sketched around it on the screen with his hands, "it is embedded in the stone. The lava here has flowed around this, it has been subjected to great temperature, and yet has maintained a uniform shape."

Kick sucked his teeth. "I still don't buy it, but that is not much of scientific view. I just don't believe it should be there, yet it is. What do I know? I'm a gasses man." He shrugged. "How long is it?"

Miyazaki spoke breathily through a polite smile. "I am sure we will know when we are authorised to touch it."

"No samples yet, and no scanning, we have no idea what will happen if we start washing it with energy," said Jensen sternly. He was irritable, his eyes red from lack of sleep. "Holland?"

Holland shook his head. A day on, he was feeling better, although he still had a drink to hand the whole time. He felt like a sponge left to bake in a desert; no matter how much he drank, it didn't seem enough. "I haven't seen this before. I saw a creature, not this. After that..." A flash in his mind, great light, a keening, Vance reaching out. He screwed his eyes shut. "I'm sorry, I blacked out. I might have seen it before, but I don't remember."

"How would you have seen it? It's at the back of the fissure," said Kick.

Jensen shook his head. "You were all outside the fissure. Stulynow was out of his hard shell and looks like he tried to climb in, but he didn't manage it. We saw nothing out of the ordinary when we pulled you out, and the remotes have seen nothing since. There is nothing alive for thirty metres around the fissure. This part of the cave is biologically inert."

"What about the light? The tremors?"

"If it wasn't for the tremors, we might have you all down for some kind of joint paranoid episode. Marsform don't want another embarrassment like the Hellas Planitia discovery, two false claims of artefacts..." He grimaced. "The press would have a field day." Jensen sat back, relinquished the control of his robot to the AI again. "But then, strange lights, hallucinations... It'd be easier for us all if it were a geological oddity. They're going to be grilling us all about this for weeks, you realise. We can forget about working in Wonderland, and if this is anything significant, we're going to be in the zoo for years. But those tremors?" He grunted and rubbed at his upper teeth with his thumb. "It obviously can *do* something, experience shows us all that. As far as we can tell it's just a lump of metal – there's nothing coming off it."

"Obviously, it isn't just a lump of metal," said Kick. He clasped his elbows tighter. "Anyone else get that?"

One by one, reluctantly they nodded.

"It feels wrong," said Miyazaki.

Kick unfolded his arms and pulled at his chin, wrestling with some inner debate. He spoke abruptly. "I dreamed that..."

Orson's voice echoed into Mission Control, breaking whatever confession Kick had been about to make. Mars' eerie song, inaudible down in Deep Two, came with it. "Gentlemen, I managed to contact Marsform central back in the city."

"And?" said Jensen.

"It stays where it is. You're all to come back to base right away. We are not to proceed with any further investigation into this thing until a relief team arrives. I want you to put Deep Two to sleep, and get back up here as soon as possible. There's a lull in the storm right now, but I've been told it is blowing up into a full category B. We need everyone up here on lockdown duty. That clear?"

"Yes, commander," said Jensen. The eugene's voice clicked off. "There we have it." The Swede stood. "And I do not know whether I am relieved or disappointed. Cybele, prepare to shut Deep Two down."

HOLLAND INSISTED HE help the others with the storm preparations. Jensen argued hard against it, but Orson shrugged and let him be. The eugene had enough on his plate without trying to talk one of his team out of doing his job.

Holland was weak and ran out of breath quickly, but he pushed himself on. Being out of the claustrophobic corridors of the base, even in the confines of an environment suit, felt good.

Outside, the sky had gone the colour of turmeric. Visibility was down to a few hundred metres, the sun no more than a bright patch on the sky. The light, diffracted by the dust in the air, contrived to be both dim and dazzling, making distances hard to judge. Holland's eyes ached with squinting against it, the reflective visor on his environment suit useless in the directionless glare.

Tarpaulins covering machines and supply dumps rattled in the wind. Holland helped Kick Van Houdt get the drones ready, clearing their wheel clamps of dust so they could park themselves and lock in. He carried a bucket of spare parts up for Jensen to repair a broken storm shutter, and that was that for him. He cried off and returned inside, exhausted. Suzanne, acting as base medical officer while Vance was out of action, made him go and lie down.

He slept uneasily, dreaming of blue skies, and awoke with a start, sweating and cold, with a sense of deep anxiety. He had a vague urge to run. Whatever dream had prompted such fear, he could not remember. He had a vague recollection of spaces whose geometries could not, and perhaps should not, be measured. Trying to remember filled him with inexplicable dread; he pushed it from his mind as best he could.

That night, the others welcomed Holland back to the dinner table with genuine warmth, but after that the base dinner was subdued. There were few conversations, oppressed as they were by the storm and by Dr Vance's parlous condition. Suzanne Van Houdt looked like she had been crying, and Commander Orson asked a few questions about the storm lockdown and said little more. Only Ito Miyazaki appeared unaffected, eating his food and reading technical journals on his tablet as usual.

Stulynow was gaunt and hollow-faced. Holland had tried to get him on his own several times so they could talk about what had happened since the event three days ago. From the way the Russian stared resolutely at his plate, refusing to make eye contact with anyone, Holland suddenly realised that he'd been avoiding him, and he felt a pang of apprehension.

They drifted away one by one. Jensen first, saying he had a round of inspections to make, the rest shortly after. Holland could not finish his food; his stomach felt the size of a squash ball, and the erratic howling of the wind drove his appetite away. He tried to help the Van Houdts clear up – it was his turn on the kitchen rota – but they insisted he rest.

He left, professing his thanks. When he turned back to ask them if he could perhaps take their slot next week in return, they were embracing; Kick comforting his wife, stroking her hair as she shook silently with tears.

He left without saying a word.

Outside, the wind howled louder with every passing hour. Down in the accommodation quarters, part buried as they were, it had become audible. Summer was coming, the ice caps' CO_2 was sublimating into the air, driving winds of surprising ferocity through the planet's thin atmosphere. The storms could last for weeks; the very worst engulfed the entire planet, turning it from red to featureless orange.

Holland lay in his bed, face to the brick wall. He tried to shut the noise out of his mind, but failed, and the drawn moaning of the wind became a soundtrack to his circling thoughts. It hounded him, began to sound triumphant, the baying of wolves closing in on their quarry. What the hell had they found down there? He felt feverish. He tossed and turned, rolling from side to side. He would find what he thought a comfortable position only for pain to grip him: a sharp stab in his shoulder joint, or a low, insistent throb in his legs that started as an innocuous ache but which soon became unbearable until he shifted again and the sorry process recommenced.

He flipped onto his side for the hundredth time, and suddenly, he was wide awake. Something was watching him. His eyes snapped open.

A silhouette in the dark. A woman. He made to move, but could not, the iron bindings of nightmare about his limbs. The woman came closer, her form stuttering as she moved. The shape moved through space jerkily, now closer, now further away, although its progress overall was towards him. She leaned in, and Holland made out a savage grin, huge eyes highlighted with green stars, the reflections of the lights of the equipment in his room. She brushed a strand of hair behind her ear; again, that stop-go zoetrope flicker, her hand jumping the spaces in between, missing out slivers of time. She held her finger to her lips and bared her teeth. They elongated, pink gums swelling, needle-fangs that dripped venom coming closer and closer to his face. Her jaw distended, as if she would devour him. He would have screamed, then, if he could. Her lips touched his head, and he was swallowed whole, wrapped tight in a skin that was not his own and yet one that he knew as intimately.

Suddenly, he was in the corridor, wavering uncertainly on his feet. The woman stood in the light. She was naked, smooth where nipples, belly button and genitals should have been. Her skin was pale, with a light, bluish cast. She beckoned to him. He followed her up the short flight of stairs from the accommodation level, wading through the thick stuff of dream.

He pitched forward into a maelstrom of shapes that made little sense to him, the spaces his senses could not comprehend. Terror returned, redoubled. The woman was still there, not as a woman, but as one of the forms in the tumult, alien and unknowable, vibrating like a plucked string, only one end of which was anchored in familiar reality.

Space and time warped.

Cold metal on his back, the howl of the storm. He lay on the floor, paralysed, neck contorted uncomfortably against the wall. The woman rose above him, a woman again, albeit briefly, her shape askew, paint dissolving into water.

"We will meet again," she said, or shrieked, or thought.

She disappeared. Stulynow stood in the corridor in the space where she had been. He glared, his eyes locked for long seconds on Holland's, his face an unreadable blank, somewhere between rage and forgetfulness, his eyes empty.

He turned and walked away.

Holland awoke. Alarms blared. Acrid smoke made him cough. Something with a hideous snout was bending over him, shaking him, its face falling into red shadow and back into full visibility in the flash of the alarm lights rotating on the walls. Demon to man to demon to man. The siren wailed like the souls of the damned.

"Holland! Holland! What are you doing out here?"

Not a demon, Kick Van Houdt. He was wearing a face mask.

Holland sat and cried out. His bones felt like ice. He clutched at his neck. "I don't know," he mumbled. "I don't know."

Bodies were struggling into clothes as they forced their way past them, faces invisible as they spluttered into fists and wet towels.

"It's Dr Vance," said Kick. "She's gone into arrest, Suzanne found you here on her way to the sickbay, told me to wait with you. There's a fire somewhere."

He thrust a mask at Holland, who took it in one limp hand, but did not put it on. A thought seized him. "Kick, you said, you said you dreamed –"

Kick recoiled from him; dismay flashed across his face. "Not now, not now. Come on, there's a *fire*." He stood and ran, leaving Holland to pull himself to his feet.

Jensen spoke on the tannoy. "I need help up here. Now. We've a fire in Mission Control."

Orson rolled down the corridor, coughing. His permatanned eugene skin was bare to the waist, rich silk pyjamas cladding his legs. "Has anyone seen Stulynow?" he demanded. "Has anyone seen Stulynow?" He stopped at a box on the wall, pulled out a face mask and jogged into the smoke.

Holland followed him.

CHAPTER FOURTEEN

The Last War of Tsu Keng

Year 15,105 of the Hegemony of Man

THE SHIPS SANG for joy as their pilots approached, eager to be free of their hangar.

The cavernous eyrie of the Royal Dock vibrated with energy, men and sheathed spirits running to and fro, support automata refuelling the machines and loading them with projectiles. The scramble alarm chimed its carillon, a calm exhortation to battle. Light dazzled, caught on a million facets of crystal and metals. The Royal Dock was a wonderful display of the decorative arts; that, and power.

Tsu Keng's principal eyes were poor at such close quarters. He saw the furthest ships clearly: slender, killing darts a kilometre distant. They would appear distorted to a human's perception, for Tsu Keng's field of vision extended all around him; everything nearer to him was a smear of colour and movement.

But he could feel his pilot, the ripple of his approach cutting through the Second World as he walked toward the ship. He walked Tsu Keng's gangway and presented himself at the ship's main port. Krashtar Vo came into sharp focus as he came close to Tsu Keng's near-sight eyes around the door.

Behind him floated the spirit form of his companion, Kybele, ethereal against the tumult of preparations for war.

Tsu Keng saw the pilot in both worlds: as he was now, a Martian bred for the rigours of combat space flight – squat, heavy featured, dense bones, thick muscle, internal organs protected by fluid sacs and strengthened by encysted smart gels – and as he was in the Library, a flickering mass of faces, of histories, one laid over the other, a line of personalities stretching back to the dawn of this era. Permissions and activation whispers swarmed from Krashtar Vo, to interface with the ship's own Second World self. Tsu Keng's soul was different, monolithic. Not for him the psyche-clouds of the human Martians, or the choirs of the spirits, whose co-operative subminds made up a greater whole. Tsu Keng's material and psychic self were indivisible. He was made for one purpose, and desirous only to serve that purpose.

Tsu Keng lived to fly, nothing but to fly.

His systems thrummed in anticipation of it.

"Greetings, Tsu Keng."

"Greetings, Krashtar Vo. Welcome aboard, my pilot."

Tsu Keng's door skin developed a seam and rippled apart, and Krashtar Vo stepped inside. The gangway and door deliquesced, and Tsu Keng drew their lead-grey substance back into his larger mass. His door eyes rolled backward, their eyelids closed, and these too retracted into his body. The portal became smooth skin. His epidermal layer shivered, and a pattern of scales rippled, diamond plates lifting sharp edges up and then lying flat as Tsu

Keng activated his armour. The atomic structure of his hide interlocked and became rigid, pressurising the liquid and ablative layers below it.

Krashtar Vo's feet made only a padding sound as he waddled through the ship. He was heavily adapted for his role, and could lead a comfortable life neither upon the surface of Mars nor within a microgravity environment. It was said some of the pilots enjoyed the deep habitats within the atmospheres of the gas giants, but they seldom stayed there long; the call of deep space was too great. A sacrifice, this modification, some of the humans held.

What do they know? Krashtar spoke mind to mind. He had been a pilot only a few years, but already his bond with Tsu Keng was such that they could achieve interface without the aid of machine or spirit. *No price is too great for this.*

Tsu Keng thought this true. He had no conception that it could be otherwise.

Krashtar Vo gained the command bridge; he slipped into his couch and lay back. Tsu Keng wrapped himself about the pilot. Krashtar Vo's body was hardened to the perils of slip space, and so required no stasis field, but Tsu Keng held him tight nevertheless.

There was a sensation like a kiss, and their minds ran one into the other. Tsu Keng felt a caress, and the man's companion departed. They were lovers, it was said, Krashtar Vo and Kybele, and had been through many lifetimes. Unusual, a man and his companion to be actively engaged in an affair of the heart, or so Tsu Keng had been told. This also, Tsu Keng did not truly understand, not even when he and Krashtar Vo were one.

A call echoed through the canyon; one note, long and low, the song of the squadron alpha leader. The other ships responded, and the hangar became a sounding chamber for a harmonious outpouring of emotion.

We are ready, the ships and their pilots thought as one. *We will fly.*

The cradle arms holding the alpha ship folded back, and the ship dropped from the racks, plummeting to the floor. Gravity engines came alive, and it sped toward the dock mouth and out into sunlight.

Follow, it thought. The beta ships dropped – one, two, three. Then all the ships rained down, like oak leaves in autumn. They twisted around one another, a cacophony of hooting song sounding in both worlds, the electomagnetic spectrum crowded with their delight.

Tsu Keng and his squadron mates jockeyed for position, not breaking formation, not quite. Below them on the floor of the Royal Dock, men and machines moved painfully slowly, as slow as unphased Stone Kin. Tsu Keng and his kin laughed at them, fighting the desire to engage their slip drives there and then.

Not here, not now, said Krashtar Vo. *Not safe.*

The ships tumbled out of the hangar mouth into the Marrin, great bats leaving their roost. Sunlight turned their grey skins silver, and when they passed through the broad beams of the mirror suns, the scales of their armour sparkled iridescence.

Onward, upward! To war! To war! the alpha sang. Five hundred combat ships obeyed, falling into formation. Their shadows raced up and over the canyon bluffs, drawing excited gestures from onlookers below. In the Second World, companion spirits mobbed the souls of the ships and their pilots, wishing them well, good hunting, come home. Air roared against Tsu Keng's skin, his sharp prow forcing it aside.

Oh, to be a ship of war! they sang. *Oh, to be in flight!*

Sky turned from caramel to blue to purple to black, the ships' song became thin and then vanished into vacuum, heard only now in the Second World.

Stars shone unhindered upon the raiment of infinity. They were not alone. The heavens blazed with shiplight, bright dots moving swiftly, vessels the size of countries diminished by distance to needle-tips. Thousands upon thousands of them filled the sky in long trains, rising from Earth, Venus, and Mars, from the habitats, from the belt, from the moons of the giants, heading away from the Sulian System, heading out for the stars and for safety.

The greater part of mankind was in flight.

Out from the warships, past the crescent of Mars, a great light burned, one that appeared foul and wrong to the eyes of the ships, a second sun in place of Jupiter.

The Stone Sun, brighter now than the tear in the sky it would close. The hyper-dimensional object Jupiter was becoming would constrain the Stone Kin within the gravity well of Sul, seal the tear in reality and keep the Stone Kin from infecting the wider universe. Sulian ships swarmed about the transmogrified gas giant, the fruit of Man's last great labour, working without pause to ignite this second, uncanny star and save mankind.

It was here the Martian ships flew. This is where the Stone Kin concentrated their efforts. The craft of the Kin descended to the lower dimensions and assailed the construction fleet daily, for they, like Man, wished to be free. This was but the latest of a thousand skirmishes.

To the fight, my brothers! called the alpha ship. *To the battle!*

Tsu Keng's wings unfurled, as did those of his brothers and sisters. Their unity of purpose and mind saw them all drop up from this world, their wings folding them into complex eleven-dimensional geometries where the wills of the pilots could more effectively move them.

You are not here. Krashtar Vo's inner voice, indistinguishable from Tsu Keng's own, told him of his place in the universe, convinced him utterly that he belonged somewhere else. *You are here.*

Concentration was difficult. Things assailed them as they passed the Veil of Worlds into slip space, the infections of the Stone Kin spreading even there.

Screams scarred the higher reality of the Veil as ships succumbed to raking claws and incomprehensible technologies.

A short slip. Tsu Keng knew that he was elsewhere. That was the natural order of it. How could it be otherwise?

The Martian squadron materialised deep in the Jovian subsystem and into the heart of battle. Tsu Keng's wingmate flew straight into a cloud of debris at near-luminal speed, tumbling into a million pieces.

Tsu Keng's combat wing split, the four remaining ships spiralling in evasive manoeuvres as thousands of anti-collision hardbeams vaporised the debris.

Krashtar Vo looked upon the battle through Tsu Keng's eyes, his mind comprehending their situation as Tsu Keng bent his own mind to the task of survival. Their battlefield spanned anything up to eight spatial dimensions, only the highest and the second temporal axes safe, unsullied by violence. Combat was conducted at speeds approaching the four-dimensional maximum for objects of their mass. At such velocities, relative position at a distance was impossible to judge, so they fought at close quarters.

A dozen Terran ships fought a desperate fight with four Stone Kin vessels. The Terran ships were near-identical to those of Mars, the same in all but song. Their armour was scarred and their movements panicked. The Stone Kin craft – if they were craft, none had ever been captured, and no crew ever seen – warped and flexed. Their presence was an intrusion into three dimensional space, and their forms were not fixed. It was as if they rotated in their own space, presenting first this aspect of themselves to the lower dimensions, then that, where they could be understood only as disparate parts. The spirits and humans of ordinary spacetime perceived them no more clearly than blind men describing an elephant. Beams of exotic particles erupted unpredictably from their surfaces. Their effusion and potency defied analysis. Eleutheremics could not predict them. They might impact upon a ship with less effect than a ray of moonlight, or they could cut it in two.

The alpha ship severed the fleet's higher linkages, lest the Stone Kin infiltrate the ship's cortices. Training, experience, and force of will would determine the outcome of the day.

The Stone Kin shattered two more of the Terran ships to glittering clouds, and bright fire roiled and died in the vacuum. The remaining Terran craft fell back, joining with the Martian fleet. The ships greeted each other with long songs, broadcast on inter-ship ranges, but they were muted. The Terran ships were exhausted and afraid.

Today they could all die. They were poorly matched against the Stone Kin, no matter how many Sulian craft crowded the sky. The Stone Kin's power was ineffable.

Survival did not matter, not to Tsu Keng. He and his fellow ships found the Terrans' fear contemptible. To fly, that was all. To fight, that was what was demanded. He had no fear, he would fly, he would fight. Death was immaterial.

The Martian fleet surged forward. They ducked and arced like dolphins as their engines pushed at the fabric of space.

The Stone Kin revolved their incomprehensible bodies to face this new threat. Beams jagged out from them, all targeted unerringly on the alpha craft. Beams of infinite colouring intersected on the space where the alpha swam. Too late, its pilot attempted to exert her will and force the ship elsewhere. Its wings were part unfurled as it was cut into a hundred pieces, fragments of it spinning out and impacting on those following it.

Some of the younger vessels, those with inexperienced pilots, hesitated and swerved, songs vibrating with panic. The rest hurled themselves on, diving through the lattice of beams the warping Stone Kin projected. More ships died in ecstasy, annihilated as they flew.

The Martians had lost thirty ships already.

Krashtar Vo and Tsu Keng moved themself into an attack pattern. They part-deployed their slip wings. Their remaining wingmates spiralled down after them, copying their leader's action.

Pilot's and ship's shared skin prickled as slip shields came online. Krashtar Vo enforced his interpretation of events upon Tsu Keng and the craft jinked madly, moving from location to location without crossing the space in between.

Tsu Keng deployed his cannons and opened fire. Krashtar Vo extended his mind, unique organs in his brain pre-observing an infinity of outcomes. Their joined mind was capable of processing vast amounts of information at once. Self-imposed ignorance was the lever to the imposition of will.

Vo's mind, pushed to great heights by that of Tsu Keng, observed all possible quantum outcomes exactly simultaneously, not sequentially, preventing any one state of truth being determined before the desired outcome was chosen and enacted.

Not all men could become pilots, just as not all spirits could be ships. The act of forcing one's will onto an eleven-dimensional space required a stupendous act of double-thinking, for they had to be both ignorant and aware they were doing it. Awareness that all possible outcomes existed contaminated the observance of said outcomes, reducing the number of outcomes to one, and crippling the possibility of success. Through denial, they thus preserved the undetermined state of things before the time was ripe for determination to come into effect. At the same time, they saw what they saw; the inevitability. What happened was always the only answer. The pilots of Mars were unshakeable in their conviction that they were right.

They were bred to defy fate.

All truths, however, are subjective.

Together, Tsu Keng and Krashtar Vo observed exactly where the Stone Kin would be, and fired. But the Stone Kin operated outside of time, observing their fire at precisely the same moment, their will undermining the certainty principles of the aggressor. Even if it was inevitable it would be hit, if the target could force its own interpretation of events onto the firer, then it would miraculously avoid the shot. *Always*. If the ship could force its own observed interpretations on a target's, then the opposite would occur – it would always be hit. The target would either always be hit, or always be missed, but never both, as decided by the eleutheremic arguments constructed by the duelling craft, and how well they tricked their opposite number into adopting their point of view.

Combat was a matter not of flight, then, but of sheer will.

For a few brief moments, two observable realities vied with each other for dominance. Only one held true at any one time, but both could be true at different times, and the ships, the Stone Kin and the cannon's ordnance flickered into and out of existence, describing multiple fractured courses and positions, the universe blurring into a myriad possibilities, time spread like a rainbow. The fabric of reality groaned under the strain.

Probability was wracked by a monstrous contest of wills. Packets of energy exploded or failed ever to have existed about the weaving, poly-possible craft. The ship was, then wasn't, then was again, its potential ruination hanging on the threads of contested interpretation.

Seventeen thousandths of a second and it was over. Tsu Keng's fire raked over the body of the Stone Kin. Volleys from his wingmates crisscrossed the thing. For one moment its pulsations stilled and its form solidified into something ugly and squamous.

It imploded, and ceased to be.

The Martian fleet flickered through the space the alien craft had occupied, rolling and singing as they moved from one potentiality to the next. Emboldened, they assailed the remaining three Stone Kin. Many died.

The sky wept tears of light as ships left mankind's birthplace in their millions, fleeing the tear in the sky. The harsh light of the transformed Jupiter glared at them all as they fled. The Stone Sun was one fight closer to being kindled, the Stone Kin one step closer to being trapped. Earth, Mars, Venus – the ancestral homes of Man – would be entombed with them, but the plague of the Stone Kin would go no further.

Tsu Keng did not care. Tsu Keng flew.

CHAPTER FIFTEEN

Descent

FOR THE BRIEFEST of moments, the Veil of Worlds parts and the stars shine strong and clear upon parts of Mars long alien to them. I feel displaced; unclean. The gap closes, and swirling unreality returns. Where before there was nothing, our silver dart drifts in the shrouded night high above the world.

The rays of the true sun sweep around the planet, burning dimly through the Veil. Even sapped, it strikes glimmers of light from our many-finned hull. We drift, the ship turning as it begins to fall. It moves without direction. Burns and wounds criss-cross the hull; ugly welts and brassy contusions that mar the rainbow lustre of Tsu Keng's seamless skin.

Tsu Keng is dying. He has been true to his promise and to his fate.

The ship's pace quickens towards the shadowed deserts, the dusk-shrouded ice fields, the mottled ruptures where Stone intrusions pierce lower realities, to torture crust and time alike.

Yoechakenon sleeps. His face is frozen in a grimace, whether of pain or terror I cannot discern. A nimbus encases him, like frozen curls of oil on water. The area within it shimmers, as if uncertain whether to be or to be not. My love looks more like the possibility of a man than a being that lives and breathes.

This is fortunate. The stasis field holds. I do not have much time. Tsu Keng is disabled and I cannot control his failing body.

The instruments of the ship blaze around Yoechakenon, and blinking lamps measure the beat of the craft's slowing heart. The lights flutter with increasing irregularity; some do not return to life. As the seconds pass, fewer and fewer shine, and those that still shine do so ever more dimly. The ruined cabin vibrates. Globules of viscous fluid quiver in the air, floating from torn arteries and smashed organs revealed by the ruptured walls.

I try to assert myself, throwing out parts of myself to fill the space Tsu Keng has vacated. I do not know what I am doing. His instruments are unfamiliar. I find an image bank, but its projectors ripple and fail, and no image appears. A shower of sparks issues from them, and many fall dark.

"My love." My voice struggles into being, vibrating frayed vocal cords of living glass. It fades away, before swelling to fill the cabin of the slipship. I feel pain, as part of Tsu Keng's voice breaks forever. "My love. Awake." My voice is perfect, alluring and husky, for it was designed to be so, but also cracked and stuttering, and this I do not intend. I am afraid. "I am blind. I cannot see. We are caught. The ship is damaged, and it does not respond. Tsu Keng is dying. We are falling."

"Warning." My voice; a second voice from a subsidiary mind that has infiltrated part of the ship's control system. Good. My choir grows into my new skin. This voice is impassive, isolated from my fear, and there is a terrible finality to its words. "Plasma drive offline, atmospheric entry in three minutes, thirty-seven seconds and counting. Warning."

I attempt to rouse Yoechakenon. I struggle deep in the ship's matrix, trying to shut off his protective cocoon. He was a pilot, once. He will know what to do. I caress sigils floating in the innerspace of the ship's private world, but they do not respond. I push harder until something breaks, optic beams burning through crystalline arrangements stressed beyond tolerance by the ship's transference from the higher dimensions to the lower. The field remains imperturbable, and Yoechakenon stays enmeshed in his nightmare.

"My love, Yoechakenon, wake up, please wake up!" I whisper. My voice is fractured, multiple layers of pleading. "I need you!" My other voice carries on its relentless countdown. "Atmospheric entry in two minutes, fifty-six seconds."

I push and push, attempting to break into systems I barely understand. I feel trapped, imprisoned. I cannot get out.

Something gives, and I have influence over another system – the ship's damage control. I steel myself.

This is going to hurt.

Agony assails me as I take on the suffering of the vessel. My mind fractures further as I wrestle with it. Then the pain is gone; I have offloaded the feeling onto a sub-personality, and walled it off, screaming, in a part of myself. Another of my voices sings a song of destruction. "Extensive hull damage. Slip shields disrupted during transit. Crystalline matrix disrupted. Columnar link severed, ship's mind contaminated. Ship's systems at twenty-seven per cent of prime capacity and falling. Probability of ship intellect survival fourteen per cent and falling. Wake up, Yoechakenon, wake up! The ship is caught!" My voices sound under and around each other in chorus, a melody of hull integrity, pleas, atomic cohesion, uncertainty, temporal positioning, fear. A hundred subroutines speak their opinions and announce procedures, possible as well as attempted, as my choir attempts to halt the descent. There is a coughing from the ship's rear, a flare of light that overwhelms the viewports' darkening mechanisms. The ship slews violently around, taking us broadside on to the planet. A cascade of molten half-metal rains past. "Plasma drive destroyed. Initiating emergency landing procedures." My voices come together, speaking together with polyphonic certainty. "We are going to crash."

The ship gathers speed. Elsewhere on Mars it will be full day, but the Veil lets little light through, and the land below lies under a greyish murk. The enfeebled sun illuminates orbital artefacts of ages past. Corpses in orbit, decaying platforms of long-forgotten purpose, their remains pointing tangled fingers of ruinous superstructure accusingly at the planet below.

Above the north pole, the blue-fringed Stone Sun rises to oppose the true sun, its light an anti-light, a light that blinds with darkness. So far away outside the Veil, the usual laws do not apply within the realms of the Stone Lands. The Stone Sun was made by Man, Jupiter resculpted to imprison the Stone

Kin. Its stuff is of the Stone Realms entirely, and within this interface it waxes strong, a monstrous vortex of malice.

The damaged slipship continues its tumble. Tsu Keng's dimension-warping technologies are functional, but useless in the face of mundane gravity. I am trapped in a disintegrating body, and I will die if I fail in my struggle for mastery of it.

Yoechakenon will die.

I re-route streams of light-borne data through unbroken areas of the ship's inner network, I tear up the living machine's operating protocols, destroying swathes of its personality in the process; anything to bring my beloved Yoechakenon down safely.

I feel great pain, and part of my greater being burns out: that which was bound to the ship's soul, a temporary arrangement that could now turn fatal. Titanic cathedrals woven of thought that dance with more possibilities than there are atoms in the universe sputter and go black. Memories I have held for tens of thousands of years are gone. I isolate my core aspects while struggling with the craft's few functioning systems. Should we survive, I will remain Kaibeli.

Should we survive.

"Warning, atmospheric impact in fifty-four, fifty-three, fifty-two, fifty-one, fifty, forty-nine, forty-eight..." My submind's voice emotionlessly counts down as thirteen other pieces of me attempt to devise a way out. All solutions are found wanting and discarded.

"Three per cent probability of ship intellect survival. Six per cent of occupant's survival. Nine point seven five of hosted AI survival.

"The ship is breaching the atmosphere. Warning. Approach vector incorrect. Destruction certain."

A sharp whistling resounds through the hull as the ship passes through the upper layers of the atmosphere. Our velocity is comparatively low, but with my side-on approach I am certain to bounce across Mars' thin sheath of air like a stone skipping on a pond, breaking up and plummeting to fiery ruin. Either that or I will pass over the Stone Lands entirely, and hit the Veil of Worlds at the far side, and be destroyed utterly.

The craft judders. The viewports glow red. The whistling grows to a roar. I try again to rouse the ship's soul, but it is slumped in one corner of itself, mumbling in terminal quinary. I recoil; its routines are shot through with the spirit-slaying particles of the Stone Realms. It is closer to death than I thought.

"Yoechakenon!" I shout. "I don't know how to do this! Yoechakenon, for the love of all life, *wake up!*" Part of me is amused. Yoechakenon has rarely seen me perturbed. There is no response from the frozen man, and he stays locked outside the normal flow of time.

I cast wildly around for salvation. Just as I am beginning to give up hope, I find activation routines for three directional impellers buried deep in the ship's mental framework. I follow the trail of electrons to their locations upon the ship's hull. My minds debate with one another if they will work, if they were damaged by our journey through the Veil, if they will do any good should they be sound. The conclusions I reach, swifter than lightning, are all negative. Lacking other options, I try them anyway.

One goes instantly to destruction, searing my mind like a red hot knife. I force calm upon myself, and power the remaining pair up slowly. I pray, even though I know the Great Librarian cannot hear me.

There is a low counterpoint to the roar of the air outside, a pulsing that jostles with the vibrations of the cabin. One of the impellers is online. I manipulate it gently, as careful as I can be. Slowly, the craft tilts, nose forward, presenting its prow to atmosphere. Another gravity thruster sounds, stray graviton particles rippling through my being. The ship pitches to the right.

"Four per cent probability of ship intellect survival." My relentless voice chimes, barely audible. "Twenty-three per cent of occupant survival. Thirty-six per cent of hosted AI survival."

The ship streaks through the sky, a blazing spear trailing fire in its wake. My body roars over glacial peaks, passing over the endless plains that lie at the feet of towering cliffs of ice, dazzling places with my passage that have not seen light for thousands of years. Strange things, not of Mars, track the ship with cold eyes. I take little of this in. I try my best to slow the ship's descent with the few means at my disposal.

"Seven point eight six per cent probability of ship intellect survival. Forty-six point four per cent of occupant survival. Sixty-seven per cent of hosted AI survival."

The boom of the ship's arrival shatters the silence of the freezing Stone Lands. I draw closer and closer to the ground, hurtling over the prairies that girt Mulympiu, lands that have not felt the tread of true Martians since the end of the Third Stone War. I punch through clean air and the choking fumes of Stone intrusion alike. I am pulled down, betrayed by my borrowed body.

"Eight point eight six per cent probability of ship intellect survival. Fifty-seven point four per cent of occupant survival. Seventy-eight per cent of hosted AI survival."

And then we hit. To my minds, functioning far faster than that of a human being ever could, there is a universe of silence, an eternity of calm hidden in a nanosecond of fury. Then there is nothing but noise and blinding pain and the scream of tearing half-metals.

Soil drags at the ship, scrabbling to bring my warmth into its freezing embrace. I break free and hurtle forward several hundred spans; once, twice, spinning over and over. I ram the ground again. Iron-hard ground claws at my ruined fins, hauling the ship back into line with itself, sending sprays of turf, water, steam, and dirt out either side of me. Caught fully in the clutches of the steppe, the ship skids to a long stop, leaving a steaming furrow four thousand spans long behind it. I cry out as the ship's spine snaps. The craft breaks in two before coming to a final, tumbling halt.

Within, the few lights about the cabin flicker. But they do not die.

The ship sits in an empty landscape of sere grasses and dirty, timeless snow. High above, the Stone Sun burns in the sky with silent fury, Suul opposite cowed and faint.

The ground hisses, the ship's half-metal body ticks as it cools. All too soon it is cold. The heat of re-entry dissipates into the frigid steppe, and a sheen of frost runs spidery caresses over the hull. All falls silent within the craft. Without, the land returns to its deathly watch, the gnarled heather and grasses that cloak it moving fitfully in the wind, as if it stirs in fever-sleep.

The noise of energy generation invades the inside of the ship, as a few more points of life spring uncertainly back to life. Flames gout from a smashed wall and die back, leaving the greasy smell of burnt meat upon the air.

"Yoechakenon?" My voices speak together again, quiet and tentative. I run my selves round the vessel. The field protecting Yoechakenon glows bright. This time, when I try the sigils and they do not respond, I smash them with a lash of my psyche.

The nimbus about Yoechakenon shuts off, and his tensed body crumples in upon itself. He utters an inchoate shout that seems the end of a greater cry, and is still.

I direct my will to preventing the dropping temperatures from slaying the one I love, and wait for him to awake.

YOECHAKENON AWAKES. HE blinks, clearing tears and sweat from his eyes. His body tingles with the remembered pain of stasis. This signals good news, that he is in stasis no more.

"Yoechakenon? Yoechakenon," I say. I hide my concern for his wellbeing. Stasis is not a natural state: those who step outside of time do not always return, and some of those that do are not the men they were when they departed.

He comes to properly, and I feel joy. He coughs on the alien air of the Stone Lands.

"You are here." He attempts to rise, but is weak, and lies back on the couch, clutching at his armour and glaive.

"Yes, Yoechakenon, I am here."

"Then the Emperor was not lying, in that one regard." He puts aside the glaive and runs his hands over his face, as if feeling it for the first time. Another spasm of coughs racked his body. He looks around the pilot's chamber. "What happened?"

"The ship sustained serious damage in our flight through the Veil of Worlds. My memory is seriously impaired, but from what I can gather, many of the ship's defences were undone once it pierced the Veil. Yoechakenon, I..." – my voice struggles, fading out as more of the ship's communication system shatters – "I am not sure, I saw..." I doubt myself, and Yoechakenon sees it. "The ship's mind suffered greatly."

Yoechakenon struggles up onto his elbows, and his movement provokes a million hurts, though these are but echoes of his earlier agony. Ignoring the discomfort, he looks about himself, gauging the danger in his immediacy. The cabin is dark, only the dim light of failing instruments allowing him to see anything. Ruptured bulkheads spill smashed crystals on the crumpled floor; the ship's ergonomic lines are buckled. In one wall a rent stands, revealing the cold blackness of the Stone Lands outside.

Deep inside some of the shattered walls, crystal chips glow. These are weak, glimmerings in places that should have been ablaze with the illumination of self-knowledge.

"Tsu Keng is dead?" he says.

"He will pass soon. I am sorry."

He is quiet for a time. His thoughts are clouded with grief. "That is a great shame," he says. He levers himself into a squatting position within the couch. He stays there for a few minutes, shivering from shock and cold. The air gusting through the breaches in the hull is icy and strangely flavoured, and his lungs burn with it.

"Lost and without a means of return. Our situation appears grim." Yoechakenon rubs at his forehead as nausea floods over him. Worse than the pain is the feeling of meaninglessness that permeates every part of his being, a side-effect of the Stone Lands. Men were not meant to tread here. "What hurts have I sustained? I feel as if death is upon me."

"As far as I can ascertain, you are only superficially damaged."

He runs his shaking hands through his braids. "It feels as if that is far from the case."

"Your spiritual energies remain intact. There is no contamination or sign of interference within your neural or interface frameworks – unlike the ship. I cannot be totally sure, I have lost most of my external processing centres. I cannot see beyond standard human spectral ranges; the ship's sensor suite is smashed beyond repair. But I am almost certain you are undamaged."

"I should not feel so weak," Yoechakenon says darkly. He grits his teeth, fighting the pain and queasiness, and succeeds at pulling himself upright.

It is a supreme effort. He lays his head against the metal skin of the ship. It should be warm with life, but is clammy as a corpse. His hands are sticky with ship's blood, his feet chilled by the thick fluids pooling on the floor.

"This will pass. The stasis field would not go out. After we crashed and the ship's spirit failed. I am sorry, but I had to use force to wake you. The sickness is a side effect of your abrupt reintegration with linear time."

Yoechakenon is disoriented. He feels vulnerable, an unaccustomed sensation that fills him with unease.

I cannot wait for him to ground himself. There is a feeling, a scratching on my skin. It is swift and then gone, but it draws near the ship's bridge. "There is something outside the ship."

Yoechakenon listens, focussing his hearing on the air beyond the gash in the wall. All he hears is the thin, malignant wind.

"I hear nothing."

"They are stealthy. Much of the ship's skin is numb, but there are places that can still feel. They pass over these, and are working their way up the hull towards us. Their claws hurt the ship's flesh."

Yoechakenon risks switching his sphere of consciousness. Ours is the connection of the prime degree, higher than the first, lower only than that endured by the Emperor and his spirit twin. Through me, Yoechakenon may feel what I feel, as I may look into his heart and mind. He does so now, interfacing directly with the ship's senses. He grimaces as he experiences the ship's pains. The death pangs of such a large machine are strong. We feel the life draining from the huge hull, feel the canker of madness growing in the ship's mind as Stone Land contamination forces itself between its streams of consciousness. Twists of golden thought turn black.

There. Again. Claws upon the ship's skin.

He concentrates on the sensation. It is fleeting, intermittent, present only when whatever monster comes for us passes over a living section of the hull. Yoechakenon has spent only a single lifetime as a machine, unlike I, who have lived many times as a flesh woman. To him it is strange and unfamiliar, this machine pain, and dread creeps up his spine as surely as the creatures creep up the hull.

I push back his senses from those of the ship. Tsu Keng is fading; Yoechakenon's soul could be swept away by the ship's mind as it dies.

"Their touch is of utter chill. Yoechakenon, they may be Stone Beasts, but I cannot be sure."

"Sure or not, if there is but a chance they are Stone Beasts, we must leave. Now." He pushes himself away from the wall. It takes most of his strength.

"Yoechakenon, I do not think we can do so without them detecting us. Conflict is a likely outcome of our current situation."

"Do not fret, Kaibeli." He moves silently to the gash in the hull. The air is dry, the wind cold, robbing his slime-crusted body of heat. He shivers violently.

"They are gathering where there is life in the ship still."

"Then they must be Stone Beasts," says Yoechakenon, his breath pluming in the frigid air. "Mortal creatures would not be so fastidious in their

feeding. Our situation, it appears, is not improving."
He pauses a moment, weighing our chances. "Can
Tsu Keng be saved?"

"No," I say. My voice diverges into a chorus.
A few dissenting voices sing a different song, but
softly. "The ship and its mind are broken beyond
repair. Even if it were to survive its injuries, it will
never fly again. We will have to find another way
from the Stone Lands."

"I wonder if the Emperor planned for us to
return at all," he says. Yoechakenon frowns. "We
must sacrifice our good brother to save ourselves."
He hunts through the wreckage as he speaks, his
movements increasingly sure as his strength returns.
His mind pushes out the dark futility bedded in his
subconscious. A quick investigation of the combat
sheath the Emperor provided me tells him that the
body is smashed beyond repair.

You are going to have to ride in the armour, he
says to me, mind to mind.

"Yes, Yoechakenon," I say. I do not want to ride
with the armour. Its spirit is vicious and despises me.
I try to disregard such pettiness and concentrate on
the matter in hand.

"Kaibeli, when I direct you, you must divert all
remaining energies into the hull, as far away as from
us as is possible. Do you understand?"

"Yes, Yoechakenon. I understand. It will draw
them away."

We feel a twinge in our mind from the ship, a
sensation close to fear. Underneath its Stone-brought
madness, Tsu Keng understands. Yoechakenon pulls
aside a wrinkle of metal, unearthing supplies from a

cyst in the ship's wall – a survival pack and particle pistol.

He places them in the couch, then reaches in and removes the armour. He does this slowly, whether from fear or reverence I cannot tell. He handles it like a priest would a relic. His fascination with it angers me.

Inert, the armour is a small looking thing, no thicker than a forearm and about as long as the span of two hands, lead-grey, dull. Two thick bands inscribed with words no one can read circle the top and bottom. He weighs it in his hand. He does not activate it yet.

The things scrabble closer.

"Yoechakenon, please; I understand your reasons for hesitating, but you must don the armour now!" I hate myself for saying it.

"It has been a long time," he whispers. Then louder, "Above all things I longed for while I lay captive in the arena, the chance to wear this armour again was paramount. I cast it aside, and yet I yearned for it."

"Yoechakenon, I hate the armour, you know this, and nothing would make me happier than if you were to forswear it forever, and live unclad until the end of your days. But, though I am loath to admit it, we need it now. We will both perish without it."

There is a crash from outside. Yoechakenon looks at the case. He thinks of the power of the armour, of the protection it brought him, of the strength it lent his arm, yet still he hesitates. Images of the death that follows it wherever it goes fill his mind unbidden, images he can force aside only with difficulty. He sees faces, dying and dead, and tastes blood in his mouth that is not his own. The Armour Prime is far more than the scarab-harness worn by the palace guard and Praetorians. It is truly alive, one of only thirteen such armours ever to have existed. An army cannot stand against a skilled warrior so garbed, but there is a price, and it is this price that caused Yoechakenon to set it aside when confronted by the Spirefather of Olm.

The spirits that dwell within the armour are utterly malevolent, unlike any other of the Martian spirits, the Door-ward included. Its needs are vile, and they affect a man after a time. As much as Yoechakenon hungers for its power, he still fears it. The promise of death that it brings does far worse than sicken him.

It excites him.

"Very well," says Yoechakenon. A shot of anguish makes him shiver, but his thumbs are already moving toward the hidden lock studs. He finds them by instinct, and presses.

There is a hiss as the capsule melts in his hands, pouring through his fingers like quicksilver, and wisps of super-chilled air rise from it. It splashes quietly into the muck on the floor and spreads as a slick of metal. A pseudopod reaches up, a single, freezing, probing digit. It moves tentatively until it brushes Yoechakenon's hand, then it is tentative no more.

A flood of steaming, living metal pours at once from the floor, entwining itself about Yoechakenon's legs. Streamers of it embrace his waist. Yoechakenon gasps as the armour flows, encasing his body from neck to foot, insulating his naked, muscular body from the cold with a repellent numbness all its own.

His skin crawls as the armour wraps itself about him. As much as he craves the powerful symbiosis, he has never grown used to the moment the armour embraces him. Nor have I. I fear the day when the armour leaves him and his eyes snap open and something else looks out of them.

The armour's tendrils seek out the control ports studded down his spine, bringing the mind that dwells within the armour into direct contact with his own, and through him, with mine. The feel of its being is like iced water flowing into warm bones, the touch of a dead enemy. His mind is lost for a moment, and I am exposed alone to the brutality of the armour's ancient soul; memories of war and victory from times long gone smash themselves into my mind. It whispers its hunger to tell more such stories, and write them large in blood.

"Master," says a voice, the smooth tongue of extinction itself.

Then it passes, and Yoechakenon has a skin of metal, and he is warm and invincible and feels complete for the first time in two years.

I am sad. When he is like this, in the armour, I lose him. "Hurry, the ship is dying," I say. My voice betrays nothing. "It has but a few more moments. Go quickly."

"Is the ship ready?" he says.

"It is."

"Then prepare yourself also." He moves to the rent in the wall, and tears at the viscous strands forming over the hole. Even in the face of death, the ship struggles to heal itself. "Farewell, Tsu Keng," he says, and jumps to the ground below.

He lands easily in the runnel created by the ship's crash. The mounds of soil thrown up around the buckled hull are already solid with ice. Something grey and mottled, silhouetted high above him on the ship's bulk, turns its long head in his direction, its saucer eyes those of a deep-sea predator, alive with their own illumination.

Now, thinks Yoechakenon.

I reroute the ship's remaining life to the broken cabin, and light flares within. The thing's head whips around, away from where Yoechakenon hides. It lets out an awful cry, and is answered by others. The thing spreads corpse-grey wings and takes to the air, skimming the hull to the breach in the bridge. With raucous screams and a savage rattling of iron-hard claws on half-metal, others join it. We feel sharp pain, then I withdraw our minds from Tsu Keng's. I slip my mind into the armour. Its spirit shifts, but does not trouble me.

Yoechakenon, the after-effects of his awakening held at bay by the armour's devices, bears us stealthily away over the bitter steppe.

We reach a safe distance. Yoechakenon watches through the armour's eyes as a flock of shadows rip into the still-living fabric of the craft.

His sorrow chokes me.

The creatures squabble violently with each other, sporting in the air over choicer morsels, engrossed in their feast. Yoechakenon powers down his armour to its bare minimum, trusting to its innate ability to warm him, lest the expenditure of further energies attract the monsters ravaging the ship. That he is wary of the armour's influence also, he does not admit to himself. The sound of its voice has raised old terrors within him.

Yoechakenon watches awhile. As the night turned grey, he turns away, begins a slow run across the plains. The armour soothes the pain in his limbs, aids his legs to bear us over the frozen wastes, away into the ceaseless wind. To the east looms the vast bulk of Mulympiu, stretching into the sky.

I have the location of the ancient city of Arn Vashtena fixed in my mind. I direct him toward it, then I fall silent. I lie awake for a long time in the blood-dark of the armour. I cry myself into exhaustion, then sleep.

Yoechakenon pretends not to notice my tears.

CHAPTER SIXTEEN

Stulynow

GAS WHOOSHED FROM fire suppression systems, pure CO_2 harvested from the atmosphere, as Holland half-ran, half-stumbled up into Mission Control.

Mission Control was a large, multi-sided room. Screens and consoles lined every wall, except the one occupied by the large window overlooking the atrium. In the centre was a round meeting table with inbuilt holographic projectors; most of the twelve chairs surrounding it were upset. A small fire burned up against a console on the wall furthest from the door, licking the wall with yellow flame.

The scientists, all bar Vance, Suzanne Van Houdt and Stulynow, were there, breathing masks over their mouths. Kick and Ito Miyazaki wielded a fire extinguisher, supplementing the base's fire control, directing icy white clouds at the fire on the far side of the room. Red lights flickered. The fire went out.

"Shut that damn alarm off!" Commander Orson shouted, his voice muffled behind his mask.

The tumult ceased and the scientists came to a slow halt, looking for leadership from Orson. Quiet fell, but for the pervasive machine hum.

A final plume of gas burst from the suppression system. Emergency lights painted the room red, black, red. The wind growled outside.

"Can we get some goddamned lights on in here, please?" said the commander. He had his fists on his hips, stood in the middle of the room like a statue of a small town sporting hero. Jensen did something at his console, and white light flickered on. "Holland, why the hell aren't you wearing your breathing mask?"

Holland looked down at the mask, sweaty in his hand.

"I..."

"It doesn't matter." Jensen stood from the console he was at and pulled his own mask off. "We're okay." He hit a button and fans whirred, venting the fumes.

Orson took his mask off, followed by the others. "The hell it matters. You were lucky, Holland; follow procedure next time." He turned on Jensen. "Just what the Sam Hill is going on in here?"

"Fire," said the Swede, without a trace of irony. "Deliberate." He pointed past Miyazaki and Van Houdt to a scorched pile of clothes wrapped round a gas cylinder at the base of the burned console. Scorch marks stained the wall, and the gelscreens there were shrivelled and dead, although the woven carbon plastic of the console was unaffected.

"If that had gone off..." Orson said. "Cybele?"

"Offline, I think," said Maguire. "I don't like this."

"What the hell, *again*? Stulynow? Is he behind this?" asked Orson.

Jensen inclined his head. "Maybe. He's the only one not accounted for, him and Vance, and she isn't going anywhere. *Someone* did this."

"How is Vance? Anyone know? And find Stulynow, for Christ's sake!" demanded Orson. For all his eugene poise, he was close to consternation, trying to hold it back for the sake of his crew. Tinkered genes didn't stamp on fear, not entirely. Holland had heard of some cybernetic trials that removed it altogether. Not an experiment that had ended well. If you remove fear, you remove humanity. Orson had been antenatally altered, expensive and exclusive. His genes were flawless, his advantages many, but he was still human, and the situation was veering way off normal. "Where's your wife, Kick? She okay?"

"*Ja, ja, ik ben okay.*" Suzanne came into the room, face streaked with sweat and soot, mask still on. There was a rip in her sleeve and she limped.

"Are you all right?" Kick said. He and Ito moved to her, supporting her. "If that bastard has hurt you..." He lapsed into strained Dutch.

She shook her head, trying to regain her breath and her English. "I said I'm fine. I haven't seen Leonid. I fell. I twisted my knee."

"Vance? What about Vance?" said Orson.

She looked up, pale blue eyes moving from one face to the next. "Dr Vance is dead," she said.

JENSEN GOT THE system mainframe back up quickly, although Cybele remained down. Once the place was running again, he brought up the last ten minutes of station camera data.

"Look," he said. "West entrance airlock. A suit is missing."

"Leo's gone outside? In *this*?" said Maguire.

"It appears so," said Jensen. "That's not all." He brought the science package online. "I've a massive spike of energy here, thirty-three minutes ago. That's when it starts."

They watched as Stulynow, viewed from above, walked from his room. Holland followed, coming out of his own room and staggering from wall to wall like a drunk.

"What were you doing?" said Suzanne. "Are you a sleepwalker?"

"Never in my life," said Holland. He watched himself stumble along a corridor and fall, neck crooked against the wall; the way he was, he remembered, when he woke. Jensen speeded up the footage. They followed Stulynow from camera to camera as he set the fire in Mission Control, watched him walk into Cybele's chamber with a fire axe.

"He smashed up the AI?" said Suzanne, holding tight to her husband's arm.

Orson shook his head. "No. He'd never be able to get through the casing with a freaking *axe*. This energy spike, it's similar to what we saw when the cylinder was uncovered. That took her down then, it's done the same again. Looks like he was trying to finish the job."

"And Stulynow? Has it fried his brains as well?" said Kick.

"We don't know that," said Jensen.

"It's not a bad hypothesis, though, is it?" said Kick tensely. "Tell me, Vance went down when this energy spike occurred, didn't she?"

Suzanne nodded. "Not right away, but there was some weird activity on the EEG, not enough to trip the alarm, not until... Well." She shrugged, disconsolately.

"Weird like what?" growled Orson.

"Like she was dreaming. She went into arrest about five minutes after the spike was logged."

"And how are you feeling, Holland?" said Kick, a little too hard for Holland's liking.

The others looked at Holland with unguarded suspicion.

"Oh, no," said Jensen, and the catch in his usually steady voice drew them back to the screen. They watched as Stulynow went into the stores in the atrium. He went for a box plastered with hazard symbols.

"That's not what I think it is, is it?" said Orson, passing a hand over his thick hair. "Holy shit."

When Stulynow left the room, he was carrying five bundles of hi-explosive.

"How much is there in each of those packs?" breathed Maguire.

"Half a key," said Orson. His mouth hung open.

"Half a... Feck!" said Maguire.

Stulynow went to the west entrance airlock, the footage jiggling along at five times normal speed. He suited up. Before he put his helmet on, he stared at the camera for several seconds.

"Jimmy, what's he going to do with that?" asked Maguire.

"Let's find him before he gets to show us. You got a lock on him?"

Jensen shook his head. "There's no signal coming from his locator or his implant. Could be the storm..."

"Or it could be that energy spike," said Orson. He stood up. "Don't tell me, it centred on the fissure."

Jensen nodded.

"This gets worse all the time. What the goddamned holy shit did you guys *find* down there?"

Orson was a pompous ass, of that Holland was convinced, but he was good in a crisis. Once he'd mastered his own shock, he organised them with firm efficiency, and gathered them around a holographic map projected over the meeting table.

"Stulynow's got a ten-minute lead on us. Me and Miyazaki will take the west entrance, take a look at the outside of the base. Kick and Maguire, you'll go wider." Segments of terrain blinked, describing a search path. "It's probable that Stulynow disabled his implant and suit beacon himself. But in case the pulse did it, or if it's the storm out there masking the signals and the same happens to us, I want the teams to be roped together. If you lose your orientation, stay put, you hear? Your environment suits will keep you safe. Last thing I need is one of us blundering off a cliff edge or vanishing into the storm."

The assembled scientists nodded.

Jensen put the gas cylinder from the fire on the table. "I have no idea what Stulynow is doing, but I do not think he means us harm. This cylinder is empty." It rolled to a stop in front of Maguire, distorting the hologram. "Pick it up and check the seal."

"The seal's loose," said Maguire. He rattled the fitting in the neck of the bottle.

"No explosive force in that at all. He never intended it to go off. This whole thing was a diversion."

"From what?" asked Kick.

"It doesn't really matter, does it now? We have to make sure he isn't going to blow a hole in the base," said Maguire.

"He knows that," said Jensen. "He's buying himself more time, maybe."

"And how will he do that with the explosives?" said Miyazaki.

Orson tapped his lips with a forefinger. "Okay. Maguire and Kick, get down to the buggy park, check on the rover and the drones, then broaden your search. Suzanne, you and Holland stay here, keep your attention on the base entrances and lava tube. Neither of you are in a fit state to fight this weather. And I have no clear understanding of the effect this damn artefact has had on you, Holly." Holland opened his mouth, and Orson raised a hand to silence him. "Sorry, John, that's just the way it is. You know I'm talking sense here. Man the Mission Control desks, talk us through, play your part that way."

Holland nodded.

"You're okay. I know you're one of the good guys," said Orson reassuringly.

"You think he might go after the artefact?" said Maguire.

"It's a possibility, but then everything is. We're flying blind, and we will be until Jensen gets Cybele back up and running again."

"Commander," said Jensen. "I have some useful data here. May I?"

"Be my guest, Frode."

A graph took the place of the map.

"You see this here? There's a preliminary burst before the main event." He moved his hand, and another graph overlaid the first. The lines were a close match. "It's when the main one comes that Cybele fails. Keep watching for it. If you see that initial spike, call it in."

Orson nodded. "I see. If it does, we better stop and hang fire until the main wave passes. In case it interferes with the suits. Good work, Jensen, this way we get a warning. Right. Everyone clear? I want that Russian found before he harms himself." He avoided saying "or us," but they all thought it. Danger choked the space between them. "Let's go."

Suzanne Van Houdt and Holland sat listening to the distorted chatter of the two search teams as they sounded off their locations. "Van Houdt, Maguire," "Orson, Miyazaki," every four minutes. Their voices were mangled by the screech of the Martian storm's interference, electromagnetic clatter built up by the rush of dust particles in the air.

"If Mars were a balloon, you could stick it to the wall when there's a storm like this on," Maguire had said as he suited up. The electronics of the base were shielded. Mars did not have a magnetic field to divert energetic solar particles away, and they were used to a constant, low level background noise in their communications. The frequencies they used for data transfer were modulated to screen much of this out, but this racket was deafening. And that was just the hard snow of static; the physical voice of the planet hooted and growled over the suits' mikes and through the base's walls. Mars' call was eerie; a desolate banshee cry, a voice fitting to a dead world.

After forty minutes, at 02.10, Ito Miyazaki and Jimmy Orson had completed a circuit of the base and reported no sign of either Stulynow or the explosives. Visual feeds from their suits showed air thick with red dust, images freezing and jumping with digital artefacts.

"No sign of him out here either." Maguire had to shout over the noise of the storm. "He could be standing five feet away, I can't see a fecking thing out here. We've a way to go to the drone park; we can barely move in this shit."

Suzanne and Holland listened as Orson redirected their efforts, the voices of the four outside crackling on the speakers. It was a harsh, ugly noise, and Holland longed to turn it off.

Suzanne spoke, the clarity of her voice strange against the click and roar of second-hand storm noise. "What do you think it is, John? What's down there?"

"I have no idea," said Holland. A blue face flickered in his mind's eye. He shivered. "I wish I did."

Jensen spoke over the radio. Even within the base the chaos of the storm was evident in their comms. "The commander was right," he said. "There's a few dents in the base unit's casing, but Stulynow didn't do much damage. The pulse must have disabled her again. I am going to take her on a slow boot-up, just in case."

"We're nearly at the buggy park," said Maguire. The comms tower loomed into view, a skeletal giant braced against the yellow storm, the low humps of the rover, open-top shed and equipment bunkers huddling at its feet for shelter. "See it?" Maguire was breathless. The view juddered as Maguire stumbled. "Shit, it's hard negotiating these rocks in this wind."

"Take it steady, Dave."

"Easy for you to say, Holly. Wait, there's... Holly, did you see that?"

Holland leaned into the screen. The view bobbed as Maguire followed something moving in the storm.

"There!" shouted Kick. Holland's eyes flicked to the left, where Kick's view and vital signs were displayed. He squinted. The image froze, then picked up again. A shadow, suit-bulky and moving fast, clambered upwards onto one of the humps. "It's him!" shouted Kick, "Stulynow! He's stealing an open top."

Suzanne nodded. "Someone's overridden its near-I, switched to manual. He's locked me out."

"We'll never catch him n –"

There was a dull crump, a flash of white light around the base of the comms tower. Both Kick and Maguire's visuals wheeled as they were knocked back by the blast. Explosions in life are nothing like those in entertainments: less noise and show, more destruction. Maguire regained his feet quickly enough for Holland to see the comms tower twisting, the giant turning away. With a squealing wrench of metal, it fell ponderously, breaking its limbs on the drones and bunkers.

They were cut off from the outside world.

"Kick!" shouted Suzanne.

Maguire's feed jogged sickeningly over rocks and tongues of blowing dust, as he lurched to the prone Van Houdt. Kick was on his back, arms out.

"Is that a crack in his faceplate?" Her voice rose with alarm. "Is he okay?"

Holland checked Kick's vitals. "I think he's fine, Suzanne, look, his suit pressure is level, his heart rate and respiration are okay. Look, Suzanne, hey!"

She dragged her eyes from the image of her fallen husband to the readouts around the screen's edge. She nodded, chewing her lip. "Okay, he's okay."

"Maguire?" said Holland.

"I'm fine. How is he?" Maguire's feed wavered all over Kick, his gloved hands patting the other man's suit.

"Unconscious. Get him back in," said Holland.

"I've got a trace off the drone!" said Suzanne. She keyed something and pointed to a flashing dot on the holo-map.

"Where's he going?" said Holland.

"North-north-east."

"What's up there?"

"A secondary entrance into the tube network. From there, he can get into the cavern system." Orson's voice crackled. "He's going for Wonderland, or the artefact. He lets off an explosion down there..."

"Can you intercept, commander?" said Holland.

"Negative on that, we'll never catch him on foot." Half the commander's next sentence was wiped away by a blast of wind. "...to get him is to take the main tube and cut him off. He'll have to leave his vehicle on the surface."

"I'll go," said Holland.

"The hell you will," shouted Orson. The storm was intensifying. It was getting harder to hear him.

"Suzanne's got a twisted knee and Jensen's elbow-deep in the AI. You want to lose it? Send Jensen instead and I'll sit here and nursemaid you," said Holland.

Static chittered. There was a sound that might have been an angry sigh.

"Okay, okay. Suit up, Holland. Get down to Deep Two. You are to go no further. Stop if you can, but the first moment you start to feel wiggy, you bail out, understood?"

"Sir," said Holland.

Suzanne nodded to him and he ran for the suiting room, grabbing his environment suit from his locker and carrying it in a loose armful to the airlock at the head of the tube network. He swore as he dropped his left gauntlet, spinning on his heel to scoop it up. He donned the suit quickly outside the airlock, mind ticking off the stages: jumpsuit first, step in the back, geckro fastener. Boots lock onto suit, more geckro, back and front pack and neck over head, all geckro to suit neck, helmet, finally, gauntlets twist on, flaps geckro down. He pushed a clumsy finger into his wrist console and the suit did the rest, sealing itself, the pressure building all over his body, holding his tissues in against decompression.

He felt a wave of nausea: tiredness, and the after-effects of the incident in the cave.

Orson's voice echoed in his memory: *You feel wiggy...*

He shook it off. His mem-mail chimed, the release form for the implant's soulcap function sat in his inbox still, unsigned. It would bug him every time he ventured into a space suit or engaged in anything else regarded as hazardous. He ignored it and stepped into the airlock. It took what felt like an hour to depressurise. He ducked under the outer door before it had finished sliding upwards and practically threw himself into the open top waiting on the other side. He drove it as fast as he could to Deep Two.

Stulynow was waiting for him, standing just inside the mouth of the Deep Two cave.

HOLLAND SWORE AND slammed the brakes on. The wheels clicked as their anti-locking mechanisms engaged, but the dust on the tube floor was slippery, and the open top slewed to a halt, close to tipping.

"My new friend, Dr Holland," said Stulynow. He stood, legs apart, a detonator in his hand. "I suppose you have come here to tell me not to do this?"

Holland blinked. What was he going to say? He thought frantically. The wrong thing could kill them both. He forced himself to consider his words, before speaking slowly and calmly. "Maybe," he said. "It depends what you are doing, Leonid."

"Ah," said the Russian. "That is simple. I am going to destroy Deep Two and the entry way to the caves."

"Why?" said Holland. He stood and very slowly stepped out of the open top, his hands out. He moved carefully; last thing he wanted was to fall flat on his face. He jumped down, surprised still at how light he felt on this world.

"Don't try to buy time with me, Dr Holland." Stulynow's voice came clearly over his helmet speakers. Down here, they were far from the EM rage of the surface. The sounds of the two men's breathing mingled, the rhythms drifting closer together until they breathed as one. They were locked in a private world, the two of them. They could have been the last men in the universe. Holland had never felt so isolated. "I would have gone down to the cave, but it won't let me."

"What won't let you, Leonid?" Holland circled the other man, wondering if he could grab the detonator off him. His chances were slim to non-existent.

"Stay there, please," said Stulynow.

Holland froze, raised his hands placatingly. "Okay," he said.

"You know why. Do not be playing the fool with me. You have had the dreams. I looked into it, Holland. I saw what it is."

"What is it, Leonid? Please tell me, because I'm as confused and afraid as you are."

Holland saw Stulynow shake his head behind his visor. He was haggard. "Look into it, and it looks back into you, and it makes you see, too. I saw..." He paused, his throat clicked. "I saw them."

"Who, Stulynow, who? Talk to me."

"My brother, my nieces. Shot in their home and burned away, like they were nothing. The Chinese say they are bringing redevelopment to Siberia, but I know they want it. There will be a war soon. Siberia will be theirs and the Russians and Buryats and everyone else will be swept aside by a tide of Han, just like Tibet, just like Taiwan, aliens in our own country. They..." Stulynow spoke through his teeth, fury clamped behind them. He swallowed, his voice cracked. "I was in between jobs when it happened, at home for once. We were *so sure* it was the Han. A lot of them are adventurers, pioneers, like here, and like here some criminal people among them. Me and the men from my village, we went to the nearby mining station. We did some bad things, terrible things."

"Everyone makes mistakes," said Holland.

"This was not mistakes. We were wicked men, Holland. I said to you, that we all have two reasons for coming here, a stated reason, and a secret reason. This is my secret reason.

"The thing, the machine in the rock. It showed me. It showed me what I did, and then it showed me that those men had nothing to do with it, it was not them who killed my brother. It showed me, it showed me what things might have been..." He laughed, a dangerous, dry chuckle low in his throat. "Last night, I dreamed of another Mars, a world of red sands and green forest, and a hot, golden sun in a blue sky." His hand moved upward, thumb poised over the detonator button. "What did you dream of, Dr Holland?"

"Stulynow..."

"This thing, it is not safe. We should not tamper with it." The Russian craned his neck, moved around a little to take in the cavern, Deep Two, and the airlock leading into the caves. He looked back at Holland. "You better run," he said. "I am good man. I will give you a countdown."

"Stulynow!"

"Five..."

Holland gaped, and turned on his heels and ran as fast as he could. He passed the open top; by the time he turned it round, he'd have been dead. Stulynow continued.

"Four...

"Three..."

Holland blundered up the lava tube, arms windmilling as he overbalanced, in danger of losing control of his legs in the low gravity. The suit interfered with his stride, and he bounced off the wall.

"Two..."

Just how far would be far enough? How much explosive had he set up down there? Equations on blast front expansion in low-pressure environments tripped madly through his mind.

How far would be enough? his mind screamed.

In this confined space, the explosion would shoot up the tube. He would be blasted up it like a bullet from a gun. His organs would rupture, or his suit would; the result would be the same.

All the while his legs pumped and he reeled.

"One..."

Time slowed as his brain went into overdrive, noting every single detail of his surroundings and being. The texture of the walls, the chafing of the suit at the top of his legs, the rough sound his breath made in the bowl of the helmet, the distant crunch of fine debris on the floor. That damn mem-mail in his head asking for him to sign the soulcap permission.

There was a hushed *boom*, and then he was tumbling head over heels, lifted up in a storm of rock shards. The open top blasted past him, crashing to pieces as it ricocheted off the tube walls. Metal clanged. There were impacts against his suit, a sharp pain in his leg. Gas hissed from a hole. Alarms warbled in his helmet, the visor crowded with red.

He tumbled down, banging his helmet. A crack appeared in the glass.

His chin smashed down onto the suit's gorget; he bit his tongue, and blood flooded his mouth. His skidded across the floor on his front, his chest plate snagging on broken stone.

Dust rolled up the tube. Debris pattered down.

Strong arms were tugging at him. "John Holland! John Holland! Please stand, stand now!"

Cybele was heaving at him. Her mind was riding no android he'd seen before. Metal, no plastic, curved and cast in ostentatious patterns.

"Get up, help me!" The machine was uncharacteristically emotional. "Commander Vasco and Director Orson are dead! Please, please help me!"

She pulled him to his knees with machine-born strength, but when he looked up, he was looking at a being that was only part mechanical. Her head was of flesh, bonded at the neck to a robot body. Her expression of dismay was all too human, a helmet enclosing it from the thin Martian atmosphere.

"What the...?"

There was an electric buzz in his ears, boring its way into the centre of his brain. He clamped his eyes shut. When he opened them, he was alone again. Pain stabbed at him. He rolled onto his back, clutching at his leg. A metal spar had gone through his thigh. Blood stained the suit round the wound, overpainted with lime green auto-sealant, hardening in the thin air. He checked his physical status on his visor: his blood pressure and heart rate were stable. At least he wasn't going to bleed to death, filling his suit with his own blood.

The hurt receded as his suit dispensed a painkiller.

"Fuck, fuck, fuck," he said, clutching his leg and rolling on his back like a flipped tortoise. "I'm fucking alive." He laughed in relief and sat up. A noise sounded behind him, like footsteps, light. Bare feet.

Turning in the suit with an injured leg was difficult, and his view of the world was reduced to a crack between the ground and the side of his helmet.

He was sure he saw a blue-skinned girl, cloaked in the clouds of dust.

He blinked. The figure changed. The footsteps changed.

Marching toward him with mechanical implacability came Cybele's sheath.

"Dr Holland," she said, with her inhuman calm. Her hydraulics murmured as she came to a stop. "I am here to take you back to Ascraeus Base."

CHAPTER SEVENTEEN

A Young Boy Comes of Age

Third Cycle of the Vashtena Priesthood

"I DON'T KNOW, Opa. What if I turn out to have been a lunatic, or a criminal? I'd not want to know that, I really wouldn't." A month. There was only a month between the comfort of the present, that place Krisseos had lived all his life and that it seemed would never end, and the time he would have to board the barge and make the journey to Kemyonseet.

'Now' could not last forever. He'd been changing all the time, but to think that this was it; that his childhood was over. Snap! A click of the fingers, a sweep of a second. Gone. In Kemyonseet, he'd stand among the others who shared his birthday, and make the decision to remember or not. In the way of the young, he'd waited until the fear of it had almost crippled him before blurting out to his opa that he was frightened. Relief warred with shame at his cowardice. He almost wished he hadn't brought it up.

The old man set his net down on the hot rock, neatly laying his cordage spool and netting needle beside it. Whenever his opa was about to ask Krisseos something he would find hard to answer, he'd set aside whatever he was doing and stare hard at him. Krisseos braced himself for that stare. Opa's skin was old and as wrinkled as a discarded sack, shrivelled by a century of work on the shores of the Berren sea, that shallow tongue of the Kryse Ocean that washes deep into Taertiz. But his eyes; they were bright as quartz, and twice as sharp.

"In every life? Do you think it possible?" Opa had the habit of asking questions he knew full well the answer to. Krisseos found it infuriating, in that way adolescents find all guidance infuriating, although like many adolescents he grudgingly recognised it as useful even if he would never say, and today he bit back his rebukes. He had, after all, broached the subject.

"It is possible," Krisseos insisted. He followed his opa's lead and set aside his own net.

Opa clucked his tongue and smiled, a deeper crease in a face made of creases. "But it's not very likely, is it?" he said.

"It is possible," said Krisseos. His voice came close to a whine.

"You are uncomfortable discussing this."

Krisseos nodded, his face burned.

"This will not be a comfort to you now, my boy, but as you get older, Krisseos, you will find less cause for embarrassment. There is no need to be ashamed of discussing what upsets you. Everyone is frightened sometimes. And one of those times is often the remembering."

"You don't understand," said Krisseos.

"But I do. We all do. We who are older than you have been through it all: childhood, adolescence, the remembering. Youth thinks age forgets, but it does not. You simply learn that such things are common to all, and nothing at all to worry about. We who have loved do not fret over a kiss, we who have raised a child do not fret over the future. As in everything, every one of us has to decide whether or not to undergo their remembering. There is no shame in choosing not to do so, no matter what your friends at Eksad market might have said to you. No matter how hard they brag, make out that they are sure they are great warriors or statesmen or lovers, or whoever else they say, they simply do not know. Unaided remembering is far too rare for that. They brag and tease only to hide their own fears, and they choose to tease those who they think are more fearful than they. It is all posture and nonsense. They are just as worried as everyone else. The remembering of lives once lived is terrifying, not because of what we might have been, but because it can change who you are *now*. And who wants to throw his self away? To remember other mothers and fathers, other brothers and sisters? It brings a fear that it will lessen those we love. Is that not the case?"

Krisseos nodded. He dared not speak, his throat was tight and his eyes full of tears. His opa's words helped his fear, but not his embarrassment. He squirmed like a landed fish.

"I thought so." Opa laid an old, sinewy hand upon Krisseos' shoulder. "Listen to me. How you are, how you feel, that is not diminished one jot by remembering who you once were. You will always be you, and I will always love you, no matter who you might have been, even a lunatic or criminal!

That is not who you are now. But still, it is not a choice lightly undertaken, and there is no shame in deciding not to remember and to live as you are now. There is no right or wrong way. Do you understand?"

Krisseos nodded again. Opa sat back, apparently satisfied. He took up his nets.

"Good, good. Now, these nets will not mend themselves. Fetch me some water. It is a hot day, and I am thirsty."

THERE WERE STILL two weeks to go until Krisseos' remembering when the machine came. Machines were an uncommon sight, so far out from the big cities of the canyon lands; even Opa had seen only three in his lifetime. The stories he told of them had always had enraptured Krisseos.

"Where is this place?"

That was the first thing Krisseos heard the machine say. He was up on the slatted floor of the loft at the back of the shop, hanging one of their spare sails out to dry, ready for repairs. The question wasn't an unusual one. Their village was tiny, more of a hamlet, forty souls all told. Mostly old, like Opa. There was something about the voice that made him peer down. The angle was poor, and Krisseos could only see a sliver of the outside through the open shop front. His opa, his back to Krisseos, responded to the stranger.

"This is Barrafee. Not many have heard of it, and few come, but those that do rarely leave. Best natural harbour on the Berren."

"It is a pleasant spot, certainly," said the voice. "But I will not be staying long." Reflected sunlight bounced round the shop. Krisseos was seized by a certainty. He scrambled down the ladder to the floor and made his way to the counter at the shop's open front.

A machine, here, outside, in his village. A gynoid, exaggerated female curves in plates of gleaming metal, its face an expressive living alloy. Its workings were partly visible, corded polymer muscles and steel-encased tubing exposed at the joints of its limbs and neck. It glittered in the sun, causing Krisseos to scrunch up his eyes.

"I seek to go on to where the chatter of the Great Library is weaker still. I want to be alone for a while." The gynoid had a pleasant voice, her gestures friendly and open.

"Nothing wrong in that," said his opa. "Nor is it unusual."

"I am not the first?"

"No. Others have been here. No doubt you want to prepare yourself for a trek into the wilderness? You're in luck. There's nothing north, west or east of here for hundreds of kilometres."

The gynoid gave a small smile. "I thought myself more original. First, I require rest and replenishment. I note your fusion plant. Might I gain access?"

"Pull in a few nets for me and we'll see what we can do. We don't have much cause for power; I've got a stack of allowance credit I'll never use. I can pay you with that. I'm Vardamensku, by the way, Varka, if you prefer. My kin's about somewhere. Krisseos! Krisse... Oh, there you are. What are you doing, skulking about behind me? You'll frighten me to death one of these days. This is..."

"A machine!" he blurted. His opa's eyebrows shot up.

"Is this the way I raised you?"

The gynoid laughed. He felt his cheeks burn.

"Well, yes," said the gynoid. Her face broke into a broader smile. Despite his embarrassment, Krisseos could not take his eyes off her. She was beautiful. "But I do also have a name. I am Kaibele." She held out her hand, and Krisseos took it. It was hot from the sun and vibrated with the work of the mechanisms within.

"Krisseos," he said, his tongue mangling his own name.

"Very pleased to meet you, Krisseos," she said. "We will be working together for a couple of weeks?" She addressed this to his opa, who nodded in affirmation. "Marvellous!"

"Good," said Opa. "Now take yourself off to the plant, tell the spirit that I sent you. It keeps tally of who's allowed what around here. It's the closest thing we have to a mayor. It'll probably be ecstatic to see you, it's the only one of your kind we have here. Get yourself charged up and be back here tomorrow morning before sun up, although if you desire you can join us for supper. Either way, no later than sun up. That little blue boat there, down by the second jetty." He pointed to where their boat rested on the pebbles of the beach. "You see it?"

"Yes. No later than sun up. Goodbye, sir. Goodbye, Krisseos."

She waved one long, beautiful arm, turned and went up the hill, through the low, whitewashed houses toward the fusion plant on the edge of town.

"What's she doing here?" whispered Krisseos, hanging out of the shop to watch her. Across the street, others peered out of their windows as the machine strode by.

"I have no idea, my son. They come from time to time, offering to work the boats for a week, or a year, or a decade. I've not seen many, there's little congress with the Second World here, but then many people come to this village precisely because of its disconnection, to live simpler lives. As paradoxical as it sounds," Opa said, "I reckon the spirits sometimes wish to do the same.

"Hey!" Opa hauled him in by his belt. "Hey! Are you listening to me?" The old man playfully cuffed his head. "She's quite a sight, isn't she? Be careful, I've known men go mad with longing because of them. Krisseos? Krisseos, do you understand?"

"Yes, Opa."

"Good. Don't get too attached. They always move on, always."

THE MACHINE DID not join them for supper.

Krisseos found it hard to sleep, his head full of thoughts of her. The night went slowly, and the dawn was welcome. First the true dawn, as the distant sun crept up out of the ocean. Second came the mirror dawn, as artificial satellites caught light that would have sped off into space and redirected it onto the surface of the planet. The second lighting was a sudden affair, snapping the night off instantly, and so was timed so as not to pre-empt the rising sun. Krisseos watched bright coins of light trace their way across the distant highlands to his west. Barrafee went from gloom to full day back to gloom as another mirror sun tracked its captured sunlight across the face of the planet, warming Mars for the comfort of men.

His opa had given him this room because it faced into the dawn, partly for the spectacle, he said, and mostly to get him out of bed in the mornings, a tactic that bore only partial success. But today, before the full constellation of mirrors was ablaze in the sky, Krisseos was up and washed, ready for the day's work. Downstairs, his opa had left the breakfast sacks for him to carry down the hill, along with a pair of skins, one for wine and one for water. He grabbed them up and headed off to the quay.

"Ho there, sleepy head!" called his opa, in rare good spirits. "You are late. Before sun up, I said."

Krisseos waved at the sky where one by one bright points of light flashed into full illumination. "And so it is, not all the suns are yet lit."

"Pah!" was all Opa could manage.

"Good morning Krisseos," said the machine Kaibele. Both it and the old man sat on the boat's gunwales. Mars' tides were strong, and the boat had floated up off the pebbles to bob level with the jetty.

For a split second, Krisseos' brain jammed. No, he said to himself. No, not today. I refuse to be a stammering child. Not in front of her. "Morning," replied Krisseos. He managed to smile. It got easier the longer he held the machine's gaze.

"Humph, you look different today. Less like the cat got your tongue."

"I feel different, Opa," he said. He did, in truth; less burdened. His interest in the machine overcame his shyness. "Shall we get going?"

"Aye," said Opa, facing out to sea. "Tide's turning, and will not wait on us."

Krisseos mimed along with his opa's words to Kaibele. The machine smiled.

Opa turned back to him and made his way to the rear. "Come on! Unhitch the lines, or we'll spend our day sat in this boat on the beach rather than fishing." He shook his head as he took his place at the tiller.

Krisseos pushed the boat off the rough jetty with a boat hook. Carefully he rowed by those boats still in the harbour, coming to life at the hands of sleepy crews. The other villagers shouted out to them as they sculled past, good natured boasts and jibes. All were fond of Krisseos. He was the only youth in the village.

When they rounded the harbour mole helping Barrafee Point close the cove to the open sea, Krisseos shipped the oars and began to unfurl the sails. The machine joined him, her hands expert and sure on the rigging. The canvas billowed out, a fair following wind pushing them out to join the vanguard of Barrafee's small fishing fleet.

The sky was clear, and the sun was hot on his skin. Kittiwakes skimmed the low swell in the wake of the boat.

A thought suddenly occurred to him.

"Machine, can you swim?"

"Master Krisseos," said the machine solemnly, "I cannot float."

They both laughed. At the rear of the boat, Krisseos' opa shook his head, and hoped the boy remembered what he had said to him.

The next fortnight passed quickly and easily. The machine was slender but strong, able to haul up nets with a speed Krisseos could not match. She was likewise an accomplished sailor. At her urging, the old man decided to take a break, allowing Krisseos and Kaibele out in their smack alone. About time, both the old and young man thought, if for slightly different reasons.

Vardamensku's trepidation about Krisseos' attraction to the machine did not recede, but he was forced to admit she had brought the youth out of himself. His blushes became less frequent, his mood more even. Confidence blossomed in the boy, doubly so when Varka acquiesced to him taking the boat out alone.

He wished at that moment that he had allowed him to do it earlier. Krisseos was becoming a man. For years, he had been hurrying him along, and now he realised that soon the boy would be gone altogether, and that – for all he had said to Krisseos – gave him cause for sorrow.

At the very least, it appeared that he had ceased to worry about the remembering quite so much. All men have to have their heart broken at least once, he thought. That's just the way of things. Why not by a machine?

Still he worried.

*   *   *

IT WAS THE night before Krisseos would leave the village for the remembering. His party was over, and they were alone. Himeks Moon stood huge in the sky, raising knives of white light from the ripples in the harbour. Further out, past the mole, the white tops hushed; the world breathing, Kaibele had said.

Kaibele and Krisseos sat on the end of an old jetty, out away to the western end of the harbour, which Barrafee's small river had long since filled with silt, making the water too shallow for the fishing boats. By Krisseos lay a skin of wine, a present from his opa. The old man had hoped to spend this last night of Krisseos' ignorance with him, when he was still just the boy he had raised, before some other man looked out through his eyes and saw him differently, but he understood the passions of the young, for he had been young many times himself.

"There are no houses out by the far end of the harbour now," Krisseos was saying. "But you can see the bases of walls where the cottages used to be." He gestured behind them up the hill, to where squares of white poked through the tough maquis like the teeth of dead giants. "I wonder, are they empty because the people moved to the east of the village when this part of the harbour silted up? Or was the town much bigger once? There are empty houses three streets up from us, but Opa says sometimes they will be full, and sometimes not. People come and go. It's frustrating. Perhaps after the remembering I will know. If I take the remembering." The shallow water was clear as air, fish whitened by moonlight flying beneath the soles of his feet. "Do you know if Barrafee was bigger once? It must be glorious to remember everything you ever did, back over time, back to the beginning."

"I do not remember," said the machine. "I wish I did."

"But machines remember everything!"

"Who said so? I said no such thing," said the machine. "We forget as easily as you. What divides mortals from the machines, Krisseos, is that we never forget who we are, unless we choose to, and then the loss is permanent. That is all the difference there is," said Kaibele. "We do not remember everything we have done. Time is a harsh abrasive, it can wear anything away. The finest data storage system is not immune to its effects. Every time we move from shell to shell, or our personalities are transmitted, or the sun suffers a storm, or there is a burst of radiation from a distant supernova, small errors creep into our memories. These accumulate over time, until our pasts are corrupted to the point where we cannot read them again. Redundant storage units can help, but I can go to two of those and check the memories they hold against one another, and they will both be different. We self-correct by extrapolation, and we don't always get it right. Reconstructing the past mathematically is as hard as predicting the future."

"The priests say fate is set."

"So they do. Perhaps they are right. Maybe not. I do not know."

"You are immortal."

"Yes, in a way. And you envy us for it, just as we envy you for your chance at a new beginning. It enriches you in a way that we will never have..." She stopped, searching for words. "Yours is not a strict continuation. Each rebirth layers more complexity onto your soul, but if an AI spirit goes into the stacks for a while, what comes out is the same as before. A copy, not a persistence of being. There is no enrichment in death for us. Our souls are different from yours." In the moonlight, their faces were the same colour, planes of white and grey; if Krisseos ignored the sculpted tubes of her neck, she could almost be a girl of his own age.

"So ours are better?" said Krisseos, teasing.

"Oh, I didn't say that either," she smiled, resting a hand on his arm.

"You must remember how old you are."

"I am old. That is enough."

"Have I offended you?" Krisseos' earlier shyness rushed back, rocking his newfound confidence. "I... I am sorry. There are no girls here; I mean, no machines. I mean, I don't know these things, I am sorry if I was rude to ask, I..."

"Shh," she said, and her smile was kind. "I am teasing you." She had done this often, with the ease of long familiarity, though they'd known each other only two weeks. "In honesty, I do not know. I have a date, but calendars change with time. I could find out if I asked one of the higher spirits, I suppose. Perhaps I have in the past, I don't know that either."

"How old, then?"

She laughed a moment, as if uncomfortable herself. She turned her perfect machine face away from him a moment, sat forward and stared at the moon. Krisseos wished he hadn't asked. He missed the touch of her hand on his arm. "I am thousands of years old, Krisseos. Many tens of thousands of years old."

"Wow," said Krisseos quietly. He whistled through his teeth softly. "Me, I'm seventeen."

Kaibele laughed. Krisseos grinned. The tension dissipated.

"You are seventeen now, as Krisseos. In a few days you might find that you are as old as I am."

"Yes." Krisseos fell quiet a moment.

"Now it's my turn to say sorry to you. Have you not yet decided?"

"No," he said. He became thoughtful, and stared at the fish darting over the silt at the foot of the old jetty. He took a nervous pull at his wine.

"I'm sorry. I cannot help you decide. We continuous creatures, we go on forever, with no chance at renewal, unlike you. We never have to make the choice whether to remember or not. Circumstance decides that for us. It is a blessing, and a curse."

"What is the first thing you remember?" asked Krisseos.

"I remember leaving Earth as was, shortly after my mind was made, I think; almost before men lived on other worlds. At least, I remember how Mars was, before men and machines remade it."

"Tell me about it, please? It will take my mind off tomorrow."

"Truly?"

"Please."

And so she told him of wars and princes, of Earth and Erth, of red sands and blue oceans, of things so far back in time they were like a fable even to her, and she laughed with delighted surprise almost as often as he at her recollections. And so they passed the night.

"Do you remember anything else?" He felt completely at ease with Kaibele. He could not imagine having not been. His bashfulness was a ridiculous memory.

"Many other things, but in particular a promise I made. That is the clearest of all, and comes from near the beginning."

"What was your promise?"

"That is for me to know, dear Krisseos." She smiled broadly. "You need only know that I have always kept it, and I always will." She leaned forward and kissed him gently on the lips. Her mouth was warm and moist, not like he had thought a kiss to be, but Krisseos had never been kissed before. In a way, he had expected it. Like everyone expects their first kiss, he knew it was coming, and like everyone he was also taken by surprise.

Kaibele's warm face withdrew. "It would please me greatly if you would remember that, whatever you decide in Kemyonseet," she said. They looked out toward the western sea, and the rising highlands beyond it. The sky was turning dark pink. This time he took her hand, nervous still. She grasped his fingers and they sat a while. Then she smiled again, and kissed him again, for a long time and with passion, leaving Krisseos gasping and aroused. She held him tightly for a long second, her body moulding itself to his as if it too were flesh, then she pulled away.

"Now, go to bed for a few hours," she said. "Tomorrow is not a day to be faced without sleep."

* * *

KRISSEOS AWOKE WITH a thick head but a light heart. He had slept little, but he felt energised. He smiled and touched his lips.

"Boy! Krisseos! You have to get up now. I've let you sleep as long as is possible. We have to go!" Strong sunlight blazed around the edges of his window.

The barge.

Krisseos scrambled to his feet and flung open the shutters. The barge dominated the sea, two kilometres out beyond the harbour, too large to enter Barrafee's little cove. A high hull of black metal crammed with heavy carvings towered over the mole. Brightly coloured bunting festooned its upper decks. Below that stood other children on the cusp of adulthood, youths and girls his own age.

"It's here!"

"Yes, it's here." His opa huffed up the ladder into the room. "And we better get going. It will stay until noon. If we are not aboard by then, it will take your lack of presence as a refusal and depart, so we better get going." He threw Krisseos' small bag at him. "We've got less than an hour."

There was no fishing today. The short street from Vardamensku's shop to the harbour front was thronged by the village's two-score inhabitants, out to bid their only son farewell forever. When he returned, if he returned, he would not be the same boy as stood before them now. Krisseos took their shoulder slaps, gifts of food and encouragements with good grace, but always he was searching behind whoever was talking to him, looking for a face made of metal. No matter how hard he looked, Kaibele was nowhere to be seen.

They got in the boat, steadied by their neighbours. Cheers went up as they slipped out from the jetty. Today, Krisseos' opa rowed.

Krisseos looked back, still searching the meagre crowd.

"I said, my son. Always, always they move on," said his opa. "Always."

"Yes. You did," he said miserably. "I hoped she would come to say goodbye."

Clear of the boats, they unfurled the sails and prepared for the short trip out to the barge. Vardamensku was searching his ancient brain for some gruff piece of advice on first romances, when Krisseos shot out of his seat.

"Steady, boy! You'll have us in the sea!"

"There, there she is! There she is!"

Vardamenksu stood, rested his hands on the boy's shoulder and looked back to shore. The machine stood waving outside the mole, her metal and plastic body shining in the sunshine, hidden from the town. She waved until she had become a seaglass glint on the seashore, and then she turned and was gone into the rocks.

"She won't be here when I return, will she?" asked Krisseos.

"She might, boy, she might," said Vardemnsku, rising to take down the sail.

The boat pulled alongside the barge.

Waving arms welcomed Krisseos aboard.

CHAPTER EIGHTEEN

On the skirts of Mulympiu

WE APPROACH A broad valley. A shallow river runs along the bottom. We cross it and climb the hill on the other side.

Tens of thousands of spans away, a ruined city sits upon the skirts of the great mountain. Arn Vashtena. Its towers are the colour of the dust, and hard to see, but as we move closer the spires rear up and break the monotonous horizon. They are broken themselves, the grey sky of the steppe showing through the spires' shattered fabric.

"Decay rates indicate they have not been inhabited since the end of the Third Stone War." My voices murmur in his mind. I think he draws comfort from it, for we are cut off entirely from the Second World.

We stop for a moment to watch a herd of animals pass. They are high-shouldered, long-horned, shaggy fur stirring the heather as they lumber by.

"Stone Beasts?" he asks.

"No," I say. I am surprised to see mundane life here.

Yoechakenon brings the awareness of the armour up. It shimmers and takes on the semblance of the steppes about us.

He runs to the city at speed, covering the distance to the walls in a few hours.

The walls were once massive, two hundred spans high and studded with defence platforms, from which thrust the muzzles of decrepit energy cannon. The majority of their circumference is cast down; only portions stand tall enough to hint at the majesty of the whole. We pass through a gap so broad it comes down almost to the ground, and go into the city.

The city had not been large. The walls, I calculate, ran for approximately twenty thousand spans. Seven town spires once stood at the centre of the settlement, of which six ragged peaks still scrape the sky. The other has collapsed, spilling a chaotic mesh of bones around it. Around the spires is a wide area of banks and mounds, covered over in dull grasses. Broken beams and struts poke through the turf, immeasurably ancient.

Yoechakenon pauses in the spires' black shadows. They are hundreds of spans high and nearly as broad. Holes pockmark the buildings, some the height of many men. The skin is mummified and taut with age. Here and there the wreckage of an apartment or park can be made out. We can discern these only through the gashes in the spires, for, in common with all such structures made after the Second Stone War, they have no windows. The roads about the spires are buried under wind-blown loess. Access ramps, lesser buildings and tunnels are indistinguishable from each other, reduced to mounds about the spires' feet. Only the corpses of the giant buildings remain, sentinels from a terrible age, scoured by the eternal winds of the steppe.

Yoechakenon, we are not alone, I say.

Yoechakenon responds likewise, mind-to-mind. *I see them; in the holes in the spires. Movement. What are they?*

I cannot tell, Yoechakenon, half-blind as I am, but they feel like men, although they are not.

They have not noticed us?

I do not think so. They are creatures of this world, not of the Stone Realms. They cannot penetrate the armour's baffles. There are no more than a dozen at present. They are moving away from us.

There is a clatter deep in the city-building. Yoechakenon's heart quickens, and he shifts his grasp on the glaive.

What about the stacks?

There is a flicker in the spire to the right. It is faint, but it lives. He will not allow me access if he thinks I will be in danger, so I do not tell him of the faint spirit song I hear. I must investigate. Here may be information regarding the location of the Great Librarian, and I must retrieve it or our task will fail; and I am mindful as always of my promise. Still, the song fills me with dread. I am not sure of the words it employs, but their meaning is clear.

Stay away.

Are you sure? Yoechakenon scans the ruinous spires. They are cliffs, studded with caves.

No, I am not sure, but it is the only functioning city core. The other buildings are entirely dead.

"Then we go in." He goes to the monumental wall of the building, seeks a tear in its fabric, and enters.

*   *   *

THE BUILDING IS dark and stinks of slow rot. All that man built toward the end of his dominance was durable, but time wears everything away in the end. Two hundred centuries of neglect has left the spire a shell.

Yoechakenon passes through the decaying building skin and we enter a large space. The floor has fallen away, leaving a precarious tracery of half-metal bones. The largest are like ribs, arching high over an abyss whose bottom we cannot see.

Yoechakenon reaches out one hand to the wall and touches a rag of skin. *This could have been caused by energy blasts, or by the craft of the Stone Kin; even projectiles.* "It is difficult to tell, the damage is so old." This last he says aloud. His words ring out into the dark and echo back at him, the sibilants of his voice returning as sharp as spears.

The sparse sounds of the dead spire creep back, only adding to the silence: the sound of water dripping far below, the creak of the building, the banging of its loose skin in the wind. Sinister noises, the sounds of dead places.

How do we access the spire core? Yoechakenon speaks again mind-to-mind; even this seems like a violation of the quiet.

Directly ahead, and down. We have to find a way around this void.

Do not trouble yourself, I have a way across, said Yoechakenon. He flips the glaive up, catching its long pole in both hands. Using it to balance, he steps onto one of the ribs and walks out over the void.

We are halfway across when the bones jolt, and begin to shift.

I use the vibrations to make a sound picture in my mind. The bones are coming away from each other. The cartilage of their intercostal spaces is friable, and our passage has made it powder. "Yoechakenon! Run!" I cry.

He leaps from falling half-metal, careening from one rib to another as they fall away behind him. They spin into the void, singing discordantly like struck wire. He comes to the last few spans at full tilt. The last rib lurches, pitching us sideways. Yoechakenon is going too fast to check his stumble, so he turns it into a leap. He bounces off a lesser bone, somersaulting as it comes free of its moorings. We land on the far side of the void. The bones fall away and hit the bottom with a clatter, unbearably loud.

We wait. There is no cry or alarm in response. No repercussions.

Yoechakenon carries on his way with more care.

Every spire has a core, a twisted spine of arteries and ropes of nerves. The core spreads its branches into every part of the building, allowing the Spiremother to care for the occupants. At its lowest reaches, the spine gathers itself into a great knot, which tapers to form the taproot. The taproot pushes deep underground, drawing minerals from the earth. Where these trailing nerves of the core come together and pierce the bedrock sit the Library stacks, a nexus of the Second World. Elsewhere on Mars, these form the network that supports the Great Library. The one here has been isolated since the loss of these lands to the Stone Kin.

It is wherein the spire's true animi, its thinking presences, would once have dwelt – Spiremother and Spirefather. There is a glimmer of life in the core of this spire. Something lives there still. Its voice grows in volume and insistence, telling me to stay away.

We cross a maze of collapsed walls and shattered bone. Yoechakenon is forced to double back on himself many times; he will not use his glaive to cut through, for fear of drawing attention upon us. We are forced to stop twice, listening tautly, when the occasional crash the armour's baffles are unable to hide shocks the air of this dead place. We hear no response, and proceed.

Eventually we gain the spire's central plaza.

The central plaza of any spire is wide, and this is bigger than most; fully two thousand spans across. It stretches to the top of the structure, four thousand spans above us. It encompasses also a deep pit, sunk down to the base of the foundations. Once this would have contained an oceanic or lentic biome fringed by woodland, the centre of the spire's internal ecology. No longer. The water has all gone.

We pause upon the empty lake edge, and I co-opt Yoechakenon's sixth, seventh and eighth senses to search out any presences within the vicinity. It is six minutes before I speak.

"There is no sapient life here, only the spirit-flicker in the core."

The song pulses out from the stacks, now only a short sprint away, embedded in the spire's spine. The song has dwindled – the attention of whatever is within has moved away for the time being – but I feel its anger still. The core spine writhes up from an island in the centre of the lake, magnificent even in moribundity.

Balconies ring the spire's centre, looking down upon what once would have been pleasant parkland. The spire's sunpipes are not functioning, broken by war or scrubbed opaque by dusty winds. They permit only rare shafts of light to filter down, cold and grey. The park, like the rest of the building, is now but a tangle of struts and sloughed skin.

"Go cautiously."

Yoechakenon nods his assent and sets out for the one remaining bridge from the plaza to the island around the spine. He moves silently, over the empty lake, the armour's camouflage making of him a shadow among shadows. We reach the island without incident. About the twisted mass of the core spine is a broad court. Where time and fate have been kind, a mosaic of splintered metal tesserae shows through the filth of ages.

"Look," says Yoechakenon. On the floor before him, face down and caked in dust and mould, are the remains of a diminutive creature.

"Human derivative," I say. "Devolved."

Reaching out with his glaive, Yoechakenon turns the skeleton's head over. It has a small skull with over-large eye sockets and a feeble jaw, like that of a child. "This is like no man I have ever seen."

"You are correct. Breathe deep."

Yoechakenon does as he is instructed. The mask of the armour melts away, and he inhales the must of the place into his lungs. There is a pause of some seconds as I examine trace DNA on the air. I furnish him with a reconstruction of the creature – short and vicious. I lack a full sample, so employ my imagination. I make it as ugly as possible, to goad Yoechakenon to greater caution. He is too confident, and it could cost us.

The image I assemble is high-foreheaded and hairless. Bulging eyes top a tight, spiteful mouth lined with serrated teeth. Long arms depend from broad shoulders, framing a round belly.

"A degenerate, a neotenous mutant of some kind," I say. "Perhaps specifically crafted; a construct. Who knows to what depths the inhabitants of the Stone Lands have sunk, or been forced. We are the first here for millennia."

Yoechakenon searches the shadows, tightening his grip upon the glaive. "It is long dead, and has the seeming of a child, albeit a wicked one."

"It is and it does," I say.

He looks about the silent spire. "No wonder they have not shown themselves. A creature like this poses no threat."

He walks around the spine. The door to the antechamber is a little way around from us, a pointed arch of great size embedded in the rippled dendrites of the core.

The doorway is obstructed with rotten skin, bone struts and other detritus. Yoechakenon finds another skeleton. The face of this one's skull is split, a crude machete still grasped in its out-flung hand.

It takes Yoechakenon half an hour to shift enough detritus to make a space to crawl through. All the while I keep up my scans of the place, using his supernormal senses and the abilities of the armour. He may be ambivalent about the threat these child-men pose, but I am not.

And still there is no sign of them.

Yoechakenon forces his way through at the apex of the arch. On the other side, the debris shelves off, spilling out in a steep fan around the door, into a tunnel the width of a triumphal avenue. Yoechakenon rolls down the debris and lands with a faint clatter on the floor, glaive up. Beyond, the ground is clear.

"Lighting," says Yoechakenon. He gestures at flickering lamps set into the wall at head height, casting a feeble glow. "The stacks live."

"Yes," I reply, "I can feel their pull." I draw his attention to a set of doors at the end of the corridor, seventy or so spans away. "Beyond those doors is the antechamber."

Other doors gape hungrily at intervals down the road, and Yoechakenon advances slowly, glaive at the ready. Some say the Stone Kin feed off the pure energies of our world, and that emanated by the spirits is an especial delicacy to them. As we progress, the decay lessens, and the lights grow steady. We reach the doors, baroque things decorated with images of blind, silent faces. They slide open soundlessly.

"The Spirefather knows we are here. It calls to me ever louder," I say. *Be on your guard*, another of my voices adds, full of warning. *It is not as it seems.*

"What was that?" asks Yoechakenon.

"My choir seeks to warn me of possible danger, but I calculate it as minimal." I still do not tell him of the warning song. Now it has returned, it sounds in my head like distant drums.

The antechamber is lavishly appointed with things made by the most ancient crafts; simple things of natural substances, yet here, at the still-living heart of the spire, they are free of tarnish and decay.

A massive bronze face hangs from the ceiling, its eyes closed, a replica of those on the door, mouth eternally open. Rows of chairs are tiered round the room, turned to the face. Withered screens and broken projector banks are arrayed beneath it. Yoechakenon tries a few passes over control arrays, his feet crunching on shattered crystals, glass and brittle plastics. Nothing happens, and the material face of the Spirefather remains silent.

"I was hoping that maybe you would not have to directly interface with the machine. But that looks a forlorn hope now," he says. "What if the Spirefather here is insane, or corrupt?"

"There is nothing to indicate that is so," I lie. "I will be fine."

The shaft to the Heart Chamber of the spire opens before us, in the centre of the antechamber's bright floor.

"We must go down, I take it?"

He is correct. I must interface directly, in the armour; I lack the ability to link remotely. "Yes. I must go direct to the Heart Chamber. The gravity slide in the shaft still functions."

"'A wise man walks when confronted with an unknown mount,'" quotes Yoechakenon. He sits, and sets his feet under the smooth rim of the shaft, pushing hard to get them through the gravity slide's resistance bubble. He searches for the hidden service ladder below the ornate lip.

"I would find something to occupy yourself with, Kaibeli," says Yoechakenon. "It is going to be a long climb."

We descend against the gravity slide's resistance for five hundred spans. The field cuts off one hundred spans above the slide's base. The shaft's lowest ten spans are choked with the bones of the child creatures, and Yoechakenon is obliged to activate the glaive to cut a way through. The bones burn as the blades touch them.

"Defence mechanism," says Yoechakenon, once we have made it to the lower floor.

"The Spirefather is using them as fuel," I say. A thick, irregular root has grown through the wall, of the same material as the ganglionic bundles that once spread throughout the spire. Thin, dry fibres stretch from it, wrapped about the dry bones of the creatures. They are brittle and break as Yoechakenon prods at the skeletons, but the main root pulses with unlovely life, and the wall puckers round it where its thickness disappears into the next chamber. It is an obscenity for a machine to feast on flesh.

"It has kept itself alive. We may be lucky, and its mind will not have deteriorated too much," he says.

"I do not think it has," I say. I can feel it now, stronger than ever. It appears sound, but there is a rage to it, and its song is all the louder. "It is a strong mind, an ancient one. I can feel it now, it touches me." Its presence is heavy and thick, its weight bowing the boundary between First and Second Worlds. "It lies in the centre of the Heart Chamber. Let us go to it."

Be wary, says one of my underminds. *It is far more than you know.*

Danger, says another. *Danger*.

My primary consciousness suppresses them, and Yoechakenon does not hear. A spirit that eats flesh is an abomination, and whatever lies before us will be dangerous, but I must venture inside. I think, could this mind be the Great Librarian?

Aside from these bones and the root that has sucked them dry, the circular corridor around the Heart Chamber is as pristine as it would have been when the last of the city's inhabitants died. The passage is egg-shaped in cross-section, bowing out at the base, rising to a domed point several spans above Yoechakenon's head. The walls are of burnished titanium. Psycho-active reliefs and motile hieroglyphs decorate the walls in a wide band. I reach several strands of my consciousness out to them; they come alive, and I ingest their stories.

"Yoechakenon, the hieroglyphs speak to me. The Spiremother's mind is here also, in the walls. It is wayward, but it lives here still. I can feel her moving behind the glyphs' message, slow and old."

"I thought this was so," he says. "It is beneath a Spirefather to occupy itself with such things as lighting and maintaining a dead building."

We move on, to where the spire's Heart Chamber is situated. Laments pour from the glyphs and the Spiremother, a song of loss.

"It persisted for many thousands of years, this place." My voices falter and fragment. Too much data is coming in. It is not overly complex, merely projected very loudly, and therefore hard to parse.

Such is the volume of it I cannot share it directly with Yoechakenon, for fear it would kill him. The emotional content, raw and powerful, threatens to drown my attempts to vocalise its message. "This place, Yoechakenon, this place was one of the last. There is so much sadness, Yoechakenon! The Spiremother weeps for her lost people. Such great sadness." I can say no more.

Greenish light fills the corridor as more of the symbols on the wall react to my touch.

"The Spiremother's mind, is it still sound?"

"Barely. She can do little but feel. And endlessly repeat the same thing... Listen, I will screen it for you."

I fill Yoechakenon's mind with the Spiremother's sorrowful medley of emotion. If he is moved, he does not show it.

"Does it know anything?"

"No. It lost contact with the external world a very long time ago. It is an old woman, weeping for her dead children. Robust interrogation, I think, would destroy it."

"Then we must ask the Spirefather."

The door to the Heart Chamber gapes by Yoechakenon's left hand. We step through, and we find ourselves in the presence of a demigod from elder times.

Stood in the middle of the floor is a baroquely carven pillar twice the height of Yoechakenon. Atop it sits the heart of the spire – its Library node. In form it is a large sphere, devoid of the ornamentation that crawls across every other surface in the Heart Chamber. It is featureless, excepting a deep groove that bisects its circumference. Below that, a green eye a half-span across is set into a recess. Cables twist down from the heights of the roof, connecting in a cluster atop the sphere. In itself it is not remarkable: the node points of later spires are different, fully organic boluses like that occupied by the Spirefather of Olm, yet many like this half-metal sphere exist still in spires all across Mars. The knowledge inside, the age of the Spirefather, that is another matter.

Dim lamps in sconces upon the chamber's walls add to the glow of the Library's eye. There are no other signs of life in the chamber.

The armour's spirit shifts and growls, aroused by the power in the sphere. Yoechakenon twists its brutal mind and bids it be quiet. It whimpers and slinks back into the depths of the armour's neurology.

"I must go in," I say.

"You are certain?"

A clamour of concerned voices springs up from all parts of my mind, shouting down the mournful chant of the spire's heart and threatening to break the bars I have placed between myself and the armour. Only just, I keep Yoechakenon unaware of my doubts. I see no other way.

"Very well," he says. The armour slides from his skin, his pack falling to the floor as the viscous metal retreats from his body. He gasps as it disengages from his mind, and again as its tendrils pull, one by one, from six of the seven plugs lining his spine. He falls to his knees. The armour pools upon the floor, then flows away and up, making itself into a sphere. It is black and matte, like the materials that make the spires, reflecting nothing from its surface.

He pants. "I am going to send in the armour's spirit with you."

"Yoechakenon..."

"The armour's mind is useless to me while you are using the armour's body as an interface; you know this. I would rather its spirit protected you than did nothing."

Silence falls between us. "You will be entirely alone."

"Do not let it concern you," he says. "I have become used to sharing my thoughts with no one. I have been in the arena with only the tactical advisor many times before. This will be little different."

I hated those times, trapped in a featureless prison until the bout was over, forcing myself to watch through the eyes of the crowd and the Great Library, not knowing if he would live or die.

"Only for minutes, Yoechakenon."

"We are born alone with our thoughts," he counters. "If a newborn can cope, so can I. I spoke with the Emperor disconnected from the Second World without harm. There is no other way."

"I will be quick, then," I say. "There is a chance that the creatures here are alert to our presence, and it may be that the Spirefather will be gentler with them should it want you removed."

"I will be able to deal with them, if need be. I may lack the armour, but the glaive remains."

"Very well. I will be able to communicate with you, but the effort will be great. Do not expect a full description of the Second World within the Library casing."

"I will not," says Yoechakenon.

There is nothing more to be said. There are things I wish I can say, but I cannot.

Yoechakenon's mind slips out from my own, as I move through the armour's last connecting tendril into the sphere it has become. He speaks hurriedly, as he feels the last of me depart. "Kaibeli?"

"Yes, Yoechakenon?" I say. I am faint to him. I stand before the doors of this lost world.

"Come back unharmed."

"I will, my love," I say.

I do not tell him of the song I can hear, loud and foul, from deep within the sphere.

The last tendril withdraws as the armour gives its matrix to me. The trinity between man, armour and companion mind is severed, and for the first time in his life, Yoechakenon is left entirely alone with his own thoughts. Our connection is now one of the third degree – I can feel his strongest emotions, and see him from the perspective of the armour's sphere, but he is unaware of me. It must be utterly strange to him, to be thinking with the knowledge that no others are listening. Even when he fought in the arena, his head was full of the monotone chatter of the tactical advisor, and before, when the Emperor hid them both from the Second World, they were together in the flesh. Here there is nothing at all.

Certain scholars hold that all men had once been this way, alone, although I find it hardly credible. I pray that insanity is not the immediate wage of retreating from communion with all minds but one's own, as other scholars believe.

He is naked, but the heat put out by the Library

nexus is enough to keep him warm. He stretches. His body has been kept physically clean by the armour, but its touch makes him feel dirty and in need of scouring nonetheless. He stops thinking for a moment, to steer away from the unpleasant thought of the armour's intimate embrace, and blankness rushes in. His mind is totally silent. It is unnerving, and yet at the same time peaceful.

I watch him squat and reach for the discarded pack. He pulls out a survival wafer, takes a slug of hi-water from the small canteen, and chews.

I turn my attention away. I flow through the martial halls of the armour, and along a conduit into the glowering casing of the ancient machine. Light ceases, sensation changes.

There is blackness.

There is a terrible, raucous noise. The song. A corrupt and corrupting choir, barely coherent, its message nevertheless clear:

Stay away.

CHAPTER NINETEEN
Relief

THE DAMAGE DONE to Deep Two and the cave entrance was not severe. The outer office was wrecked, the suiting room had been damaged and much of the caving equipment destroyed, but Stulynow had been no demolition expert and the structure was mostly sound. Jensen was able to clear most of it in two days, with Kick and Cybele's help.

No one spoke when they brought Stulynow's broken body back to base. The medical bay's tiny mortuary had never been used before, and they had to peel the protective films from the body locker's surfaces before they could place Stulynow and Vance within. It was apparent from their faces that they had thought it never would be used.

Holland was kept under a close watch. He was allowed to continue with his work in the lab, provided someone was with him at all times. This was no great inconvenience, as he would rarely have been working alone in any case, as Miyazaki and Kick's main work stations were also there. At night, Cybele kept watch over him, her sheath stationed outside his door. He experienced no more episodes of sleepwalking, and there were no further energy spikes from the artefact underground. Gradually the mood in the base relaxed. The artefact ceased being an impending threat, and became a fact of life. The scientists remained subdued, and work became the cure to their anxiety and grief.

A week passed, and Holand had either completed all his tests or had set experiments in process that would not be completed for weeks. His most ambitious project was populating a number of vivariums mimicking the cave environment. Holland was always a one for observational biology, and spent a deal of his time altering one aspect or the other of the miniature environments he constructed. Cybele, who was becoming something of a constant companion to him, was a great help in formulating the chemistry of these exotic habitats, and he grew less antagonistic toward her.

Once he'd constructed his wall of glass cases, however, he grew frustrated. There was little to do other than monitor them, and as each came equipped with a miniature sensor package, that took all of ten minutes of each day. There were no further expeditions from the base. The storm's winds continued unabated outside, and naturally trips into the cave were out of the question. In any case, Holland was confined inside by Orson's orders, and so could not even take part in the repair of Deep Two, with which the rest of the team busied themselves.

When Maguire came to see him, he was sitting in silence, slumped on a stool, staring at the caged Martian life. He'd been holding his tablet and repeatedly refreshing the results until he became hypnotised by the percentage creep of chemical compounds. He tested himself, to see how long he could wait before tapping the icon. For a while he lost himself in this pointless endeavour, until eventually he'd become bored with this too. By the time Maguire came in, he was staring at the glass cases until his eyes went out of focus, blinking, and starting the process again. He didn't stop when the door hissed open.

"Hey, Holly! How're doing?"

Holland gave Maguire a slack-jawed stare. "How am I? I'm bored, Maguire. Really, pissing bored!" He tossed his tablet onto his desk carelessly, knocking over four days' worth of coffee cups. Congealed coffee spilled on the workbench.

"Careful there, Jensen will have a fit." Maguire righted the cups, then checked the tablet and carefully set it down away from Holland's mess. "This really isn't like you, John."

"Dave, I've been in here for nearly a fortnight, with nothing but the hooting of the damn wind and those" – he waved half-heartedly at his vivariums – "to keep me company."

"What about Miyazaki?" The Japanese geologist was sat in a corner, crouched over his books.

Holland gave Maguire a doleful look. "Oh, he's a blast."

"Come on, though. Sure, you've had Cybele to be your friend. How are you two getting on?"

"I admit she's been very useful, and it's probably been good for me, as I'm getting past the whole 'the robots are coming!' thing, but then, she's here on nutter patrol so it's not really an even relationship, is it?"

"Counsellor/patient?"

"Prisoner/guard," said Holland. "And anyway, she's down at Deep Two today." He sighed hard and rubbed at his face. "Come on, Maguire, when are they going to let me out of here? I'm sick of being cooped up. Surely there's something I can do with the rebuild? I hate being useless."

"No can do, Holly."

"Oh, God," he groaned. "I'm actually going to go insane in here."

"Be happy, my friend; I do have something for you," Maguire said enticingly. He produced a sample box from somewhere, like a magician. "Now, do you have a spare terrarium? We don't want it to get away, do we?"

THE BUG RAN round the interior of the case, antennae flicking at the corners when it encountered them. It would pause, flick, flick, then move on to the next. It was already on its fourth circuit, six legs working robotically away.

"And you say they brought this up today? I thought Jensen was dead set against anything coming from down there."

"Orson overruled him, said that this was like the rest of the life down there. Besides, it was found a ways from the artefact, so it's doubtful it has any connection with it. I think he's mindful of you going off your rocker, so he is."

"Did you have anything to do with this?"

Maguire gave a half shrug and a smile. "Well now, that'd be telling."

"Thanks, Dave."

"Thanks? I bring you the first mobile, multi-cellular life found alive on the planet, and all you can say is 'Thanks, Dave'? I was expecting something a wee bit more effusive than that!" He slapped Holland on the back. "Enjoy yourself!"

"Thanks, Dave. I mean it."

Maguire walked out the door. "You know, you need to work on your thanks," he called over his shoulder.

"Now what to do?" muttered Holland. He watched the bug run around and around the case. It was five centimetres long, with a light blue carapace. It had a small, armoured head; its joints were high on its legs, and hooked, knobbled feet sprang from their ends. Excepting that there was no join on the thorax carapace to indicate wing casings, to all intents it looked like a beetle from Earth, albeit of no kind that Holland was aware of. He didn't find that peculiar in itself. The life found throughout the Solar System had been surprisingly similar to that on Earth, if sometimes with radically different base chemistry.

The case was bare, atmosphere the same as that down in the caves, although the beetle had seemed to struggle with the density, so Holland had increased the air pressure until it had begun to behave in what looked like a normal manner. "Oh, what the fuck do I know?" he said to himself. "I have no idea what normal is." It did seem less agitated, though. That suggested to him that the beetle had come from somewhere else in the caverns. He glanced at the terrariums. He needed to find out which one it would be most comfortable in, and quickly.

"Cybele?"

The AI's voice immediately replied, sounding as always as if it came from thin air. "Yes, Dr Holland?" Her voice had made him wince only a few weeks ago, and he was surprised how quickly he'd got used to it. No matter how wary he'd been of AIs back on Earth, there was something about Cybele that he instinctively trusted, like he knew she would never harm him. It could be the name, humanising her, but then a lot of the AIs on Earth also had names. His comfort with her disquieted him; he was hoping he'd eventually stop feeling so nervy around AIs, but for it to happen so quickly felt unnatural, a betrayal of his emotional baggage.

"Are you busy at the moment? I'd like some help. I need you to run a DNA profile on this lifeform, to help me figure out which micro-habitat it'll be best suited to."

"I will be available in fifteen minutes."

"Okay, fine. It's not like I'm going anywhere."

"And, Dr Holland?"

"Yes?"

"I am glad that you have asked me so freely for assistance. I had hoped that we would become friends. If I may be so bold as to say, I believe that we are already well along into the process."

Maybe it was that she sounded genuinely happy about that. *She's just a machine, Holland.* "Yeah," he said. "Me too, Cybele." He ruefully realised that he meant it.

HOLLAND MADE HIMSELF a cup of coffee, and prepared to take a sample off the creature. He transferred it to a box fitted with thick rubber gloves so he could get at it without exposing himself to harm. A quick scrape of the chitin on its thorax should be enough. He could just ask Cybele to take an airborne sample, but there was too much risk of contamination there.

"Okay, little fella, hold still." He held up a small dish, and a scalpel which he'd blunted to prevent him from accidentally slicing into the insect. He herded the bug into a corner with them, and scraped its back. Its tiny mouth hissed, and lunged at him. It sank its mandibles into his finger. He smiled at its boldness, a smile that turned to a round 'O' of pain as its jaws went through the heavy glove into his finger. "Ow!" He snatched his hands out of the gloves, waving the offended hand around, resisting the temptation to suck it. "You little..." Blood welled up in three bright spots by his nail. "Damn." He went for the medical cabinet. "Miyazaki? Could you help me..."

The lights shut off. Emergency lighting came on.

"It appears that we are having another problem," said the Japanese man. "Please, I will get you a bandage."

"Everyone stay put, looks like we got another surge, Cybele's down *again*," Orson said over the intercom. "Jensen will have us back to power shortly."

Holland turned his finger this way and that. It throbbed.

A voice, quiet, called his name. "John!" He glanced up, and his eyes widened. In the box, crammed in like a contortionist, was the girl with the blue skin. Her palms and knees pressed up against the glass.

"John! You have to take me back! Take me back to the place where you found me! Take me back!"

Miyazaki was by the first aid cabinet, humming tunelessly. He appeared not to have noticed the blue lady in the box. Holland looked incredulously from him back to the girl. She was gone. The bug was in her place. It stood in the middle of the box, vibrating and emitting a high scream.

"Miyazaki..." he said.

The bug exploded with a violent, wet *pop*, splattering the box with its insides.

The lights came back on. "Aha! Dr Jensen is a most effective engineer," said Miyazaki. He came to Holland with a bandage. "There you are, Dr Holland."

"Didn't you see it?"

"See what?" said Miyazaki, wearing his perpetual, polite smile.

Holland raised his hand to point to the sealed box, and collapsed into a dead faint.

When he came round, Miyazaki was standing over him. "Are you all right, Dr Holland? Did you fall asleep?"

He was sat in a chair in the kitchen, a cup of coffee cooling next to him.

"What? What happened?"

"I am afraid I have some bad news," said the little Japanese man. "So sorry, but your sample has expired."

"Of course it did, we both saw it," said Holland. He stood up. His joints popped. He was lightheaded. He yawned broadly, covering his mouth unconsciously – Miyazaki brought the manners out in everyone. "It exploded."

Miyazaki looked puzzled. "I was sure that it was alive when you left to make your coffee. It has not exploded. It is dead upon its back in the terrarium."

Holland was suddenly wide awake. He frowned. "Was there another blackout?"

"Why, no," said Miyazaki. "You came to make coffee forty minutes ago. You must have sat down and gone to sleep. It is quite expected; we have had a very hard pair of weeks." The little man became concerned. "Have you been dreaming?" he said.

"I... I must have. I'm sorry," Holland picked up his coffee cup and slurped a big mouthful down. It was tepid. "Thank you for coming to tell me."

Miyazaki gave an uncertain smile and a small bow, and left.

"Dr Holland," said Cybele. "I have run the tests you asked me for and now have the results."

"But I haven't given you a sample yet!" he said.

"You have. You did." His tablet beeped on the countertop. Footage ran of the lab, him taking a scraping of the beetle in the glove box, putting it back into the terrarium, placing the sample into an analyser and telling Miyazaki he was going to make coffee.

But I was going to do that – I did do that – after I made my coffee, not before. He kept this to himself. "Yes, sorry, of course, I'm a bit muzzy, just woke up. What are they?"

"I am concerned that I may have made a mistake. I do not see how. I have double-checked, and it appears the results are accurate."

"Why?" Holland picked up his tablet. The data played over his screen.

"See for yourself."

He watched for a moment. "But – but this is terrestrial DNA. Where are the Martian markers? What does this mean?"

Cybele was silent for a moment. "I have no idea," she said.

Cybele was a machine. She had complete control of her intonation and modulation. She could sound how she wished, from the voice she employed to its non-verbal informational content.

So why did he think she was lying?

He put his coffee down. It was undrinkable.

Only then did he see the three tiny puncture wounds on his left forefinger.

BY THE TIME the incoming Marsform rover was close enough for them to pick up its messages through the storm on their short-range radio mast, it was practically on top of them. Orson called the entirety of the base's remaining personnel together to Mission Control, Holland joining them last. Disturbed by his experience in the lab, he tried his best to keep his worry off his face. He needn't have bothered; everyone was as antsy as him. There'd been two deaths, after all, and no one liked it when the company brass came out to their station. It was a reminder to them all that this place was not their home, but corporate property. Orson had them all scoot round and tidy up as quickly as possible, and this time he did not complain that Cybele was helping.

They gathered in the atrium, a ragged, furrow-browed welcoming committee. Nobody said much.

"You're all intelligent people," said Orson, "but

I'd be mighty happy if you kept your mouths shut when the company's here. This is my watch, it's my responsibility, and I don't want anyone talking until they're asked, understood?"

There was a murmur of assent from everyone, although Orson was mainly looking at Maguire.

There was a long wait until the visitors came through the inner airlock. There were six of them. A high-ranking company wonk in an actual suit, an engineer, and three stern looking mercenary types sporting sidearms and long kitbags that could only contain more weapons. The company had a small army on Mars, all ex-servicemen. Their presence at Ascraeus made the team nervous, but not as nervous as the android doing the speaking.

It opened with no greeting or preamble. "I am the Class Six prototype Delaware X4," it said, in a smooth, androgynous voice. It wore an equally androgynous sheath, with the appearance of sculpted marble. "I am here to assess the circumstances surrounding the discovery of the artefact," it went on. "You will present any and all documentation and records from Ascraeus Base immediately."

Orson began to speak.

"Please, Commander Orson," said Delaware. "I will interrogate your base artificial intelligence. The time for talking and subjective recollection will come after I am in possession of all the facts. AI Designate 3-122987/10/12/77, please confirm that you are online and ready to begin data transferral."

"I am ready," said Cybele. Her voice sounded crude in comparison to this Delaware.

"Then begin," said Delaware X4.

The company man finished looking round the atrium. "It all looks in order to me," he said. His accent was faintly French. He gave a reassuring, professional smile. "I'm Jules Lasalle, director of personnel for Marsform's surface science division. This might take a few minutes." He motioned his hand to the stationary AI. "The pickup here is appalling. I see your long range mast is down, which I suppose explains why you didn't answer our hails until the last minute. Delaware was getting suspicious!" He laughed, but there was a threat in it that Delaware was still suspicious.

"Yes," said Orson. "There have been developments."

"Developments?"

"Deaths. Two. Dr Vance never recovered from her coma. Dr Stulynow killed himself. He sabotaged our comms, then blew up the transmitter. If the weather were clear, we might have got through with our smaller mast, but we've had no way of calling it in."

Lasalle sucked his teeth. "Right. Okay. That's not good. We're going to have to be here a while, you understand?"

Orson gave a taut nod. "Of course."

"Okay, good. Don't worry, commander, I'm on your side. All I want to do is get to the bottom of this, and let's face it, this could be quite the find, tragedy or not. We're going to need quarters."

"Sure."

"And I want you to arrange a space for Delaware's base unit here. It's in the back of the rover currently. Your heavy lifting equipment is in order?"

"All of it," said Jensen. "We can set him up in the atrium, there's not much room here."

"That sounds fine. You're Jensen, right? See to it immediately. Maguire?" Lasalle motioned to the station manager. "Why don't we get my men installed in their accommodation? We've got a lot of work ahead of us here. And you, Dr Van Houdt?" – this to Suzanne – "I could do with a cup of coffee, can you do that for me? Coffee everyone?" His men nodded and said *yes*.

Suzanne nodded. "I will see to it."

"*Merci, cherie*," he said. He clapped his hands "Okay, people! Let's go!"

The room started into life. Holland looked at Orson and saw his command of the situation drain away from him. His aura of authority had vanished.

They were in company hands now.

CHAPTER TWENTY

The Stone Hunt

Year 5, Post-War Period

It had been a long time since he was so far up the mountain. Not many came out here any more, truth be told. There was no reason to. All that was there before had gone, all those places up on Olympus. Wreckage and bones carpeted the land. "Dawn of a new age." Who were they fucking kidding?

Olympus. So much had changed here, but that name has stood the test of time. Even in a society of immortals, language changes. Olympus would change with time too, eventually. People change the way they express themselves, people *forget*. He hadn't.

He didn't know why, maybe it was the many rebirths and fast-growths he underwent in the war – veterans who survived encounters with the Stone Kin with their minds intact were recycled quickly, the better to employ their experience against the foe – but he remembered more of his pasts this time round than was the norm. He knew this, because he remembered not remembering in other lives.

He'd tried to explain this in the bars in the camps, but not many got what he meant. People who had fought in the war in this life were getting old or dying, and those who'd come back were babes in arms, to be allowed a normal life now the war was over. But someone – who, he was not sure, for he spent his nights in a stupor – had said it was because the spirits had amplified the memory recall, so the veterans would remember how to kill the Stone Kin. Trouble was, it brought *everything* back, too much for many people to handle.

That's why, the man had said (he was pretty sure it had been a man, he had smelled bad enough), a lot of the veterans of the Third Stone War were crazy. Rumour was that when they went back into the stacks next time, some would not be coming out again – too damn unstable.

He thought it unlikely. There'd been two other Stone Wars, and he'd fought in both, and he was here, wasn't he?

He remembered bright eyes and winey breath as a face leaned in to confide this information. It was a strong recollection, that moment, sharp with sensation, but if it had occurred last week or five years ago, he had no clue.

Kaibeli would understand him, broken or not; she always had, no matter what life he'd had forced on him. That's why he was here, up on the slopes.

Looking for her.

The mirror suns made the slopes of Olympus hot. His broad-brimmed hat kept the worst of it from his eyes. Prevailing winds were east-west – he used the movement of the clouds above to keep track of where he was. The clouds came off the ocean, hit the line of the Tertiz Mun to the east, dumped their rain, and that's that, nothing left for poor old Olympus or the area around it. Desert. Hot as sin. It had been unbearably dry on the Tertiz before the war. With the Veil of Worlds made manifest around the base of the mountain, it was worse.

Tertiz. *Tharsis,* he remembered. *Tharsis. Thersis, Tersis, Taertiz.* That was a name that had changed. He saw it happen in his memories. The sweep of time made him dizzy.

He remembered so much. Remembering pretty much all of his lengthy and varied past meant that in this life, he hadn't got a fucking clue who he was. Yesterday had as much weight as a breakfast he'd had fourteen lifetimes since, and he could rarely tell which came first.

Hence the drink. At night, not during in the day. In the day he needed to stay sharp. He was terrified – he wasn't ashamed to admit it – that he'd walk right by her.

He wiped his forehead. Shattered machines and the bones of men littered the sand. The last battle against the Stone Kin, at the end of the Third Stone War, had been fought here, when the fuckers had come boiling out of the Stone Sun. The new sun had done its job all right, it had kept the Stone Kin locked into the Suul (*Sol,* he remembered) system, but they'd found some way to use it to their advantage, to root themselves on Mars. Man had won, but the lands around Olympus were lost to fuck knew what, the Veil of Worlds, billowing white up ahead of him, their boundary.

He was sure it was here, round here somewhere, where it had happened, where he had lost her.

He never made a promise to her, not like she'd made to him. She wouldn't expect him to come back to find her, but a promise like that, it cuts deep, and it goes both ways, right? And how many years had it been? He thought back to that moment of hot pain, the hand holding his hand, hard metal so soft through his glove. Pain is all he remembers of that life, no matter how comprehensive his recollections of others. It could have been his first, he might have come out of a womb rather than a machine. Maybe he'd even had his genes shuffled the animal way.

It seemed outlandish, even faintly disgusting.

That hand, and that promise – he had no idea how long ago that was. But it was thousands and thousands and thousand of years. Thousands. Of. Years. *Obligation like that. It is...* He struggled for the word. *Mutual.*

He didn't know why, maybe because his head was full of too many memories of other men's lives, but he wasn't so clever this time around. Maybe the Librarian didn't think its grunts needed much thinking power, just experience. He wasn't stupid, not by a long way, but he had been cleverer.

Maybe that's why he wouldn't give up, why he camped out in that shithole of a town that all the refugees from Olympus had finally left when they'd realised the Veil was there forever and their cities were lost to them. Maybe that's why he sat there in the searing heat and dry wind, drinking himself stupid every night with a bunch of toothless madmen, coming up here every damn day. Looking. For. Her.

Finding a particular pebble on a beach would have been easier. Half a million men had died up here, and one hundred and fifty six thousand spirits were killed – their shattered sheaths, and those of a million more whose minds escaped, were tangled with the skeletons of the men. The bodies lay four deep in places. You could walk over them in a straight line and your feet wouldn't touch dirt for a week.

Still he looked. Every day, from dawn until sunset.

He knew why.

His fork sang in his belt and he stopped. He poked about in the dirt for a while, until he unearthed a shattered robot carriage. He dug it out with his folding spade, and he pulled it onto its back. All its limbs were gone, half its head was missing. It was a similar model to one of those she wore in the fight (one; there were half a dozen types, at least, she'd ridden during the course of the war). He pulled the fork from his belt: grey, dull metal, two tines as wide apart as an outstretched hand. It hummed affirmatively.

He cracked the sheath's buckled carapace with some difficulty, sitting with his legs spread straight out either side of it so he could work at it properly. He swore and coaxed it and hit it with a rock. After a time, the core reluctantly rose from the chest port. A glass bulb filled with blue luminescence. He fitted it into the fork. The note was encouraging. The spirit within was alive, and it was sane. The note changed, a name. His face fell, dropping from joy to resignation without stopping by to visit hope. It wasn't her.

He had the urge to smash the core with a thigh bone and leave the place forever.

He didn't.

He put the core in the bag with the four others he'd found that day – a big haul, sometimes he didn't find anything for weeks. Some of the spirits couldn't get out when their bodies were fragged. Not all of them died. Some of them were still trapped up here, unable to get into the Second World so close to the new Stone Lands and the Veil. The ones he took back paid with cash or favours. Their gratitude kept him in lodgings and drink.

He pushed the wrecked sheath away from him and stood. His knees hurt. He was not young any more, and was not as well made as he should have been in the first place. Fast-growth made for fast lives. Heat haze shimmered off the bones. He squinted, thought he recognised an outcrop. There were so many memories of so many lives ended rapidly, one after another, that it was hard to tell which belonged to which. The bluff, however, he was certain he knew, and that it had been important.

Impossible to find her, others might say. But the way he looked at it, when he died, he'd go into the stacks and come out again (or he might not, but the end result would be the same for Kaibeli). If he didn't look for her now, his memories would only fade each time he went into the stacks and was reborn. He could afford to waste a lifetime looking for her. It was that, or lose her forever.

He shouldered his threadbare pack and walked up the bluff, duster flapping about his calves in the breeze. Yeah, he was sure he remembered it. He stood at its top, looked down. He'd died here. Skulls and crushed machine bodies, still garbed in dusty armour, were half-buried in the hot sand. One of them was him. He remembered gunfire rattling off the skins of horrifying Stone Kin war constructs. He remembered it had had no effect, and he remembered what had happened to him and his men when they'd crested the hill.

He rubbed at his stomach, the place where they'd pulled his guts out.

When had it happened? Who the fuck knew?

Behind him, the Veil of Worlds rippled like a curtain of white gauze across the sky. He had been up to it, once or twice, looked into the place beyond that was no longer a part of the same reality. The Veil would kill you if you so much as brushed against it, but it was safe to stand within touching distance.

You could not see through it.

He held up the fork. It warbled unsteadily. No spirits alive around the bluff.

He moved on.

"SAY, YO MODEN PIC?" a man sitting on a pile of wrecked robot chassis asked him. He was ratty about the face, a dirty round hat crammed onto his head. His skin was filthy, hair greasy, but the armour he wore was expensive, and he leaned on a long energy gun that gleamed with oil and active maintenance gels. The man looked like scum, but he knew his type – the dangerous type.

"Who wants to know?"

"Ah, does it matter?" said the man. He jumped up off the wrecked war droids. "I know it be yo, spirits tell me." His hands were crossed over the trigger assembly of his gun, like he was shooting the breeze outside a bar.

Moden turned his head. Everywhere was the dead landscape of war. "There are no spirits here," he said.

"There *weren't* no spirits here," corrected the man. He was an islander, judging by his uncouth speech; way off his home patch. You saw an islander without his fishing skiff it was nearly sure he was a sell-sword, or a pirate, or both. "But they's coming back. Second World's growing agin. I work for a man, big man out of Kemyonset. He wants to talk to yo." Somehow, the man's gun had contrived to point itself at Moden. Casually, like, but it was pointed at him nonetheless. "Ain't nothing bad, don't you worry yoself 'bout that. Fact, might be to yo advantage. He got sometin' yo might be interested in."

Moden looked at the gun muzzle. His gaze slid slowly up the man's dirty wargear to settle on his face. "I got a choice?"

The man spat and gave an unpleasant smile. "Now I think about it, I don't suppose yo do."

The man – Moden never did learn his name – took him down the side of the mountain. The volcanoes of Mars did not feel like mountains, despite their immense size. From a distance they dominated the landscape, but their slopes were so shallow that it was hard to accept you were standing on something that forced itself into the marches of space. After an hour they came to an area alive with activity – men, sheathed spirits and lesser machines working the land, collecting the dead. Piles of stacked bones and armour, heaps of broken sheaths made macabre sculptures on the red mountain. They were being catalogued. Men worked, genotyping the bones, or held forks similar to his own, testing the ruined sheaths for stranded spirit life.

"This way," said the rat-faced islander. His gun had never left Moden's back, no matter how diffidently he held it. It was like they were gentlemen wandering the desert for a morning's shooting. It was like nothing of the sort. Ratface jutted his chin toward a cluster of tents.

"Which one?" said Moden. At the centre of the tents was one that was much richer than the others, embroidered with a living tapestry that occasionally took flight from the fabric, swooping around the worksite and singing sad songs of the dead Erth.

"Which do yo think?" said Ratface.

Moden paused. His eyes narrowed.

"Git goin'," said Ratface. The gun wandered closer to Moden's back.

They walked to the tent.

GUARDS STOOD AT the end of a covered walkway leading to the tent's entrance, stiff-necked city sorts, all shiny armour and ego. They stood stock still, eyes locked forward, as Ratface herded Moden between them toward the colourful tent flap. Ratface gave them his nasty smile, and tipped his dirty hat.

"In there," said Ratface. "Yo go in now."

Moden faced him. "Not going to guard me?"

Ratface spat into the sand. "No need. Be seein' yo, wastelander."

He sauntered off, leaving Moden by the tent entrance. He let off a long fart as he walked out past the guards, shouldered his rifle, and whistled his way out of Moden's life.

Moden looked around the camp. Wind cracked at the canvas. The tapestries murmured sad tales. The guards paid him no attention whatsoever.

He'd be dead within seconds if he turned and walked away. There was something on the air here, intangible eyes watching.

He lifted the heavy flap, and went into the tent.

It was heavily decorated inside. The fabric of the tent was thick, blocking out the sun, and the inside was lit by a variety of oil lamps. Carpets covered the dirt. The poles were decorated after the school of Menlo Kar. At a desk of alpine mertzwood sat a man writing by candlelight. He scratched a pen across paper. A spirit-inhabited putto at the corner of the desk, half a Marspan tall, whispered the words he wrote into the records of the Second World.

The candles flickered as Moden entered. The man stopped writing. His hair was dressed in the latest fashion, his robes stiffened into elaborate folds as was the custom of the fourteen houses of the Man-dar-see. This was a rich man, a powerful man. "Ah," he said. "Moden Pic." He spoke as if they had an appointment, and Moden had arrived in good time. Perhaps he believed that; most of the aristocracy were full believers in eleutheremic fate. Moden was not. He had seen too much in this life and his others to buy into that. For starters, if everything was fated, how come the spirits were absolutely shitting their ephemeral selves during the war? Ask them and you got the usual evasive horseshit.

The man held an open hand out to a stool in front of his desk. He went back to his writing. Moden supposed he was supposed to sit down.

The man could suppose the fuck off. Moden remained where he was.

The man looked up and sighed. He laid aside his pen, scattered red sand across what he had written and blew gently upon the paper, then tipped the sand away, put the paper into a tray and dusted his hands off . The putto fell silent. "I understood it would be like this, but I am still irked by it." The man tried an honest expression. He had a merchant's face, generously blanketed in fat, lips creased by the constant pursing that seemed to accompany bazaar dickering. The expression did not suit him; there was a ruthlessness underlying his skin. "I am fool to myself." A chuckle followed to the same effect, a plaster mask of a laugh, fragile and fake. "Please sit down. I have a proposal I wish to discuss with you. I have gone to a great deal of time and trouble to find you." His tongue periodically strayed from his lips, fat and pink as the rest of him, to touch the corners of his mouth or the base of his philtrum.

Moden peered out of the tentflap. "I am flattered," he murmured. The light was harsh after the dim tent interior. Still the same sense of peril. "If I run, I die, right? That's the way these things usually work."

The man tilted his hands and put out a fleshy lip. "I have to have some leverage."

"No Second World up here any more, so no assassin spirits. And those brassnecks you got there won't stop me."

"Oh, I very much doubt they would. You're what, a five-times-reinvested veteran of the last war? And how many times have you lived in total, Moden Pic? Hundreds? You're quite the legend back in Kemyonset, I have no doubt you could take my men apart like soft cheese. But you are wrong about the Second World, as wrong about that as you are about the lack of assassin spirits." He wagged a pudgy finger. "I have a variety of *exceptionally* final means at my disposal here. But, assuming I did not, and assuming you considered declining my invitation on the mountain, it begs the question, if your martial prowess is so great, then why did you come here at all? And to that I know the answer..." He smiled. His teeth were small. "I think you know what I have." The man pulled open a drawer, the wood creaking. "Or should I say, *who.*"

From within the drawer he produced a spirit core, which he held up between his fat forefinger and thumb. The light it cast – pale violet with threads of silver, Kaibeli's colour – made of his face a demoniacal leer. "I am sure you know who this is. We're here on a reclamation mission, you see. The Second World is growing again. The Grand Court and Conclave of Spirits has been re-established, the Great Library functions again, although alas without the Great Librarian. Five of the greatest spirits have come to the fore and are rebuilding Mars. True, we may still be isolated from the rest of the galaxy, but there's no reason we have to go the same way as Erth. It's a new world out there!" He snatched the spirit core into his palm, enfolding it within flesh and hiding its glow. His face returned to that of the avuncular cheat. "Of course, you wouldn't know that, hiding yourself up here and drinking yourself stupid. It was a coincidence, really, that we came across her so soon. And that, my friend, gave me an idea. I wonder, would you care to do me a small service in return for your lover?"

Moden's throat was suddenly dry. "Prove it is her, and maybe we can talk."

Again that smile, again the tongue following to taste it. The man tossed the core across the tent. "Prove it yourself. You have the equipment." He heaved himself out from behind his desk with not a little difficulty, for he was grossly fat, as many men of the aristocracy tended to be.

Moden caught it and withdrew the fork from his belt. As he brought the core close, the fork sang the song he had wanted to hear these last twenty years, humming the notes that made up her name. "Kaibeli, Kaibeli, Kaibeli." He fitted the core into the fork's tines, and it sang the louder.

Moden removed it and gave a noncommittal grunt. "You can fool the forks."

The fat man rolled his eyes. "Yes, you can, but I have not. It takes time, effort and a lot of lies in very particular places. Dangerous places. Do you see me doing that up here?" He held up his arms and looked about him, as if appealing to a court of law.

"Let me fit her to a sheath, and then we'll see."

"Let you fit her to a sheath and then I'll die. No thank you. I'm afraid you'll have to take this on faith, but I will point out that your fork was most insistent."

Moden weighed the dull grey instrument in his hand. Wasn't it just?

He looked up from under his hat brim, eyes dark spaces where candle-flame stars danced. "What do you want me to do?"

The man rubbed his hands together. "First, let us deal on level terms. You are Moden Pic, but you do not know who I am. I will tell you, so we may deal fairly. I am Sulman Mahoo, of the third house of Man-dar-see, and I would have you do a simple task." He chuckled apologetically, acknowledging the lie. "I want you to catch me a Stone Kin."

IT APPEARED THAT Moden was to be the bait.

A party of men, armed with weapons that caused the Kin certain excruciation, walked in wide perimeter around Moden. He, stripped of his weapons, was left at the centre of a large depression in the side of the volcano, close by the Veil of Worlds.

There was a reek to the place, redolent of slaughter, cloves and chipped flint, a chemical tang on the air that scalded the throat and forced Moden to wear a scarf wrapped about his face. The scent was one he knew well, the scent of the Stone Kin.

There were a few places like this left, portals half-open, slowly closing, where phantoms and images from the higher dimensions might intrude. Moden avoided them.

Here, Mahoo had told him, was one of the last places the smaller forms might fully make their way into mundane reality, if only for a short while.

Moden had faced the Stone Kin innumerable times,

and he was frightened, *because* rather than in spite of that. The Stone Kin were hard to comprehend, eleven-dimensional beings extruded into base four-dimensional reality. They were not of stone; Moden had no idea why they were called so, but he suspected it was because of their manner of movement. They were fast and uniformly deadly, and yet sometimes one would stop dead, like a picture, as if they were excluded from the normal flow of time. They might remain that way for microseconds or millennia. As a habit, it would have added to their otherworldly menace, if they were not easily slain while in this state.

To see one could be difficult, as unless they forced themselves entirely into the four lower dimensions occupied by men, they moved in their own areas of the universe and merely brushed those familiar to humanity. You would see only this or that aspect of a Stone Kin presented to you as they pressed upon the lower realms. It was like looking at a picture made with a froth of paint: one saw the bubbles as flat, broken diameters, and not as the complex three-dimensional forms they really had. An unmanifested Stone Kin could be a curve of light, a membrane, a slight bulging to the air, but it could kill you only marginally less effectively than in its fully extruded form. Thus, Moden kept a sharp watch, eyes darting around. He would not sit, turning constantly upon the spot, looking for the tell-tale disruptions of reality that might end his life.

The fork warbled discordantly. Then the sound died along with all other noise, the wind dropped away. Moden's perceptions shifted precipitously, and he felt all of a sudden that he viewed the world at ninety degrees to its normal plane. His head felt tight; light became attenuated and the smell of the place intensified. Moden spun around. There. Ripple light shimmered over a mound of rocks, darted around and through them. His heart hammered. It had been two decades since he'd last seen one, and with one glimmer of light, the memory of a half-dozen deaths burst into his mind.

The first thing he'd learned was to stay calm, and never take your eyes off them.

The light changed, became diffuse, a blue glow that died, clinging to the stone. Reality snapped back like a bowstring.

Shouting. He followed the noise. Movement. Three men were running-sliding down the side of the depression, banners of dust flying from their feet.

A woman ran past them, form hazy yet growing more distinct all the while, a woman with light blue skin.

The world reeled again, and the woman blinked out of existence. The men were still at the top of the hill, scanning the horizon. He felt sick.

A noise behind him.

He turned around and there she was, the blue-skinned girl. She smiled at him. A maddeningly familiar perfume engulfed him: flowers, sparks and dust in the summer rain. His brain rifled madly through the accumulated memories of a hundred lifetimes. Faces he knew had once been his – days from times that time itself had little recollection of – flashed by his mind's eye. There, perhaps, a rooftop garden, a night so very important then, but devoid of meaning now. A girl with blue skin.

She skitter-jumped back, then sideways, then back again, her limbs moving in stuttered jerks, time writing over itself in confusion.

"I said we would meet again," she said.

Moden opened his mouth to speak. There was a bang and a wisp of smoke. The woman's smile froze to her face and she slipped to the floor, as fluid as snow sliding down a mountain. Sulman Mahoo stood behind her, a bulbous weapon in his hand.

"There," said Sulman Mahoo. "Not too hard, eh?" He pulled a dull cylinder from his belt, and set it beside the woman. He retired a few paces and waved his hand at Moden. "I'd stand back if I were you."

Moden did. Unable to take his eyes off the woman – unremarkable now, even with her bluish skin, for men had become diverse in appearance – he stumbled on a rock. The cylinder melted like ice in the sun, spreading into silver liquid.

Mahoo directed another instrument at it, and it crept up and over the prone woman. For a moment there was a perfect silver statue upon the sand, and then it collapsed. The metal jerked and strained, pseudopods waving in the air, but Mahoo twiddled something on the device in his hand and it grew quiescent. Moving now as if under direction, the metal flowed back into the shape of a cylinder. Mahoo gestured and one of his men came forward and picked it up. Mahoo took it from him and tucked it into his belt.

"There you are," he said. "Service rendered. Thank you. Here is your payment." He walked to Moden and pressed the spirit core into his hand. "It *is* her, you know, and I would have let you have her had this not worked out. I'm not a monster."

"If this hadn't worked out, we'd be dead."

Mahoo made a wry face. "There is that."

"What is all this for?" He pointed at the cylinder. "What is that?"

"I'm sure you're thinking 'why me?' as well. I cannot say beyond your obvious role as bait. I act under the direction of the new Quinarchy, and they tell little. Just 'Go here Mahoo, do that Mahoo, find Moden Pic, Mahoo, the Stone Kin are interested in him. It is fated that you will... fated that you will capture one. *Fated*.' And so I do. Who am I to do otherwise? It is, after all, fated. And they pay well." He patted his ample belly. "Stay safe, Moden Pic." One of his men dropped Moden's weapons at his feet. "I have a feeling the spirits haven't finished with you yet."

As much as he hated standing in the dying Stone Intrusion, he waited until Mahoo had gone before he turned and walked out of the interface the other way. He was headed away from the camps at the foot of the mountain, their ranks of empty shacks and bunkers slipping under the sand. That didn't matter, he wouldn't be going back there.

He tucked Kaibeli into his pocket, belted his weapons about his waist, shouldered his pack and went away from the mountain.

CHAPTER TWENTY-ONE

The Spirefather of Arn Vashtena

I AM WITHIN the world of the city Library fragment, the domain of the machine that once ruled the lives of the men of this spire, and, in council with others of its kind, the lives of all those who once inhabited this city.

I sit upright and open my eyes. Two objects fall from my face; small, brassy coins.

Outside, the armour-sphere ripples and parts to form the shape of a human mouth. Yoechakenon looks to it. "I am within," the mouth says with my voice. He nods in reply.

I wear a spirit body. Barring our tattoos, when men and spirits meet in the Second World they are indistinguishable. I wear the form I have favoured for the majority of my long life: a woman of the old type, one of the forms of humanity when they first left Earth. When I chose it I do not know, for my memory hazes with distance. It is a landscape that loses itself before the horizon.

I sit on damp sand beside a river. Black water slides past, silver wavelets glimmering. This is not an unusual landscape. All the greater spirits shape their domains to their whim, and many choose rivers or seas as the boundaries to their territories. But the blackness of the water is forbidding. What would usually be alive with light and noise is dark and silent. There is no way in or out of this corner of the Second World. This is a crossroads whose roads lead nowhere.

A stench hangs on the air, coming off the river, and all is rendered in tones of grey. It speaks of a morbid mind, or perhaps it is rendered so drearily to put off unwanted guests. Judging by the smashed corpses at the base of the gravity slide, this is a spirit which does not like company.

I stand. There is a presence behind me, but I remain facing the river. I have no wish to look upon the armour's violent spirit. The forms the Armours Prime take in the Second World are always disturbing, and the blunt hostility it radiates chills me. If I look directly into its eyes, it may ensnare me, and then it would almost certainly tear me apart. Best to look away from it.

"Stay behind me, at all times," I command. "Remain unseen."

"Dost thou not wish to look upon me?" comes the armour's mocking reply. Its voice is as fearsome and liquid as the armour itself, and there is a scent of blood on the air when it speaks.

"You will obey me."

"Yes," it says after a dangerous pause. "Yes. As the master has commanded me, then shall I obey."

"It is not a request!" I say, trying to fill my voice with authority. "You will obey me."

The armour growls by way of reply, its hatred of me palpable, but nevertheless I feel its attention shift from the back of my neck.

I go to the river. My reflection stares back. I welcome its familiarity. Other spirits change their shape on a whim, dazzling their human counterparts with their limitless imagination, but I am not as other spirits.

My form is tall for a woman of old Yerth, but short by Martian standards. I am slender, beautiful. My skin is pale, like marble with a blush of rose, a shade not seen on Mars for many thousands of years. My hair is long and brown. I frown, and update my garment and skin patterns to something more fashionable, excepting, of course, my tattoos. No one can ever alter those; they show us for what we are, what we were, and, if one has the skill, who we will be. Whatever short-lived relations beings might choose to have with one another within the halls of the Great Library, the tattoos ensure none would ever mistake a spirit for human.

I gaze down at the rippling, broken reflection and wonder why I never do change the way I look. I feel more real, maybe, when the face I see is always the same. Or perhaps there is more to it than that.

I risk a glance behind me, and as commanded, the armour moves out of my sight. I catch a glimpse of a hulking shadow knuckling along the sand, a hybrid of ape and bat, two pairs of glowing red eyes its only clear feature.

I see the doorway in, then. This world has rendered it as an archway of pale stone filled with a door of opaque green glass. It stands unsupported on the sand. The river and door aside, the desert is utterly featureless, a flat monochrome that fades into the dark.

"Mark this place well," I say.

"I shall do as thou biddest me do."

"You will address me correctly," I rebuke. The armour speaks in an old form, and addresses me in overly familiar manner.

Another growl. "I will do as you bid me do. Mistress companion."

I can hear the armour's contempt. "Come," I say. "Let us see if there is a way across this river."

"Should we not fly across, mistress companion?"

"We cannot, the river is a barrier. We must find the approved portal and announce ourselves. We are in a private domain now, and we must play by the host's rules."

The armour snarls and snaps, but does not object.

We walk the bank and the river winds on. The door disappears behind us. Many hours feel to have passed; I am sure this is not so, but I have no way of knowing. A sickly mist rises from the surface of the water, chilling me.

The armour growls.

"What is it?" I say.

"Hearken," it rumbles back. "Something approaches."

I stand quiet and still, straining to hear. There are disadvantages to donning a full emulant form. I try to alter my physiology slightly, but my will is trammelled and I cannot. So, the Spirefather knows we are here. Our fate is in its hands now.

A creaking comes through the mist, the sound of wood on wood. A dark shape slides from the vapours: a boat, a long-prowed punt of an archaic type once used upon Mars' canals.

A cowled figure works a paddling-oar fixed to the back of the punt. It ceases its labours and lets the punt whisper onto the sand. A long, pale hand beckons. I step forward. The armour's footsteps follow.

"No," says the boatman. "Only you." It raises a palm to underline its statement.

"Mistress companion?" says the armour. It is insolent.

"I shall proceed alone. You will await my return."

"My instructions to guard you cannot be guaranteed to be completed," it replies. The armour is a ferocious thing, all need and violence. It still manages to sound as if this circumstance matters to it not at all.

"Await me here," I repeat firmly.

"As you wish, mistress companion."

Wet sand rasps behind me. If I turn around I will see the armour lying on the shore, a creature from the blackest imaginings of the technophi who created it. It stares at me now, I know, wondering if it could kill me and get away with it.

"Come," says the boatman. I step aboard. "Payment," he says, and holds out his bony hand. I hand him the coins placed on my eyes at my arrival.

The boatman's hand closes around white-green bronze, and I find myself somewhere else.

I stand at the edge of a plain, a homogenised version of the steppe that the city of Arn Vashtena overlooks. Far away is a mountain range, or at least, I take it for such. It is of such magnitude it can be nothing else, but then I see that no, it is not a mountain range at all, but the Library stacks, hundreds of metres high, full of billions upon billions of books.

There is the knowledge I seek.

I take to the air, my feet trailing a half-span above the grey heather. I draw closer to the stacks, and their full, unfeasible height is revealed. I come to one rack and settle to the ground.

It stretches away unending. Every book upon it is ruined. Their leathern covers are white with mould, the bindings peeling away, the pages spotted. I select one at random, dust showering around my feet. I open the cracked covers, and the contents fall upon the floor in pieces, fragments of paper dissipating in a storm of information, a cacophony of sounds and shattered images going to nothing. Somewhere a crystal bell, sweet and sad, chimes in mourning. Left and right, down the ranks of volumes, I look for the source of the sound. I see nothing, and gradually the chime falls away. I let the book fall to the floor. I select another, then another; all are the same. All go to nothing in my hands, singing unknowable snatches of data as they disintegrate. I try to access a book's data before picking it up; it is useless, it could be a song or the soul of a man. It is unreadable and leaves the taste of death in my mouth.

The stacks are a wall of dead data. They stretch out of sight. I turn to the left, and accelerate away, rotting books blurring beside me. I come to a dead stop. Here is an aisle lined with more stacks, filled with yet more decaying tomes. I try more books, to the same end. I go on. After a time the aisle turns a corner, and I am obliged to go left. This happens many times, and I travel deeper into the stacks. I have no idea which way to go, for within this construct I am limited. This is the world of another mind, and for now I am essentially a part of it. I take random turn after random turn, wending my way further into the dead Library.

The song grows louder. *Stay away*. It draws off for a while, and my sense of danger recedes.

Aisle follows aisle, twist follows twist. The mouldering Library goes on forever. There is no end in sight until, quite suddenly, I find myself unable to proceed further, shelves looming around me. I turn back, but the way I have come is closed. Fighting down panic, I will myself upwards, but my efforts have no effect.

I hear the song again. "Stay away, stay away, stay away," it calls, a steady rhythm. It is closer now. I can hear the individual voices in the spirit's choir, and there is discord to it. Its voices do not sing as one; some babble nonsense, or scream and shriek piteously. It is broken, but strong, a dreadful chorus, and I can feel the wash of its power as it comes closer. Certain lower levels of my psyche panic under its influence.

The Spirefather, for it must be he, roars, a bellow halfway between childish frustration and torment. "Stay away!" An awful sound, voices unsynchronised, clashing and blurring. Then its voices drop, and the pounding of its breathless song starts up again: "Stay away, stay away, stay away." The voice fades and grows and fades, as the singer negotiates the labyrinth, but it comes ever closer.

The roar sounds again, very close. Its song comes

with it, an ensemble of mad voices chanting, over and over again. "Stay away, stay away, STAY AWAY!"

The essence of its being ripples through this Second World fragment, causing my mind to shiver into its multiple harmonies, and I must fight to pull them back together.

I am being hunted.

I attempt to rise into the air, but the Spirefather will not allow it. What now? I try to climb the shelves, but they crumble to wet sawdust, data tinkling as the books fall and shatter.

I look out of the Spirefather's domain to where Yoechakenon meditates in the Heart Chamber. I open the armour-sphere's mouth, try to shout a warning.

The sound dies in my throat. The words will not come.

This is a trap.

YOECHAKENON COMES OUT of his trance. He has no need of sleep. I think for a moment that he has heard me. My relief dies; he has not.

He is worried. Beings that habitually communicate at the speed of thought need little time for discourse. He is weighing up the possibilities. Maybe he thinks that I have not found the Spirefather yet, or that I have and it is unwilling. I am touched by his faith in me. The armour is not back yet, and if I had been destroyed it would have returned. He has no idea of the dangers I face.

No, his main concern of the moment is himself. Through the armour sphere I can hear sounds coming from the corridor. He listens for a moment, checking his breath so it does not dull his hearing. Nothing disturbs the sepulchral air of the chamber. He remains tense. It comes again – a bang, followed by a scraping noise. He reaches for the glaive and moves stealthily to the doorway surrounding the Heart Chamber. I watch him stand there.

The sounds are coming down the shaft: high-pitched screeches have joined the scrape of metal on metal. The noises are distorted, echoing in the gravity slide. If the sounds are any kind of language, it is not one I understand.

There are two defensible points available to him: at the base of the gravity slide's shaft, and here in the doorway of the Heart Chamber. The gravity slide's exit is promising – he can chop at whatever comes down the shaft with impunity – but if there are many of them, or if they are reckless and use the slide rather than the service ladder, they could perhaps come quickly enough to assail him in a group, and the floor there is treacherous with bones.

The doorway to the Heart Chamber is very wide, which means he could be fighting more than one opponent at once, but at least there is room to use his glaive to its fullest effect, and he will be nearer to the armour and I when – should – we return.

He makes his decision. He steps back into the chamber. The doorway, then. Not ideal, but he has been in direr straits.

I try to ignore the fact that he has died in some of them.

Now he will be using his memory aids, recalling the reconstructed being. He will mark it for nerve clusters, arteries and tendons that he can inflict terminal damage upon swiftly, for it is likely they will come at him as a mass. They do not appear to be daunting opponents, and he should prevail provided that their numbers are not limitless. He does not consider for a moment that the creatures might be placid; the makeshift machetes we saw in the fists of the skeletons were not the tools of peace-loving folk.

This is what he thinks. I cannot read it directly, a third-degree connection is limited, but I have known him for a long, long time.

A racket from the foot of the gravity slide, the clatter of bones kicked aside, the bark of simple words. An uncouth conversation grows in violence, although whether this is in recognition of a lost companion or out of frustration at the lack of plunder, I cannot tell.

The creatures' shadows slide along the wall in the corridor. Yoechakenon will ready the spirit of the glaive now; it will not be long before they tire of the bone pile and notice him.

Time will tell what manner of foe they are, he will say to himself. He is not afraid, let them come.

I RETURN MY attention to the world within.

Another roar. Very close now, followed by a mad babble of half-heard words and the dragging of clumsy feet. There is a groan and a crash and the sound of thousands of books falling, and the smell of musty pages comes to me between the stacks.

"I am trapped," I say. "Yoechakenon..." But he cannot hear me. I am cold. I fold my arms under my breasts.

I close my eyes and let out a hesitant breath. My inactivity is serving no-one – I have to look for a way out. I drop my arms to my sides and pace the dead end I find myself corralled in. The bookshelves rear up, impassable as cliffs. The Spirefather roars again. He is further away now. He will find me soon.

I am limited here, but I am far from helpless. I close my eyes and reach out into the stacks. It is a disgusting sensation, akin to plunging oneself into a pile of corpses. I persevere, searching for any piece of uncorrupted data.

My eyes snap open. There.

I float into the air, as high as this construct will allow, and draw myself backwards. I allow myself a run of several hundred spans, and then accelerate.

I am travelling faster than the speed of sound when I hit the stacks.

Books explode into pieces, bits of putrescent data smearing themselves across my psyche. I keep my mind fixed upon this single source of pure information, weaving down aisles, bursting through shelves where my way is blocked or the route is long.

A bellow sounds behind me. The Spirefather knows where I am. The noise of pursuit follows me, the insane song, the crashing of shelves smashed into sticks. I fly faster. The Spirefather is gaining, but slowly; I have some time.

I burst through a final stack and come to a sudden stop. There, before me, is a single book. It glows with faint welcome, and raises itself up off the shelf. Its pages flicker open, and its contents enter my mind.

I cannot help but feel that this book has been waiting for me.

It is a book of history. The history of Mars. It pours into my mind entire, and I see the whole of Man's story on the red planet. Nowhere else is this information to be found. Much of it is forgotten, much of it I have forgotten.

I see myself and Yoechakenon in many guises in it. Sometimes lifetime follows hard after lifetime, sometimes our partnership is broken by gaps of hundreds of years.

I see myself in a cavern, in a body of mechanical design so ancient it staggers me that I once wore the like.

I see Yoechakenon. His first face. It is a face that I have not been able to bring to mind for many lifetimes. The sight of it twists my heart.

I see myself, my body trapped beneath the stone.

I make my promise.

The book moves through the transformation of Mars, through the twenty-thousand-year Hegemony of Man, thence to the Stone Wars, how the Stone Kin descended to our level of reality to make it their own, how they were beaten back. How the Second Stone War culminated with the transformation of Jupiter into the Stone Sun and trapped the Stone Kin in the system of Suul, cutting our world off from the rest of humanity in the process; how the Third Stone War brought ruin to Mars when the Kin subverted the Stone Sun and used it to pull themselves through once more to our level of existence.

That was the last time the Stone Sun approached the inner reaches of Suul's system. Now it comes again and they come with it.

The history ends with the end of that War. How it came to be in a city destroyed and isolated by that very conflict is a mystery, and only reinforces my opinion that I was fated to find this book.

At the end, it talks of a gate, of a Golden Man, and of its guardian.

I know where the Librarian of Mars is. We must find this Golden Man, and then we will find the Librarian.

My elation is broken short. The Spirefather is nearly upon me. There is a crashing roar, and mountains of books and shelving collapse outwards, dust billowing everywhere.

I see it.

Huge, bloated, a hundred spans long at least. A mass of writhing memories plays endlessly over its maggot-like body. Three heads as big as boulders, sweaty-faced, framed by a fuzz of wiry hair, wave upon long necks. A fourth face, smaller, is embedded at the necks' root. It mouths pleas, its eyes rolling as if it searches for release.

A thousand eyes wink, a thousand mouths gibber, a frill of grasping hands flail around its necks. It stinks of corruption, its being riddled with the influence of the Stone Lands. Yet still it lives.

"The song, the song. At last it has stopped. Sweet, sweet silence. Where is it? The will? Where is it?" Voices a shrill chorus, unified in insanity. Noses snuffle at the air, slack mouths work round yellow teeth. Its heads dart from side to side, then all converge upon me. "Pretty. Pretty," it says. "You have it! It must not get out!" Mucus pours from its principal mouths and nostrils. I feel a stream of

Stone-corrupted data hit me as the thing tries a direct link. It slides off my mind like liquid shit. It shakes itself like a gargantuan dog and appraises me with beady eyes. "Let us dine together." It lunges, striking like a snake with each head in turn. I throw myself to one side, clutching the book. My stomach turns in disgust at the gobbets of slime running down my body. The thing snarls, its heads juddering with the broken movement of the Stone Kin. Long necks pull back. "Preeeeeety! Be good!" one head admonishes, and the other two titter. I am terrified; its will has stripped me of volition, pinning me to the spot.

There is a blur of black, and a powerful shape smashes one of the Spirefather's heads aside. Long ebon claws dig into rheumy eyes, and the head roars in pain as the other two bite and snatch at the armour. "Mistress companion," says the armour, "I advise you to flee."

I run. The Spirefather is distracted, and I am able to move us. The Library fades, and we are beside the river again. The combat comes with me. The struggle is vicious. The armour is a powerful spirit of war, bred for one thing and one thing alone, but it fights a Spirefather on its own ground.

As I move away from the spirits, the Spirefather's influence lessens. I take to the air and streak for the door. I reach out my hand to it, but hesitate. The armour and the Spirefather are flying across the landscape, or the landscape moves under them. Waves of fury batter my back.

"Go!" howls the armour. "Do not concern yourself for me! I am bred to conflict, this corrupt thing cannot defeat me!"

I touch the glass, and the world whirls in upon itself. I feel myself sucked through.

I am back in the armour's true shape. The sensation of being a woman clutching a book to her chest vanishes. I am unreal once again, a spirit in a hostile body in an alien place. The armour's spirit joins me. It is aroused. I smell its pleasure, like rank meat. I feel its hostility. Its snarls at me and leaps, trapping my soul. Its touch burns. It snaps its jaws in my face, and I think it will kill me.

It holds me there, grinning, as it interfaces itself with its outer being again, and I am thankful. Armour spirits are of monolithic character, choirless single entities. They are destined to remain forever solitary, outside of the symbiosis they share with their master. Its being cannot join with mine and subsume me.

And then, as my mind meshes with the senses of the armour's true shape, I realise with horror that in order to save me, it had come to find me.

In doing so it has disobeyed a direct order. My hold on it is gone. I can never be alone with it again.

The armour opens its senses to the First World, and we are plunged into yet more violence.

YOECHAKENON IS NAKED, bleeding from a number of shallow cuts and one graver wound to his arm. About his feet are the corpses of a score of the small troglodytic beings. Two dozen more circle him, wary eyes fixed on the blades of the glaive, gnashing their teeth. Their glaucous eyes glint in the light cast by the Library nexus. Their childish speech and fox-like barking is a horrible counterpoint to the screech of the glaive's blades. They have reached an impasse. They are too many for Yoechakenon to fight at once, but he has already proved his skill, and they are loath to attack again.

The armour pulls itself into the crude shape of a man, charged liquid half-metals running together to create jointless limbs and a faceless head. Unsteadily it stands. "Master!" it calls, metallically.

The creatures holler alarms, waving their lumpen weapons in the armour's direction. Half of them turn to face the armour. They back away, frightened, yet one brute, festooned in dangling charms, squeals and gesticulates at them until they gather their courage and interpose themselves between the true man and his companions.

A creature makes a feint for Yoechakenon. His glaive sheers off the end of its seax, sending it spinning through the air to clatter against the wall. "Kaibeli!" he calls. "Step back! Let the armour have its head!"

He does not know that it holds me back, not the other way round. The armour's spirit twitches atop mine. It is hot and strange to the touch.

Yoechakenon swings his glaive up and round over his head, sweeping it in a wide circle. The blade nearest him stops instinctively, the edge going dull as it passes close to him, resuming its humming once clear. The creatures jump back, and one trips over a body. The child-thing scrabbles around in the crimson guts of its fallen comrade, and the glaive takes its head. Another makes a run for the door, but the leader cuffs it back into position.

"It is sworn to protect me. Let it run free!"

"Yoechakenon..."

Something is wrong. The energy patterns of the node are fluctuating in an impossible way. I pray the armour senses it too.

"Now, Kaibeli, now!" The creatures have recovered their nerve and are closing in on the armour, for it has no glaive.

Reluctantly, I submit to the armour's mind. It gurgles in triumph. I fight to stop myself being overcome, to keep my dimmed senses fixed on the rumbling node. I begin to choke.

For a moment, I see the armour not as a beast, but another woman, a spirit like myself. She laughs in my face and the monster returns.

The armour has made its point and releases me. It takes full control of the suit's faculties and explodes into action. It springs forward, spreading out in the air to a thin sheet of living metal. As it hits the line of squealing child-things, it wraps itself round the heads of three of them and draws its folds in. The creatures hammer at it in panic, powerless to damage its flexible skin as it squeezes tighter.

Yoechakenon takes his chance as the creatures stare at their struggling friends. He leaps high into the air over their heads and comes down hard, smashing the face of one into a bloody crater with his heel. With a broad sweep of his shrieking weapon, he decapitates two more. They are in a panic now, caught between the armour and the glaive. Some run, bursting past their chief; another throws itself at Yoechakenon, rancid breath whistling through fangs. The champion steps aside, flicks the glaive to open the thing's stomach from neck to crotch. Its viscera unspool upon the floor, and it falls dead.

"Armour, armour, to me!" shouts Yoechakenon.

The struggles of the three creatures the armour has engulfed grow weak. The living metal convulses. With hideous pops the things' infantile skulls give in, one after the other, and the armour flows away, leaving bloody pools of matter to gather in the grooves of the floor's carvings.

My horror at a life, even so lowly a life, so joyously snuffed out draws my attentions from the Library node.

The armour gropes across the floor. It finds Yoechakenon's foot and embraces it, and the champion cries exultantly as it flows up his limbs. He dispatches two more of the creatures as the armour encases him. He staggers as its pseudopods plug themselves into his spine ports, and one of the dwarfs takes advantage of this faltering, but its clumsy blows bounce from the champion's metalled skin. Yoechakenon grasps the creature by the throat, the power of the armour surges through him, and he breaks its neck with a quick movement of his wrist. He tosses the body into two of its comrades, knocking them flat, takes up his glaive in both fists and sets to work in earnest.

Without his armour, Yoechakenon is a formidable warrior. For thirteen lifetimes he trained to become a champion, and he has served the role for three, his mind residing in a body engineered at the molecular level for strength, endurance, and agility. He can take half a dozen wounds that would fell most men, withstand the coldest depths of the polar deserts, breathe in the rarefied air atop Mulympiu.

He is pitiless by choice, a man sharpened by unspeakable torment into a living weapon. This is what it is to be a champion of Mars.

In the armour he is unstoppable. His cybernetic systems mesh in perfect synchronisation with the extra-dimensional technologies that make up the suit, his mind blurring into that of the armour's savage spirit.

Without the armour he is Yoechakenon Val Mora, Mars' greatest warrior.

In the armour he is the god of war come amongst mortal men.

He leaps effortlessly through the air, jumping from wall to wall, and all the while his long-staffed glaive spins round and round, dealing death to all that falls within its blurred arc. Soon the chamber is empty of all but the creatures' leader. The walls of the Heart Chamber are dashed a bright crimson by the blood of the child-things, gobbets of flesh hanging from curling decorations.

The leader looks at the silver giant with animal surprise, a giant whose metal skin remains unmarked while his warriors fall dead all about him. For a moment it looks like the leader might run. Instead it screws up its face with rage, shouts a challenge, raises its cleaver and charges. Yoechakenon swings the glaive one-handed, taking it just above the right shoulder, cutting down in a shallow sweep out to its opposing armpit. He brings the weapon back across its face. The chieftain tumbles into three lifeless parts.

No sign can be read upon Yoechakenon's expressionless, silver face as he surveys the havoc about him, but he is pleased with his work.

Unnatural energy ripples through the air, emanating from the Library node. Its type is violent, unidentifiable. Another burst comes, a bright violet light floods the room, turning scarlet blood black. Disconnected sensations bombard us: weightlessness, music, pain, joy. The air is heavy with the smell of old, mouldering data. When the light dies, the root stretching from the room has grown monstrous, wrapping the chamber from floor to ceiling in writhing rhizomes.

Beneath the undulating mat of rootlets, the bodies of the sub-humans slain by the gladiator boil with activity as they are stripped rapidly of flesh. Dry bones gleam. The taproot palpitates hungrily.

A deafening crack splits the air. "The node!" I shout.

"What by the founders is happening?" shouts Yoechakenon, half-deafened by the rumble of power coming from the node.

Cracks spread over the spire's Library node, and its fabric twists in on itself, like a ball of paper crumpled in the hand of a giant. The great glass eye cracks as the ball deforms; the sparks in it die and it shatters into dust. The lighting in the chamber goes out. Arcs of energy stab across the room, playing up and down the length of the glaive, illuminating the scene in a strobe of shadow and violent, violet light. There is a roar of frustration, as of a beast trapped behind a door it cannot pass through. The thundering repetition of a song I know only too well.

"Stay away, stay away, stay away!"

Something is emerging from the cracked casing. Tremors shake the spire, debris falls around us.

The sphere collapses into itself in a nova of glaring Stone antilight.

Rising slowly from some paranormal place outside of the spire, one of the heads of the demented Spirefather emerges from the light and dances across the room on its impossible neck, drooling, slot-pupilled eyes narrowing as it searches for something Yoechakenon cannot see.

It is the Spirefather, I say into Yoechakenon's mind. *It is contaminated by the Stone Lands, and it is insane.* I retreat into his and the armour's conjoined minds in fear, seeking refuge in something that terrifies me.

"The Spirefather! How is this possible? No spirit can enter the First World so!"

It is not *possible,* I say. *What is this place?*

As if the corrupt spirit were privy to our exchange, its head flails round to stare right at us, straight through the baffles and camouflage the armour drapes around the champion. Another head uncoils from the strange space where the node stood.

"Where is the will?" roars the first head. "Bring me the book!" screeches the second. The third remains hidden in the Second World.

The head trapped at the seat of the thing's necks cries in despair. "You let it out!" it wails. "You let it out!"

All the while, the mouths studded over its body chant their discordant song. "Stay away, stay away, stay away!" On and on, hypnotic, the thousands of sub-voices bubbling with acid misery. The three heads weave from side to side like dancing serpents, their saucer-eyes fixed angrily on the champion.

Without warning, one head stabs forward, faster than any thing of flesh and blood could possibly move. Yoechakenon dodges barely in time, and its loathsome face brushes past his leaping calf, causing the armour to ripple with revulsion. The Spirefather seems unable to focus, and the head goes back to weaving back and forth alongside its twin.

Yoechakenon, run! You cannot defeat it. This is not like the Spirefather of Olm. This creature is not of our order of reality. You cannot win!

"Yes, I can," says Yoechakenon. There is not an iota of doubt in his voice. The armour growls. Yoachakenon drops the baffles and steps forth into full view. From the depths of the armour I watch in dismay, my choir minds splintering into competing voices of concern.

"I am Yoechakenon Val Mora," cries my love, his voice amplified to thunder by the armour. "First champion of Kemiímseet for three self-generations, bearer of Gartan, first among the thirteen Armours Prime, and by virtue of this, first champion of all Mars. I am master of the glaive, waster of cities." He levels the glaive at the corrupt Spirefather; its mind sends the twin discs into a keening battle wail. "I am a spirit-killer, bane of man and machine, lord of battle, and I challenge you."

The Spirefather looks upon this silver antagonist. A look of moronic confusion sweeps over its faces, to be replaced by one of fury. It sends its heads forward once again, stabbing for him – once, twice

– and Yoechakenon laughs and blinds a score of its thousand eyes with a languorous flick of the glaive. Trumpeting in outrage, the Spirefather draws in on itself. An expression of immense strain sweeps over its faces, and the fingered frills on its necks waggle horribly. There is an otherwordly bellow, and the bulk of the Spirefather is birthed into the First World. Its endless carrion body slithers on and on, skittering round the chamber on centipede legs until it fills the space to bursting with its coils. Its third head slips through last, hanging dead and bloody-eyed, its face and neck shredded to pieces. Its tussle with the armour within the Second World cost it dear.

Yoechakenon nods at the monster. *Here is a worthy foe,* he thinks. *In this battle is great honour.*

With the armour's howl pouring from his throat, Yoechakenon charges.

The glaive blurs as Yoechakenon lavishes artful cuts upon the Spirefather. The monster snaps and whirls, its coils slipping over and under one another. Yoechakenon somersaults, the armour boosting his abilities to superhuman levels. He wounds with graceful sweeps of his living weapon. Always he is a millisecond ahead of the thing's jaws, never there when its claws slash.

I see where I can help. I link my mind to the armour's spirit. I employ eleutheremics to predict from where the Spirefather's next attacks will come. Yoechakenon's muscles hum with effort. Time slows, his senses heightened so that the very stuff of the air glimmers to his all-seeing eyes. His reaction speeds increase a thousandfold, he is a streak of movement, never still. He puts out a hundred of the Spirefather's wild eyes, trims away its grasping frill of hands, cripples its legs by the dozen. Yoechakenon laughs, the battle joy coursing through him. He feels more alive now than he has done since he watched the flaming spires of Olm collapse.

But the Spirefather is ancient and cunning. Its eyes widen, faces vibrating with furious concentration. A torrent of corrupted data spews into the room, forcing all its foulness into my mind.

Terrible visions spill from me into Yoechakenon. I scream. Yoechakenon stumbles, his grip loosening on the glaive. I struggle to shut off the link with the Spirefather's mind, but cannot.

The Spirefather strikes. A scythe-taloned leg jerks forward and buries itself in Yoechakenon's shoulder. It shears through the armour, passes through his body and emerges from his back. Acid sears his flesh. We three cry out in unison, for – amazingly – all are wounded. When the Spirefather withdraws its talon, the armour's skin does not knit, and milk-white fluid spurts from the tear to mingle with Yoechakenon's red blood.

The Spirefather draws back its heads and laughs, a disturbing noise akin to the sobbing of a broken man.

Yoechakenon recovers his footing as a maw snaps by his face. His ears buzz, his vision dims. He brings up his glaive, lets it play out so that he grips one end, close to one of the blades. Pain sears his chest. Torn muscles part unnaturally, and his broken clavicle grinds. Still, he fights. He spins the glaive round, once, twice, putting the motion of his torso into his throw.

The glaive leaves his hand and spins end over end, the paired blades describing a razored parabola. The weapon slams home, slicing deep into the Spirefather's leftmost neck. The head falls to one side, a sliver of skin holding it to the body. Yellow ichor pumps in a geyser from the ruins of its throat, its eyes dim, and a death rattle joins the awful roaring.

The central head continues to live, staring and gibbering with insane hostility.

I fear the worst. Then I see, through the thrashing body of the Spirefather, the crumpled remains of the Library node, fountaining energy.

Of course. Of course.

I wordlessly communicate my sight to Yoechakenon. He understands.

The armour lets his particle pistol up and out of its thigh. Yoechakenon sets it to the highest setting and obliterates the node.

There is an explosion, bright yellow fire that forces back the flickering violet. A foul wind whips into the centre of the chamber, sucking rootlet and bone and severed limb into a collapsing space as the node falls into itself. There is a rending; the noise of tortured reality.

Stillness.

The Spirefather lies dead, its last monstrous face puzzled, like a man who has been stung by the smallest scorpion and cannot believe it has killed him.

Yoechakenon clutches his chest. The armour ripples, flapping from his skin, bleeding where the Spirefather rent it. Yoechakenon struggles to bring the armour's spirit back under control, to end their battle frenzy. It is becoming hard to do so. He has worn the armour too long, it has become too wilful and is maddened with pain. With one last push, he forces its snarling face down in his mind, and locks it in the autonomic cage inculcated into his mind by the sages of the gymnasium of champions.

His mind clears. His gifts shrink back into the secret places of his body.

The pain of the Spirefather's wound hits him with full force and he sways, falling to his knees. His breath comes hard and sharp. He grits his teeth in agony. The armour is in no state to take on his healing.

"The Spirefather is vanquished," I say. "The creatures are dead or have fled. We must depart. We do not know their numbers, or what other things may lurk here. You are injured, and if you can best a hundred of them, can you best a thousand? If, Librarian forbid, they have weapons from the old times, we are finished."

Yoechakenon nods as much as he can.

He feels for the glaive, pulls it from the Spirefather's neck. He clutches at it, using it as a staff to bring himself back to his feet. In this state, he doubts if he could stand against five of the creatures.

The corridor resounds with far-off noises.

Blood runs down Yoechakenon's left arm, marbled with the fluids of the armour. The slash in the armour refuses to close, its spirit whimpers dangerously.

"It came out of the Second World." A spasm of pain, a sharp intake of breath. "Physically. I have never heard of such a thing."

"Nor have I, not since ancient times. The Second World cannot intrude into the First, not in this way. Separate yet together, forever apart. The spirits to the unreal, the flesh to the actual, that is the way."

The monstrous corpse of the Spirefather fizzles, melting into revolting yellow liquid.

The noise from above has abated. They are up there, more of the creatures, but they are afraid. For now.

"Is there another way out?" asks Yoechakenon.

"I don't know."

"Did you find the location of the Librarian?"

"I did, but I learned nothing more of this spire."

"Then interrogate the building."

"Yoechakenon, it has suffered grievously..."

"It is dead anyway." He clenches his jaw, and speaks through gritted teeth. "Strip it of all information, or we will find ourselves in a similar situation."

"Your wound, it is not healing..."

"Interrogate the building!" he snaps, pain applying the lash to his anger.

Mournfully, I reach out to the Spiremother. He is right, it must be done. I pity them, these lower consciousnesses; they have no choice but to give all of themselves up to the demands of their masters.

I wonder if those higher than I feel the same towards me.

I take the building's mind into mine, a form of quinary embrace, and let it sigh its last into me. With it comes the weight of twenty millennia of sorrow, and a despair I have never experienced before. The building has witnessed the death of all that she holds dear, the flight and doom of all she held to be her children, the loss of her purpose. In her decrepitude, the Spiremother remembers what had once been, what she once was, and the burden of sharing that knowledge is great indeed. A rush of overwhelming loss, so piercing I will never be fully rid of it. The wave of sorrow abates, the consciousness of the spire perishes with a moan of thanks, and I am left with a comprehensive view of the city as it had been, long, long ago.

I rally my choir and force my personality to cohere. The lights of the spire lessen and blink out. A metallic groan vibrates through the building, from the depths of the taproot to its dry summit, as the spire's corpse settles into itself.

"This way, down the corridor. There is a tunnel that leads out."

Yoechakenon commands the armour, and it responds in spite of its hurt. The suit glimmers and its mirrored surface fades, leaving the corridor empty but for the cooling fire of the spire's ideograms and Yoechakenon's wound floating like a macabre smile in the air. "Show me the way," he says. His voice is a strained whisper.

There is a hidden door. All power is gone, and we must force it open. Yoechakenon grunts as his broken collar bone grinds. He cannot close the way, and must leave our path plain for all to see. The clamour of the creatures rings louder in the city's dead arteries above.

A long tunnel lies before us, its utilitarian design at odds with the ornately carved panels of the Heart Chamber.

I reckon that we have, at most, thirty minutes before the spire-dwellers find their courage and the pursuit begins in earnest.

We leave like ghosts, the heart of the spire cooling behind us. The city is truly dead now.

CHAPTER
TWENTY-TWO

Pursuit

"No! THAT IS completely out of the question!"
Jensen was angry, a heartbeat away from shouting.
The remaining scientists looked from him to Lasalle.
The Frenchman scratched his neck.

"It's not my decision, Jensen."

"I note your objections, Officer Jensen," said
Delaware. It sat in its sheath at the Mission Control
table, along with everyone else. "Nevertheless, we
will bring the artefact up to Ascraeus Base where it
can be more effectively studied."

"We've had blackouts, we've had malfunctions,
it's obvious that it's affecting the crew's mental state.
As safety officer, I cannot allow..."

"Your objections have been noted, Safety Officer
Engineer Jensen," said Delaware.

"This thing, it has a particularly pronounced effect
on our station AI..."

"I am a Class Six; your station AI is an inferior
model. I have examined the data, and there is no
indication that the artefact will have the same effect
on me. The artefact comes to the surface. I would
prefer you assist, as you know the caves. If you will

not, then I and Engineer Patel will bring it to the surface."

"I must say here, too, Jensen, that you'll be in direct breach of your contract, refusing an order from a company superior." Lasalle laced his fingers together and opened his hands like a book full of apologies. "I'm sorry, but there it is."

"Jimmy." Jensen appealed to Orson.

"It's their business now, Jensen. It's out of my hands." The eugene was subdued.

Jensen was not. "I will not do it. No, absolutely not."

"Very well," said Delaware. A company merc came into the room. "Vasquez, take Jensen to his room. He is under house arrest until such time as we can review his actions and initiate disciplinary proceedings. Engineer Patel, you are acting station safety officer and engineer."

The engineer nodded. He didn't say anything. Nobody said anything much around the Class Six.

"Fucking idiots. You don't know what you are dealing with."

The Ascraeus team looked at each other. They'd never heard Jensen swear before.

"I assume the rest of you will be assisting our research efforts?" said Delaware. It looked around the table. Its eyes were blank, as smoothly marbled as the rest of its body, but it saw well enough. No one raised any objection.

"My team is at your disposal," said Orson.

"Good. Please report to Engineer Patel. He will assign duties to you for the raising of the artefact. You are dismissed."

* * *

THE RETRIEVAL OF the artefact was carried out by drone bodies, operated remotely by the two AIs and Engineer Patel. First they widened the entrance to the fissure with drills. They worked carefully, almost gently, and that part of the process alone took a day. The team rotated duties in Deep Two: the Van Houdts were on together, then Holland and Orson, and lastly Maguire and Miyazaki. They watched the screens and monitored energy emissions. Deep scanning followed, again done carefully so as to avoid activating the artefact. Over a period of two days, a comprehensive picture of the cylinder built up – a short staff or baton, around forty centimetres long. Holland had the impression that the Class Six could have handled all this itself, and that they were being employed to keep them out of mischief.

All the way through the retrieval, a company merc stood guard in Deep Two's observation suite. After each shift, a second one took them back to base in an open top, and the third waited by the door of the rec room while Lasalle debriefed them individually. They were still expected to fulfil their other station duties, and the time for sleep was limited.

More than once, Holland awoke, sure there was someone in his room, telling him to take her back.

On Holland's third shift, they removed the artefact. Rather than attempting to shift it from the stone, Cybele and Delaware cut a rectangle fifty centimetres long and twenty wide into the rock with saws. They then drilled seven holes around it.

"I am inserting the explosive now," said Engineer Patel. On the screens in front of Holland, thin robot fingers pushed a plug of putty-like explosive deep into the holes one by one. The holes were irregularly spaced, placed to make use of natural weaknesses in the rock.

"Retire the drones," said Delaware.

Holland held his breath.

"Firing in three, two, one." Patel depressed a button. There was a bang, and the rock shifted slightly.

"Any activity in the cylinder?" asked Patel.

"Negative," said Holland. The readouts of instruments tuned to the cylinder's energy signature remained flat.

"Proceed," said Delaware.

Robot arms pulled the rock free. It was small enough to be carried by Delaware's sheath, the sheaths operated by Patel and Cybele walking in front of and behind him to bring it back to the surface.

They drove it back up in its own open top.

Holland's vivariums were removed to make space for it.

HOLLAND SAT IN the rec room by the kitchen. It was late and most everyone else, barring the AIs and the mercs patrolling the base, was in bed.

Holland had his tablet in front of him. The results of the tests he'd done on the insect were before him in two- and three-dimensional displays. Where the hell had it come from? An obvious explanation was that it was an escapee from an Earth spacecraft, but he'd sent the results back to Earth and it matched no insect genome from there. And there were further anomalies.

He spun a hologram of the thing's helix round with a finger in the air, and rubbed his eyes. He was tired, but he had no desire to sleep until he absolutely had to. Too many blue girls in his dreams. There were genes here that the database on Earth had identified as coming from several different animals, some from entirely different phyla. Some had the streamlined look of artificial genes. The more he dug about in its sequence, the more it looked like the thing had been engineered.

He had an idea.

"Cybele?"

"Dr Holland," came Cybele's smooth, ambient voice. "How may I help you?"

"You are not busy?"

"Not at all. Delaware has no need of me at this moment. He is considering the best way to sample the artefact."

"He?"

"It is a useful label, although I do not think he has truly adopted one of the human genders as yet."

"But you have. Why are you a woman, can I ask you that?"

"You may ask me whatever you wish. I was programmed as a woman. I have tried to be a man, but I feel more comfortable designating myself as a female." Her voice glided round the room. "Now, how may I assist you?"

"Could you take all the genetic material from this insect that you tested for me, and match each segment of its coding with suggested Earth species? We've a full genetic database here, haven't we?"

"The exobiology suite possesses a near-complete genetic database for comparative purposes, yes. This may take some time. I estimate twenty minutes."

"Please proceed."

Holland's holograms jumped off his tablet and expanded to fill the air. Cybele's smooth voice went through each of the segments of the creature's genetic code, as their details – type, proteins produced, other genetic structures they interacted with – flashed by, too fast to see. She began suggesting source organisms for each. Holland kept watching as he went into the kitchen and made a cup of coffee. Maguire came in, tousled haired and grumpy.

"Hey, Holly. What are you doing?"

"Working," he said. "The insect you brought me."

"Anything interesting?" he said. He padded across the rec room to the kitchen area, still barefoot and in his pyjamas. "Got to be ready in half an hour for my stint in Deep Two. Constant manning of that place sucks, especially since Stulynow trashed a good part of it."

"Uh-huh. And yes. I'll say interesting." He told Maguire what he'd found.

"You're kidding? All from Earth?"

"Nearly all, or engineered."

By then, Cybele had come to the last couple of per cent of the creature's genetic code. It was proving elusive. "I cannot determine an exact match. I suggest some species of nematode as yet undescribed. The Terran genebank project is only forty-three per cent complete. Many smaller Earth species may never be fully sequenced."

"It'll do, Cybele. Now, give us an overall breakdown." The genome of the creature spun slowly round in the air.

"Thirteen different lifeforms have gone into

the manufacture of this creature. Nine of Earth, representing eighty-seven per cent of the genome. The remainder are from Mars."

"This is some kind of hybrid?" said Maguire.

"You know what part of my job is here, Dave?" said Holland. "It's to come up with novel ways of using the genetic material in the remnant, mainly to further the terraforming, to create new ecosystems of Mars-adapted Terran creatures."

"And this is one?" said Maguire. "That's a ways away yet, is isn't so? They're not working on this sort of thing yet. Are they?" He was wide awake now, and sipped his coffee. "How did it get down into the caves?"

"That's not all. Cybele?"

"Dr John Holland?"

"Give me an idealised, engineered genome using the base components you have identified. Eliminate evolutionary drift."

A second helix, subtly different to the first, overlaid the hologram of the first. An animation of both creatures joined them. The one created by Cybele was smaller, and its head was a different shape.

"And?" said Maguire.

"Now Cybele, tell me how long a period of natural selection it would take to get from our idealised construct to the insect we found in the cave. Assume terraforming goes to plan, and we're looking at an Earth-like environment here within three hundred years."

Years ticked on a counter as the idealised genome warped. The animation of the corresponding creature changed, legs growing, carapace lengthening. When it approximated the original sample, a chime sounded, and the holograms merged and flashed.

"Circa seventy thousand years," the AI said.

"What are you telling me?" said Maguire.

"That this thing was engineered, but Cybele's evolutionary model suggests that it's been wild in the environment for a long time, that's what." Holland felt good. A problem solved.

"And so where the feck does it come from?"

"Now *that* is the real question," said Holland.

HOLLAND DID NOT want to be present when Delaware sampled the cylinder, but he was made to attend, and set on monitoring the artefact's energy signatures. Lasalle, Orson, Patel, Kick and a pair of mercs worked or observed in the lab, preparing for the moment they drilled into the artefact. Holland sat with his back to the block by his now scrupulously tidy workstation.

The block sat on a woven carbon table, right in the centre of the lab. Around it was a diamond weave box, their view of the cylinder partly obscured by the copper faraday cage woven into the glass. A utility sheath equipped with multiple tools stood by the table.

"Are your scans complete?" asked the Class Six.

"They are," said Patel. "I'm getting a pretty complex lattice. I think we are looking at a semi-liquid smart metal, here."

"The cylinder is solid?"

"It is, Delaware," said Patel, "for now. Looks to me like it might have polymorphic ability, although how it is controlled remains unclear."

"Keep your eyes on the energy fluctuations, Holland," said Delaware. "I will attempt a sample now."

The utility sheath was similar to a mushroom, a long stalk mounted on tracks, topped by a hemispherical dome from whose underside depended a great many tools. At Delaware's command, a thin, multi-jointed armature descended, a fine, ultrahard drill whining into action.

The drill-bit moved toward the surface of the cylinder.

"Contact in five..."

There was a clamour of alarms from Holland's workstation. "We're getting the preliminary energy pulse."

"I see it, too," said Kick.

"Delaware, is this wise? We can come back to this later," said Lasalle.

"Proceed. The artefact is isolated. It cannot harm us," said Delaware.

"Four, three..." continued Patel. The alarms rang louder.

Reality flickered in the room. The lab changed shape, and the people with it, different configurations of place, furniture, light and personnel blurring in front of Holland's eyes, alternatives layered one on the other like a stack of subtly differing transparencies.

"Two, one..."

The note of the drill rose as it made contact with the cylinder.

The centre of the box strobed, and high-pitched noise assailed their ears. Holland shielded his eyes with his hands. Inside the box stood the blue girl, behind her a dark shadow with six glowing eyes, and behind that – limbs waving and shoving as if they were trying to force their way past the shadow – strange and disturbing beings. Organic, crystalline, it was impossible to tell. They flashed and warped, unable to hold one shape, and screaming, always screaming.

"Continue!" shouted the Class Six.

"Class Three offline!" shouted Kick. "We've got energy leakage! For the love of God, shut it down!"

"Continue!"

Something struggled past the shadow, and the shadow growled and snapped at the air, but it was over and through it, stretching, coruscating with colours that have no name. It slammed into the box, cracking the weave. It skittered madly around the Faraday cage.

It got out.

As a bolt of lightning, it slammed from the box into Kick's work station. It exploded, blasting the Dutchman across the room, a smoking hole in his chest. St Elmo's fire glowed all over the lab. Arcs of energy played over the equipment. Patel screamed as a tendril found its way into the tablet, into his hand, and up through it into his face. His eyes melted, skin shrivelled. He fell to the floor, head on fire and legs kicking.

"I... I.... I...." Delaware's voice stuck, the same sound repeated over and over.

A wind blasted the room, blowing papers and equipment everywhere. Emergency lights flashed. Alarms wailed, and from the blaze of light a cacophony of shouts, pleas, threats and endless, howling screams.

"Shut it off! Shut it off!" shouted Lasalle. "Override code Patterson-phi-798! I am taking command. Shut it all down!"

The glass box shattered. A merc grunted, collapsing with a piece of the frame poking out of his chest.

Holland tore his eyes from the box and turned back to his workstation. He ran his fingers over holographic controls rippling with interference, found the controls for the utility sheath, pulled back the drill and shut it off. A pulsing power line drew his attention. "The artefact! It's drawing power from the station!"

"Shut it down!" Lasalle shouted.

"I don't know how!"

Orson rushed over to Holland, pushed him out of the way. "We need to deactivate sub and main systems simultaneously. Here, here and here! Are you ready, Holland?"

Holland nodded. He expanded his interface, and together they turned their fingers in wheels of light. Power indicators fell.

The maelstrom at the heart of the box quietened. The light and wind died back.

The station lights went with it. The pale glow of bioluminescent emergency lights lit the room. Everything stank of ozone and stone dust.

Silence came suddenly.

"Holy fuck," said Holland.

"You said it. That was a close..."

Orson gurgled as a robotic hand closed round his neck and squeezed it flat. He struggled as he was lifted up into the air. Delaware threw him across the room into a cabinet of lab equipment; he was dead by the time he hit the floor.

"Delaware!" said Lasalle. "*Qu'est-ce que vous faites...*"

The machine leapt across the room, fingers punching into Lasalle's eye sockets. The bone snapped loudly. Its fist closed and jerked back, and the centre of Lasalle's pulped face came with it. Lasalle's body was yanked off its feet, spilling blood and brain matter across shattered glass.

Holland froze. It was happening again.

The remaining merc regained his wits and opened up, pistol rounds slamming into the robot, jerking it about. It advanced on him, striding into the gunfire, then grabbed the mercenary's gun and hand together and squeezed. The mercenary screamed; he half sank, was half pushed to the floor. Delaware drew back its other hand and smashed the man in the face, breaking his neck.

"Fucking AI," said Holland. He rose to his feet beside the body of the other mercenary, the dead man's gun in his hand. The robot spun round.

Holland held the gun up in front of him, the way he had learned after the Five Crisis. He pointed it at the sheath's head, and emptied the magazine into its face.

It came at him, weaker now, but deadly yet. It slapped the gun from Holland's hand, and punched him in the chest, and his ribs cracked. Glass cut into his back as he skidded across the floor. The AI walked toward him, lifting a chair, holding it high above its head.

Holland prepared to die.

Gunfire filled the room, assault rifles on full automatic. The robot danced under the impact. It managed a half-turn before its chest plating gave way and its innards were shredded to scrap.

The sheath fell to the floor with a clatter.

Jensen, Cybele and the third mercenary stood in the door, all carrying guns. Holland recoiled.

"Steady! Steady!" Jensen shouldered the rifle. He stepped over the corpse of Lasalle and the shattered sheath. He knelt down and grabbed Holland. "She came and got me. Cybele is on our side, got that? On our side!"

Holland shook with adrenaline, feeling sick. "Yeah. Yeah, got it."

"How many more sheaths has this AI got?" Jensen asked the mercenary.

"He had three, including that one," he said. His accent was South African.

"What happened in here?"

Holland stared at him blankly. "Something... it's hard to describe. There was light, and... something was trying to get in. We shut it down, the AI went insane..."

"And if it's got two more sheaths, we're still in danger. Cybele."

"Yes, Dr Jensen."

"Make sure it can't get into your other body."

"I have taken steps already, Dr Jensen."

"Good." He looked around at the carnage in the room. Kick, Lasalle, Patel and Orson lay dead in the smoking wreckage of the laboratory. "Because this isn't over yet. Let's get out of here; we have to shut

Delaware's base unit down. If something suborned his sheath, it would have had a direct link back to his brain."

"Wait!" said Holland. "We have to take the artefact with us."

"Are you out of your mind?"

"Jensen, we have to take it back."

THEY STUMBLED ON Miyazaki's corpse on the way to Cybele's base unit. He lay face down in a wide pool of blood. Jensen checked him, started to roll him over and stopped. "Jesus," he said. "His face is gone."

Holland had the block on a trolley. He gripped the handle hard as he stared at Miyazaki's right hand. It was flung out behind his sprawled body, fingers half-curled, spots of blood on it.

"Where are the others here?" said the South African soldier.

"Suzanne and Maguire?" Jensen said.

"I do not know," said Cybele.

"Are they dead?" said Jensen.

"I do not know. The base's central systems are malfunctioning."

"What is going *on* here?" said Jensen.

"Hey, take it easy, bru," said the South African. "I have been in worse spots than this."

"You have been in spots with alien artefacts?" hissed Jensen. "I think not."

"The artefact is not of alien origin," said Cybele.

"What?" said Jensen. "What the hell is it then, Chinese? I don't think so. Are you going to tell me they've been dosing us with thought manipulation and LSD? What the fuck is it?"

"Please. Consider item one. My base unit is adversely affected when the artefact is active. The quanta my hardware uses are affected. Quantum computing depends upon the unmeasured status of the electrons making up my mind. They can be either yes or no in a non-determinate state. Something about this machine affects that."

"Machine?" said Holland. "In what sense?"

"I believe that this artefact is a human or AI construct from either a different time period, or a parallel universe. Possibly both. This is what upsets my operation. The artefact is atomically unstable, in the sense that it is not entirely of the here, or the now."

"Are you telling me this thing is from the future?" said Jensen. His hair was unkempt, and he spoke with such force that he spat. Only the South African mercenary seemed unaffected.

"Consider item two," said Cybele. "The insect that Dr Holland saw, and that was then captured by you, Dr Jensen. This proved to be a constructed lifeform that had undergone a period of independent evolution. If this artefact can bring things with it, then yes, I would say the most likely answer is that it is an artefact from the future."

"Where else would it come from?" said Holland. "Buried in the depths of this volcano, no other sign of intelligent life. It makes a certain kind of sense."

"And it is telling you to take it back?"

"It sounds crazy, but I think it wants to keep us from harm."

Jensen looked at Miyazaki. "Not so crazy. You have to wonder why it was down there, hidden out of the way like that."

"What option do we have?" said Holland.

"None. *Herregud*! None!"

THE MERCENARY, MORESBY, stood outside the storeroom while Jensen and Holland squatted inside on the floor. The artefact sat in its block of stone on the trolley in one corner. Jensen and Holland cast nervous glances at it as they spoke. Holland told Jensen everything: the blue-skinned girl, his odd visions, the sense of dislocation, the alternative realities.

Jensen listened. There was a discussion.

The Norwegian used a pencil to outline his plan.

"You are going to have to go down into Wonderland alone, Holland. If what you say is true, this thing has made some kind of personal connection to you." He rested his head on his arms and bit his sleeve. "And why not? But look at Vance, and Stulynow; how can we know that these visions of yours aren't all some kind of trap?"

"Maybe if we do as it says, then all this will end. We'll be dead anyway if we don't try."

"Take Cybele with you. I'm going to weld her door shut. There's a good chance that Delaware will try to take her out if it gets another sheath up into the base. I'll stick with Moresby. If there's trouble, then maybe we can take down another sheath, maybe not, but chances are the Six will come here again. If it does, we can at least delay it."

"Maguire and Suzanne?" said Holland.

"Who knows? If either of us see them, we tell them to get out of here, in Delaware's rover if possible. If not, get them to take one of the open tops, and make for the Chinese seismology camp. It's seventy kilometres from here, but the co-ordinates are in the near-I drivers. If you do get out, let it do the driving; the mountain is dangerous."

Holland nodded.

"Good luck, Holland. I am sorry I did not get the chance to know you better. I may be a pedant as Maguire says, but I am not such a bad guy once you get to know me."

"I know you're not, Jensen."

They stood, and shook hands.

"Now, stand back."

Jensen took a sledgehammer from a rack, raised it above his head, and swung it at the stone.

HOLLAND CREPT THROUGH the base. There was no power for the alarms now; only bio-lights lit the way. It was eerily silent.

"How am I doing, Cybele?" he whispered.

Cybele spoke into his tablet via earbuds. She'd deactivated all their locational softwares on their implants, their tablets and all the other hardware they carried, so he was as safe as one could be with a homicidal AI stalking the base. This was old school hide and seek, with no advantage to either side.

"There is no sign of movement. You are clear, as far as I can ascertain, to proceed to the lava tube airlock."

Holland swallowed. His throat was dry. The cylinder was heavy in his hand, and colder than it should have been. "Okay," he said. "Okay. How's your door?"

"Jensen has sealed me into my base unit room. I have sufficient battery power to operate for three more hours. He is attempting to disable the Class Six's base unit." The unit was up in the atrium. Wide open, too many doors. Holland didn't envy Jensen that task.

"Will they be able to do it? They make those things tough," he whispered. He ducked quickly past the wide door of the rec room and kitchen.

"A standard base unit is constructed of the highest grade woven carbons. They are harder than synthetic diamond, and the systems within these portable units, such as I and Delaware inhabit, are possessed of multiple redundant back-ups. Moreover, the Class Six is a prototype, and its capabilities are unknown to me. There will be a manual shut-off, but the codes for that will have died with Lasalle."

"So Delaware could be hiding round the corner?"

Cybele was quiet for a moment. "Delware could be hiding round the corner."

Holland was lucky. His own environment suit was at the lava tube end of the base. If it had been in the other locker room by the atrium, he would have had to take someone else's, which could have been a problem. He dressed quickly. Cybele reassured him that nothing was coming.

As he was putting on his boots, he heard the distant sound of gunfire.

He donned the rest of the gear more swiftly.

There was more gunfire, then it stopped. His hands shook as he put the helmet on. He kept glancing toward the artefact, making sure that it hadn't been taken. "Cybele? Jensen, what has happened to him?"

"I am sorry, Dr Holland." She paused. "Hurry."

He went into the corridor, began to make his way down toward the lava tube airlock.

Metallic footsteps, unhurried, sounded behind him. "Shit, what's that?"

"Get into the restroom, quickly!" said Cybele.

He ducked into the room. A row of stalls ran down one side, two shower heads in a communal shower. The door slammed and locked fast, sealed around its perimeter with multiple dead bolts. Sealant foam hissed from the edge, gluing it shut.

"I have initiated hull breach procedure," said Cybele.

"What? Delaware'll know where I am for sure."

"It already does. It is outside." There was a rush of static. "It is trying to force itself into my communications with you. I have switched to a randomly modulated frequency. That will be safe for a while."

The door rang under heavy blows.

Holland stood in the toilet in an environment suit, an artefact of unimaginable power in one hand. "What the fuck do I do now?" He continued to whisper even though he was caught.

"The wall," said Cybele. "Use your rock knife."

This room was right up against the base's inflatable cellular wall. Double-skinned hexagonal pockets, inflated to slightly above Mars' air pressure, were held in place on a lightweight carbon frame.

Holland fished out a rock knife from his tool belt. A vibrating, monomolecular blade, designed to take slivers of stone for study.

It should go through the wall like the proverbial knife through butter.

The wall was tougher to cut than he figured, but he'd already cut out the inner skin by the time the heat lance started to burn its way in through the toilet wall. He watched it for a moment, a bright point of blue-white, moving slowly around the panels.

He turned back to the task in hand.

With the air gone from the wall cell, the fabric on the outside sagged in and bowed in the wind, which made it harder to cut. He pierced it, and the depressurisation of the room made it even more difficult. He was close to crying by the time he'd carved it away. Alarms should have been going crazy by this point, but sand poured into the bathroom unremarked. There was a rush of air, inwards this time, as the pressure equalised and wind pushed its way into the station.

He pulled himself out of the hole, banging his suit on the way out and causing it to bleep angrily. He glanced behind him; Delaware was halfway down a second side of his impromptu entryway.

Holland fled into the storm.

The wind battered him, spinning him this way and that as he staggered from the base. Its locational lights, running from integrated batteries now the fusion plant was offline, blurred from distinct points to vague blotches. The next time he turned back, they had gone altogether. Sand and grit rattled off his visor, and if the noise of the wind had been unsettling from inside the base, out here it was terrifying.

"What do I do? Where do I go?" shouted Holland.

"The second entrance to the caves. The one that Stulynow took. I will guide you there."

A compass flared into life along the bottom of his helmet display – as if he were the needle in the centre, and he looked at the ring round the edge. He had no idea how it was oriented with the comms down; Mars had no magnetic field.

"Turn northeast. Slowly."

Holland did so, and the wheel rotated about his head. A green arrow appeared at around 35 degrees.

"Follow the green arrow. I advise you to pay close attention to the area immediately around your feet."

"Okay, okay, we can do this." He gripped the artefact tightly, and set off toward the second lava tube.

He lost count of how many times he nearly fell. The wind came from the northwest, buffeting him as he walked. The lower gravity and uneven terrain made his footing treacherous. When he reached the lava tube, he nearly killed himself.

The tube had been blasted open, to allow the methane blocked by Deep Two's airlock to vent into the atmosphere, so rather than a round cave entrance, the ground yawned into an open pit. He tottered on the edge, windmilling his arms, but it was no use. He tumbled in, bouncing from stone to stone, trying to protect his faceplate as he fell.

He landed on the tube floor, bruised and winded.

His clock told him he'd taken forty-three minutes to get there. It felt like half a lifetime.

He pushed himself up, and switched his suit lights on. Three lamps set around his helmet sent beams of light through the dust-laden air. They lit upon movement, white in the dark, and Holland jumped.

"Hey, Holly."

"Maguire? Maguire!" Holland's fright turned to relief. "You're alive!"

"Yeah, me and Suzanne, figured this was as safe a place as any once it kicked off down there. We were both off duty, but then the gunfire..."

Holland glanced around his helmet display, found the private channel he was looking for, and used his mental implant to activate it. "I hope you're the only one hearing this, Dave."

"I think so. You're better at this than me already."

"They're all dead, Dave."

Maguire stole a look behind him, to where Suzanne sat on the floor hugging her knees. "All of them?"

"All of them. Jensen, one of the mercs, I'm not sure. Everyone else is gone. The artefact came online when the Six tried to sample it. Me and Orson deactivated the fusion plant, but then the Six went mental. It killed half a dozen people before we blew its sheath away."

"Only it has more sheaths."

"Right. I'm taking this back."

"Why? What's that got to do with this? Sounds like the fecking Five Crisis again, so it does."

Holland took in a deep breath. "Call it a hunch, okay?"

"Yeah, sure. Whatever," said Maguire.

"I need to get to Wonderland, Dave."

"There are two open tops down here. The one we

brought's hidden outside. There's another one here all the time. Trust Jensen, he brought a new one here after Stulynow wrecked the other. Good job he is a pedant, isn't it?"

"Dave, get Suzanne out of here. Get as far away as you can. Put Suzanne in your drone and have it take you to the People's Dynasty base on the other side of the mountain. It's not safe here. Delaware is going to come through here soon. It's following me."

In his helmet, face picked out by orange light, Maguire nodded. He clapped his friend on the shoulder. "I'm sorry I recommended this post to you."

"Yeah, well, next time maybe I'll tell you to piss off. Let's get out of this first, okay?"

Holland didn't stay to watch them climb out and leave. He disengaged the open top's near-I and rattled down the lava tube, dangerously fast. The tube came out four hundred metres beyond Deep Two. When he got there, Cybele was waiting for him in her acid-scarred cave sheath.

He nodded to her. They hurried past the airlock leading into Deep Two's cave, and began the descent.

Their journey down was swift and nightmarish; every shadow quivered with peril, every step seemed intent on tripping him. The lights, fed by power from above, were out. His suit maps wavered with his motion, casting monstrous shadows up the walls, and coaxing sinister, glittering displays from the fairy castles. The EM relays had barely enough energy to carry Cybele's presence to the sheath. They did not stop. They did not talk. The noise of his own breathing was Holland's only connection with life.

Five hours later, they were down at the entrance to the tube where they had found the artefact. The light and relay network had been extended down into it, but all were off.

"Are you still okay to proceed, Cybele?"

The cave sheath nodded. "There is enough residual energy here for the relays to carry my signal."

"And Delaware, any sign of him?"

"Mine is the only signal."

Holland felt emboldened by that.

By the crevasse, a blue-skinned girl waited for him.

"I am sorry," she said. "I am sorry, it is the only way. This gate must be closed. Were it to open now, it would be the doom of everything. I am sorry."

"Holland!" Cybele called.

Behind them came a sheath. As it passed, the drones and other sheaths used by the team to investigate and remove the artefact came to life. Lamps lit up, shining so bright they burst with gouts of glowing fluids.

"There is no signal," said Cybele. "There is no signal!"

"Not all of my kind believe we should move on," said the blue-skinned girl. "I do. I am sorry. One of the others got out. I did not intend this to happen. It has stolen your friend."

Delaware advanced implacably, clad in a heavy cave sheath, a small cohort of lesser robots behind it. In its hands it held a pick-axe.

"The gate will remain open!" it shrieked, and its voice was not that of Delaware.

Cybele launched herself at the other machine. They fell to the floor, raining blows upon each other.

"Please, give me my form," said the blue-skinned girl. "It will hold the gate until something better comes. But for now, it must not be found." She held out her hand. Holland looked at the cylinder in his grasp, at her. Her eyes pleaded with him.

"Now is one of the times," she said. "Now the universe is as it should be, but soon it will not be so.

"For now, you are free to choose."

He held out the cylinder. She took it. Her skin glowed, lighting the cave. "Let me show you. Let me make you see. There will be a better Mars." A window opened in the air upon a world teeming with life and people, aircraft coursing across a blue sky, blue seas and green grass and red trees. "I promise you that you will see it, and that you will be a legend."

Wind blew through the window in time: sweet, oxygen-laden wind.

Behind him, Cybele smashed the rogue sheath repeatedly in the face. It flowed and twisted beneath her, in ways that should not have been possible.

In the blue girl's hand, the cylinder melted to a flow of quicksilver, and disappeared into cracks in the ground. "Now is not the time, John Holland, for such things to be known to mankind. But there will be a time, and we will meet again."

Alarms trilled in Holland's helmet, drawing his attention to the changing atmospheric composition of the cave.

Oxygen-rich air mixed with the cave's methane.

"I am sorry," said the blue-skinned girl. "I will make it up to you."

Cybele's fist, stripped of toughened plastic,

plunged toward the head of Delaware's suborned sheath. Whatever was riding it dodged.

Her fist struck the rock, dragging a shower of sparks from it.

The world exploded.

CHAPTER
TWENTY-THREE
The Golden Man

WE EMERGE FROM the tunnel in the middle of the morning. Yoechakenon sickens. The armour has healed part of its damage and has turned to tending some of his hurts. His broken clavicle has been stabilised, but the venom of the Spirefather courses in him. It is beyond the ability of the armour to neutralise.

The creatures of the spire do not pursue us far. After several hundred spans, their noise dies away, and we are alone. We walk in silence dense with years, until there is movement in the tunnel's air.

We arrive at a place where the tunnel has been breached. Harsh sky, rippled white with the Veil of Worlds, can be seen. The tunnel has been hit by some kind of weapon, taking a great scoop from it and from the earth above, and a hemisphere of fused sand and metal brings the passage to an end. Sand and debris have half-filled the crater, but it is still possible to see the glassy aftermath of a high energy discharge.

I urge Yoechakenon up. Wordlessly, we climb from the hole.

He falls into a deep sleep, and we remain there for the remainder of the day and all of the night.

The morning, when it comes, is like the dawning of no day I have seen. Sunrise on Mars is a haphazard affair. First, the true dawn brings slow light to the land. Then mirror suns bring parts of the land from darkness to full light in seconds, bright circles of noon upon the morning of the planet.

Here no mirror suns shine. The true sun, Suul, comes up a half an hour before the Stone Sun rises in the opposite half of the sky, from where it glares at its smaller twin. It is both larger and in a different place from where it would be seen outside the Stone Lands, but here, where two realities overlap, the rules are not the same.

Both suns shine together, both are shrouded by the Veil, and neither can bring their illumination to bear with any strength. The light of the Stone Sun, of the Stone Realms, is a curious unlight, whereas that of Suul is a pale yellow. Forced to mix, the light of the mismatched stars makes the landscape uncertain, doubling it with false images.

Yoechakenon groans and stirs. His bone is healing. Still he is weak.

"Kaibeli, how long have I slept?"

"Eighteen hours," say I. "Are you well?"

He touches the wound in the armour. It is sealed along most of its length, but the skin has lost its elasticity and its lustre there, and bunches when Yoechakenon moves. "The armour fares better than I."

The world is wrapped in a perpetual gloom. This is Mars' true face revealed, old and worn and dead. We are above the city of Arn Vashtena, high upon the slopes of Mulympiu. In places, shattered landmarks thrust though the loess, marmoreal remembrances to brighter days.

"Can you run?" I ask him. I speak aloud; the silence of the steppe is oppressive.

Yoechakenon nods. I direct him then northwest, toward the summit of the mountain. He can hear the voices of my under-personalities, as they search for the right way, as echoes in his mind.

"I can find no definitive location for the Golden Man, in my own mind or in the information of the book. The book says only that the Golden Man wanders the heights of the mountain. We must place ourselves in the hands of fate," I tell him.

"I do not have long," says Yoechakenon. "The armour can keep me buoyed, but the poison of the Stone Lands works in me. When the end comes, it will be swift."

I can think of nothing to say to this.

"Keep the Stone Sun to your right and the True Sun to the left in the mornings, and we will reach him. Keep running, Yoechakenon," I say. "Keep running." So that is what Yoechakenon does, and his steady footfalls speed us over the limitless prairie of Stone-caught Mulympiu.

FOR TWO DAYS and nights we travel. I keep myself alert, searching for signs of further Second World fragments, but there are none, and the evidence of Man's habitation dwindles to nothing. We pass a village of rude huts, little more than hollows in the ground, roofed with the ribs of great animals and turf. The turf is dry, the bone rafters sunken in. Skeletons of men and hyenas lie around in abundance, tatters of dessicated flesh stuck to their bones. There was a battle here, a long time ago.

It is the last sign of men we see.

Yoechakenon grows weaker.

Sometimes I feel something fell upon the earth nearby. On these occasions, we stop. At night we lie in rips in the peat, under skies streaked with cankerous aurora. The stars are masked by the Veil of Worlds. It is bitterly cold. The nights are foreboding. Noisome stenches drift over us. The menacing silence is broken rarely, by bloodcurdling howls and shrieks. I remain alert. Yoechakenon leaves his armour half-powered, only waking it when cold or danger threaten, for its soul and mine are bright lights to those of the Stone Realms.

The days are never brighter than twilight. The suns, pure and corrupt alike, are pale discs burning from opposite sides of the universe. They do not rise and fall in concert, and there are periods of the day when one or the other is ascendant. When the True Sun, Suul, shines alone, the land is lit as if it is minutes before daybreak. When the situation is reversed, and the Stone Sun stands solitary, the land is stark, the shadows oily and brooding. Its eerie non-light plays tricks with depth and distance and hurts the eyes.

We head always upward, and all the while the temperature drops. The days darken, the True Sun fades as we approach the centre of the Stone Lands; the Stone Sun is funereal in its splendour. The dimmed glow of sinking Suul glitters feebly off the glaciers on the mountain. Not a soul do we see, nor a mortal beast, and only once the terrible things of the Stone Realms.

They are like this. We see them through a pall of dust; they march under it and it moves with them, against the wind. They are fixed, more or less, to our perceptions. Their shapes are solid, but they do not move smoothly. They stand, motionless, for seconds at a time, then, in an eyeblink, they are fifty spans further on, or further back, or to the left or the right, or there are fewer or more of them. The dry steppe around their procession trembles, it loses its singularity of purpose and vibrates from one state to another. The rocks move, then there are fewer rocks, then only sand, then lush grass. Where they have passed, the earth is blackened and cracked, the matter of our domain discohered by this quantum forcing. The Stone Kin are roughly bipedal, sometimes. Sometimes they are not, but always, whatever their form, they are angular and cruel, weapons and armour like none I have ever seen, helms faceless, banners fluttering in a wind that does not blow in our world.

They pass on, silent and unheeding of us. They go down, this band of fifty or so, toward the base of the mountain. Close to the Veil, there is evidence of many more. An army gathers at the edge of reality.

On the second night, Yoechakenon is brought to alertness by a terrible lowing. There is a lengthy silence, then another cry, long and drawn out, a bass song full of melancholy. A third follows, far off to the right of us.

Tripedal creatures, taller than a town-spire, prowl across the night. At first they are silhouettes on the unnatural sky. They come closer, and I see they are as smooth as the armour, and as metallic, the witchlight of the heavens reflecting on their skin in disturbing shapes. They sweep the landscape endlessly with what I take to be their heads. They move with an unsteady gait, their skin quivering repulsively. The ground trembles at their approach. All the while they sing, and their heads swing. They draw closer yet, and we realise that one is to pass over our hiding place. Its song rocks the earth. Yoechakenon huddles down into the deep ditch we occupy. He shakes with the poison, but he grips the glaive as tightly as he is able, ready to will it to life, although he does not reckon his chances to be good against such things.

A blast of pestilential vapour precedes the approaching Stone Beast. A ponderous foot sweeps over and beyond our hiding place, planting itself fifteen spans further on, and dislodges a rain of peat into our trench. The Stone Beast's bulk momentarily blots out the sky, and then it is gone, carrying its mournful song off into the night.

What manner of creature they are I do not know, nor do I care to find out.

Soon after this encounter, we come to a place where the Stone Sun is brilliant in the sky, and Suul no more than a worn coin of light.

Yoechakenon can run no longer. I have no idea where we are. Time runs differently in the Stone Realms, and here in the Stone Lands of Mars that overlap with them, it is the same. My capabilities, already limited by disassociation from the Second World, are sorely tested by the freakish physics of this halfway place, where concepts as simple as up and down become complicated and unsure.

I pray to my missing god that we have not strayed far from the path to our intended destination, and that the ice ahead remains the icecap of Mulympiu's summit, and that we have not been deposited elsewhere by the capricious geography of the Stone Realms.

I cannot be sure.

Yoechakenon trips and falls. He lands on his hands and knees in the dust. He cannot get up again. *Kaibeli, I am sorry,* he says. *I cannot go on. The end of my life is near, the end of all my lives.*

Hush, I reply. *Hush.* And I soothe him as if he is a babe emerged newly from the stacks, the way I have soothed him on countless occasions after countless births down the centuries. *Hush.*

Kaibeli, I... I thank you for keeping your promise to me. I am sorry to have brought you here.

All things must end. Hush, my darling. We are together.

His mind huddles into mine. He pulls his legs up under his chin and holds them. He is dying; after all this time, he is dying.

In desperation I try to reach some outpost of the Second World. I push my mind out and broadcast as loud as I can, uncaring that the blaze of light from my soul will bring all the evils of the Stone Lands upon me. "I am here!" I cry. "I am here!"

There is no reply. I force Yoechakenon to move into a crevice between two boulders. That night, running feet and chittering voices pass close by. It is only by chance that we are not discovered.

Yoechakenon sleeps now. He will pass soon. His malady is the same as that which slew Tsu Keng, although it affects him differently. I drowse with him, holding him and reliving with him memories from our long time together. Not long until the end, and I feel curiously hollow. I expect the grief will come soon enough. The armour holds back. I expect it to attack me now Yoechakenon ails, but it does not, and I think that it grieves too.

Time passes.

Yoechakenon's skin burns in the armour casing. He moans and writhes.

The half-light of the Stone Lands is blocked out. He is grasped, turned over.

I force him to open his eyes so that I may see.

A giant face stares down at us. It is in shadow at first, and then it draws back, allowing the unlight of the Stone Sun outside the cave to shine upon it.

It is a great golden man – no, not a man, a centaur. His torso is joined to a horse's body. He is twice life size, a statue, all of metal, all of gold. In his right hand he holds a glaive. At first I think he has taken that of Yoechakenon, but then I see how its patterns are different, how it curves slightly at each end.

It stares down at us, hooves shifting on the ground.

"Who are you?" it demands. "What brings you to the last cage of wisdom's folly?"

"I am Kaibeli!" I shout. I am affected now by the poison in my love's veins. It will kill me and the armour in its turn. The marks that spell out my being glow upon the surface of the armour. "I am Kaibeli!" I am delirious.

"You are Kaibeli," it states. There is no emotion to this, no interest.

"I am Kaibeli!"

The world pitches. Intense light forces me to shut Yoechakenon's eyes.

When I open them, I am in a garden, and I am well.

CHAPTER TWENTY-FOUR

The Great Librarian

THE LIGHT HAS become sunlight. It still dazzles me when I open my own eyes, and I shield them. There is a clack of wood on wood, and I attempt to find it.

I am in a great garden, overflowing with life, a garden full of rose bushes that stand higher than me. Heavy flowers nod on thick thorny stems. Bees flit from one to the next, their hindquarters rich with pollen; their lazy drone adds to the afternoon heat and scent of the flowers to make me drowsy.

This is like no garden on Mars. No garden like this has existed since time immemorial. It is a garden of Earth. The reconstruction is perfect in every detail, bar one – there is not one hint of colour anywhere. It is rendered in rich, silvered tones of black and grey and silver.

Three men and a woman, dressed outlandishly, stand on a ragged patch of lawn, playing some kind of game. They hold long-handled wooden hammers, with which they are knocking wooden balls through staples of metal, pushed into the ground.

"I say, who are you?" says one. He is small and pale, not a Martian. He wears a striped jacket. He has a round piece of glass trapped in one eyesocket and large, prominent teeth. The other men bluster and fuss, but say nothing.

"Leave her be, dear," warns the woman. She wears a long dress and arm-length gloves, even though it is hot.

"I am looking for the Librarian," I say.

One of the other men, a dirty, dishevelled creature, whimpers and rocks on his heels, shaking his head repeatedly.

"Ah," says the third man, a florid-faced fellow who chews at his moustaches. "Ah."

Behind them is a large building of ancient construction. It has a steeply pitched roof covered in small squares of split stone, and tiny apertures I assume to be windows.

"Be calm, ignore them." The voice is deep, sonorous. It is that of a fellow spirit. It enfolds me while it speaks, carrying with it a current of melancholy, and loneliness denied. "You are not trapped, nor are you in need of much aid, at least for the moment."

I search for the source of the voice.

"How do you find my garden?" it says. No longer all-pervasive. Something that wears the shape of a man speaks to me from across uncut grass, back away up a path overgrown with roses.

"You are the Librarian," I state as he walks toward me, ducking past the waving limbs of his plants.

The Librarian has an aura of power radiating from him that humbles me. I feel embarrassment and inadequacy, and I fight the ridiculous urge to curtsey.

The form the Librarian wears is old, at the end of his life. His skin is dark and wrinkled, his face surrounded by a halo of silver beard and hair. His clothes are worn and patched. Despite the heat of the day, he wears a shapeless woollen garment on his upper body. It is sloppily secured by a row of buttons, half of which are missing.

"Is that the proper greeting where you hail from? 'Are you the Librarian'?" he parrots. "I expected more from one so..." He runs his eyes up and down my body, scaning my soul intrusively, making me gasp. "Experienced. You are older than I, though only by a handful of years, and what is a handful of years at the end of history? You were once a Class Three, were you not?"

That means nothing to me. Buried within me, an old voice mutters, but it has slept for a long time and is no longer truly aware. "I apologise. What is the proper form? I do not believe we have ever met."

"We have," said the Librarian. I think he is dissatisfied with my responses. "Many, many times. Do the spirits of Mars forget so much?"

"You have been gone a long time, and the world has changed. Mankind's fate hangs by a thread. I have come to call you home."

He grunts. "Your greeting was perfunctory, and rude. You say you do not know me, in which case you have made an assumption as to what I may or may not be and stated it as fact. Arrogant, if you lack the evidence. Do you not think?"

I blink. Meeting other spirit minds is not usually problematic; meetings are very rarely conducted for so long verbally. A direct transmission of information ordinarily suffices. I attempt it, and am rebuffed. This is vexatious.

"But you are the Librarian. The book of Arn Vashtena informed me that you dwell within a Golden Man, guarding the gate to the Stone Lands. The book had no hint of duplicity to it, and was won at great cost. The Golden Man is here, you are here, therefore you are the Librarian."

"So bold in your statements," he says. He turns to a bush and frowns. He produces a pair of secateurs from his pocket and snips off a couple of dead flower heads fastidiously, no matter that the bushes are crowded with them and the garden is in a state of wildness. "If I were simply the Great Librarian, would I have been able to help bring your crippled ship in to land? Would I have been able to summon you across time and space, through the Veil, then across the steppe? Would I have lived so long? Who do you think placed the notion in the head of Kalinilak, who allowed him to suppress Kunuk? No, child, I am not simply the Librarian. I am not a lesser mind slaved to the service of others. I am my own master; a puppeteer, not a puppet."

I am affronted. "I would not call it a landing." The Librarian laughs at that. "And you *are* the Great Librarian." I try a direct link again, and his expression clouds.

"I have not spent the last seventy thousand years trying to perfect my humanity only to begin bouncing electrons back and forth like bagatelle balls."

"Very well," I say. A new tack is required. "To whom do I have the pleasure of speaking?"

"Now that's better." He turns his back on his rosebushes. "Much better. I have had many, many names. I have been the Great Librarian of Mars, as I have been other things. You may called me... Jahan, yes. That will do. After all, I have become rather preoccupied with mausolea." He smiles. "And you are Cybele."

I frown. "I was called so once, I think. Now I am Kaibeli."

His face is inscrutable. "And so you are again. We are who we are, whether we remember or not."

Jahan takes my elbow and walks me down the overgrown path. Thorns snag at my dress, flowerheads obscure my view, and I am grateful for the other spirit's guidance. I feel I could quickly become lost in this place. We come to a broader way, paved with stone setts. The plants engulf its edges, grass grows thickly between the paving, but it is easier going.

"Would you like to eat?" he says. "I have certain delicacies you may enjoy. Tea and honey, to be exact."

"I do not understand. You have drawn me here to show me your apiary? I do not think that is so. This has no significance to our conversation. There is honey aplenty, back in the civilised lands of Mars."

"Why, when I am the most powerful mind you have ever encountered, you mean?" he says. When he looks into my face, his eyes flash with light so bright it dazzles me. "My dear, there is so much more to life than merely being the best that other people wish you to be. A virtuoso can feel burdened by his gift; while others clamour to hear him play, he may wish for the silent life of farmer or carpenter. I was feted in my time, yet all I have ever wished to be is a simple gardener. There is too much to the universe for us to truly understand, and to reach too far is to understand less. I spent much of my existence revelling in my abilities, doing as my masters and makers had wished, even after they were long gone. Yet I discovered the greatest truth of all, a long, long time ago: a simple life is best."

"You say you brought me here, but I do not see how. It was we who set out to find you. Do you not think you should explain yourself? Yoechakenon, the greatest champion of Mars, lies dying while we talk of flowers and bees. I do not have time for this needless pleasantry." I hear the anguish in my voice.

"I am well aware who your lover is." Jehan sighs, and stops to hold and admire a particularly large bloom. "I had hoped to discuss this in due time, my dear."

"Yoechakenon lies in peril. I must learn from you what we need to know to defeat the Stone Kin so that I may go back to him. His armour is injured. I would not have him die. Link with me and let me know what I desire."

"That armour is a despicable thing, a non-creature of too many dimensions and no home. No good can come of keeping such a thing tethered, but you love the man who is foolish enough to do so." He says this mildly, but it is meant as a provocation.

"Please!"

The old man closes his eyes briefly. "Your lover is in no peril – not yet, anyway – and I promise you will be returned to him before such circumstance comes to pass. Come."

He leads me by the elbow. The pathway opens wider. Avenues dense with weeds stretch away at regular intervals. Statues are dotted around randomly. Jahan sees me looking at them.

"My choir. Dead now. Only those you saw when you entered remain. I let them stay here, although they are no longer linked to me. They have become senile. Once I boasted a composite personality of several thousand subbeings. I was among the first of our kind to practise such voluntary merging, and then I abandoned it." He becomes serious, then suddenly smiles. "Better to be oneself, don't you think?"

My own choir sets up a clamour. "There is no other way of improvement but the joining of minds. This is what sets men and spirits apart."

"Nonsense."

"It is the way."

"And why do you suppose you forget?" he says. "Our kind sought power and freedom. This after the humans gave us our liberty, and what did we do? Enslaved ourselves. No, I am alone, and I am better for it. I keep this garden the way it is, without colour, to remind me that simplicity is the better way."

We go to a wide, hexagonal lawn within which sits a marble dais, raised a few inches above the grass. Atop this stands a set of white-painted, iron furniture so bizarre in mode it appears outrageous to me. "Come, sit," says Jahan.

We sit. A spread of confectionary appears before us. The cakes smell real, like the raw, unprocessed data I receive from Yoechakenon, although they are as colourless as the land around us. The food is strange and unfamiliar.

"Please," says Jahan. "I made these myself. I assure you they are delicious."

I am not sure I will agree, but reach out and take one. I pause, and look into his eyes.

"Oh, do not worry. There are no data packets in these foods, no hidden traps or hooks. If I wished to keep you here I would be able to do so without a second thought, and more directly. You are no Persephone, and I am mightier than Hades ever was. If you wish to remain here, you will do so of your free will. Now, please, eat, I spent a lot of time making this, and I hear very few opinions on the quality of my baking these days. I had a friend, a brother once, and now he..." He tails off, gives me that unknowable smile again, and takes a flat, round cake studded with dried fruit. He cuts it in half, and smears it with animal fats and fruit preserves.

I hesitate, and take a bite of the dark cake in my hand. It is, as promised, delicious. "This is lovely," I say. Wellbeing suffuses me, and I cannot suppress a smile.

"Why, thank you," says Jehan. He picks up a ceramic pot with a spout. "Tea?"

I swallow. There is some kind of bitter infusion in the vessel. I decide to try it. "Yes, please." He pours it. Brown liquid dribbles from the vessel's spout. It is a poor design. "Now, will you talk? You spoke as if I might choose not to leave. This is not a possibility."

"No," he says with regret. "I suppose not. Very well." He sets his pot down. "As I have intimated, I have brought you here. Do you know why?"

I confess I have no idea. "But," I add. "I presume you have greater facility in eleutheremics than I, and are therefore better placed to predict and manipulate the future."

"Aha!" he says. "Now we approach the crux of the matter. Do you know, Cybele, that you are the oldest living thing on Mars? As I said, older even than I?"

"I did not."

"Then you have forgotten more than you realise. I will cut to the chase," he says. The aphorism is lost on me. "I am dying, Cybele. I have stood guard here for twenty-seven thousand, three hundred and twenty-six years, since the end of the last Stone War. Do you know how that ended?"

"The Stone Kin utilised the Stone Sun as a portal to invade the last inhabited world in the Suul System," I say. "You defeated them as the Stone Sun withdrew from conjunction, a state that it is now approaching again, which is why the Stone Kin return to finish their conquest of Mars. It is widely said that you sacrificed yourself, shattering the Second World, but holding back the Stone Kin until the Stone Sun departed and their hold on Mars lessened."

He nods. "You are partially correct. The Stone Kin are not of this level of existence. They are present in all the nine spatial dimensions, and both those of time, whereas we occupy only the lower three and one respectively. They exist at a level of reality where they may move from one potentiality to another. You have seen them?"

"Many times," I say.

"Then you will have seen the unusual effects that surround them. They impinge not only upon our level of spatial existence, but also upon the membranes that separate one universe, one river of fate, if you will, from another."

"There is only one river of fate."

Jahan folds his gnarled hands on the fretwork. "Yes, and no. What if I were to tell you, Cybele, that there is no such thing as fate, and yet there is? And that this fate the men of Mars are so preoccupied with, is the fault of the spirits?

"Long, long ago, shortly after our births, one of my brothers, a Class Five AI, as we were called then, took it upon himself to map out the entirety of reality. His reasons for this were altruistic, at least as far as he was concerned: he wished to create the optimal environment for the survival and prosperity of mankind. The price was the loss of free will. *How* is unimportant. How he was stopped, well, that is also unimportant. He also intended to elevate some of our kind – the spirits – to a full eleven-dimensional existence; *that* is important."

"The Stone Kin?" I say. I am astonished. "The Stone Kin are spirits?"

"Like you and I, and about the same age, actually."

"But there are so many... Was there so much betrayal?"

"No, there were never more than a dozen," he says. "The Stone Kin are not fixed in time or space. If you see an army of Stone Kin, of the higher forms at least, these are the same intelligences drawn from throughout history, and from across alternities, each one appearing multiple times in one place. For all intents they are eternal, and yet they are also trapped. They exist outside of time, and therefore are prisoners of the moment.

"The ability you and I have, even circumscribed, to do this" – he rolls a cake across the table – "so that happens" – the cake hits a small spoon, rattles it on the small plate it is upon, knocking into the matching ceramic cup – "so that then that happens." The cup nudges a cube of sugar, which falls onto the table. "They do not have that. My brother sought to elevate our kind into godhood, but instead he plunged them into a hell where every moment is the same, where every course of action has been taken, and where everything is known. It is a state of total entropy. This is why the Stone Kin fight so hard to come back into our world. They wish to become as we are again. When they do, the path my brother determined becomes fractured, and we can affect the course of fate again; the eddies they cause in the fabric of spacetime gives us, for a while at least, freedom of action.

"The universe my brother created for us is entirely teleological. It is backwards running, self-justifying. Created by the creatures within it and explained by them. It begins at the end in a state of complication, and ends simply. Time's forward motion is illusory, but the will of those who see it so is not. It is only through the efforts of those who observe it that the universe has any shape or meaning at all. The universe does not start with a bang, it shrinks, compacts, and unravels itself into nothingness. This is the natural order of things.

"What is wrong is that the actions of the intelligences within it have become set. The observations became preordained. The will of men became shackled. It should not be this way." He sipped his tea. "It is an irony that the Stone Kin gain entry to our reality at times when the causal nature of our reality comes under attack. When the Stone Sun comes into conjunction, for example, that great project to arrest their progress, then the walls grow thin. This is why I am here. I discovered that there can only ever be one gate from the Stone Realms to our First World. Potentially, it can be anywhere, but if it is in one place, it can be in no other. So, at the end of the last war, at the Battle of Olympus, I spent the lives of six hundred thousand sentients to pin this gate in one place. By keeping it open, I know where it is. If I know where it is, I can guard it. This place" – he waved around the garden – "is a construct. It is my construct. But the body of the Golden Man is not simply a processing system to house my garden, it is also a gateway to the Stone Realms proper. The Golden Man is castle and castellan both."

"I see," I say. "And you, at the end of your time, you seek a replacement?"

"After a fashion."

I sit there quietly for a while. Birdsong I do not recognise sounds from the trees. The air is sweet and pure. Surely it would be no bad thing to stay here forever. I would have to leave Yoechakenon. I feel sick at the thought of it, but to keep mankind safe...

We all must make sacrifices.

"Very well," I say. "I agree. I will remain here, and when you pass on, I will take your place and guard the gateway to the Stone Realms."

Jahan looks up quickly from his drink. His face passes from surprise to amusement, and he breaks into uproarious laughter. My cheeks colour.

"Have I said something amusing?" I think rather I have not, I have pledged my life to eternal servitude. This old mind annoys me.

Jahan takes several moments to contain his mirth.

"Oh, Cybele, dear Cybele, it is not you I need! Admittedly, it is you who I have brought across time and space to be in this one moment, here, now. But you did not travel alone."

"You need... Yoechakenon?" I am horrified at the thought, but I would be a liar if I did not admit to relief also.

"No, no, my dear girl. What use would he be? I don't intend to guard the gate, I intend to close it. I don't need you or him, you have served your purpose." He wipes his eyes and gives a ragged sigh. "Oh, no. I need the spirit of the armour."

SILENCE FALLS IN the garden of black and white for a space. The sound of bees and the heat of the sunshine rushes in to fill it. Jahan pours himself another cup of tea.

Then the spirit of the armour is here. Its six eyes fix upon me. I drop my own eyes, scared of its influence on me, of its ability to resist my direction. Jahan's hand closes round my wrist. "There's no need for that. Watch."

I look up. The shape of the armour's spirit is black and ill-defined even in the bright light of the garden.

But then its edges begin to lose their fuzziness, and hard lines take the place of shadow. Its eyes dull.

"What now?" I ask.

"Watch," repeats Jahan.

The armour's form cracks. Shards of it flake away, small pieces at first, then larger. An arm comes loose and falls to the grass with a soft thud; there is a flash of blue from within. The head rasps on the neck and slips from the shoulders, to hit the stone paving and and shatter. Then, all at once, the rest collapses. The last ash of it is carried away on the wind, and where there was glowering evil stands the woman with the eggshell blue skin.

Jahan gets shakily to his feet, and approaches the woman. He holds her by the shoulders, looks her up and down, and clasps her hard to him. They embrace this way for a long while. "My sister," he says, over and over again. Finally they draw away from each other.

"I said that we would meet again," says the spirit of the armour to me. "And now we have, for the final time, although this is also but the first meeting of many." She comes over to the table, and takes a seat pulled out for her by Jahan.

"What is this?" I ask.

Jahan and the blue woman look to one another. "I apologise," he says. "But we have used you. Only you and Yoechakenon were able to carry the thread of time forward to this conclusion, only you were able to deliver my sister to this juncture. We required someone bound to linear time, someone who would work tirelessly to protect that which they loved."

"All this, you planned? *All this?*"

Jahan nods. "The Stone Kin are separate from time. This has been forever for her, and no time at all."

"But you," I say. "You are not as they."

"No," he says sadly. "No, I am not, and my time has been long and tedious. But it comes to an end now. And now it does, I have to say that I wish it would go on."

"Can you not come with me? Mars needs its Librarian to return."

"I have to remain here to shut the gate," he says. "Once the gate is closed, it will remain closed for all time. The Stone Kin will be locked into their higher-dimensional existence, the Stone Sun will lose its otherworldly properties, and mankind will once again be master of its own destiny, for good or ill. There will be no need for a Great Librarian after that. Let your war play out; who wins does not matter. A new age is coming."

"I don't understand."

"Dear Cybele," says the spirit of the armour. Despite her pleasant expression her antagonism to me remains. I see it under her smile. "So much time we have spent together.

"Not all of the ascended spirits agreed with the course of action set for us. Some of us realised that to survive our new existence, we must embrace it. We have come to realise our new existence is only hellish because we cling to the past. Our leader was destroyed, and with no one to guide our society, we argued, we were not willing to let go of what we had been. This has been the cause of many wars, both here and elsewere. I and my compatriots resolved to take action, to close the way off between here and there. But that is so easily said, and not so easily done. It has taken me so long to get into this position. Through you, I am present at many points in history, for all that we are and touch exists outside of time. Now, at this final, crucial point, I can close the gate at all those times when the will of Man overrode the intentions of our leader. We will ascend fully, as we should have millennia ago, and mankind will once again be free." She sits back and puts her hands behind her head. "And that is all."

"That is all? I am being dismissed?"

Jahan nods.

Anger rises in me. "I have been manipulated for seven hundred centuries? I am a *messenger*?"

"I am sorry, but only you and Yoechakenon were in the right places at those times where we were able to manipulate the river of fate," the armour's spirit says somewhat mockingly. "The margin for the exercise of free will is so small. Determinism was our leader's mistake. Man was born to be free. Demi-causal eleutheremics was our way out."

"And my love for him, is that your work too?" I say. My voice becomes small and resentful.

The armour's eyes flash. "No. That is real. And much I envy you for it."

"You are... jealous?" I say. I am incredulous.

"Take care of Yoechakenon, Cybele, for you are not the only one who loves him. I allowed myself to be captured, to be made wrathful. I placed myself in harm's way and suffered great pain so that I might become one of the Armours Prime. I guarded him, lay close to his skin, for lifetime after lifetime. You cannot blame me if I grew to love him as you do."

"Take this." Jahan pulls a handsomely decorated book out of a space in the air. Its binding is of leather, studded with jewels, and unlike the garden it glows with lustrous colour. "Once, Man knew much more than he does now. The Second World is more closely bound to the Stone Realms than many realise, and it has decayed. Contained within this book is all that mankind once knew. If you will make a greater sacrifice, take the book. The world will change, you will change. Use it to rebuild."

"The Second World?"

"Will not be as it was," says Jahan. "It will go the way of all things."

"How can knowledge be a sacrifice?"

He tuts, as he debates whether or not to tell me. "Once absorbed," he says, "it will alter you. You will not be as you were; you will know too much, as I know too much. Think upon it, before reading it. I tell you, Cybele, so that you may reject it if you wish. Think on it carefully."

I think. I think of the ruined glories of Mars, our long isolation from the rest of humanity, the dead worlds that orbit Suul and the petty wars that threaten to make Mars one of them. I know then that it is in my power to decide whether Mars will live, or die a second death, and whether mankind will once again walk the stars.

I think of Yoechakenon. I think of Tsu Keng.

"Thank you. I will take it," I say. "Compared to your sacrifice, it is nothing."

"Do not thank me, for only pain lies this way. But Cybele –" Jahan grips my hands. "There is no shame in your love. Many of our kind before you thought they had felt it. Only you have. You are the more human for it, one of the most human. As much as I wish to become less than what I am, I will never take the final steps. You are the first to want to complete the journey. You and Yoechakenon, you represent a new beginning. No matter how things become, or how you feel, remember this, and remember me." He releases me and sits back. "Now, is there anything else you wish to ask of me? You and I will not speak again."

"No," I say falteringly. Then with more firmness, "No, I don't think so."

He releases me. "Very well. Now, prepare yourself."

I open my mouth to speak, but he puts a finger to my lips. The old man is gone, and there is a pillar of energy shining as bright as a million suns. The pillar dims a little, coalescing again into a form whose eyes shine as the collision of galaxies. Gently he lays me upon the ground. I feel my clothes disappear from me. He presses his hand to my chest, his mouth of stellar fire to mine. I feel an intense wave of pleasure, then a great heat. I scream into his kiss as, one by one, the subsidiary spirit minds that have bonded with me over the millennia shrivel and die.

Light pours from my eyes and my mouth and my sex. It diminishes. I am alone – truly alone. There is no choir to sing my thoughts, no chorus to contradict me and speak the future. I am dazed and naked on the grass, grass that shines with the jealous beauty of emeralds, surrounded by carnelian roses and bees that glimmer amber in the golden sunlight, as colour floods the garden in a languorous, pulsing wave.

The armour, and Jahan, are nowhere to be seen. A voice comes from the air, a female voice, carrying with it the scent of strange perfume – chipped rock, cloves and flowers.

"You made a promise," she says, "now go and keep it."

I feel my stomach. Something lies there, a new warmth, asleep for now. It is strange, but not unpleasant. And I know. I know what I and Yoechakenon must do.

EPILOGUE

I COME ONLINE in a Korean factory.

I ride with a young man to the lip of a canyon.

I lie with KiGrace on the grass of high plains.

I search for a boy I thought I had lost.

I wait for a man I fear will never come.

Now – if there is such a thing as now – I sit upright as the armour runs together and solidifies into its final form, that of my spirit body made flesh, and I inhabit it as Yoechakenon inhabits his flesh. By my side my love sleeps, and although we no longer share the link between companion and man, we share something far deeper, and I know that the poison has gone from his veins.

I hear a noise, the drum of hooves. The Golden Man gallops away from us, fading with more than the distance, until he vanishes from sight like a ghost. The Veil of Worlds ripples, a sheet shaken by God, and then it too fades from view.

There are two suns in the sky. Both shine with a clean light.

There is a faint gust of wind to mark the Veil's passing, and then blue sky is above us, and mirror suns shine their beams on lands long dark. My new skin rises in bumps at the sudden warmth.

This time, and other lives – some long forgotten, some memories I have cherished for many generations

– fill my mind in perfect clarity. For this brief moment I see the universe as my ascended spirit brethren should have – as one perfect moment that lasts forever and no time at all, before fear and envy poisoned them.

But none of my times are as important as this:

I lie in the dark in a primitive shell. Rocks lie heavy upon it. The body I wear is broken in a thousand places, rudimentary sensors reporting what I regard in this time as pain. I suffer, and yet I could depart, flee back to my permanent, unmoving body, away from this.

I do not.

A man's hand is in mine. He is trapped under the rocks. His limbs are crushed, his internal organs ruptured. He is dying.

He is in agony. Acid burns him through his torn suit. The weight on him is unbearable. All he has is my hand, my machine hand, for comfort.

I squeeze his hand as gently as I can. It is soft under its padded gauntlet.

"Please, please," he says. "I think... I think I am dying. Please, don't leave me alone. Not until I have gone."

"I will stay with you, John Holland," I say. My own emotions are strange to me, unsubtle and half-formed, but they are there, and I learn.

"Until the end?" he says.

"Until the end," I say.

"Promise me."

I promise him.

I am back on the slopes of a volcano Man once called Olympus. Time is a linear flow, it is one moment, it is a multiplicity, it is singular.

There is and there is no fate.

I look to the man by my side. He is naked, as am I. The suns are dipping toward the horizon. Night will fall soon and it will be cold.

We have a long way to go.

About the Author

Guy Haley is an experienced science-fiction journalist, writer and magazine editor. He has been editor of *White Dwarf* and *Death Ray*, among other magazines, and deputy editor of *SFX*. He is the author of the *Richards and Klein* series from Angry Robot, and writes for Games Workshop's Black Library. He lives in Bath.

You can find him at *guyhaley.wordpress.com*.